selected short stories

selected short stories of
Anton Chekhov

maple press

Published by

MAPLE PRESS PRIVATE LIMITED
office: A-63, Sector 58, Noida 201301, U.P., India
phone: +91 120 455 3581, 455 3583
email: info@maplepress.co.in
website: www.maplepress.co.in

Reprint 2021 in India

ISBN: 978-93-80816-09-8

Contents

The Bishop

I

The evening service was being celebrated on the eve of Palm Sunday in the Old Petrovsky Convent. When they began distributing the palm it was close upon ten o'clock, the candles were burning dimly, the wicks wanted snuffing; it was all in a sort of mist. In the twilight of the church the crowd seemed heaving like the sea, and to Bishop Pyotr, who had been unwell for the last three days, it seemed that all the faces--old and young, men's and women's--were alike, that everyone who came up for the palm had the same expression in his eyes. In the mist he could not see the doors; the crowd kept moving and looked as though there were no end to it. The female choir was singing, a nun was reading the prayers for the day.

How stifling, how hot it was! How long the service went on! Bishop Pyotr was tired. His breathing was laboured and rapid, his throat was parched, his shoulders ached with weariness, his legs were trembling. And it disturbed him unpleasantly when a religious maniac uttered occasional shrieks in the gallery. And then all of a sudden, as though in a dream or delirium, it seemed to the bishop as though his own mother Marya Timofyevna, whom he had not seen for nine years, or some old woman just like his mother, came up to him out of the crowd, and, after taking a palm branch from him, walked away looking at him all the while good-humouredly with a kind, joyful smile until she was lost in the crowd. And for some reason tears flowed down his face. There was peace in his heart, everything was well, yet he kept gazing fixedly towards the left choir, where the prayers were being read, where in the dusk of evening you could not recognize anyone, and--wept. Tears glistened on his face and on his beard. Here someone close at hand was weeping, then someone else farther away, then others and still others, and little by little the church was filled with soft weeping. And a little later, within five minutes, the nuns' choir was singing; no one was weeping and everything was as before.

Soon the service was over. When the bishop got into his carriage to drive home, the gay, melodious chime of the heavy, costly bells was filling the whole garden in the moonlight. The white walls, the white crosses on the tombs, the white birch-trees and black shadows, and the far-away moon in the sky exactly over the convent, seemed now living their own life, apart and incomprehensible, yet very near to man. It was the beginning of April, and after the warm spring day it turned cool; there was a faint touch of frost, and the breath of spring could be felt in the soft, chilly air. The road from the convent to the town was sandy, the horses had to go at a walking pace, and on both sides of the carriage in the brilliant, peaceful moonlight there were people trudging along home from church through the sand. And all was silent, sunk in thought; everything around seemed kindly, youthful, akin, everything--trees and sky and even the moon, and one longed to think that so it would be always.

At last the carriage drove into the town and rumbled along the principal street. The shops were already shut, but at Erakin's, the millionaire shopkeeper's, they were trying the new electric lights, which flickered brightly, and a crowd of people were gathered round. Then came wide, dark, deserted streets, one after another; then the highroad, the open country, the fragrance of pines. And suddenly there rose up before the bishop's eyes a white turreted wall, and behind it a tall belfry in the full moonlight, and beside it five shining, golden cupolas: this was the Pankratievsky Monastery, in which Bishop Pyotr lived. And here, too, high above the monastery, was the silent, dreamy moon. The carriage drove in at the gate, crunching over the sand;

here and there in the moonlight there were glimpses of dark monastic figures, and there was the sound of footsteps on the flag-stones...

"You know, your holiness, your mamma arrived while you were away," the lay brother informed the bishop as he went into his cell.

"My mother? When did she come?"

"Before the evening service. She asked first where you were and then she went to the convent."

"Then it was her I saw in the church, just now! Oh, Lord!"

And the bishop laughed with joy.

"She bade me tell your holiness," the lay brother went on, "that she would come to-morrow. She had a little girl with her--her grandchild, I suppose. They are staying at Ovsyannikov's inn."

"What time is it now?"

"A little after eleven."

"Oh, how vexing!"

The bishop sat for a little while in the parlour, hesitating, and as it were refusing to believe it was so late. His arms and legs were stiff, his head ached. He was hot and uncomfortable. After resting a little he went into his bedroom, and there, too, he sat a little, still thinking of his mother; he could hear the lay brother going away, and Father Sisoy coughing the other side of the wall. The monastery clock struck a quarter.

The bishop changed his clothes and began reading the prayers before sleep. He read attentively those old, long familiar prayers, and at the same time thought about his mother. She had nine children and about forty grandchildren. At one time, she had lived with her husband, the deacon, in a poor village; she had lived there a very long time from the age of seventeen to sixty. The bishop remembered her from early childhood, almost from the age of three, and--how he had loved her! Sweet, precious childhood, always fondly remembered!

Why did it, that long-past time that could never return, why did it seem brighter, fuller, and more festive than it had really been?

When in his childhood or youth he had been ill, how tender and sympathetic his mother had been! And now his prayers mingled with the memories, which gleamed more and more brightly like a flame, and the prayers did not hinder his thinking of his mother.

When he had finished his prayers he undressed and lay down, and at once, as soon as it was dark, there rose before his mind his dead father, his mother, his native village Lesopolye... the creak of wheels, the bleat of sheep, the church bells on bright summer mornings, the gypsies under the window--oh, how sweet to think of it! He remembered the priest of Lesopolye, Father Simeon--mild, gentle, kindly; he was a lean little man, while his son, a divinity student, was a huge fellow and talked in a roaring bass voice. The priest's son had flown into a rage with the cook and abused her: "Ah, you Jehud's ass!" and Father Simeon overhearing it, said not a word, and was only ashamed because he could not remember where such an ass was mentioned in the Bible. After him the priest at Lesopolye had been Father Demyan, who used to drink heavily, and at times drank till he saw green snakes, and was even nicknamed Demyan Snakeseer. The schoolmaster at Lesopolye was Matvey Nikolaitch, who had been a divinity student, a kind and intelligent man, but he, too, was a drunkard; he never beat the schoolchildren, but for some reason he always had hanging on his wall a bunch of birch-twigs, and below it an utterly meaningless inscription in Latin: "Betula kinderbalsamica secuta." He had a shaggy black dog whom he called Syntax.

And his holiness laughed. Six miles from Lesopolye was the village Obnino with a wonder-working ikon. In the summer they used to carry the ikon in procession about the neighbouring villages and ring the bells the whole day long; first in one village and then in another, and it used to seem to the bishop then that joy was quivering in the air, and he (in those days his name was Pavlusha) used to follow the ikon, bareheaded and barefoot, with naive faith, with a naive smile, infinitely happy. In Obnino, he remembered now, there were always a lot of people, and the priest there, Father Alexey, to save time during mass, used to make his deaf nephew Ilarion read the names of those for whose health or whose souls' peace prayers were asked. Ilarion used to read them, now and then getting a five or ten kopeck piece for the service, and only when he was grey and bald, when life was nearly over, he suddenly saw written on one of the pieces of paper: "What a fool you are, Ilarion." Up to fifteen at least Pavlusha was undeveloped and idle at his lessons, so much so that they thought of taking him away from the clerical school and putting him into a shop; one day, going to the post at Obnino for letters, he had stared a long time at the post-office clerks and asked: "Allow me to ask, how do you get your salary, every month or every day?"

His holiness crossed himself and turned over on the other side, trying to stop thinking and go to sleep.

"My mother has come," he remembered and laughed.

The moon peeped in at the window, the floor was lighted up, and there were shadows on it. A cricket was chirping. Through the wall Father Sisoy was snoring in the next room, and his aged snore had a sound that suggested loneliness, forlornness, even vagrancy. Sisoy had once been housekeeper to the bishop of the diocese, and was called now "the former Father Housekeeper"; he was seventy years old, he lived in a monastery twelve miles from the town and stayed sometimes in the town, too. He had come to the Pankratievsky Monastery three days before, and the bishop had kept him that he might talk to him at his leisure about matters of business, about the arrangements here...

At half-past one they began ringing for matins. Father Sisoy could be heard coughing, muttering something in a discontented voice, then he got up and walked barefoot about the rooms.

"Father Sisoy," the bishop called.

Sisoy went back to his room and a little later made his appearance in his boots, with a candle; he had on his cassock over his underclothes and on his head was an old faded skull-cap.

"I can't sleep," said the bishop, sitting up. "I must be unwell. And what it is I don't know. Fever!"

"You must have caught cold, your holiness. You must be rubbed with tallow." Sisoy stood a little and yawned. "O Lord, forgive me, a sinner."

"They had the electric lights on at Erakin's today," he said; "I don't like it!"

Father Sisoy was old, lean, bent, always dissatisfied with something, and his eyes were angry-looking and prominent as a crab's.

"I don't like it," he said, going away. "I don't like it. Bother it!"

II

Next day, Palm Sunday, the bishop took the service in the cathedral in the town, then he visited the bishop of the diocese, then visited a very sick old lady, the widow of a general, and at last drove home. Between one and two o'clock he had welcome visitors dining with him--his mother and his niece Katya, a child of eight years old. All dinner-time the spring sunshine was streaming in at the windows, throwing bright light on the white tablecloth and on Katya's red hair. Through the double windows they could hear the noise of the rooks and the notes of the starlings in the garden.

"It is nine years since we have met," said the old lady. "And when I looked at you in the monastery yesterday, good Lord! you've not changed a bit, except maybe you are thinner and your beard is a little longer. Holy Mother, Queen of Heaven! Yesterday at the evening service no one could help crying. I, too, as I looked at you, suddenly began crying, though I couldn't say why. His Holy Will!"

And in spite of the affectionate tone in which she said this, he could see she was constrained as though she were uncertain whether to address him formally or familiarly, to laugh or not, and that she felt herself more a deacon's widow than his mother. And Katya gazed without blinking at her uncle, his holiness, as though trying to discover what sort of a person he was. Her hair sprang up from under the comb and the velvet ribbon and stood out like a halo; she had a turned-up nose and sly eyes. The child had broken a glass before sitting down to dinner, and now her grandmother, as she talked, moved away from Katya first a wineglass and then a tumbler. The bishop listened to his mother and remembered how many, many years ago she used to take him and his brothers and sisters to relations whom she considered rich; in those days she was taken up with the care of her children, now with her grandchildren, and she had brought Katya...

"Your sister, Varenka, has four children," she told him; "Katya, here, is the eldest. And your brother-in-law Father Ivan fell sick, God knows of what, and died three days before the Assumption; and my poor Varenka is left a beggar."

"And how is Nikanor getting on?" the bishop asked about his eldest brother.

"He is all right, thank God. Though he has nothing much, yet he can live. Only there is one thing: his son, my grandson Nikolasha, did not want to go into the Church; he has gone to the university to be a doctor. He thinks it is better; but who knows! His Holy Will!"

"Nikolasha cuts up dead people," said Katya, spilling water over her knees.

"Sit still, child," her grandmother observed calmly, and took the glass out of her hand. "Say a prayer, and go on eating."

"How long it is since we have seen each other!" said the bishop, and he tenderly stroked his mother's hand and shoulder; "and I missed you abroad, mother, I missed you dreadfully."

"Thank you."

"I used to sit in the evenings at the open window, lonely and alone; often there was music playing, and all at once I used to be overcome with homesickness and felt as though I would give everything only to be at home and see you."

His mother smiled, beamed, but at once she made a grave face and said:

"Thank you."

His mood suddenly changed. He looked at his mother and could not understand how she had come by that respectfulness, that timid expression of face: what was it for? And he did not recognize her. He felt sad and vexed. And then his head ached just as it had the day before; his legs felt fearfully tired, and the fish seemed to him stale and tasteless; he felt thirsty all the time...

After dinner two rich ladies, landowners, arrived and sat for an hour and a half in silence with rigid countenances; the archimandrite, a silent, rather deaf man, came to see him about business. Then they began ringing for vespers; the sun was setting behind the wood and the day was over. When he returned from church, he hurriedly said his prayers, got into bed, and wrapped himself up as warm as possible.

It was disagreeable to remember the fish he had eaten at dinner. The moonlight worried him, and then he heard talking. In an adjoining room, probably in the parlour, Father Sisoy was talking politics:

"There's war among the Japanese now. They are fighting. The Japanese, my good soul, are the same as the Montenegrins; they are the same race. They were under the Turkish yoke together."

And then he heard the voice of Marya Timofyevna:

"So, having said our prayers and drunk tea, we went, you know, to Father Yegor at Novokatnoye, so..."

And she kept on saying, "having had tea" or "having drunk tea," and it seemed as though the only thing she had done in her life was to drink tea.

The bishop slowly, languidly, recalled the seminary, the academy. For three years he had been Greek teacher in the seminary: by that time he could not read without spectacles. Then he had become a monk; he had been made a school inspector. Then he had defended his thesis for his degree. When he was thirty-two he had been made rector of the seminary, and consecrated archimandrite: and then his life had been so easy, so pleasant; it seemed so long, so long, no end was in sight. Then he had begun to be ill, had grown very thin and almost blind, and by the advice of the doctors had to give up everything and go abroad.

"And what then?" asked Sisoy in the next room.

"Then we drank tea..." answered Marya Timofyevna.

"Good gracious, you've got a green beard," said Katya suddenly in surprise, and she laughed.

The bishop remembered that the grey-headed Father Sisoy's beard really had a shade of green in it, and he laughed.

"God have mercy upon us, what we have to put up with this girl!" said Sisoy, aloud, getting angry. "Spoilt child! Sit quiet!"

The bishop remembered the perfectly new white church in which he had conducted the services while living abroad, he remembered the sound of the warm sea. In his flat he had five lofty light rooms; in his study he had a new writing-table, lots of books. He had read a great deal and often written. And he remembered how he had pined for his native land, how a blind beggar woman had played the guitar under his window every day and sung of love, and how, as he listened, he had always for some reason thought of the past. But eight years had passed and he had been called back to Russia, and now he was a suffragan bishop, and all the past had retreated far away into the mist as though it were a dream...

Father Sisoy came into the bedroom with a candle.

"I say!" he said, wondering, "are you asleep already, your holiness?"

"What is it?"

"Why, it's still early, ten o'clock or less. I bought a candle to-day; I wanted to rub you with tallow."

"I am in a fever..." said the bishop, and he sat up. "I really ought to have something. My head is bad..."

Sisoy took off the bishop's shirt and began rubbing his chest and back with tallow.

"That's the way... that's the way..." he said. "Lord Jesus Christ... that's the way. I walked to the town to-day; I was at what's-his-name's--the chief priest Sidonsky's... I had tea with him. I don't like him. Lord Jesus Christ... That's the way. I don't like him."

III

The bishop of the diocese, a very fat old man, was ill with rheumatism or gout, and had been in bed for over a month. Bishop Pyotr went to see him almost every day, and saw all who came to ask his help. And now that he was unwell he was struck by the emptiness, the triviality of everything which they asked and for which they wept; he was vexed at their ignorance, their timidity; and all this useless, petty business oppressed him by the mass of it, and it seemed to him that now he understood the diocesan bishop, who had once in his young days written on "The Doctrines of the Freedom of the Will," and now seemed to be all lost in trivialities, to have forgotten everything, and to have no thoughts of religion. The bishop must have lost touch with Russian life while he was abroad; he did not find it easy; the peasants seemed to him coarse, the women who sought his help dull and stupid, the seminarists and their teachers uncultivated and at times savage. And the documents coming in and going out were reckoned by tens of thousands; and what documents they were! The higher clergy in the whole diocese gave the priests, young and old, and even their wives and children, marks for their behaviour--a five, a four, and sometimes even a three; and about this he had to talk and to read and write serious reports. And there was positively not one minute to spare; his soul was troubled all day long, and the bishop was only at peace when he was in church.

He could not get used, either, to the awe which, through no wish of his own, he inspired in people in spite of his quiet, modest disposition. All the people in the province seemed to him little, scared, and guilty when he looked at them. Everyone was timid in his presence, even the old chief priests; everyone "flopped" at his feet, and not long previously an old lady, a village priest's wife who had come to consult him, was so overcome by awe that she could not utter a single word, and went empty away. And he, who could never in his sermons bring himself to speak ill of people, never reproached anyone because he was so sorry for them, was moved to fury with the people who came to consult him, lost his temper and flung their petitions on the floor. The whole time he had been here, not one person had spoken to him genuinely, simply, as to a human being; even his old mother seemed now not the same! And why, he wondered, did she chatter away to Sisoy and laugh so much; while with him, her son, she was grave and usually silent and constrained, which did not suit her at all. The only person who behaved freely with him and said what he meant was old Sisoy, who had spent his whole life in the presence of bishops and had outlived eleven of them. And so the bishop was at ease with him, although, of course, he was a tedious and nonsensical man.

After the service on Tuesday, his holiness Pyotr was in the diocesan bishop's house receiving petitions there; he got excited and angry, and then drove home. He was as unwell as before; he longed to be in bed, but he had hardly reached home when he was informed that a young merchant called Erakin, who subscribed liberally to charities, had come to see him about a very important matter. The bishop had to see him. Erakin stayed about an hour, talked very loud, almost shouted, and it was difficult to understand what he said.

"God grant it may," he said as he went away. "Most essential! According to circumstances, your holiness! I trust it may!"

After him came the Mother Superior from a distant convent. And when she had gone they began ringing for vespers. He had to go to church.

In the evening the monks sang harmoniously, with inspiration. A young priest with a black beard conducted the service; and the bishop, hearing of the Bridegroom who comes at midnight and of the Heavenly Mansion adorned for the festival, felt no repentance for his sins, no tribulation, but peace at heart and tranquillity. And he was carried back in thought to the distant past, to his childhood and youth, when, too, they used to sing of the Bridegroom and of the Heavenly Mansion; and now that past rose up before him--living, fair, and joyful as in all likelihood it never had been. And perhaps in the other world, in the life to come, we shall think of the distant past, of our life here, with the same feeling. Who knows? The bishop was sitting near the altar. It was dark; tears flowed down his face. He thought that here he had attained everything a man in his position could attain; he had faith and yet everything was not clear, something was lacking still. He did not want to die; and he still felt that he had missed what was most important, something of which he had dimly dreamed in the past; and he was troubled by the same hopes for the future as he had felt in childhood, at the academy and abroad.

"How well they sing to-day!" he thought, listening to the singing. "How nice it is!"

IV

On Thursday he celebrated mass in the cathedral; it was the Washing of Feet. When the service was over and the people were going home, it was sunny, warm; the water gurgled in the gutters, and the unceasing trilling of the larks, tender, telling of peace, rose from the fields outside the town. The trees were already awakening and smiling a welcome, while above them the infinite, fathomless blue sky stretched into the distance, God knows whither.

On reaching home his holiness drank some tea, then changed his clothes, lay down on his bed, and told the lay brother to close the shutters on the windows. The bedroom was darkened. But what weariness, what pain in his legs and his back, a chill heavy pain, what a noise in his ears! He had not slept for a long time--for a very long time, as it seemed to him now, and some trifling detail which haunted his brain as soon as his eyes were closed prevented him from sleeping.

As on the day before, sounds reached him from the adjoining rooms through the walls, voices, the jingle of glasses and teaspoons... Marya Timofyevna was gaily telling Father Sisoy some story with quaint turns of speech, while the latter answered in a grumpy, ill-humoured voice: "Bother them! Not likely! What next!" And the bishop again felt vexed and then hurt that with other people his old mother behaved in a simple, ordinary way, while with him, her son, she was shy, spoke little, and did not say what she meant, and even, as he fancied, had during all those three days kept trying in his presence to find an excuse for standing up, because she was embarrassed at sitting before him. And his father? He, too, probably, if he had been living, would not have been able to utter a word in the bishop's presence...

Something fell down on the floor in the adjoining room and was broken; Katya must have dropped a cup or a saucer, for Father Sisoy suddenly spat and said angrily:

"What a regular nuisance the child is! Lord forgive my transgressions! One can't provide enough for her."

Then all was quiet, the only sounds came from outside. And when the bishop opened his eyes he saw Katya in his room, standing motionless, staring at him. Her red hair, as usual, stood up from under the comb like a halo.

"Is that you, Katya?" he asked. "Who is it downstairs who keeps opening and shutting a door?"

"I don't hear it," answered Katya; and she listened.

"There, someone has just passed by."

"But that was a noise in your stomach, uncle."

He laughed and stroked her on the head.

"So you say Cousin Nikolasha cuts up dead people?" he asked after a pause.

"Yes, he is studying."

"And is he kind?"

"Oh, yes, he's kind. But he drinks vodka awfully."

"And what was it your father died of?"

"Papa was weak and very, very thin, and all at once his throat was bad. I was ill then, too, and brother Fedya; we all had bad throats. Papa died, uncle, and we got well."

Her chin began quivering, and tears gleamed in her eyes and trickled down her cheeks.

"Your holiness," she said in a shrill voice, by now weeping bitterly, "uncle, mother and all of us are left very wretched... Give us a little money... do be kind... uncle darling..."

He, too, was moved to tears, and for a long time was too much touched to speak. Then he stroked her on the head, patted her on the shoulder and said:

"Very good, very good, my child. When the holy Easter comes, we will talk it over... I will help you... I will help you..."

His mother came in quietly, timidly, and prayed before the ikon. Noticing that he was not sleeping, she said:

"Won't you have a drop of soup?"

"No, thank you," he answered, "I am not hungry."

"You seem to be unwell, now I look at you. I should think so; you may well be ill! The whole day on your legs, the whole day... And, my goodness, it makes one's heart ache even to look at you! Well, Easter is not far off; you will rest then, please God. Then we will have a talk, too, but now I'm not going to disturb you with my chatter. Come along, Katya; let his holiness sleep a little."

And he remembered how once very long ago, when he was a boy, she had spoken exactly like that, in the same jestingly respectful tone, with a Church dignitary... Only from her extraordinarily kind eyes and the timid, anxious glance she stole at him as she went out of the room could one have guessed that this was his mother. He shut his eyes and seemed to sleep, but twice heard the clock strike and Father Sisoy coughing the other side of the wall. And once more his mother came in and looked timidly at him for a minute. Someone drove up to the steps, as he could hear, in a coach or in a chaise. Suddenly a knock, the door slammed, the lay brother came into the bedroom.

"Your holiness," he called.

"Well?"

"The horses are here; it's time for the evening service."

"What o'clock is it?"

"A quarter past seven."

He dressed and drove to the cathedral. During all the "Twelve Gospels" he had to stand in the middle of the church without moving, and the first gospel, the longest and the most beautiful, he read himself. A mood of confidence and courage came over him. That first gospel, "Now is the Son of Man glorified," he knew by heart; and as he read he raised his eyes from time to time, and saw on both sides a perfect sea of lights and heard the splutter of candles, but, as in past years, he could not see the people, and it seemed as though these were all the same people as had been round him in those days, in his childhood and his youth; that they would always be the same every year and till such time as God only knew.

His father had been a deacon, his grandfather a priest, his great-grandfather a deacon, and his whole family, perhaps from the days when Christianity had been accepted in Russia, had belonged to the priesthood; and his love for the Church services, for the priesthood, for the peal of the bells, was deep in him, ineradicable, innate. In church, particularly when he took part in the service, he felt vigorous, of good cheer, happy. So it was now. Only when the eighth gospel had been read, he felt that his voice had grown weak, even his cough was inaudible. His head had begun to ache intensely, and he was troubled by a fear that he might fall down.

And his legs were indeed quite numb, so that by degrees he ceased to feel them and could not understand how or on what he was standing, and why he did not fall...

It was a quarter to twelve when the service was over. When he reached home, the bishop undressed and went to bed at once without even saying his prayers. He could not speak and felt that he could not have stood up. When he had covered his head with the quilt he felt a sudden longing to be abroad, an insufferable longing! He felt that he would give his life not to see those pitiful cheap shutters, those low ceilings, not to smell that heavy monastery smell. If only there were one person to whom he could have talked, have opened his heart!

For a long while he heard footsteps in the next room and could not tell whose they were. At last the door opened, and Sisoy came in with a candle and a tea-cup in his hand.

"You are in bed already, your holiness?" he asked. "Here I have come to rub you with spirit and vinegar. A thorough rubbing does a great deal of good. Lord Jesus Christ!... That's the way... that's the way... I've just been in our monastery... I don't like it. I'm going away from here to-morrow, your holiness; I don't want to stay longer. Lord Jesus Christ... That's the way..."

Sisoy could never stay long in the same place, and he felt as though he had been a whole year in the Pankratievsky Monastery. Above all, listening to him it was difficult to understand where his home was, whether he cared for anyone or anything, whether he believed in God... He did not know himself why he was a monk, and, indeed, he did not think about it, and the time when he had become a monk had long passed out of his memory; it seemed as though he had been born a monk.

"I'm going away to-morrow; God be with them all."

"I should like to talk to you... I can't find the time," said the bishop softly with an effort. "I don't know anything or anybody here..."

"I'll stay till Sunday if you like; so be it, but I don't want to stay longer. I am sick of them!"

"I ought not to be a bishop," said the bishop softly. "I ought to have been a village priest, a deacon... or simply a monk... All this oppresses me... oppresses me."

"What? Lord Jesus Christ... That's the way. Come, sleep well, your holiness!... What's the good of talking? It's no use. Good-night!"

The bishop did not sleep all night. And at eight o'clock in the morning he began to have hemorrhage from the bowels. The lay brother was alarmed, and ran first to the archimandrite, then for the monastery doctor, Ivan Andreyitch, who lived in the town. The doctor, a stout old man with a long grey beard, made a prolonged examination of the bishop, and kept shaking his head and frowning, then said:

"Do you know, your holiness, you have got typhoid?"

After an hour or so of hemorrhage the bishop looked much thinner, paler, and wasted; his face looked wrinkled, his eyes looked bigger, and he seemed older, shorter, and it seemed to him that he was thinner, weaker, more insignificant than any one, that everything that had been had retreated far, far away and would never go on again or be repeated.

"How good," he thought, "how good!"

His old mother came. Seeing his wrinkled face and his big eyes, she was frightened, she fell on her knees by the bed and began kissing his face, his shoulders, his hands. And to her, too, it seemed that he was thinner, weaker, and more insignificant than anyone, and now she forgot that he was a bishop, and kissed him as though he were a child very near and very dear to her.

"Pavlusha, darling," she said; "my own, my darling son!... Why are you like this? Pavlusha, answer me!"

Katya, pale and severe, stood beside her, unable to understand what was the matter with her uncle, why there was such a look of suffering on her grandmother's face, why she was saying such sad and touching things. By now he could not utter a word, he could understand nothing, and he imagined he was a simple ordinary man, that he was walking quickly, cheerfully through the fields, tapping with his stick, while above him was the open sky bathed in sunshine, and that he was free now as a bird and could go where he liked!

"Pavlusha, my darling son, answer me," the old woman was saying. "What is it? My own!"

"Don't disturb his holiness," Sisoy said angrily, walking about the room. "Let him sleep... what's the use... it's no good..."

Three doctors arrived, consulted together, and went away again. The day was long, incredibly long, then the night came on and passed slowly, slowly, and towards morning on Saturday the lay brother went in to the old mother who was lying on the sofa in the parlour, and asked her to go into the bedroom: the bishop had just breathed his last.

Next day was Easter Sunday. There were forty-two churches and six monasteries in the town; the sonorous, joyful clang of the bells hung over the town from morning till night unceasingly, setting the spring air aquiver; the birds were singing, the sun was shining brightly. The big market square was noisy, swings were going, barrel organs were playing, accordions were squeaking, drunken voices were shouting. After midday people began driving up and down the principal street.

In short, all was merriment, everything was satisfactory, just as it had been the year before, and as it will be in all likelihood next year.

A month later a new suffragan bishop was appointed, and no one thought anything more of Bishop Pyotr, and afterwards he was completely forgotten. And only the dead man's old mother, who is living to-day with her son-in-law the deacon in a remote little district town, when she goes out at night to bring her cow in and meets other women at the pasture, begins talking of her children and her grandchildren, and says that she had a son a bishop, and this she says timidly, afraid that she may not be believed...

And, indeed, there are some who do not believe her.

The Letter

The clerical superintendent of the district, his Reverence Father
Fyodor Orlov, a handsome, well-nourished man of fifty, grave and
important as he always was, with an habitual expression of dignity
that never left his face, was walking to and fro in his little drawing-
room, extremely exhausted, and thinking intensely about the same
thing: "When would his visitor go?" The thought worried him and did
not leave him for a minute. The visitor, Father Anastasy, the priest of
one of the villages near the town, had come to him three hours before
on some very unpleasant and dreary business of his own, had stayed
on and on, was now sitting in the corner at a little round table with
his elbow on a thick account book, and apparently had no thought of
going, though it was getting on for nine o'clock in the evening.

Not everyone knows when to be silent and when to go. It not
infrequently happens that even diplomatic persons of good worldly
breeding fail to observe that their presence is arousing a feeling akin
to hatred in their exhausted or busy host, and that this feeling is being
concealed with an effort and disguised with a lie. But Father Anastasy
perceived it clearly, and realized that his presence was burdensome and
inappropriate, that his Reverence, who had taken an early morning
service in the night and a long mass at midday, was exhausted and
longing for repose; every minute he was meaning to get up and go, but
he did not get up, he sat on as though he were waiting for something.
He was an old man of sixty-five, prematurely aged, with a bent and
bony figure, with a sunken face and the dark skin of old age, with
red eyelids and a long narrow back like a fish's; he was dressed in a
smart cassock of a light lilac colour, but too big for him (presented to

him by the widow of a young priest lately deceased), a full cloth coat with a broad leather belt, and clumsy high boots the size and hue of which showed clearly that Father Anastasy dispensed with galoshes. In spite of his position and his venerable age, there was something pitiful, crushed and humiliated in his lustreless red eyes, in the strands of grey hair with a shade of green in it on the nape of his neck, and in the big shoulder-blades on his lean back... He sat without speaking or moving, and coughed with circumspection, as though afraid that the sound of his coughing might make his presence more noticeable.

The old man had come to see his Reverence on business. Two months before he had been prohibited from officiating till further notice, and his case was being inquired into. His shortcomings were numerous. He was intemperate in his habits, fell out with the other clergy and the commune, kept the church records and accounts carelessly --these were the formal charges against him; but besides all that, there had been rumours for a long time past that he celebrated unlawful marriages for money and sold certificates of having fasted and taken the sacrament to officials and officers who came to him from the town. These rumours were maintained the more persistently that he was poor and had nine children to keep, who were as incompetent and unsuccessful as himself. The sons were spoilt and uneducated, and stayed at home doing nothing, while the daughters were ugly and did not get married.

Not having the moral force to be open, his Reverence walked up and down the room and said nothing or spoke in hints.

"So you are not going home to-night?" he asked, stopping near the dark window and poking with his little finger into the cage where a canary was asleep with its feathers puffed out.

Father Anastasy started, coughed cautiously and said rapidly:

"Home? I don't care to, Fyodor Ilyitch. I cannot officiate, as you know, so what am I to do there? I came away on purpose that I might not have to look the people in the face. One is ashamed not to officiate, as you know. Besides, I have business here, Fyodor Ilyitch. To-morrow after breaking the fast I want to talk things over thoroughly with the Father charged with the inquiry."

"Ah!...." yawned his Reverence, "and where are you staying?"

"At Zyavkin's."

Father Anastasy suddenly remembered that within two hours his Reverence had to take the Easter-night service, and he felt so ashamed of his unwelcome burdensome presence that he made up his mind to go away at once and let the exhausted man rest. And the old man got up to go. But before he began saying good-bye he stood clearing his throat for a minute and looking searchingly at his Reverence's back, still with the same expression of vague expectation in his whole figure; his face was working with shame, timidity, and a pitiful forced laugh such as one sees in people who do not respect themselves. Waving his hand as it were resolutely, he said with a husky quavering laugh:

"Father Fyodor, do me one more kindness: bid them give me at leave-taking... one little glass of vodka."

"It's not the time to drink vodka now," said his Reverence sternly. "One must have some regard for decency."

Father Anastasy was still more overwhelmed by confusion; he laughed, and, forgetting his resolution to go away, he dropped back on his chair. His Reverence looked at his helpless, embarrassed face and his bent figure and he felt sorry for the old man.

"Please God, we will have a drink to-morrow," he said, wishing to soften his stem refusal. "Everything is good in due season."

His Reverence believed in people's reforming, but now when a feeling of pity had been kindled in him it seemed to him that this disgraced, worn-out old man, entangled in a network of sins and weaknesses, was hopelessly wrecked, that there was no power on earth that could straighten out his spine, give brightness to his eyes and restrain the unpleasant timid laugh which he laughed on purpose to smooth over to some slight extent the repulsive impression he made on people.

The old man seemed now to Father Fyodor not guilty and not vicious, but humiliated, insulted, unfortunate; his Reverence thought of his wife, his nine children, the dirty beggarly shelter at Zyavkin's; he thought for some reason of the people who are glad to see priests drunk and persons in authority detected in crimes; and thought that the very best thing Father Anastasy could do now would be to die as soon as possible and to depart from this world for ever.

There were a sound of footsteps.

"Father Fyodor, you are not resting?" a bass voice asked from the passage.

"No, deacon; come in."

Orlov's colleague, the deacon Liubimov, an elderly man with a big bald patch on the top of his head, though his hair was still black and he was still vigorous-looking, with thick black eyebrows like a Georgian's, walked in. He bowed to Father Anastasy and sat down.

"What good news have you?" asked his Reverence.

"What good news?" answered the deacon, and after a pause he went on with a smile: "When your children are little, your trouble is small; when your children are big, your trouble is great. Such goings on, Father Fyodor, that I don't know what to think of it. It's a regular farce, that's what it is."

He paused again for a little, smiled still more broadly and said:

"Nikolay Matveyitch came back from Harkov to-day. He has been telling me about my Pyotr. He has been to see him twice, he tells me."

"What has he been telling you, then?"

"He has upset me, God bless him. He meant to please me but when I came to think it over, it seems there is not much to be pleased at. I ought to grieve rather than be pleased... 'Your Petrushka,' said he, 'lives in fine style. He is far above us now,' said he. 'Well thank God for that,' said I. 'I dined with him,' said he, 'and saw his whole manner of life. He lives like a gentleman,' he said; 'you couldn't wish to live better.' I was naturally interested and I asked, 'And what did you have for dinner?' 'First,' he said, 'a fish course something like fish soup, then tongue and peas,' and then he said, 'roast turkey.' 'Turkey in Lent? that is something to please me,' said I. 'Turkey in Lent? Eh?'"

"Nothing marvellous in that," said his Reverence, screwing up his eyes ironically. And sticking both thumbs in his belt, he drew himself up and said in the tone in which he usually delivered discourses or gave his Scripture lessons to the pupils in the district school: "People who do not keep the fasts are divided into two different categories: some do not keep them through laxity, others through infidelity. Your Pyotr does not keep them through infidelity. Yes."

The deacon looked timidly at Father Fyodor's stern face and said:

"There is worse to follow... We talked and discussed one thing and another, and it turned out that my infidel of a son is living with some madame, another man's wife. She takes the place of wife and hostess in his flat, pours out the tea, receives visitors and all the rest of it, as though she were his lawful wife. For over two years he has been keeping up this dance with this viper. It's a regular farce. They have been living together for three years and no children."

"I suppose they have been living in chastity!" chuckled Father Anastasy, coughing huskily. "There are children, Father Deacon-- there are, but they don't keep them at home! They send them to the Foundling! He-he-he!..." Anastasy went on coughing till he choked.

"Don't interfere, Father Anastasy," said his Reverence sternly.

"Nikolay Matveyitch asked him, 'What madame is this helping the soup at your table?'" the deacon went on, gloomily scanning Anastasy's bent figure. "'That is my wife,' said he. 'When was your wedding?' Nikolay Matveyitch asked him, and Pyotr answered, 'We were married at Kulikov's restaurant.'"

His Reverence's eyes flashed wrathfully and the colour came into his temples. Apart from his sinfulness, Pyotr was not a person he liked. Father Fyodor had, as they say, a grudge against him. He remembered him a boy at school--he remembered him distinctly, because even then the boy had seemed to him not normal. As a schoolboy, Petrushka

had been ashamed to serve at the altar, had been offended at being
addressed without ceremony, had not crossed himself on entering the
room, and what was still more noteworthy, was fond of talking a great
deal and with heat--and, in Father Fyodor's opinion, much talking was
unseemly in children and pernicious to them; moreover Petrushka
had taken up a contemptuous and critical attitude to fishing, a pursuit
to which both his Reverence and the deacon were greatly addicted.
As a student Pyotr had not gone to church at all, had slept till midday,
had looked down on people, and had been given to raising delicate
and insoluble questions with a peculiarly provoking zest.

"What would you have?" his Reverence asked, going up to the
deacon and looking at him angrily. "What would you have? This was
to be expected! I always knew and was convinced that nothing good
would come of your Pyotr! I told you so, and I tell you so now. What
you have sown, that now you must reap! Reap it!"

"But what have I sown, Father Fyodor?" the deacon asked softly,
looking up at his Reverence.

"Why, who is to blame if not you? You're his father, he is your
offspring! You ought to have admonished him, have instilled the fear
of God into him. A child must be taught! You have brought him into
the world, but you haven't trained him up in the right way. It's a sin!
It's wrong! It's a shame!"

His Reverence forgot his exhaustion, paced to and fro and went
on talking. Drops of perspiration came out on the deacon's bald head
and forehead. He raised his eyes to his Reverence with a look of guilt,
and said:

"But didn't I train him, Father Fyodor? Lord have mercy on us,
haven't I been a father to my children? You know yourself I spared
nothing for his good; I have prayed and done my best all my life to
give him a thorough education. He went to the high school and I got
him tutors, and he took his degree at the University. And as to my
not being able to influence his mind, Father Fyodor, why, you can
judge for yourself that I am not qualified to do so! Sometimes when

he used to come here as a student, I would begin admonishing him in my way, and he wouldn't heed me. I'd say to him, 'Go to church,' and he would answer, 'What for?' I would begin explaining, and he would say, 'Why? what for?' Or he would slap me on the shoulder and say, 'Everything in this world is relative, approximate and conditional. I don't know anything, and you don't know anything either, dad.'"

Father Anastasy laughed huskily, cleared his throat and waved his fingers in the air as though preparing to say something. His Reverence glanced at him and said sternly:

"Don't interfere, Father Anastasy."

The old man laughed, beamed, and evidently listened with pleasure to the deacon as though he were glad there were other sinful persons in this world besides himself. The deacon spoke sincerely, with an aching heart, and tears actually came into his eyes. Father Fyodor felt sorry for him.

"You are to blame, deacon, you are to blame," he said, but not so sternly and heatedly as before. "If you could beget him, you ought to know how to instruct him. You ought to have trained him in his childhood; it's no good trying to correct a student."

A silence followed; the deacon clasped his hands and said with a sigh:

"But you know I shall have to answer for him!"

"To be sure you will!"

After a brief silence his Reverence yawned and sighed at the same moment and asked:

"Who is reading the 'Acts'?"

"Yevstrat. Yevstrat always reads them."

The deacon got up and, looking imploringly at his Reverence, asked:

"Father Fyodor, what am I to do now?"

"Do as you please; you are his father, not I. You ought to know best."

"I don't know anything, Father Fyodor! Tell me what to do, for goodness' sake! Would you believe it, I am sick at heart! I can't sleep now, nor keep quiet, and the holiday will be no holiday to me. Tell me what to do, Father Fyodor!"

"Write him a letter."

"What am I to write to him?"

"Write that he mustn't go on like that. Write shortly, but sternly and circumstantially, without softening or smoothing away his guilt. It is your parental duty; if you write, you will have done your duty and will be at peace."

"That's true. But what am I to write to him, to what effect? If I write to him, he will answer, 'Why? what for? Why is it a sin?'"

Father Anastasy laughed hoarsely again, and brandished his fingers.

"Why? what for? why is it a sin?" he began shrilly. "I was once confessing a gentleman, and I told him that excessive confidence in the Divine Mercy is a sin; and he asked, 'Why?' I tried to answer him, but----" Anastasy slapped himself on the forehead. "I had nothing here. He-he-he-he!..."

Anastasy's words, his hoarse jangling laugh at what was not laughable, had an unpleasant effect on his Reverence and on the deacon. The former was on the point of saying, "Don't interfere" again, but he did not say it, he only frowned.

"I can't write to him," sighed the deacon.

"If you can't, who can?"

"Father Fyodor!" said the deacon, putting his head on one side and pressing his hand to his heart. "I am an uneducated slow-witted man, while the Lord has vouchsafed you judgment and wisdom. You know everything and understand everything. You can master anything, while I don't know how to put my words together sensibly. Be generous. Instruct me how to write the letter. Teach me what to say and how to say it..."

"What is there to teach? There is nothing to teach. Sit down and write."

"Oh, do me the favour, Father Fyodor! I beseech you! I know he will be frightened and will attend to your letter, because, you see, you are a cultivated man too. Do be so good! I'll sit down, and you'll dictate to me. It will be a sin to write to-morrow, but now would be the very time; my mind would be set at rest."

His Reverence looked at the deacon's imploring face, thought of the disagreeable Pyotr, and consented to dictate. He made the deacon sit down to his table and began.

"Well, write... 'Christ is risen, dear son...' exclamation mark. 'Rumours have reached me, your father,' then in parenthesis, 'from what source is no concern of yours...' close the parenthesis... Have you written it? 'That you are leading a life inconsistent with the laws both of God and of man. Neither the luxurious comfort, nor the worldly splendour, nor the culture with which you seek outwardly to disguise it, can hide your heathen manner of life. In name you are a Christian, but in your real nature a heathen as pitiful and wretched as all other heathens--more wretched, indeed, seeing that those heathens who know not Christ are lost from ignorance, while you are lost in that, possessing a treasure, you neglect it. I will not enumerate here your vices, which you know well enough; I will say that I see the cause of your ruin in your infidelity. You imagine yourself to be wise, boast of your knowledge of science, but refuse to see that science without faith, far from elevating a man, actually degrades him to the level of a lower animal, inasmuch as...'" The whole letter was in this strain.

When he had finished writing it the deacon read it aloud, beamed all over and jumped up.

"It's a gift, it's really a gift!" he said, clasping his hands and looking enthusiastically at his Reverence. "To think of the Lord's bestowing a gift like that! Eh? Holy Mother! I do believe I couldn't write a letter like that in a hundred years. Lord save you!"

Father Anastasy was enthusiastic too.

"One couldn't write like that without a gift," he said, getting up and wagging his fingers--"that one couldn't! His rhetoric would trip any philosopher and shut him up. Intellect. Brilliant intellect! If you weren't married, Father Fyodor, you would have been a bishop long ago, you would really!"

Having vented his wrath in a letter, his Reverence felt relieved; his fatigue and exhaustion came back to him. The deacon was an old friend, and his Reverence did not hesitate to say to him:

"Well deacon, go, and God bless you. I'll have half an hour's nap on the sofa; I must rest."

The deacon went away and took Anastasy with him. As is always the case on Easter Eve, it was dark in the street, but the whole sky was sparkling with bright luminous stars. There was a scent of spring and holiday in the soft still air.

"How long was he dictating?" the deacon said admiringly. "Ten minutes, not more! It would have taken someone else a month to compose such a letter. Eh! What a mind! Such a mind that I don't know what to call it! It's a marvel! It's really a marvel!"

"Education!" sighed Anastasy as he crossed the muddy street; holding up his cassock to his waist. "It's not for us to compare ourselves with him. We come of the sacristan class, while he has had a learned education. Yes, he's a real man, there is no denying that."

"And you listen how he'll read the Gospel in Latin at mass to-day! He knows Latin and he knows Greek... Ah Petrushka, Petrushka!" the deacon said, suddenly remembering. "Now that will make him scratch his head! That will shut his mouth, that will bring it home to him! Now he won't ask 'Why.' It is a case of one wit to outwit another! Haha-ha!"

The deacon laughed gaily and loudly. Since the letter had been written to Pyotr he had become serene and more cheerful. The consciousness of having performed his duty as a father and his faith in the power of the letter had brought back his mirthfulness and good-humour.

"Pyotr means a stone," said he, as he went into his house. "My Pyotr is not a stone, but a rag. A viper has fastened upon him and he pampers her, and hasn't the pluck to kick her out. Tfoo! To think there should be women like that, God forgive me! Eh? Has she no shame? She has fastened upon the lad, sticking to him, and keeps him tied to her apron strings... Fie upon her!"

"Perhaps it's not she keeps hold of him, but he of her?"

"She is a shameless one anyway! Not that I am defending Pyotr... He'll catch it. He'll read the letter and scratch his head! He'll burn with shame!"

"It's a splendid letter, only you know I wouldn't send it, Father Deacon. Let him alone."

"What?" said the deacon, disconcerted.

"Why... Don't send it, deacon! What's the sense of it? Suppose you send it; he reads it, and... and what then? You'll only upset him. Forgive him. Let him alone!"

The deacon looked in surprise at Anastasy's dark face, at his unbuttoned cassock, which looked in the dusk like wings, and shrugged his shoulders.

"How can I forgive him like that?" he asked. "Why I shall have to answer for him to God!"

"Even so, forgive him all the same. Really! And God will forgive you for your kindness to him."

"But he is my son, isn't he? Ought I not to teach him?"

"Teach him? Of course--why not? You can teach him, but why call him a heathen? It will hurt his feelings, you know, deacon..."

The deacon was a widower, and lived in a little house with three windows. His elder sister, an old maid, looked after his house for him, though she had three years before lost the use of her legs and was confined to her bed; he was afraid of her, obeyed her, and did nothing without her advice. Father Anastasy went in with him. Seeing his table already laid with Easter cakes and red eggs, he began weeping for some reason, probably thinking of his own home, and to turn these tears into a jest, he at once laughed huskily.

"Yes, we shall soon be breaking the fast," he said. "Yes... it wouldn't come amiss, deacon, to have a little glass now. Can we? I'll drink it so that the old lady does not hear," he whispered, glancing sideways towards the door.

Without a word the deacon moved a decanter and wineglass towards him. He unfolded the letter and began reading it aloud. And now the letter pleased him just as much as when his Reverence had dictated it to him. He beamed with pleasure and wagged his head, as though he had been tasting something very sweet.

"A-ah, what a letter!" he said. "Petrushka has never dreamt of such a letter. It's just what he wants, something to throw him into a fever..."

"Do you know, deacon, don't send it!" said Anastasy, pouring himself out a second glass of vodka as though unconsciously. "Forgive him, let him alone! I am telling you... what I really think. If his own father can't forgive him, who will forgive him? And so he'll live without forgiveness. Think, deacon: there will be plenty to chastise him without you, but you should look out for some who will show mercy to your son! I'll... I'll... have just one more. The last, old man... Just sit down and write straight off to him, 'I forgive you Pyotr!' He will under-sta-and! He will fe-el it! I understand it from myself, you see old man... deacon, I mean. When I lived like other people, I hadn't much to trouble about, but now since I lost the image and semblance, there is only one thing I care about, that good people should forgive me. And remember, too, it's not the righteous but sinners we must forgive. Why should you forgive your old woman if she is not sinful? No, you must forgive a man when he is a sad sight to look at... yes!"

Anastasy leaned his head on his fist and sank into thought.

"It's a terrible thing, deacon," he sighed, evidently struggling with the desire to take another glass--"a terrible thing! In sin my mother bore me, in sin I have lived, in sin I shall die... God forgive me, a sinner! I have gone astray, deacon! There is no salvation for me! And it's not as though I had gone astray in my life, but in old age--at death's door... I..."

The old man, with a hopeless gesture, drank off another glass, then got up and moved to another seat. The deacon, still keeping the letter in his hand, was walking up and down the room. He was thinking of his son. Displeasure, distress and anxiety no longer troubled him; all that had gone into the letter. Now he was simply picturing Pyotr; he imagined his face, he thought of the past years when his son used to come to stay with him for the holidays. His thoughts were only of what was good, warm, touching, of which one might think for a whole lifetime without wearying. Longing for his son, he read the letter through once more and looked questioningly at Anastasy.

"Don't send it," said the latter, with a wave of his hand.

"No, I must send it anyway; I must... bring him to his senses a little, all the same. It's just as well..."

The deacon took an envelope from the table, but before putting the letter into it he sat down to the table, smiled and added on his own account at the bottom of the letter:

"They have sent us a new inspector. He's much friskier than the old one. He's a great one for dancing and talking, and there's nothing he can't do, so that all the Govorovsky girls are crazy over him. Our military chief, Kostyrev, will soon get the sack too, they say. High time he did!" And very well pleased, without the faintest idea that with this postscript he had completely spoiled the stern letter, the deacon addressed the envelope and laid it in the most conspicuous place on the table.

Easter Eve

I was standing on the bank of the River Goltva, waiting for the ferry-boat from the other side. At ordinary times the Goltva is a humble stream of moderate size, silent and pensive, gently glimmering from behind thick reeds; but now a regular lake lay stretched out before me. The waters of spring, running riot, had overflowed both banks and flooded both sides of the river for a long distance, submerging vegetable gardens, hayfields and marshes, so that it was no unusual thing to meet poplars and bushes sticking out above the surface of the water and looking in the darkness like grim solitary crags.

The weather seemed to me magnificent. It was dark, yet I could see the trees, the water and the people... The world was lighted by the stars, which were scattered thickly all over the sky. I don't remember ever seeing so many stars. Literally one could not have put a finger in between them. There were some as big as a goose's egg, others tiny as hempseed... They had come out for the festival procession, every one of them, little and big, washed, renewed and joyful, and everyone of them was softly twinkling its beams. The sky was reflected in the water; the stars were bathing in its dark depths and trembling with the quivering eddies. The air was warm and still... Here and there, far away on the further bank in the impenetrable darkness, several bright red lights were gleaming...

A couple of paces from me I saw the dark silhouette of a peasant in a high hat, with a thick knotted stick in his hand.

"How long the ferry-boat is in coming!" I said.

"It is time it was here," the silhouette answered.

"You are waiting for the ferry-boat, too?"

"No I am not," yawned the peasant--"I am waiting for the illumination. I should have gone, but to tell you the truth, I haven't the five kopecks for the ferry."

"I'll give you the five kopecks."

"No; I humbly thank you... With that five kopecks put up a candle for me over there in the monastery... That will be more interesting, and I will stand here. What can it mean, no ferry-boat, as though it had sunk in the water!"

The peasant went up to the water's edge, took the rope in his hands, and shouted; "Ieronim! Ieron--im!"

As though in answer to his shout, the slow peal of a great bell floated across from the further bank. The note was deep and low, as from the thickest string of a double bass; it seemed as though the darkness itself had hoarsely uttered it. At once there was the sound of a cannon shot. It rolled away in the darkness and ended somewhere in the far distance behind me. The peasant took off his hat and crossed himself.

"'Christ is risen," he said.

Before the vibrations of the first peal of the bell had time to die away in the air a second sounded, after it at once a third, and the darkness was filled with an unbroken quivering clamour. Near the red lights fresh lights flashed, and all began moving together and twinkling restlessly.

"Ieron--im!" we heard a hollow prolonged shout.

"They are shouting from the other bank," said the peasant, "so there is no ferry there either. Our Ieronim has gone to sleep."

The lights and the velvety chimes of the bell drew one towards them... I was already beginning to lose patience and grow anxious, but behold at last, staring into the dark distance, I saw the outline of something very much like a gibbet. It was the long-expected ferry. It moved towards us with such deliberation that if it had not been that its lines grew gradually more definite, one might have supposed that it was standing still or moving to the other bank.

"Make haste! Ieronim!" shouted my peasant. "The gentleman's tired of waiting!"

The ferry crawled to the bank, gave a lurch and stopped with a creak. A tall man in a monk's cassock and a conical cap stood on it, holding the rope.

"Why have you been so long?" I asked jumping upon the ferry.

"Forgive me, for Christ's sake," Ieronim answered gently. "Is there no one else?"

"No one..."

Ieronim took hold of the rope in both hands, bent himself to the figure of a mark of interrogation, and gasped. The ferry-boat creaked and gave a lurch. The outline of the peasant in the high hat began slowly retreating from me--so the ferry was moving off. Ieronim soon drew himself up and began working with one hand only. We were silent, gazing towards the bank to which we were floating. There the illumination for which the peasant was waiting had begun. At the water's edge barrels of tar were flaring like huge camp fires. Their reflections, crimson as the rising moon, crept to meet us in long broad streaks. The burning barrels lighted up their own smoke and the long shadows of men flitting about the fire; but further to one side and behind them from where the velvety chime floated there was still the same unbroken black gloom. All at once, cleaving the darkness, a rocket zigzagged in a golden ribbon up the sky; it described an arc and, as though broken to pieces against the sky, was scattered crackling into sparks. There was a roar from the bank like a far-away hurrah.

"How beautiful!" I said.

"Beautiful beyond words!" sighed Ieronim. "Such a night, sir! Another time one would pay no attention to the fireworks, but to-day one rejoices in every vanity. Where do you come from?"

I told him where I came from.

"To be sure... a joyful day to-day..." Ieronim went on in a weak sighing tenor like the voice of a convalescent. "The sky is rejoicing and the earth and what is under the earth. All the creatures are keeping holiday. Only tell me kind sir, why, even in the time of great rejoicing, a man cannot forget his sorrows?"

I fancied that this unexpected question was to draw me into one of those endless religious conversations which bored and idle monks are so fond of. I was not disposed to talk much, and so I only asked:

"What sorrows have you, father?"

"As a rule only the same as all men, kind sir, but to-day a special sorrow has happened in the monastery: at mass, during the reading of the Bible, the monk and deacon Nikolay died."

"Well, it's God's will!" I said, falling into the monastic tone. "We must all die. To my mind, you ought to rejoice indeed... They say if anyone dies at Easter he goes straight to the kingdom of heaven."

"That's true."

We sank into silence. The figure of the peasant in the high hat melted into the lines of the bank. The tar barrels were flaring up more and more.

"The Holy Scripture points clearly to the vanity of sorrow and so does reflection," said Ieronim, breaking the silence, "but why does the heart grieve and refuse to listen to reason? Why does one want to weep bitterly?"

Ieronim shrugged his shoulders, turned to me and said quickly:

"If I died, or anyone else, it would not be worth notice perhaps; but, you see, Nikolay is dead! No one else but Nikolay! Indeed, it's hard to believe that he is no more! I stand here on my ferry-boat and every minute I keep fancying that he will lift up his voice from the bank. He always used to come to the bank and call to me that I might not be afraid on the ferry. He used to get up from his bed at night on purpose for that. He was a kind soul. My God! how kindly and gracious! Many a mother is not so good to her child as Nikolay was to me! Lord, save his soul!"

Ieronim took hold of the rope, but turned to me again at once.

"And such a lofty intelligence, your honour," he said in a vibrating voice. "Such a sweet and harmonious tongue! Just as they will sing immediately at early matins: 'Oh lovely! oh sweet is Thy Voice!' Besides all other human qualities, he had, too, an extraordinary gift!"

"What gift?" I asked.

The monk scrutinized me, and as though he had convinced himself that he could trust me with a secret, he laughed good-humouredly.

"He had a gift for writing hymns of praise," he said. "It was a marvel, sir; you couldn't call it anything else! You would be amazed if I tell you about it. Our Father Archimandrite comes from Moscow, the Father Sub-Prior studied at the Kazan academy, we have wise monks and elders, but, would you believe it, no one could write them; while Nikolay, a simple monk, a deacon, had not studied anywhere, and had not even any outer appearance of it, but he wrote them! A marvel! A real marvel!" Ieronim clasped his hands and, completely forgetting the rope, went on eagerly:

"The Father Sub-Prior has great difficulty in composing sermons; when he wrote the history of the monastery he worried all the brotherhood and drove a dozen times to town, while Nikolay wrote canticles! Hymns of praise! That's a very different thing from a sermon or a history!"

"Is it difficult to write them?" I asked.

"There's great difficulty!" Ieronim wagged his head. "You can do nothing by wisdom and holiness if God has not given you the gift. The monks who don't understand argue that you only need to know the life of the saint for whom you are writing the hymn, and to make it harmonize with the other hymns of praise. But that's a mistake, sir. Of course, anyone who writes canticles must know the life of the saint to perfection, to the least trivial detail. To be sure, one must make them harmonize with the other canticles and know where to begin and what to write about. To give you an instance, the first response begins everywhere with 'the chosen' or 'the elect.'... The first line must always begin with the 'angel.' In the canticle of praise to Jesus the Most

42

Sweet, if you are interested in the subject, it begins like this: 'Of angels Creator and Lord of all powers!' In the canticle to the Holy Mother of God: 'Of angels the foremost sent down from on high,' to Nikolay, the Wonder-worker-- 'An angel in semblance, though in substance a man,' and so on. Everywhere you begin with the angel. Of course, it would be impossible without making them harmonize, but the lives of the saints and conformity with the others is not what matters; what matters is the beauty and sweetness of it. Everything must be harmonious, brief and complete. There must be in every line softness, graciousness and tenderness; not one word should be harsh or rough or unsuitable. It must be written so that the worshipper may rejoice at heart and weep, while his mind is stirred and he is thrown into a tremor. In the canticle to the Holy Mother are the words: 'Rejoice, O Thou too high for human thought to reach! Rejoice, O Thou too deep for angels' eyes to fathom!' In another place in the same canticle: 'Rejoice, O tree that bearest the fair fruit of light that is the food of the faithful! Rejoice, O tree of gracious spreading shade, under which there is shelter for multitudes!'"

Ieronim hid his face in his hands, as though frightened at something or overcome with shame, and shook his head.

"Tree that bearest the fair fruit of light... tree of gracious spreading shade..." he muttered. "To think that a man should find words like those! Such a power is a gift from God! For brevity he packs many thoughts into one phrase, and how smooth and complete it all is! 'Light-radiating torch to all that be...' comes in the canticle to Jesus the Most Sweet. 'Light-radiating!' There is no such word in conversation or in books, but you see he invented it, he found it in his mind! Apart from the smoothness and grandeur of language, sir, every line must be beautified in every way, there must be flowers and lightning and wind and sun and all the objects of the visible world. And every exclamation ought to be put so as to be smooth and easy for the ear. 'Rejoice, thou flower of heavenly growth!' comes in the hymn to Nikolay the Wonder-worker. It's not simply 'heavenly flower,' but 'flower of heavenly growth.' It's smoother so and sweet to the ear. That was just as Nikolay wrote it! Exactly like that! I can't tell you how he used to write!"

"Well, in that case it is a pity he is dead," I said; "but let us get on, father, or we shall be late."

Ieronim started and ran to the rope; they were beginning to peal all the bells. Probably the procession was already going on near the monastery, for all the dark space behind the tar barrels was now dotted with moving lights.

"Did Nikolay print his hymns?" I asked Ieronim.

"How could he print them?" he sighed. "And indeed, it would be strange to print them. What would be the object? No one in the monastery takes any interest in them. They don't like them. They knew Nikolay wrote them, but they let it pass unnoticed. No one esteems new writings nowadays, sir!"

"Were they prejudiced against him?"

"Yes, indeed. If Nikolay had been an elder perhaps the brethren would have been interested, but he wasn't forty, you know. There were some who laughed and even thought his writing a sin."

"What did he write them for?"

"Chiefly for his own comfort. Of all the brotherhood, I was the only one who read his hymns. I used to go to him in secret, that no one else might know of it, and he was glad that I took an interest in them. He would embrace me, stroke my head, speak to me in caressing words as to a little child. He would shut his cell, make me sit down beside him, and begin to read..."

Ieronim left the rope and came up to me.

"We were dear friends in a way," he whispered, looking at me with shining eyes. "Where he went I would go. If I were not there he would miss me. And he cared more for me than for anyone, and all because I used to weep over his hymns. It makes me sad to remember. Now I feel just like an orphan or a widow. You know, in our monastery they are all good people, kind and pious, but... there is no one with softness and refinement, they are just like peasants. They all speak loudly, and tramp heavily when they walk; they are noisy, they clear their throats, but Nikolay always talked softly, caressingly, and if he noticed that anyone was asleep or praying he would slip by like a fly or a gnat. His face was tender, compassionate..."

Ieronim heaved a deep sigh and took hold of the rope again. We were by now approaching the bank. We floated straight out of the darkness and stillness of the river into an enchanted realm, full of stifling smoke, crackling lights and uproar. By now one could distinctly see people moving near the tar barrels. The flickering of the lights gave a strange, almost fantastic, expression to their figures and red faces. From time to time one caught among the heads and faces a glimpse of a horse's head motionless as though cast in copper.

"They'll begin singing the Easter hymn directly,..." said Ieronim, "and Nikolay is gone; there is no one to appreciate it... There was nothing written dearer to him than that hymn. He used to take in every word! You'll be there, sir, so notice what is sung; it takes your breath away!"

"Won't you be in church, then?"

"I can't;... I have to work the ferry..."

"But won't they relieve you?"

"I don't know... I ought to have been relieved at eight; but, as you see, they don't come!... And I must own I should have liked to be in the church..."

"Are you a monk?"

"Yes... that is, I am a lay-brother."

The ferry ran into the bank and stopped. I thrust a five-kopeck piece into Ieronim's hand for taking me across and jumped on land. Immediately a cart with a boy and a sleeping woman in it drove creaking onto the ferry. Ieronim, with a faint glow from the lights on his figure, pressed on the rope, bent down to it, and started the ferry back...

I took a few steps through mud, but a little farther walked on a soft freshly trodden path. This path led to the dark monastery gates, that looked like a cavern through a cloud of smoke, through a disorderly crowd of people, unharnessed horses, carts and chaises. All this crowd was rattling, snorting, laughing, and the crimson light and wavering shadows from the smoke flickered over it all... A perfect chaos! And in this hubbub the people yet found room to load a little cannon and to sell cakes. There was no less commotion on the other side of the wall in the monastery precincts, but there was more regard for decorum and order. Here there was a smell of juniper and incense. They talked loudly, but there was no sound of laughter or snorting. Near the tombstones and crosses people pressed close to one another with Easter cakes and bundles in their arms. Apparently many had come from a long distance for their cakes to be blessed and now were exhausted. Young lay brothers, making a metallic sound with their boots, ran busily along the iron slabs that paved the way from the monastery gates to the church door. They were busy and shouting on the belfry, too.

"What a restless night!" I thought. "How nice!"

One was tempted to see the same unrest and sleeplessness in all nature, from the night darkness to the iron slabs, the crosses on the tombs and the trees under which the people were moving to and fro. But nowhere was the excitement and restlessness so marked as in the church. An unceasing struggle was going on in the entrance between the inflowing stream and the outflowing stream. Some were going in, others going out and soon coming back again to stand still for a little and begin moving again. People were scurrying from place to place, lounging about as though they were looking for something. The stream flowed from the entrance all round the church, disturbing even the front rows, where persons of weight and dignity were standing. There could be no thought of concentrated prayer. There were no prayers at all, but a sort of continuous, childishly irresponsible joy, seeking a pretext to break out and vent itself in some movement, even in senseless jostling and shoving.

The same unaccustomed movement is striking in the Easter service itself. The altar gates are flung wide open, thick clouds of incense float in the air near the candelabra; wherever one looks there are lights, the gleam and splutter of candles... There is no reading; restless and lighthearted singing goes on to the end without ceasing. After each hymn the clergy change their vestments and come out to burn the incense, which is repeated every ten minutes.

I had no sooner taken a place, when a wave rushed from in front and forced me back. A tall thick-set deacon walked before me with a long red candle; the grey-headed archimandrite in his golden mitre hurried after him with the censer. When they had vanished from sight the crowd squeezed me back to my former position. But ten minutes had not passed before a new wave burst on me, and again the deacon appeared. This time he was followed by the Father Sub-Prior, the man who, as Ieronim had told me, was writing the history of the monastery.

As I mingled with the crowd and caught the infection of the universal joyful excitement, I felt unbearably sore on Ieronim's account. Why did they not send someone to relieve him? Why could not someone of less feeling and less susceptibility go on the ferry? 'Lift up thine eyes, O Sion, and look around,' they sang in the choir, 'for thy children have come to thee as to a beacon of divine light from north and south, and from east and from the sea...'

I looked at the faces; they all had a lively expression of triumph, but not one was listening to what was being sung and taking it in, and not one was 'holding his breath.' Why was not Ieronim released? I could fancy Ieronim standing meekly somewhere by the wall, bending forward and hungrily drinking in the beauty of the holy phrase. All this that glided by the ears of the people standing by me he would have eagerly drunk in with his delicately sensitive soul, and would have been spell-bound to ecstasy, to holding his breath, and there would not have been a man happier than he in all the church. Now he was plying to and fro over the dark river and grieving for his dead friend and brother.

The wave surged back. A stout smiling monk, playing with his rosary and looking round behind him, squeezed sideways by me, making way for a lady in a hat and velvet cloak. A monastery servant hurried after the lady, holding a chair over our heads.

I came out of the church. I wanted to have a look at the dead Nikolay, the unknown canticle writer. I walked about the monastery wall, where there was a row of cells, peeped into several windows, and, seeing nothing, came back again. I do not regret now that I did not see Nikolay; God knows, perhaps if I had seen him I should have lost the picture my imagination paints for me now. I imagine the lovable poetical figure solitary and not understood, who went out at nights to call to Ieronim over the water, and filled his hymns with flowers, stars and sunbeams, as a pale timid man with soft mild melancholy features. His eyes must have shone, not only with intelligence, but with kindly tenderness and that hardly restrained childlike enthusiasm which I could hear in Ieronim's voice when he quoted to me passages from the hymns.

When we came out of church after mass it was no longer night. The morning was beginning. The stars had gone out and the sky was a morose greyish blue. The iron slabs, the tombstones and the buds on the trees were covered with dew There was a sharp freshness in the air. Outside the precincts I did not find the same animated scene as I had beheld in the night. Horses and men looked exhausted, drowsy, scarcely moved, while nothing was left of the tar barrels but heaps of black ash. When anyone is exhausted and sleepy he fancies that nature, too, is in the same condition. It seemed to me that the trees and the young grass were asleep. It seemed as though even the bells were not pealing so loudly and gaily as at night. The restlessness was over, and of the excitement nothing was left but a pleasant weariness, a longing for sleep and warmth.

Now I could see both banks of the river; a faint mist hovered over it in shifting masses. There was a harsh cold breath from the water. When I jumped on to the ferry, a chaise and some two dozen men and women were standing on it already. The rope, wet and as I fancied drowsy, stretched far away across the broad river and in places disappeared in the white mist.

"Christ is risen! Is there no one else?" asked a soft voice.

I recognized the voice of Ieronim. There was no darkness now to hinder me from seeing the monk. He was a tall narrow-shouldered man of five-and-thirty, with large rounded features, with half-closed listless-looking eyes and an unkempt wedge-shaped beard. He had an extraordinarily sad and exhausted look.

"They have not relieved you yet?" I asked in surprise.

"Me?" he answered, turning to me his chilled and dewy face with a smile. "There is no one to take my place now till morning. They'll all be going to the Father Archimandrite's to break the fast directly."

With the help of a little peasant in a hat of reddish fur that looked like the little wooden tubs in which honey is sold, he threw his weight on the rope; they gasped simultaneously, and the ferry started.

We floated across, disturbing on the way the lazily rising mist. Everyone was silent. Ieronim worked mechanically with one hand. He slowly passed his mild lustreless eyes over us; then his glance rested on the rosy face of a young merchant's wife with black eyebrows, who was standing on the ferry beside me silently shrinking from the mist that wrapped her about. He did not take his eyes off her face all the way.

There was little that was masculine in that prolonged gaze. It seemed to me that Ieronim was looking in the woman's face for the soft and tender features of his dead friend.

The Murder

I

The evening service was being celebrated at Progonnaya Station. Before the great ikon, painted in glaring colours on a background of gold, stood the crowd of railway servants with their wives and children, and also of the timbermen and sawyers who worked close to the railway line. All stood in silence, fascinated by the glare of the lights and the howling of the snow-storm which was aimlessly disporting itself outside, regardless of the fact that it was the Eve of the Annunciation. The old priest from Vedenyapino conducted the service; the sacristan and Matvey Terehov were singing.

Matvey's face was beaming with delight; he sang stretching out his neck as though he wanted to soar upwards. He sang tenor and chanted the "Praises" too in a tenor voice with honied sweetness and persuasiveness. When he sang "Archangel Voices" he waved his arms like a conductor, and trying to second the sacristan's hollow bass with his tenor, achieved something extremely complex, and from his face it could be seen that he was experiencing great pleasure.

At last the service was over, and they all quietly dispersed, and it was dark and empty again, and there followed that hush which is only known in stations that stand solitary in the open country or in the forest when the wind howls and nothing else is heard and when all the emptiness around, all the dreariness of life slowly ebbing away is felt.

Matvey lived not far from the station at his cousin's tavern. But he did not want to go home. He sat down at the refreshment bar and began talking to the waiter in a low voice.

"We had our own choir in the tile factory. And I must tell you that though we were only workmen, our singing was first-rate, splendid. We were often invited to the town, and when the Deputy Bishop, Father Ivan, took the service at Trinity Church, the bishop's singers sang in the right choir and we in the left. Only they complained in the town that we kept the singing on too long: 'the factory choir drag it out,' they used to say. It is true we began St. Andrey's prayers and the Praises between six and seven, and it was past eleven when we finished, so that it was sometimes after midnight when we got home to the factory. It was good," sighed Matvey. "Very good it was, indeed, Sergey Nikanoritch! But here in my father's house it is anything but joyful. The nearest church is four miles away; with my weak health I can't get so far; there are no singers there. And there is no peace or quiet in our family; day in day out, there is an uproar, scolding, uncleanliness; we all eat out of one bowl like peasants; and there are beetles in the cabbage soup... God has not given me health, else I would have gone away long ago, Sergey Nikanoritch."

Matvey Terehov was a middle-aged man about forty-five, but he had a look of ill-health; his face was wrinkled and his lank, scanty beard was quite grey, and that made him seem many years older. He spoke in a weak voice, circumspectly, and held his chest when he coughed, while his eyes assumed the uneasy and anxious look one sees in very apprehensive people. He never said definitely what was wrong with him, but he was fond of describing at length how once at the factory he had lifted a heavy box and had ruptured himself, and how this had led to "the gripes," and had forced him to give up his work in the tile factory and come back to his native place; but he could not explain what he meant by "the gripes."

"I must own I am not fond of my cousin," he went on, pouring himself out some tea. "He is my elder; it is a sin to censure him, and I fear the Lord, but I cannot bear it in patience. He is a haughty, surly, abusive man; he is the torment of his relations and workmen, and constantly out of humour. Last Sunday I asked him in an amiable way,

'Brother, let us go to Pahomovo for the Mass!' but he said 'I am not going; the priest there is a gambler;' and he would not come here to-day because, he said, the priest from Vedenyapino smokes and drinks vodka. He doesn't like the clergy! He reads Mass himself and the Hours and the Vespers, while his sister acts as sacristan; he says, 'Let us pray unto the Lord'! and she, in a thin little voice like a turkey-hen, 'Lord, have mercy upon us!...' It's a sin, that's what it is. Every day I say to him, 'Think what you are doing, brother! Repent, brother!' and he takes no notice."

Sergey Nikanoritch, the waiter, poured out five glasses of tea and carried them on a tray to the waiting-room. He had scarcely gone in when there was a shout:

"Is that the way to serve it, pig's face? You don't know how to wait!"

It was the voice of the station-master. There was a timid mutter, then again a harsh and angry shout:

"Get along!"

The waiter came back greatly crestfallen.

"There was a time when I gave satisfaction to counts and princes," he said in a low voice; "but now I don't know how to serve tea... He called me names before the priest and the ladies!"

The waiter, Sergey Nikanoritch, had once had money of his own, and had kept a buffet at a first-class station, which was a junction, in the principal town of a province. There he had worn a swallow-tail coat and a gold chain. But things had gone ill with him; he had squandered all his own money over expensive fittings and service; he had been robbed by his staff, and getting gradually into difficulties, had moved to another station less bustling. Here his wife had left him, taking with her all the silver, and he moved to a third station of a still lower class, where no hot dishes were served. Then to a fourth. Frequently changing his situation and sinking lower and lower, he had at last come to Progonnaya, and here he used to sell nothing but tea and cheap vodka, and for lunch hard-boiled eggs and dry sausages, which smelt of tar, and which he himself sarcastically said were only fit for the orchestra. He was bald all over the top of his head, and had prominent blue eyes and thick bushy whiskers, which he often combed out, looking into the little looking-glass. Memories of the past haunted him continually; he could never get used to sausage "only fit for the orchestra," to the rudeness of the station-master, and to the peasants who used to haggle over the prices, and in his opinion it was as unseemly to haggle over prices in a refreshment room as in a chemist's shop. He was ashamed of his poverty and degradation, and that shame was now the leading interest of his life.

"Spring is late this year," said Matvey, listening. "It's a good job; I don't like spring. In spring it is very muddy, Sergey Nikanoritch. In books they write: Spring, the birds sing, the sun is setting, but what is there pleasant in that? A bird is a bird, and nothing more. I am fond of good company, of listening to folks, of talking of religion or singing something agreeable in chorus; but as for nightingales and flowers-- bless them, I say!"

He began again about the tile factory, about the choir, but Sergey Nikanoritch could not get over his mortification, and kept shrugging his shoulders and muttering. Matvey said good-bye and went home.

There was no frost, and the snow was already melting on the roofs, though it was still falling in big flakes; they were whirling rapidly round and round in the air and chasing one another in white clouds along the railway line. And the oak forest on both sides of the line, in the dim light of the moon which was hidden somewhere high up in the clouds, resounded with a prolonged sullen murmur. When a violent storm shakes the trees, how terrible they are! Matvey walked along the causeway beside the line, covering his face and his hands, while the wind beat on his back. All at once a little nag, plastered all over with snow, came into sight; a sledge scraped along the bare stones of the causeway, and a peasant, white all over, too, with his head muffled up, cracked his whip. Matvey looked round after him, but at once, as though it had been a vision, there was neither sledge nor peasant to be seen, and he hastened his steps, suddenly scared, though he did not know why.

Here was the crossing and the dark little house where the signalman lived. The barrier was raised, and by it perfect mountains had drifted and clouds of snow were whirling round like witches on broomsticks. At that point the line was crossed by an old highroad, which was still called "the track." On the right, not far from the crossing, by the roadside stood Terehov's tavern, which had been a posting inn. Here there was always a light twinkling at night.

When Matvey reached home there was a strong smell of incense in all the rooms and even in the entry. His cousin Yakov Ivanitch was still reading the evening service. In the prayer-room where this was going on, in the corner opposite the door, there stood a shrine of old-fashioned ancestral ikons in gilt settings, and both walls to right and to left were decorated with ikons of ancient and modern fashion, in shrines and without them. On the table, which was draped to the floor, stood an ikon of the Annunciation, and close by a cyprus-wood cross and the censer; wax candles were burning. Beside the table was a reading desk. As he passed by the prayer-room, Matvey stopped and glanced in at the door. Yakov Ivanitch was reading at the desk at that moment, his sister Aglaia, a tall lean old woman in a dark-blue dress and white kerchief, was praying with him. Yakov Ivanitch's daughter Dashutka, an ugly freckled girl of eighteen, was there, too, barefoot as usual, and wearing the dress in which she had at nightfall taken water to the cattle.

"Glory to Thee Who hast shown us the light!" Yakov Ivanitch boomed out in a chant, bowing low.

Aglaia propped her chin on her hand and chanted in a thin, shrill, drawling voice. And upstairs, above the ceiling, there was the sound of vague voices which seemed menacing or ominous of evil. No one had lived on the storey above since a fire there a long time ago. The windows were boarded up, and empty bottles lay about on the floor between the beams. Now the wind was banging and droning, and it seemed as though someone were running and stumbling over the beams.

Half of the lower storey was used as a tavern, while Terehov's family lived in the other half, so that when drunken visitors were noisy in the tavern every word they said could be heard in the rooms. Matvey lived in a room next to the kitchen, with a big stove, in which, in old days, when this had been a posting inn, bread had been baked every day. Dashutka, who had no room of her own, lived in the same room behind the stove. A cricket chirped there always at night and mice ran in and out.

Matvey lighted a candle and began reading a book which he had borrowed from the station policeman. While he was sitting over it the service ended, and they all went to bed. Dashutka lay down, too. She began snoring at once, but soon woke up and said, yawning:

"You shouldn't burn a candle for nothing, Uncle Matvey."

"It's my candle," answered Matvey; "I bought it with my own money."

Dashutka turned over a little and fell asleep again. Matvey sat up a good time longer--he was not sleepy--and when he had finished the last page he took a pencil out of a box and wrote on the book:

"I, Matvey Terehov, have read this book, and think it the very best of all the books I have read, for which I express my gratitude to the non-commissioned officer of the Police Department of Railways, Kuzma Nikolaev Zhukov, as the possessor of this priceless book."

He considered it an obligation of politeness to make such inscriptions in other people's books.

II

On Annunciation Day, after the mail train had been sent off, Matvey was sitting in the refreshment bar, talking and drinking tea with lemon in it.

The waiter and Zhukov the policeman were listening to him.

"I was, I must tell you," Matvey was saying, "inclined to religion from my earliest childhood. I was only twelve years old when I used to read the epistle in church, and my parents were greatly delighted, and every summer I used to go on a pilgrimage with my dear mother. Sometimes other lads would be singing songs and catching crayfish, while I would be all the time with my mother. My elders commended me, and, indeed, I was pleased myself that I was of such good behaviour. And when my mother sent me with her blessing to the factory, I used between working hours to sing tenor there in our choir, and nothing gave me greater pleasure. I needn't say, I drank no vodka, I smoked no tobacco, and lived in chastity; but we all know such a mode of life is displeasing to the enemy of mankind, and he, the unclean spirit, once tried to ruin me and began to darken my mind, just as now with my cousin. First of all, I took a vow to fast every Monday and not to eat meat any day, and as time went on all sorts of fancies came over me. For the first week of Lent down to Saturday the holy fathers have ordained a diet of dry food, but it is no sin for the weak or those who work hard even to drink tea, yet not a crumb passed into my mouth till the Sunday, and afterwards all through Lent I did not allow myself a drop of oil, and on Wednesdays and Fridays I did not touch a morsel at all. It was the same in the lesser fasts. Sometimes in St. Peter's fast our factory lads would have fish soup, while I would sit a little apart from them and suck a dry crust. Different people have different powers, of course, but I can say of myself I did not find fast days hard, and, indeed, the greater the zeal the easier it seems. You are only hungry on the first days of the fast, and then you get used to it; it goes on getting easier, and by the end of a week you don't mind it at all, and there is a numb feeling in your legs as though you were not on earth, but in the clouds. And, besides that, I laid all sorts of penances on myself; I used to get up in the night and pray, bowing down to the ground, used to drag heavy stones from place to place, used to go out barefoot in the snow, and I even wore chains, too. Only, as time went on, you know,

I was confessing one day to the priest and suddenly this reflection occurred to me: why, this priest, I thought, is married, he eats meat and smokes tobacco--how can he confess me, and what power has he to absolve my sins if he is more sinful that I? I even scruple to eat Lenten oil, while he eats sturgeon, I dare say. I went to another priest, and he, as ill luck would have it, was a fat fleshy man, in a silk cassock; he rustled like a lady, and he smelt of tobacco too. I went to fast and confess in the monastery, and my heart was not at ease even there; I kept fancying the monks were not living according to their rules. And after that I could not find a service to my mind: in one place they read the service too fast, in another they sang the wrong prayer, in a third the sacristan stammered. Sometimes, the Lord forgive me a sinner, I would stand in church and my heart would throb with anger. How could one pray, feeling like that? And I fancied that the people in the church did not cross themselves properly, did not listen properly; wherever I looked it seemed to me that they were all drunkards, that they broke the fast, smoked, lived loose lives and played cards. I was the only one who lived according to the commandments. The wily spirit did not slumber; it got worse as it went on. I gave up singing in the choir and I did not go to church at all; since my notion was that I was a righteous man and that the church did not suit me owing to its imperfections--that is, indeed, like a fallen angel, I was puffed up in my pride beyond all belief. After this I began attempting to make a church for myself. I hired from a deaf woman a tiny little room, a long way out of town near the cemetery, and made a prayer-room like my cousin's, only I had big church candlesticks, too, and a real censer. In this prayer-room of mine I kept the rules of holy Mount Athos-- that is, every day my matins began at midnight without fail, and on the eve of the chief of the twelve great holy days my midnight service lasted ten hours and sometimes even twelve. Monks are allowed by rule to sit during the singing of the Psalter and the reading of the Bible, but I wanted to be better than the monks, and so I used to stand all through. I used to read and sing slowly, with tears and sighing, lifting up my hands, and I used to go straight from prayer to work without sleeping; and, indeed, I was always praying at my work, too. Well, it got all over the town 'Matvey is a saint; Matvey heals the sick and senseless.' I never had healed anyone, of course, but we all know wherever any heresy or false doctrine springs up there's no keeping the female sex away. They are just like flies on the honey. Old maids and females of all sorts came trailing to me, bowing down to my feet, kissing my hands and crying out I was a saint and all the rest of it, and one even saw a halo round my head. It was too crowded in the prayer-room. I took a bigger room, and then we had a regular tower of Babel. The devil got hold of me completely and screened the light from my eyes with his unclean hoofs. We all behaved as though we were frantic. I read, while the old maids and other females sang, and then after standing on their legs for twenty-four hours or longer without eating or drinking, suddenly a trembling would come over them as though they were in a fever; after that, one would begin screaming and then another--it was horrible! I, too, would shiver all over like a Jew in a frying-pan, I don't know myself why, and our legs began to prance about. It's a strange thing, indeed: you don't want to, but you prance about and waggle your arms; and after that, screaming and shrieking, we all danced and ran after one another --ran till we dropped; and in that way, in wild frenzy, I fell into fornication."

The policeman laughed, but, noticing that no one else was laughing, became serious and said:

"That's Molokanism. I have heard they are all like that in the Caucasus."

"But I was not killed by a thunderbolt," Matvey went on, crossing himself before the ikon and moving his lips. "My dead mother must have been praying for me in the other world. When everyone in the town looked upon me as a saint, and even the ladies and gentlemen of good family used to come to me in secret for consolation, I happened to go into our landlord, Osip Varlamitch, to ask forgiveness --it was the Day of Forgiveness--and he fastened the door with the hook, and we were left alone face to face. And he began to reprove me, and I must tell you Osip Varlamitch was a man of brains, though without education, and everyone respected and feared him, for he was a man of stern, God-fearing life and worked hard. He had been the mayor of the town, and a warden of the church for twenty years maybe, and had done a great deal of good; he had covered all the New Moscow Road with gravel, had painted the church, and had decorated the columns to look like malachite. Well, he fastened the door, and-- 'I have been wanting to get at you for a long time, you rascal,...' he said. 'You think you are a saint,' he said. 'No you are not a saint, but a backslider from God, a heretic and an evildoer!...' And he went on and on... I can't tell you how he said it, so eloquently and cleverly, as though it were all written down, and so touchingly. He talked for two hours. His words penetrated my soul; my eyes were opened. I listened, listened and --burst into sobs! 'Be an ordinary man,' he said, 'eat and drink, dress and pray like everyone else. All that is above the ordinary is of the devil. Your chains,' he said, 'are of the devil; your fasting is of the devil; your prayer-room is of the devil. It is all pride,' he said. Next day, on Monday in Holy Week, it pleased God I should fall ill. I ruptured myself and was taken to the hospital. I was terribly worried, and wept bitterly and trembled. I thought there was a straight road before me from the hospital to hell, and I almost died. I was in misery on a bed of sickness for six months, and when I was discharged the first thing I did I confessed, and took the sacrament in the regular way and became a man again. Osip Varlamitch saw me off home and exhorted me: 'Remember, Matvey, that anything above the ordinary is of the devil.' And now I eat and drink like everyone else and pray like everyone else... If it happens now that the priest smells of tobacco or vodka I don't venture to blame him, because the priest, too, of course, is an ordinary man. But as soon as I am told that in the town or in the village a saint has set up who does not eat for weeks, and makes rules of his own, I know whose work it is. So that is how I carried on in the past, gentlemen. Now, like Osip Varlamitch, I am continually exhorting my cousins and reproaching them, but I am a voice crying in the wilderness. God has not vouchsafed me the gift."

Matvey's story evidently made no impression whatever. Sergey Nikanoritch said nothing, but began clearing the refreshments off the counter, while the policeman began talking of how rich Matvey's cousin was.

"He must have thirty thousand at least," he said.

Zhukov the policeman, a sturdy, well-fed, red-haired man with a full face (his cheeks quivered when he walked), usually sat lolling and crossing his legs when not in the presence of his superiors. As he talked he swayed to and fro and whistled carelessly, while his face had a self-satisfied replete air, as though he had just had dinner. He was making money, and he always talked of it with the air of a connoisseur. He undertook jobs as an agent, and when anyone wanted to sell an estate, a horse or a carriage, they applied to him.

"Yes, it will be thirty thousand, I dare say," Sergey Nikanoritch assented. "Your grandfather had an immense fortune," he said, addressing Matvey. "Immense it was; all left to your father and your uncle. Your father died as a young man and your uncle got hold of it all, and afterwards, of course, Yakov Ivanitch. While you were going pilgrimages with your mama and singing tenor in the factory, they didn't let the grass grow under their feet."

"Fifteen thousand comes to your share," said the policeman swaying from side to side. "The tavern belongs to you in common, so the capital is in common. Yes. If I were in your place I should have taken it into court long ago. I would have taken it into court for one thing, and while the case was going on I'd have knocked his face to a jelly."

Yakov Ivanitch was disliked because, when anyone believes differently from others, it upsets even people who are indifferent to religion. The policeman disliked him also because he, too, sold horses and carriages.

"You don't care about going to law with your cousin because you have plenty of money of your own," said the waiter to Matvey, looking at him with envy. "It is all very well for anyone who has means, but here I shall die in this position, I suppose..."

Matvey began declaring that he hadn't any money at all, but Sergey Nikanoritch was not listening. Memories of the past and of the insults which he endured every day came showering upon him. His bald head began to perspire; he flushed and blinked.

"A cursed life!" he said with vexation, and he banged the sausage on the floor.

III

The story ran that the tavern had been built in the time of Alexander I, by a widow who had settled here with her son; her name was Avdotya Terehov. The dark roofed-in courtyard and the gates always kept locked excited, especially on moonlight nights, a feeling of depression and unaccountable uneasiness in people who drove by with posting-horses, as though sorcerers or robbers were living in it; and the driver always looked back after he passed, and whipped up his horses. Travellers did not care to put up here, as the people of the house were always unfriendly and charged heavily. The yard was muddy even in summer; huge fat pigs used to lie there in the mud, and the horses in which the Terehovs dealt wandered about untethered, and often it happened that they ran out of the yard and dashed along the road like mad creatures, terrifying the pilgrim women. At that time there was a great deal of traffic on the road; long trains of loaded waggons trailed by, and all sorts of adventures happened, such as, for instance, that thirty years ago some waggoners got up a quarrel with a passing merchant and killed him, and a slanting cross is standing to this day half a mile from the tavern; posting-chaises with bells and the heavy _dormeuses_ of country gentlemen drove by; and herds of homed cattle passed bellowing and stirring up clouds of dust.

selected short stories

When the railway came there was at first at this place only a platform, which was called simply a halt; ten years afterwards the present station, Progonnaya, was built. The traffic on the old posting-road almost ceased, and only local landowners and peasants drove along it now, but the working people walked there in crowds in spring and autumn. The posting-inn was transformed into a restaurant; the upper storey was destroyed by fire, the roof had grown yellow with rust, the roof over the yard had fallen by degrees, but huge fat pigs, pink and revolting, still wallowed in the mud in the yard. As before, the horses sometimes ran away and, lashing their tails dashed madly along the road. In the tavern they sold tea, hay oats and flour, as well as vodka and beer, to be drunk on the premises and also to be taken away; they sold spirituous liquors warily, for they had never taken out a licence.

The Terehovs had always been distinguished by their piety, so much so that they had even been given the nickname of the "Godlies." But perhaps because they lived apart like bears, avoided people and thought out all their ideas for themselves, they were given to dreams and to doubts and to changes of faith and almost each generation had a peculiar faith of its own. The grandmother Avdotya, who had built the inn, was an Old Believer; her son and both her grandsons (the fathers of Matvey and Yakov) went to the Orthodox church, entertained the clergy, and worshipped before the new ikons as devoutly as they had done before the old. The son in old age refused to eat meat and imposed upon himself the rule of silence, considering all conversation as sin; it was the peculiarity of the grandsons that they interpreted the Scripture not simply, but sought in it a hidden meaning, declaring that every sacred word must contain a mystery.

Avdotya's great-grandson Matvey had struggled from early childhood with all sorts of dreams and fancies and had been almost ruined by it; the other great-grandson, Yakov Ivanitch, was orthodox, but after his wife's death he gave up going to church and prayed at home. Following his example, his sister Aglaia had turned, too; she did not go to church herself, and did not let Dashutka go. Of Aglaia it was told that in her youth she used to attend the Flagellant meetings in Vedenyapino, and that she was still a Flagellant in secret, and that was why she wore a white kerchief.

Yakov Ivanitch was ten years older than Matvey--he was a very handsome tall old man with a big grey beard almost to his waist, and bushy eyebrows which gave his face a stern, even ill-natured expression. He wore a long jerkin of good cloth or a black sheepskin coat, and altogether tried to be clean and neat in dress; he wore galoshes even in dry weather. He did not go to church, because, to his thinking, the services were not properly celebrated and because the priests drank wine at unlawful times and smoked tobacco. Every day he read and sang the service at home with Aglaia. At Vedenyapino they left out the "Praises" at early matins, and had no evening service even on great holidays, but he used to read through at home everything that was laid down for every day, without hurrying or leaving out a single line, and even in his spare time read aloud the Lives of the Saints. And in everyday life he adhered strictly to the rules of the church; thus, if wine were allowed on some day in Lent "for the sake of the vigil," then he never failed to drink wine, even if he were not inclined.

He read, sang, burned incense and fasted, not for the sake of receiving blessings of some sort from God, but for the sake of good order. Man cannot live without religion, and religion ought to be expressed from year to year and from day to day in a certain order, so that every morning and every evening a man might turn to God with exactly those words and thoughts that were befitting that special day and hour. One must live, and, therefore, also pray as is pleasing to God, and so every day one must read and sing what is pleasing to God--that is, what is laid down in the rule of the church. Thus the first chapter of St. John must only be read on Easter Day, and "It is most meet" must not be sung from Easter to Ascension, and so on. The consciousness of this order and its importance afforded Yakov Ivanitch great gratification during his religious exercises. When he was forced to break this order by some necessity--to drive to town or to the bank, for instance his conscience was uneasy and he fit miserable.

When his cousin Matvey had returned unexpectedly from the factory and settled in the tavern as though it were his home, he had from the very first day disturbed his settled order. He refused to pray with them, had meals and drank tea at wrong times, got up late, drank milk on Wednesdays and Fridays on the pretext of weak health; almost every day he went into the prayer-room while they were at prayers and cried: "Think what you are doing, brother! Repent, brother!" These words threw Yakov into a fury, while Aglaia could not refrain from beginning to scold; or at night Matvey would steal into the prayer-room and say softly: "Cousin, your prayer is not pleasing to God. For it is written, First be reconciled with thy brother and then offer thy gift. You lend money at usury, you deal in vodka--repent!"

In Matvey's words Yakov saw nothing but the usual evasions of empty-headed and careless people who talk of loving your neighbour, of being reconciled with your brother, and so on, simply to avoid praying, fasting and reading holy books, and who talk contemptuously of profit and interest simply because they don't like working. Of course, to be poor, save nothing, and put by nothing was a great deal easier than being rich.

But yet he was troubled and could not pray as before. As soon as he went into the prayer-room and opened the book he began to be afraid his cousin would come in and hinder him; and, in fact, Matvey did soon appear and cry in a trembling voice: "Think what you are doing, brother! Repent, brother!" Aglaia stormed and Yakov, too, flew into a passion and shouted: "Go out of my house!" while Matvey answered him: "The house belongs to both of us."

Yakov would begin singing and reading again, but he could not regain his calm, and unconsciously fell to dreaming over his book. Though he regarded his cousin's words as nonsense, yet for some reason it had of late haunted his memory that it is hard for a rich man to enter the kingdom of heaven, that the year before last he had made a very good bargain over buying a stolen horse, that one day when his wife was alive a drunkard had died of vodka in his tavern...

He slept badly at nights now and woke easily, and he could hear that Matvey, too, was awake, and continually sighing and pining for his tile factory. And while Yakov turned over from one side to another at night he thought of the stolen horse and the drunken man, and what was said in the gospels about the camel.

It looked as though his dreaminess were coming over him again. And as ill-luck would have it, although it was the end of March, every day it kept snowing, and the forest roared as though it were winter, and there was no believing that spring would ever come. The weather disposed one to depression, and to quarrelling and to hatred and in the night, when the wind droned over the ceiling, it seemed as though someone were living overhead in the empty storey; little by little the broodings settled like a burden on his mind, his head burned and he could not sleep.

IV

On the morning of the Monday before Good Friday, Matvey heard from his room Dashutka say to Aglaia:

"Uncle Matvey said, the other day, that there is no need to fast."

Matvey remembered the whole conversation he had had the evening before with Dashutka, and he felt hurt all at once.

"Girl, don't do wrong!" he said in a moaning voice, like a sick man. "You can't do without fasting; our Lord Himself fasted forty days. I only explained that fasting does a bad man no good."

"You should just listen to the factory hands; they can teach you goodness," Aglaia said sarcastically as she washed the floor (she usually washed the floors on working days and was always angry with everyone when she did it). "We know how they keep the fasts in the factory. You had better ask that uncle of yours--ask him about his

'Darling,' how he used to guzzle milk on fast days with her, the viper.
He teaches others; he forgets about his viper. But ask him who was it
he left his money with--who was it?"

Matvey had carefully concealed from everyone, as though it were
a foul sore, that during that period of his life when old women and
unmarried girls had danced and run about with him at their prayers
he had formed a connection with a working woman and had had a
child by her. When he went home he had given this woman all he
had saved at the factory, and had borrowed from his landlord for
his journey, and now he had only a few roubles which he spent on
tea and candles. The "Darling" had informed him later on that the
child was dead, and asked him in a letter what she should do with
the money. This letter was brought from the station by the labourer.
Aglaia intercepted it and read it, and had reproached Matvey with his
"Darling" every day since.

"Just fancy, nine hundred roubles," Aglaia went on. "You gave
nine hundred roubles to a viper, no relation, a factory jade, blast
you!" She had flown into a passion by now and was shouting shrilly:
"Can't you speak? I could tear you to pieces, wretched creature! Nine
hundred roubles as though it were a farthing You might have left it
to Dashutka--she is a relation, not a stranger--or else have it sent to
Byelev for Marya's poor orphans. And your viper did not choke, may
she be thrice accursed, the she-devil! May she never look upon the
light of day!"

Yakov Ivanitch called to her: it was time to begin the "Hours." She
washed, put on a white kerchief, and by now quiet and meek, went into
the prayer-room to the brother she loved. When she spoke to Matvey
or served peasants in the tavern with tea she was a gaunt, keen-eyed,
ill-humoured old woman; in the prayer-room her face was serene and
softened, she looked younger altogether, she curtsied affectedly, and
even pursed up her lips.

Yakov Ivanitch began reading the service softly and dolefully, as
he always did in Lent. After he had read a little he stopped to listen

to the stillness that reigned through the house, and then went on reading again, with a feeling of gratification; he folded his hands in supplication, rolled his eyes, shook his head, sighed. But all at once there was the sound of voices. The policeman and Sergey Nikanoritch had come to see Matvey. Yakov Ivanitch was embarrassed at reading aloud and singing when there were strangers in the house, and now, hearing voices, he began reading in a whisper and slowly. He could hear in the prayer-room the waiter say:

"The Tatar at Shtchepovo is selling his business for fifteen hundred. He'll take five hundred down and an I.O.U. for the rest. And so, Matvey Vassilitch, be so kind as to lend me that five hundred roubles. I will pay you two per cent a month."

"What money have I got?" cried Matvey, amazed. "I have no money!"

"Two per cent a month will be a godsend to you," the policeman explained. "While lying by, your money is simply eaten by the moth, and that's all that you get from it."

Afterwards the visitors went out and a silence followed. But Yakov Ivanitch had hardly begun reading and singing again when a voice was heard outside the door:

"Brother, let me have a horse to drive to Vedenyapino."

It was Matvey. And Yakov was troubled again. "Which can you go with?" he asked after a moment's thought. "The man has gone with the sorrel to take the pig, and I am going with the little stallion to Shuteykino as soon as I have finished."

"Brother, why is it you can dispose of the horses and not I?" Matvey asked with irritation.

"Because I am not taking them for pleasure, but for work."

"Our property is in common, so the horses are in common, too, and you ought to understand that, brother."

A silence followed. Yakov did not go on praying, but waited for Matvey to go away from the door.

"Brother," said Matvey, "I am a sick man. I don't want possession --let them go; you have them, but give me a small share to keep me in my illness. Give it me and I'll go away."

Yakov did not speak. He longed to be rid of Matvey, but he could not give him money, since all the money was in the business; besides, there had never been a case of the family dividing in the whole history of the Terehovs. Division means ruin.

Yakov said nothing, but still waited for Matvey to go away, and kept looking at his sister, afraid that she would interfere, and that there would be a storm of abuse again, as there had been in the morning. When at last Matvey did go Yakov went on reading, but now he had no pleasure in it. There was a heaviness in his head and a darkness before his eyes from continually bowing down to the ground, and he was weary of the sound of his soft dejected voice. When such a depression of spirit came over him at night, he put it down to not being able to sleep; by day it frightened him, and he began to feel as though devils were sitting on his head and shoulders.

Finishing the service after a fashion, dissatisfied and ill-humoured, he set off for Shuteykino. In the previous autumn a gang of navvies had dug a boundary ditch near Progonnaya, and had run up a bill at the tavern for eighteen roubles, and now he had to find their foreman in Shuteykino and get the money from him. The road had been spoilt by the thaw and the snowstorm; it was of a dark colour and full of holes, and in parts it had given way altogether. The snow had sunk away at the sides below the road, so that he had to drive, as it were, upon a narrow causeway, and it was very difficult to turn off it when he met anything. The sky had been overcast ever since the morning and a damp wind was blowing...

A long train of sledges met him; peasant women were carting bricks. Yakov had to turn off the road. His horse sank into the snow up to its belly; the sledge lurched over to the right, and to avoid falling out he bent over to the left, and sat so all the time the sledges moved slowly by him. Through the wind he heard the creaking of the sledge poles and the breathing of the gaunt horses, and the women saying about him, "There's Godly coming," while one, gazing with compassion at his horse, said quickly:

"It looks as though the snow will be lying till Yegory's Day! They are worn out with it!"

Yakov sat uncomfortably huddled up, screwing up his eyes on account of the wind, while horses and red bricks kept passing before him. And perhaps because he was uncomfortable and his side ached, he felt all at once annoyed, and the business he was going about seemed to him unimportant, and he reflected that he might send the labourer next day to Shuteykino. Again, as in the previous sleepless night, he thought of the saying about the camel, and then memories of all sorts crept into his mind; of the peasant who had sold him the stolen horse, of the drunken man, of the peasant women who had brought their samovars to him to pawn. Of course, every merchant tries to get as much as he can, but Yakov felt depressed that he was in trade; he longed to get somewhere far away from this routine, and he felt dreary at the thought that he would have to read the evening service that day. The wind blew straight into his face and soughed in his collar; and it seemed as though it were whispering to him all these thoughts, bringing them from the broad white plain... Looking at that plain, familiar to him from childhood, Yakov remembered that he had had just this same trouble and these same thoughts in his young days when dreams and imaginings had come upon him and his faith had wavered.

He felt miserable at being alone in the open country; he turned back and drove slowly after the sledges, and the women laughed and said:

"Godly has turned back."

At home nothing had been cooked and the samovar was not heated on account of the fast, and this made the day seem very long. Yakov Ivanitch had long ago taken the horse to the stable, dispatched the flour to the station, and twice taken up the Psalms to read, and yet the evening was still far off. Aglaia has already washed all the floors, and, having nothing to do, was tidying up her chest, the lid of which was pasted over on the inside with labels off bottles. Matvey, hungry and melancholy, sat reading, or went up to the Dutch stove and slowly scrutinized the tiles which reminded him of the factory. Dashutka was asleep; then, waking up, she went to take water to the cattle. When she was getting water from the well the cord broke and the pail fell in. The labourer began looking for a boathook to get the pail out, and Dashutka, barefooted, with legs as red as a goose's, followed him about in the muddy snow, repeating: "It's too far!" She meant to say that the well was too deep for the hook to reach the bottom, but the labourer did not understand her, and evidently she bothered him, so that he suddenly turned around and abused her in unseemly language. Yakov Ivanitch, coming out that moment into the yard, heard Dashutka answer the labourer in a long rapid stream of choice abuse, which she could only have learned from drunken peasants in the tavern.

"What are you saying, shameless girl!" he cried to her, and he was positively aghast. "What language!"

And she looked at her father in perplexity, dully, not understanding why she should not use those words. He would have admonished her, but she struck him as so savage and benighted; and for the first time he realized that she had no religion. And all this life in the forest, in the snow, with drunken peasants, with coarse oaths, seemed to him as savage and benighted as this girl, and instead of giving her a lecture he only waved his hand and went back into the room.

At that moment the policeman and Sergey Nikanoritch came in again to see Matvey. Yakov Ivanitch thought that these people, too, had no religion, and that did not trouble them in the least; and human life began to seem to him as strange, senseless and unenlightened as a dog's. Bareheaded he walked about the yard, then he went out on to the road, clenching his fists. Snow was falling in big flakes at the time. His beard was blown about in the wind. He kept shaking his head, as though there were something weighing upon his head and shoulders, as though devils were sitting on them; and it seemed to him that it was not himself walking about, but some wild beast, a huge terrible beast, and that if he were to cry out his voice would be a roar that would sound all over the forest and the plain, and would frighten everyone...

V

When he went back into the house the policeman was no longer there, but the waiter was sitting with Matvey, counting something on the reckoning beads. He was in the habit of coming often, almost every day, to the tavern; in old days he had come to see Yakov Ivanitch, now he came to see Matvey. He was continually reckoning on the beads, while his face perspired and looked strained, or he would ask for money or, stroking his whiskers, would describe how he had once been in a first-class station and used to prepare champagne-punch for officers, and at grand dinners served the sturgeon-soup with his own hands. Nothing in this world interested him but refreshment bars, and he could only talk about things to eat, about wines and the paraphernalia of the dinner-table. On one occasion, handing a cup of tea to a young woman who was nursing her baby and wishing to say something agreeable to her, he expressed himself in this way:

"The mother's breast is the baby's refreshment bar."

Reckoning with the beads in Matvey's room, he asked for money; said he could not go on living at Progonnaya, and several times repeated in a tone of voice that sounded as though he were just going to cry:

"Where am I to go? Where am I to go now? Tell me that, please."

Then Matvey went into the kitchen and began peeling some boiled potatoes which he had probably put away from the day before. It was quiet, and it seemed to Yakov Ivanitch that the waiter was gone. It was past the time for evening service; he called Aglaia, and, thinking there was no one else in the house sang out aloud without embarrassment. He sang and read, but was inwardly pronouncing other words, "Lord, forgive me! Lord, save me!" and, one after another, without ceasing, he made low bows to the ground as though he wanted to exhaust himself, and he kept shaking his head, so that Aglaia looked at him with wonder. He was afraid Matvey would come in, and was certain that he would come in, and felt an anger against him which he could overcome neither by prayer nor by continually bowing down to the ground.

Matvey opened the door very softly and went into the prayer-room.

"It's a sin, such a sin!" he said reproachfully, and heaved a sigh. "Repent! Think what you are doing, brother!"

Yakov Ivanitch, clenching his fists and not looking at him for fear of striking him, went quickly out of the room. Feeling himself a huge terrible wild beast, just as he had done before on the road, he crossed the passage into the grey, dirty room, reeking with smoke and fog, in which the peasants usually drank tea, and there he spent a long time walking from one corner to the other, treading heavily, so that the crockery jingled on the shelves and the tables shook. It was clear to him now that he was himself dissatisfied with his religion, ant could not pray as he used to do. He must repent, he must think things over, reconsider, live and pray in some other way. But how pray? And perhaps all this was a temptation of the devil, and nothing of this was necessary?... How was it to be? What was he to do? Who could guide him? What helplessness! He stopped and, clutching at his head, began to think, but Matvey's being near him prevented him from reflecting calmly. And he went rapidly into the room.

Matvey was sitting in the kitchen before a bowl of potato, eating. Close by, near the stove, Aglaia and Dashutka were sitting facing one another, spinning yarn. Between the stove and the table at which Matvey was sitting was stretched an ironing-board; on it stood a cold iron.

"Sister," Matvey asked, "let me have a little oil!"

"Who eats oil on a day like this?" asked Aglaia.

"I am not a monk, sister, but a layman. And in my weak health I may take not only oil but milk."

"Yes, at the factory you may have anything."

Aglaia took a bottle of Lenten oil from the shelf and banged it angrily down before Matvey, with a malignant smile evidently pleased that he was such a sinner.

"But I tell you, you can't eat oil!" shouted Yakov.

Aglaia and Dashutka started, but Matvey poured the oil into the bowl and went on eating as though he had not heard.

"I tell you, you can't eat oil!" Yakov shouted still more loudly; he turned red all over, snatched up the bowl, lifted it higher that his head, and dashed it with all his force to the ground, so that it flew into fragments. "Don't dare to speak!" he cried in a furious voice, though Matvey had not said a word. "Don't dare!" he repeated, and struck his fist on the table.

Matvey turned pale and got up.

"Brother!" he said, still munching--"brother, think what you are about!"

"Out of my house this minute!" shouted Yakov; he loathed Matvey's wrinkled face, and his voice, and the crumbs on his moustache, and the fact that he was munching. "Out, I tell you!"

"Brother, calm yourself! The pride of hell has confounded you!"

"Hold your tongue!" (Yakov stamped.) "Go away, you devil!"

"If you care to know," Matvey went on in a loud voice, as he, too, began to get angry, "you are a backslider from God and a heretic. The accursed spirits have hidden the true light from you; your prayer is not acceptable to God. Repent before it is too late! The deathbed of the sinner is terrible! Repent, brother!"

Yakov seized him by the shoulders and dragged him away from the table, while he turned whiter than ever, and frightened and bewildered, began muttering, "What is it? What's the matter?" and, struggling and making efforts to free himself from Yakov's hands, he accidentally caught hold of his shirt near the neck and tore the collar; and it seemed to Aglaia that he was trying to beat Yakov. She uttered a shriek, snatched up the bottle of Lenten oil and with all her force brought it down straight on the skull of the cousin she hated. Matvey reeled, and in one instant his face became calm and indifferent. Yakov, breathing heavily, excited, and feeling pleasure at the gurgle the bottle had made, like a living thing, when it had struck the head, kept him from falling and several times (he remembered this very distinctly) motioned Aglaia towards the iron with his finger; and only when the blood began trickling through his hands and he heard Dashutka's loud wail, and when the ironing-board fell with a crash, and Matvey rolled heavily on it, Yakov left off feeling anger and understood what had happened.

"Let him rot, the factory buck!" Aglaia brought out with repulsion, still keeping the iron in her hand. The white bloodstained kerchief slipped on to her shoulders and her grey hair fell in disorder. "He's got what he deserved!"

Everything was terrible. Dashutka sat on the floor near the stove with the yarn in her hands, sobbing, and continually bowing down, uttering at each bow a gasping sound. But nothing was so terrible to Yakov as the potato in the blood, on which he was afraid of stepping, and there was something else terrible which weighed upon him like a bad dream and seemed the worst danger, though he could not take it in for the first minute. This was the waiter, Sergey Nikanoritch, who was standing in the doorway with the reckoning beads in his hands, very pale, looking with horror at what was happening in the kitchen. Only when he turned and went quickly into the passage and from there outside, Yakov grasped who it was and followed him.

Wiping his hands on the snow as he went, he reflected. The idea flashed through his mind that their labourer had gone away long before and had asked leave to stay the night at home in the village; the day before they had killed a pig, and there were huge bloodstains in the snow and on the sledge, and even one side of the top of the well was splattered with blood, so that it could not have seemed suspicious even if the whole of Yakov's family had been stained with blood. To conceal the murder would be agonizing, but for the policeman, who would whistle and smile ironically, to come from the station, for the peasants to arrive and bind Yakov's and Aglaia's hands, and take them solemnly to the district courthouse and from there to the town, while everyone on the way would point at them and say mirthfully, "They are taking the Godlies!"--this seemed to Yakov more agonizing than anything, and he longed to lengthen out the time somehow, so as to endure this shame not now, but later, in the future.

"I can lend you a thousand roubles,..." he said, overtaking Sergey Nikanoritch. "If you tell anyone, it will do no good... There's no bringing the man back, anyway;" and with difficulty keeping up with the waiter, who did not look round, but tried to walk away faster than ever, he went on: "I can give you fifteen hundred..."

He stopped because he was out of breath, while Sergey Nikanoritch walked on as quickly as ever, probably afraid that he would be killed, too. Only after passing the railway crossing and going half the way from the crossing to the station, he furtively looked round and walked more slowly. Lights, red and green, were already gleaming in the station and along the line; the wind had fallen, but flakes of snow were still coming down and the road had turned white again. But just at the station Sergey Nikanoritch stopped, thought a minute, and turned resolutely back. It was growing dark.

"Oblige me with the fifteen hundred, Yakov Ivanitch," he said, trembling all over. "I agree."

VI

Yakov Ivanitch's money was in the bank of the town and was invested in second mortgages; he only kept a little at home, Just what was wanted for necessary expenses. Going into the kitchen he felt for the matchbox, and while the sulphur was burning with a blue light he had time to make out the figure of Matvey, which was still lying on the floor near the table, but now it was covered with a white sheet, and nothing could be seen but his boots. A cricket was chirruping. Aglaia and Dashutka were not in the room, they were both sitting behind the counter in the tea-room, spinning yarn in silence. Yakov Ivanitch crossed to his own room with a little lamp in his hand, and pulled from under the bed a little box in which he kept his money. This time there were in it four hundred and twenty one-rouble notes and silver to the amount of thirty-five roubles; the notes had an unpleasant heavy smell. Putting the money together in his cap, Yakov Ivanitch went out into the yard and then out of the gate. He walked, looking from side to side, but there was no sign of the waiter.

"Hi!" cried Yakov.

A dark figure stepped out from the barrier at the railway crossing and came irresolutely towards him.

"Why do you keep walking about?" said Yakov with vexation, as he recognized the waiter. "Here you are; there is a little less than five hundred... I've no more in the house."

"Very well;... very grateful to you," muttered Sergey Nikanoritch, taking the money greedily and stuffing it into his pockets. He was trembling all over, and that was perceptible in spite of the darkness. "Don't worry yourself, Yakov Ivanitch... What should I chatter for: I came and went away, that's all I've had to do with it. As the saying is, I know nothing and I can tell nothing..." And at once he added with a sigh "Cursed life!"

For a minute they stood in silence, without looking at each other.

"So it all came from a trifle, goodness knows how,..." said the waiter, trembling. "I was sitting counting to myself when all at once a noise... I looked through the door, and just on account of Lenten oil you... Where is he now?"

"Lying there in the kitchen."

"You ought to take him somewhere... Why put it off?"

Yakov accompanied him to the station without a word, then went home again and harnessed the horse to take Matvey to Limarovo. He had decided to take him to the forest of Limarovo, and to leave him there on the road, and then he would tell everyone that Matvey had gone off to Vedenyapino and had not come back, and then everyone would think that he had been killed by someone on the road. He knew there was no deceiving anyone by this, but to move, to do something, to be active, was not as agonizing as to sit still and wait. He called Dashutka, and with her carried Matvey out. Aglaia stayed behind to clean up the kitchen.

When Yakov and Dashutka turned back they were detained at the railway crossing by the barrier being let down. A long goods train was passing, dragged by two engines, breathing heavily, and flinging puffs of crimson fire out of their funnels.

The foremost engine uttered a piercing whistle at the crossing in sight of the station.

"It's whistling,..." said Dashutka.

The train had passed at last, and the signalman lifted the barrier without haste.

"Is that you, Yakov Ivanitch? I didn't know you, so you'll be rich."

And then when they had reached home they had to go to bed.

Aglaia and Dashutka made themselves a bed in the tea-room and lay down side by side, while Yakov stretched himself on the counter. They neither said their prayers nor lighted the ikon lamp before lying down to sleep. All three lay awake till morning, but did not utter a single word, and it seemed to them that all night someone was walking about in the empty storey overhead.

Two days later a police inspector and the examining magistrate came from the town and made a search, first in Matvey's room and then in the whole tavern. They questioned Yakov first of all, and he testified that on the Monday Matvey had gone to Vedenyapino to confess, and that he must have been killed by the sawyers who were working on the line.

And when the examining magistrate had asked him how it had happened that Matvey was found on the road, while his cap had turned up at home--surely he had not gone to Vedenyapino without his cap?-- and why they had not found a single drop of blood beside him in the snow on the road, though his head was smashed in and his face and chest were black with blood, Yakov was confused, lost his head and answered:

"I cannot tell."

And just what Yakov had so feared happened: the policeman came, the district police officer smoked in the prayer-room and Aglaia fell upon him with abuse and was rude to the police inspector; and afterwards when Yakov and Aglaia were led out to the yard, the peasants crowded at the gates and said, "They are taking the Godlies!" and it seemed that they were all glad.

At the inquiry the policeman stated positively that Yakov and Aglaia had killed Matvey in order not to share with him, and that Matvey had money of his own, and that if it was not found at the search evidently Yakov and Aglaia had got hold of it. And Dashutka was questioned. She said that Uncle Matvey and Aunt Aglaia quarrelled and almost fought every day over money, and that Uncle Matvey was rich, so much so that he had given someone--"his Darling"--nine hundred roubles.

Dashutka was left alone in the tavern. No one came now to drink tea or vodka, and she divided her time between cleaning up the rooms, drinking mead and eating rolls; but a few days later they questioned the signalman at the railway crossing, and he said that late on Monday evening he had seen Yakov and Dashutka driving from Limarovo. Dashutka, too, was arrested, taken to the town and put in prison. It soon became known, from what Aglaia said, that Sergey Nikanoritch had been present at the murder. A search was made in his room, and money was found in an unusual place, in his snowboots under the stove, and the money was all in small change, three hundred one-rouble notes. He swore he had made this money himself, and that he hadn't been in the tavern for a year, but witnesses testified that he was poor and had been in great want of money of late, and that he used to go every day to the tavern to borrow from Matvey; and the policeman described how on the day of the murder he had himself gone twice to the tavern with the waiter to help him to borrow. It was recalled at this juncture that on Monday evening Sergey Nikanoritch had not been there to meet the passenger train, but had gone off somewhere. And he, too, was arrested and taken to the town.

The trial took place eleven months later.

Yakov Ivanitch looked much older and much thinner, and spoke in a low voice like a sick man. He felt weak, pitiful, lower in stature that anyone else, and it seemed as though his soul, too, like his body, had grown older and wasted, from the pangs of his conscience and from the dreams and imaginings which never left him all the while he was in prison. When it came out that he did not go to church the president of the court asked him:

"Are you a dissenter?"

"I can't tell," he answered.

He had no religion at all now; he knew nothing and understood nothing; and his old belief was hateful to him now, and seemed to him darkness and folly. Aglaia was not in the least subdued, and she still went on abusing the dead man, blaming him for all their misfortunes. Sergey Nikanoritch had grown a beard instead of whiskers. At the trial he was red and perspiring, and was evidently ashamed of his grey prison coat and of sitting on the same bench with humble peasants. He defended himself awkwardly, and, trying to prove that he had not been to the tavern for a whole year, got into an altercation with every witness, and the spectators laughed at him. Dashutka had grown fat in prison. At the trial she did not understand the questions put to her, and only said that when they killed Uncle Matvey she was dreadfully frightened, but afterwards she did not mind.

All four were found guilty of murder with mercenary motives. Yakov Ivanitch was sentenced to penal servitude for twenty years;

Aglaia for thirteen and a half; Sergey Nikanoritch to ten; Dashutka to six.

VII

Late one evening a foreign steamer stopped in the roads of Due in Sahalin and asked for coal. The captain was asked to wait till morning, but he did not want to wait over an hour, saying that if the weather changed for the worse in the night there would be a risk of his having to go off without coal. In the Gulf of Tartary the weather is liable to violent changes in the course of half an hour, and then the shores of Sahalin are dangerous. And already it had turned fresh, and there was a considerable sea running.

A gang of convicts were sent to the mine from the Voevodsky prison, the grimmest and most forbidding of all the prisons in Sahalin. The coal had to be loaded upon barges, and then they had to be towed by a steam-cutter alongside the steamer which was anchored more than a quarter of a mile from the coast, and then the unloading and reloading had to begin--an exhausting task when the barge kept rocking against the steamer and the men could scarcely keep on their legs for sea-sickness. The convicts, only just roused from their sleep, still drowsy, went along the shore, stumbling in the darkness and clanking their fetters. On the left, scarcely visible, was a tall, steep, extremely gloomy-looking cliff, while on the right there was a thick impenetrable mist, in which the sea moaned with a prolonged monotonous sound, "Ah!... ah!... ah!... ah!..." And it was only when the overseer was lighting his pipe, casting as he did so a passing ray of light on the escort with a gun and on the coarse faces of two or three of the nearest convicts, or when he went with his lantern close to the water that the white crests of the foremost waves could be discerned.

One of this gang was Yakov Ivanitch, nicknamed among the convicts the "Brush," on account of his long beard. No one had addressed him by his name or his father's name for a long time now; they called him simply Yashka.

He was here in disgrace, as, three months after coming to Siberia, feeling an intense irresistible longing for home, he had succumbed to temptation and run away; he had soon been caught, had been sentenced to penal servitude for life and given forty lashes. Then he was punished by flogging twice again for losing his prison clothes, though on each occasion they were stolen from him. The longing for home had begun from the very time he had been brought to Odessa, and the convict train had stopped in the night at Progonnaya; and Yakov, pressing to the window, had tried to see his own home, and could see nothing in the darkness. He had no one with whom to talk of home. His sister Aglaia had been sent right across Siberia, and he did not know where she was now. Dashutka was in Sahalin, but she had been sent to live with some ex-convict in a far away settlement; there was no news of her except that once a settler who had come to the Voevodsky Prison told Yakov that Dashutka had three children. Sergey Nikanoritch was serving as a footman at a government official's at Due, but he could not reckon on ever seeing him, as he was ashamed of being acquainted with convicts of the peasant class.

The gang reached the mine, and the men took their places on the quay. It was said there would not be any loading, as the weather kept getting worse and the steamer was meaning to set off. They could see three lights. One of them was moving: that was the steam-cutter going to the steamer, and it seemed to be coming back to tell them whether the work was to be done or not. Shivering with the autumn cold and the damp sea mist, wrapping himself in his short torn coat, Yakov Ivanitch looked intently without blinking in the direction in which lay his home. Ever since he had lived in prison together with men banished here from all ends of the earth--with Russians, Ukrainians, Tatars, Georgians, Chinese, Gypsies, Jews-- and ever since he had listened to their talk and watched their sufferings, he had begun to turn again to God, and it seemed to him at last that he had learned the true faith for which all his family, from his grandmother Avdotya down, had so thirsted, which they had sought so long and which they had never found. He knew it all now and understood where God was, and how He was to be served, and the only thing he could not understand was why men's destinies were so diverse, why this simple faith which other men receive from God for nothing and together with their lives, had cost him such a price that his arms and legs trembled like a drunken man's from all the horrors and agonies which as far as he could see would go on without a break to the day of his death. He looked with strained eyes into the darkness, and it seemed to him that through the thousand miles of that mist he could see home, could see his native province, his district, Progonnaya, could see the darkness, the savagery, the heartlessness, and the dull, sullen, animal indifference of the men he had left there. His eyes were dimmed with tears; but still he gazed into the distance where the pale lights of the steamer faintly gleamed, and his heart ached with yearning for home, and he longed to live, to go back home to tell them there of his new faith and to save from ruin if only one man, and to live without suffering if only for one day.

The cutter arrived, and the overseer announced in a loud voice that there would be no loading.

"Back!" he commanded. "Steady!"

They could hear the hoisting of the anchor chain on the steamer. A strong piercing wind was blowing by now; somewhere on the steep cliff overhead the trees were creaking. Most likely a storm was coming.

Uprooted

An Incident of My Travels

I was on my way back from evening service. The clock in the belfry of the Svyatogorsky Monastery pealed out its soft melodious chimes by way of prelude and then struck twelve. The great courtyard of the monastery stretched out at the foot of the Holy Mountains on the banks of the Donets, and, enclosed by the high hostel buildings as by a wall, seemed now in the night, when it was lighted up only by dim lanterns, lights in the windows, and the stars, a living hotch-potch full of movement, sound, and the most original confusion. From end to end, so far as the eye could see, it was all choked up with carts, old-fashioned coaches and chaises, vans, tilt-carts, about which stood crowds of horses, dark and white, and horned oxen, while people bustled about, and black long-skirted lay brothers threaded their way in and out in all directions. Shadows and streaks of light cast from the windows moved over the carts and the heads of men and horses, and in the dense twilight this all assumed the most monstrous capricious shapes: here the tilted shafts stretched upwards to the sky, here eyes of fire appeared in the face of a horse, there a lay brother grew a pair of black wings... There was the noise of talk, the snorting and munching of horses, the creaking of carts, the whimpering of children. Fresh crowds kept walking in at the gate and belated carts drove up.

The pines which were piled up on the overhanging mountain, one above another, and leaned towards the roof of the hostel, gazed into the courtyard as into a deep pit, and listened in wonder; in their dark thicket the cuckoos and nightingales never ceased calling... Looking at the confusion, listening to the uproar, one fancied that in this living hotch-potch no one understood anyone, that everyone was looking for something and would not find it, and that this multitude of carts, chaises and human beings could not ever succeed in getting off.

More than ten thousand people flocked to the Holy Mountains for the festivals of St. John the Divine and St. Nikolay the wonder-worker. Not only the hostel buildings, but even the bakehouse, the tailoring room, the carpenter's shop, the carriage house, were filled to overflowing... Those who had arrived towards night clustered like flies in autumn, by the walls, round the wells in the yard, or in the narrow passages of the hostel, waiting to be shown a resting-place for the night. The lay brothers, young and old, were in an incessant movement, with no rest or hope of being relieved. By day or late at night they produced the same impression of men hastening somewhere and agitated by something, yet, in spite of their extreme exhaustion, their faces remained full of courage and kindly welcome, their voices friendly, their movements rapid... For everyone who came they had to find a place to sleep, and to provide food and drink; to those who were deaf, slow to understand, or profuse in questions, they had to give long and wearisome explanations, to tell them why there were no empty rooms, at what o'clock the service was to be where holy bread was sold, and so on. They had to run, to carry, to talk incessantly, but more than that, they had to be polite, too, to be tactful, to try to arrange that the Greeks from Mariupol, accustomed to live more comfortably than the Little Russians, should be put with other Greeks, that some shopkeeper from Bahmut or Lisitchansk, dressed like a lady, should not be offended by being put with peasants There were continual cries of: "Father, kindly give us some kvass! Kindly give us some hay!" or "Father, may I drink water after confession?" And the lay brother would have to give out kvass or hay or to answer: "Address yourself to the priest, my good woman, we have not the authority to give permission." Another question would follow, "Where is the priest then?" and the lay brother would have to explain where was the priest's cell. With all this bustling activity, he yet had to make time to go to service in the church, to serve in the part devoted to the gentry, and to give full answers to the mass of necessary and unnecessary questions which pilgrims of the educated class are fond of showering about them. Watching them during the course of twenty-four hours, I found it hard to imagine when these black moving figures sat down and when they slept.

When, coming back from the evening service, I went to the hostel in which a place had been assigned me, the monk in charge of the sleeping quarters was standing in the doorway, and beside him, on the steps, was a group of several men and women dressed like townsfolk.

"Sir," said the monk, stopping me, "will you be so good as to allow this young man to pass the night in your room? If you would do us the favour! There are so many people and no place left--it is really dreadful!"

And he indicated a short figure in a light overcoat and a straw hat. I consented, and my chance companion followed me. Unlocking the little padlock on my door, I was always, whether I wanted to or not, obliged to look at the picture that hung on the doorpost on a level with my face. This picture with the title, "A Meditation on Death," depicted a monk on his knees, gazing at a coffin and at a skeleton laying in it. Behind the man's back stood another skeleton, somewhat more solid and carrying a scythe.

"There are no bones like that," said my companion, pointing to the place in the skeleton where there ought to have been a pelvis. "Speaking generally, you know, the spiritual fare provided for the people is not of the first quality," he added, and heaved through his nose a long and very melancholy sigh, meant to show me that I had to do with a man who really knew something about spiritual fare.

While I was looking for the matches to light a candle he sighed once more and said:

"When I was in Harkov I went several times to the anatomy theatre and saw the bones there; I have even been in the mortuary. Am I not in your way?"

My room was small and poky, with neither table nor chairs in it, but quite filled up with a chest of drawers by the window, the stove and two little wooden sofas which stood against the walls, facing one another, leaving a narrow space to walk between them. Thin rusty-looking little mattresses lay on the little sofas, as well as my belongings. There were two sofas, so this room was evidently intended for two, and I pointed out the fact to my companion.

"They will soon be ringing for mass, though," he said, "and I shan't have to be in your way very long."

Still under the impression that he was in my way and feeling awkward, he moved with a guilty step to his little sofa, sighed guiltily and sat down. When the tallow candle with its dim, dilatory flame had left off flickering and burned up sufficiently to make us both visible, I could make out what he was like. He was a young man of two-and-twenty, with a round and pleasing face, dark childlike eyes, dressed like a townsman in grey cheap clothes, and as one could judge from his complexion and narrow shoulders, not used to manual labour. He was of a very indefinite type; one could take him neither for a student nor for a man in trade, still less for a workman. But looking at his attractive face and childlike friendly eyes, I was unwilling to believe he was one of those vagabond impostors with whom every conventual establishment where they give food and lodging is flooded, and who give themselves out as divinity students, expelled for standing up for justice, or for church singers who have lost their voice... There was something characteristic, typical, very familiar in his face, but what exactly, I could not remember nor make out.

For a long time he sat silent, pondering. Probably because I had not shown appreciation of his remarks about bones and the mortuary, he thought that I was ill-humoured and displeased at his presence. Pulling a sausage out of his pocket, he turned it about before his eyes and said irresolutely:

"Excuse my troubling you,... have you a knife?"

I gave him a knife.

"The sausage is disgusting," he said, frowning and cutting himself off a little bit. "In the shop here they sell you rubbish and fleece you horribly... I would offer you a piece, but you would scarcely care to consume it. Will you have some?"

In his language, too, there was something typical that had a very great deal in common with what was characteristic in his face, but what it was exactly I still could not decide. To inspire confidence and to show that I was not ill-humoured, I took some of the proffered sausage. It certainly was horrible; one needed the teeth of a good house-dog to deal with it. As we worked our jaws we got into conversation; we began complaining to each other of the lengthiness of the service.

"The rule here approaches that of Mount Athos," I said; "but at Athos the night services last ten hours, and on great feast-days --fourteen! You should go there for prayers!"

"Yes," answered my companion, and he wagged his head, "I have been here for three weeks. And you know, every day services, every day services. On ordinary days at midnight they ring for matins, at five o'clock for early mass, at nine o'clock for late mass. Sleep is utterly out of the question. In the daytime there are hymns of praise, special prayers, vespers... And when I was preparing for the sacrament I was simply dropping from exhaustion." He sighed and went on: "And it's awkward not to go to church... The monks give one a room, feed one, and, you know, one is ashamed not to go. One wouldn't mind standing it for a day or two, perhaps, but three weeks is too much--much too much I Are you here for long?"

"I am going to-morrow evening."

"But I am staying another fortnight."

"But I thought it was not the rule to stay for so long here?" I said.

"Yes, that's true: if anyone stays too long, sponging on the monks, he is asked to go. Judge for yourself, if the proletariat were allowed to stay on here as long as they liked there would never be a room vacant, and they would eat up the whole monastery. That's true. But the monks make an exception for me, and I hope they won't turn me out for some time. You know I am a convert."

"You mean?"

"I am a Jew baptized... Only lately I have embraced orthodoxy."

Now I understood what I had before been utterly unable to understand from his face: his thick lips, and his way of twitching up the right corner of his mouth and his right eyebrow, when he was talking, and that peculiar oily brilliance of his eyes which is only found in Jews. I understood, too, his phraseology... From further conversation I learned that his name was Alexandr Ivanitch, and had in the past been Isaac, that he was a native of the Mogilev province, and that he had come to the Holy Mountains from Novotcherkassk, where he had adopted the orthodox faith.

Having finished his sausage, Alexandr Ivanitch got up, and, raising his right eyebrow, said his prayer before the ikon. The eyebrow remained up when he sat down again on the little sofa and began giving me a brief account of his long biography.

"From early childhood I cherished a love for learning," he began in a tone which suggested he was not speaking of himself, but of some great man of the past. "My parents were poor Hebrews; they exist by buying and selling in a small way; they live like beggars, you know, in filth. In fact, all the people there are poor and superstitious; they don't like education, because education, very naturally, turns a man away from religion... They are fearful fanatics... Nothing would induce my parents to let me be educated, and they wanted me to take to trade, too, and to know nothing but the Talmud... But you will agree, it is not everyone who can spend his whole life struggling for a crust of bread, wallowing in filth, and mumbling the Talmud. At times officers and country gentlemen would put up at papa's inn, and they used to talk a great deal of things which in those days I had never dreamed of; and, of course, it was alluring and moved me to envy. I used to cry and entreat them to send me to school, but they taught me to read Hebrew and nothing more. Once I found a Russian newspaper, and took it home with me to make a kite of it. I was beaten for it, though

I couldn't read Russian. Of course, fanaticism is inevitable, for every people instinctively strives to preserve its nationality, but I did not know that then and was very indignant..."

Having made such an intellectual observation, Isaac, as he had been, raised his right eyebrow higher than ever in his satisfaction and looked at me, as it were, sideways, like a cock at a grain of corn, with an air as though he would say: "Now at last you see for certain that I am an intellectual man, don't you?" After saying something more about fanaticism and his irresistible yearning for enlightenment, he went on:

"What could I do? I ran away to Smolensk. And there I had a cousin who relined saucepans and made tins. Of course, I was glad to work under him, as I had nothing to live upon; I was barefoot and in rags... I thought I could work by day and study at night and on Saturdays. And so I did, but the police found out I had no passport and sent me back by stages to my father..."

Alexandr Ivanitch shrugged one shoulder and sighed.

"What was one to do?" he went on, and the more vividly the past rose up before his mind, the more marked his Jewish accent became. "My parents punished me and handed me over to my grandfather, a fanatical old Jew, to be reformed. But I went off at night to Shklov. And when my uncle tried to catch me in Shklov, I went off to Mogilev; there I stayed two days and then I went off to Starodub with a comrade."

Later on he mentioned in his story Gonel, Kiev, Byelaya, Tserkov, Uman, Balt, Bendery and at last reached Odessa.

"In Odessa I wandered about for a whole week, out of work and hungry, till I was taken in by some Jews who went about the town buying second-hand clothes. I knew how to read and write by then, and had done arithmetic up to fractions, and I wanted to go to study somewhere, but I had not the means. What was I to do? For six months I went about Odessa buying old clothes, but the Jews paid me no wages, the rascals. I resented it and left them. Then I went by steamer to Perekop."

"What for?"

"Oh, nothing. A Greek promised me a job there. In short, till I was sixteen I wandered about like that with no definite work and no roots till I got to Poltava. There a student, a Jew, found out that I wanted to study, and gave me a letter to the Harkov students. Of course, I went to Harkov. The students consulted together and began to prepare me for the technical school. And, you know, I must say the students that I met there were such that I shall never forget them to the day of my death. To say nothing of their giving me food and lodging, they set me on the right path, they made me think, showed me the object of life. Among them were intellectual remarkable people who by now are celebrated. For instance, you have heard of Grumaher, haven't you?"

"No, I haven't."

"You haven't! He wrote very clever articles in the _Harkov Gazette_, and was preparing to be a professor. Well, I read a great deal and attended the student's societies, where you hear nothing that is commonplace. I was working up for six months, but as one has to have been through the whole high-school course of mathematics to enter the technical school, Grumaher advised me to try for the veterinary institute, where they admit high-school boys from the sixth form. Of course, I began working for it. I did not want to be a veterinary surgeon but they told me that after finishing the course at the veterinary institute I should be admitted to the faculty of medicine without examination. I learnt all Kuehner; I could read Cornelius Nepos, _a livre ouvert_; and in Greek I read through almost all Curtius. But, you know, one thing and another,... the students leaving and the uncertainty of my position, and then I heard that my mamma had come and was looking for me all over Harkov. Then I went away. What was I to do? But luckily I learned that there was a school of mines here on the Donets line. Why should I not enter that? You know the school of mines qualifies one as a mining foreman--a splendid berth. I know of mines where the foremen get a salary of fifteen hundred a year. Capital... I entered it..."

With an expression of reverent awe on his face Alexandr Ivanitch enumerated some two dozen abstruse sciences in which instruction was given at the school of mines; he described the school itself, the construction of the shafts, and the condition of the miners... Then he told me a terrible story which sounded like an invention, though I could not help believing it, for his tone in telling it was too genuine and the expression of horror on his Semitic face was too evidently sincere.

"While I was doing the practical work, I had such an accident one day!" he said, raising both eyebrows. "I was at a mine here in the Donets district. You have seen, I dare say, how people are let down into the mine. You remember when they start the horse and set the gates moving one bucket on the pulley goes down into the mine, while the other comes up; when the first begins to come up, then the second goes down--exactly like a well with two pails. Well, one day I got into the bucket, began going down, and can you fancy, all at once I heard, Trrr! The chain had broken and I flew to the devil together with the bucket and the broken bit of chain... I fell from a height of twenty feet, flat on my chest and stomach, while the bucket, being heavier, reached the bottom before me, and I hit this shoulder here against its edge. I lay, you know, stunned. I thought I was killed, and all at once I saw a fresh calamity: the other bucket, which was going up, having lost the counter-balancing weight, was coming down with a crash straight upon me... What was I to do? Seeing the position, I squeezed closer to the wall, crouching and waiting for the bucket to come full crush next minute on my head. I thought of papa and mamma and Mogilev and Grumaher... I prayed... But happily... it frightens me even to think of it..."

Alexandr Ivanitch gave a constrained smile and rubbed his forehead with his hand.

"But happily it fell beside me and only caught this side a little... It tore off coat, shirt and skin, you know, from this side... The force of it was terrific. I was unconscious after it. They got me out and sent me to the hospital. I was there four months, and the doctors there said I should go into consumption. I always have a cough now and a pain in my chest. And my psychic condition is terrible... When I am alone in a room I feel overcome with terror. Of course, with my health in that state, to be a mining foreman is out of the question. I had to give up the school of mines..."

"And what are you doing now?" I asked.

"I have passed my examination as a village schoolmaster. Now I belong to the orthodox church, and I have a right to be a teacher. In Novotcherkassk, where I was baptized, they took a great interest in me and promised me a place in a church parish school. I am going there in a fortnight, and shall ask again."

Alexandr Ivanitch took off his overcoat and remained in a shirt with an embroidered Russian collar and a worsted belt.

"It is time for bed," he said, folding his overcoat for a pillow, and yawning. "Till lately, you know, I had no knowledge of God at all. I was an atheist. When I was lying in the hospital I thought of religion, and began reflecting on that subject. In my opinion, there is only one religion possible for a thinking man, and that is the Christian religion. If you don't believe in Christ, then there is nothing else to believe in,... is there? Judaism has outlived its day, and is preserved only owing to the peculiarities of the Jewish race. When civilization reaches the Jews there will not be a trace of Judaism left. All young Jews are atheists now, observe. The New Testament is the natural continuation of the Old, isn't it?"

I began trying to find out the reasons which had led him to take so grave and bold a step as the change of religion, but he kept repeating the same, "The New Testament is the natural continuation of the Old"--a formula obviously not his own, but acquired-- which did not explain the question in the least. In spite of my efforts and artifices, the reasons remained obscure. If one could believe that he had embraced Orthodoxy from conviction, as he said he had done, what was the nature and foundation of this conviction it was impossible to grasp from his words. It was equally impossible to assume that he had changed his religion from interested motives: his cheap shabby clothes, his going on living at the expense of the convent, and the uncertainty of his future, did not look like interested motives. There was nothing for it but to accept the idea that my companion had been impelled to change his religion by the same restless spirit which had flung him like a chip of wood from town to town, and which he, using the generally accepted formula, called the craving for enlightenment.

Before going to bed I went into the corridor to get a drink of water. When I came back my companion was standing in the middle of the room, and he looked at me with a scared expression. His face looked a greyish white, and there were drops of perspiration on his forehead.

"My nerves are in an awful state," he muttered with a sickly smile," awful I It's acute psychological disturbance. But that's of no consequence."

And he began reasoning again that the New Testament was a natural continuation of the Old, that Judaism has outlived its day... Picking out his phrases, he seemed to be trying to put together the forces of his conviction and to smother with them the uneasiness of his soul, and to prove to himself that in giving up the religion of his fathers he had done nothing dreadful or peculiar, but had acted as a thinking man free from prejudice, and that therefore he could boldly remain in a room all alone with his conscience. He was trying to convince himself, and with his eyes besought my assistance.

Meanwhile a big clumsy wick had burned up on our tallow candle. It was by now getting light. At the gloomy little window, which was turning blue, we could distinctly see both banks of the Donets River and the oak copse beyond the river. It was time to s sleep.

"It will be very interesting here to-morrow," said my companion when I put out the candle and went to bed. "After early mass, the procession will go in boats from the Monastery to the Hermitage."

Raising his right eyebrow and putting his head on one side, he prayed before the ikons, and, without undressing, lay down on his little sofa.

"Yes," he said, turning over on the other side.

"Why yes?" I asked.

"When I accepted orthodoxy in Novotcherkassk my mother was looking for me in Rostov. She felt that I meant to change my religion," he sighed, and went on: "It is six years since I was there in the province of Mogilev. My sister must be married by now."

After a short silence, seeing that I was still awake, he began talking quietly of how they soon, thank God, would give him a job, and that at last he would have a home of his own, a settled position, his daily bread secure... And I was thinking that this man would never have a home of his own, nor a settled position, nor his daily bread secure. He dreamed aloud of a village school as of the Promised Land; like the majority of people, he had a prejudice against a wandering life, and regarded it as something exceptional, abnormal and accidental, like an illness, and was looking for salvation in ordinary workaday life. The tone of his voice betrayed that he was conscious of his abnormal position and regretted it. He seemed as it were apologizing and justifying himself.

Not more than a yard from me lay a homeless wanderer; in the rooms of the hostels and by the carts in the courtyard among the pilgrims some hundreds of such homeless wanderers were waiting for the morning, and further away, if one could picture to oneself the whole of Russia, a vast multitude of such uprooted creatures was pacing at that moment along highroads and side-tracks, seeking something better, or were waiting for the dawn, asleep in wayside inns and little taverns, or on the grass under the open sky... As I fell asleep I imagined how amazed and perhaps even overjoyed all these people would have been if reasoning and words could be found to prove to them that their life was as little in need of justification as any other. In my sleep I heard a bell ring outside as plaintively as though shedding bitter tears, and the lay brother calling out several times:

"Lord Jesus Christ, Son of God, have mercy upon us! Come to mass!"

When I woke up my companion was not in the room. It was sunny and there was a murmur of the crowds through the window. Going out, I learned that mass was over and that the procession had set off for the Hermitage some time before. The people were wandering in crowds upon the river bank and, feeling at liberty, did not know what to do with themselves: they could not eat or drink, as the late mass was not yet over at the Hermitage; the Monastery shops where pilgrims are so fond of crowding and asking prices were still shut. In spite of their exhaustion, many of them from sheer boredom were trudging to the Hermitage. The path from the Monastery to the Hermitage, towards which I directed my steps, twined like a snake along the high steep bank, going up and down and threading in and out among the oaks and pines. Below, the Donets gleamed, reflecting the sun; above, the rugged chalk cliff stood up white with bright green on the top from the young foliage of oaks and pines, which, hanging one above another, managed somehow to grow on the vertical cliff without falling. The pilgrims trailed along the path in single file, one behind another. The majority of them were Little Russians from the neighbouring districts, but there were many from a distance, too, who had come on foot from the provinces of Kursk and Orel; in the long string of varied colours there were Greek settlers, too, from Mariupol, strongly built, sedate and friendly people, utterly unlike their weakly and degenerate compatriots who fill our southern seaside towns. There were men from the Donets, too, with red stripes on their breeches, and emigrants from the Tavritchesky province. There were a good many pilgrims of a nondescript class, like my Alexandr Ivanitch; what sort of people they were and where they came from it was impossible to tell from their faces, from their clothes, or from their speech. The path ended at the little landing-stage, from which a narrow road went to the left to the Hermitage, cutting its way through the mountain. At the landing-stage stood two heavy big boats of a forbidding aspect, like the New Zealand pirogues which one may see in the works of Jules Verne. One boat with rugs on the seats was destined for the clergy and the singers, the other without rugs for the public. When the procession was returning I found myself among the elect who had succeeded in squeezing themselves into the second. There were so many of the elect that the boat scarcely moved, and one had to stand all the way without stirring and to be careful that one's hat was not crushed. The route was lovely. Both banks--one high, steep and white, with overhanging pines and oaks, with the crowds hurrying back along the path, and the other shelving, with green meadows and an oak copse bathed in sunshine--looked as happy and rapturous as though the May morning owed its charm only to them. The reflection of the sun in the rapidly flowing Donets quivered and raced away in all directions, and its long rays played on the chasubles, on the banners and on the drops splashed up by the oars. The singing of the Easter hymns, the ringing of the bells, the splash of the oars in the water, the calls of the birds, all mingled in the air into something tender and harmonious. The boat with the priests and the banners led the way; at its helm the black figure of a lay brother stood motionless as a statue.

When the procession was getting near the Monastery, I noticed Alexandr Ivanitch among the elect. He was standing in front of them all, and, his mouth wide open with pleasure and his right eyebrow cocked up, was gazing at the procession. His face was beaming; probably at such moments, when there were so many people round him and it was so bright, he was satisfied with himself, his new religion, and his conscience.

When a little later we were sitting in our room, drinking tea, he still beamed with satisfaction; his face showed that he was satisfied both with the tea and with me, that he fully appreciated my being an intellectual, but that he would know how to play his part with credit if any intellectual topic turned up...

"Tell me, what psychology ought I to read?" he began an intellectual conversation, wrinkling up his nose.

"Why, what do you want it for?"

"One cannot be a teacher without a knowledge of psychology. Before teaching a boy I ought to understand his soul."

I told him that psychology alone would not be enough to make one understand a boy's soul, and moreover psychology for a teacher who had not yet mastered the technical methods of instruction in reading, writing, and arithmetic would be a luxury as superfluous as the higher mathematics. He readily agreed with me, and began describing how hard and responsible was the task of a teacher, how hard it was to eradicate in the boy the habitual tendency to evil and superstition, to make him think honestly and independently, to instil into him true religion, the ideas of personal dignity, of freedom, and so on. In answer to this I said something to him. He agreed again. He agreed very readily, in fact. Obviously his brain had not a very firm grasp of all these "intellectual subjects."

Up to the time of my departure we strolled together about the Monastery, whiling away the long hot day. He never left my side a minute; whether he had taken a fancy to me or was afraid of solitude, God only knows! I remember we sat together under a clump of yellow acacia in one of the little gardens that are scattered on the mountain side.

"I am leaving here in a fortnight," he said; "it is high time."

"Are you going on foot?"

"From here to Slavyansk I shall walk, then by railway to Nikitovka; from Nikitovka the Donets line branches off, and along that branch line I shall walk as far as Hatsepetovka, and there a railway guard, I know, will help me on my way."

I thought of the bare, deserted steppe between Nikitovka and Hatsepetovka, and pictured to myself Alexandr Ivanitch striding along it, with his doubts, his homesickness, and his fear of solitude... He read boredom in my face, and sighed.

"And my sister must be married by now," he said, thinking aloud, and at once, to shake off melancholy thoughts, pointed to the top of the rock and said:

"From that mountain one can see Izyum."

As we were walking up the mountain he had a little misfortune. I suppose he stumbled, for he slit his cotton trousers and tore the sole of his shoe.

"Tss!" he said, frowning as he took off a shoe and exposed a bare foot without a stocking. "How unpleasant!... That's a complication, you know, which... Yes!"

Turning the shoe over and over before his eyes, as though unable to believe that the sole was ruined for ever, he spent a long time frowning, sighing, and clicking with his tongue.

I had in my trunk a pair of boots, old but fashionable, with pointed toes and laces. I had brought them with me in case of need, and only wore them in wet weather. When we got back to our room I made up a phrase as diplomatic as I could and offered him these boots. He accepted them and said with dignity:

"I should thank you, but I know that you consider thanks a convention."

He was pleased as a child with the pointed toes and the laces, and even changed his plans.

"Now I shall go to Novotcherkassk in a week, and not in a fortnight," he said, thinking aloud. "In shoes like these I shall not be ashamed to show myself to my godfather. I was not going away from here just because I hadn't any decent clothes..."

When the coachman was carrying out my trunk, a lay brother with a good ironical face came in to sweep out the room. Alexandr Ivanitch seemed flustered and embarrassed and asked him timidly:

"Am I to stay here or go somewhere else?"

He could not make up his mind to occupy a whole room to himself, and evidently by now was feeling ashamed of living at the expense of the Monastery. He was very reluctant to part from me; to put off being lonely as long as possible, he asked leave to see me on my way.

The road from the Monastery, which had been excavated at the cost of no little labour in the chalk mountain, moved upwards, going almost like a spiral round the mountain, over roots and under sullen overhanging pines...

The Donets was the first to vanish from our sight, after it the Monastery yard with its thousands of people, and then the green roofs... Since I was mounting upwards everything seemed vanishing into a pit. The cross on the church, burnished by the rays of the setting sun, gleamed brightly in the abyss and vanished. Nothing was left but the oaks, the pines, and the white road. But then our carriage came out on a level country, and that was all left below and behind us. Alexandr Ivanitch jumped out and, smiling mournfully, glanced at me for the last time with his childish eyes, and vanished from me for ever...

The impressions of the Holy Mountains had already become memories, and I saw something new: the level plain, the whitish-brown distance, the way side copse, and beyond it a windmill which stood with out moving, and seemed bored at not being allowed to wave its sails because it was a holiday.

The Cook's Wedding

Grisha, a fat, solemn little person of seven, was standing by the kitchen door listening and peeping through the keyhole. In the kitchen something extraordinary, and in his opinion never seen before, was taking place. A big, thick-set, red-haired peasant, with a beard, and a drop of perspiration on his nose, wearing a cabman's full coat, was sitting at the kitchen table on which they chopped the meat and sliced the onions. He was balancing a saucer on the five fingers of his right hand and drinking tea out of it, and crunching sugar so loudly that it sent a shiver down Grisha's back. Aksinya Stepanovna, the old nurse, was sitting on the dirty stool facing him, and she, too, was drinking tea. Her face was grave, though at the same time it beamed with a kind of triumph. Pelageya, the cook, was busy at the stove, and was apparently trying to hide her face. And on her face Grisha saw a regular illumination: it was burning and shifting through every shade of colour, beginning with a crimson purple and ending with a deathly white. She was continually catching hold of knives, forks, bits of wood, and rags with trembling hands, moving, grumbling to herself, making a clatter, but in reality doing nothing. She did not once glance at the table at which they were drinking tea, and to the questions put to her by the nurse she gave jerky, sullen answers without turning her face.

"Help yourself, Danilo Semyonitch," the nurse urged him hospitably. "Why do you keep on with tea and nothing but tea? You should have a drop of vodka!"

And nurse put before the visitor a bottle of vodka and a wine-glass, while her face wore a very wily expression.

"I never touch it... No..." said the cabman, declining. "Don't press me, Aksinya Stepanovna."

"What a man!... A cabman and not drink!... A bachelor can't get on without drinking. Help yourself!"

The cabman looked askance at the bottle, then at nurse's wily face, and his own face assumed an expression no less cunning, as much as to say, "You won't catch me, you old witch!"

"I don't drink; please excuse me. Such a weakness does not do in our calling. A man who works at a trade may drink, for he sits at home, but we cabmen are always in view of the public. Aren't we? If one goes into a pothouse one finds one's horse gone; if one takes a drop too much it is worse still; before you know where you are you will fall asleep or slip off the box. That's where it is."

"And how much do you make a day, Danilo Semyonitch?"

"That's according. One day you will have a fare for three roubles, and another day you will come back to the yard without a farthing. The days are very different. Nowadays our business is no good. There are lots and lots of cabmen as you know, hay is dear, and folks are paltry nowadays and always contriving to go by tram. And yet, thank God, I have nothing to complain of. I have plenty to eat and good clothes to wear, and... we could even provide well for another..." (the cabman stole a glance at Pelageya) "if it were to their liking..."

Grisha did not hear what was said further. His mamma came to the door and sent him to the nursery to learn his lessons.

"Go and learn your lesson. It's not your business to listen here!"

When Grisha reached the nursery, he put "My Own Book" in front of him, but he did not get on with his reading. All that he had just seen and heard aroused a multitude of questions in his mind.

"The cook's going to be married," he thought. "Strange--I don't understand what people get married for. Mamma was married to papa, Cousin Verotchka to Pavel Andreyitch. But one might be married to papa and Pavel Andreyitch after all: they have gold watch-chains and nice suits, their boots are always polished; but to marry that dreadful cabman with a red nose and felt boots... Fi! And why is it nurse wants poor Pelageya to be married?"

When the visitor had gone out of the kitchen, Pelageya appeared and began clearing away. Her agitation still persisted. Her face was red and looked scared. She scarcely touched the floor with the broom, and swept every corner five times over. She lingered for a long time in the room where mamma was sitting. She was evidently oppressed by her isolation, and she was longing to express herself, to share her impressions with some one, to open her heart.

"He's gone," she muttered, seeing that mamma would not begin the conversation.

"One can see he is a good man," said mamma, not taking her eyes off her sewing. "Sober and steady."

"I declare I won't marry him, mistress!" Pelageya cried suddenly, flushing crimson. "I declare I won't!"

"Don't be silly; you are not a child. It's a serious step; you must think it over thoroughly, it's no use talking nonsense. Do you like him?"

"What an idea, mistress!" cried Pelageya, abashed. "They say such things that... my goodness..."

"She should say she doesn't like him!" thought Grisha.

"What an affected creature you are... Do you like him?"

"But he is old, mistress!"

"Think of something else," nurse flew out at her from the next room. "He has not reached his fortieth year; and what do you want a young man for? Handsome is as handsome does... Marry him and that's all about it!"

"I swear I won't," squealed Pelageya.

"You are talking nonsense. What sort of rascal do you want? Anyone else would have bowed down to his feet, and you declare you won't marry him. You want to be always winking at the postmen and tutors. That tutor that used to come to Grishenka, mistress... she was never tired of making eyes at him. O-o, the shameless hussy!"

"Have you seen this Danilo before?" mamma asked Pelageya.

"How could I have seen him? I set eyes on him to-day for the first time. Aksinya picked him up and brought him along... the accursed devil... And where has he come from for my undoing!"

At dinner, when Pelageya was handing the dishes, everyone looked into her face and teased her about the cabman. She turned fearfully red, and went off into a forced giggle.

"It must be shameful to get married," thought Grisha. "Terribly shameful."

All the dishes were too salt, and blood oozed from the half-raw chickens, and, to cap it all, plates and knives kept dropping out of Pelageya's hands during dinner, as though from a shelf that had given way; but no one said a word of blame to her, as they all understood the state of her feelings. Only once papa flicked his table-napkin angrily and said to mamma:

"What do you want to be getting them all married for? What business is it of yours? Let them get married of themselves if they want to."

After dinner, neighbouring cooks and maidservants kept flitting into the kitchen, and there was the sound of whispering till late evening. How they had scented out the matchmaking, God knows. When Grisha woke in the night he heard his nurse and the cook whispering together in the nursery. Nurse was talking persuasively, while the cook alternately sobbed and giggled. When he fell asleep after this, Grisha dreamed of Pelageya being carried off by Tchernomor and a witch.

Next day there was a calm. The life of the kitchen went on its accustomed way as though the cabman did not exist. Only from time to time nurse put on her new shawl, assumed a solemn and austere air, and went off somewhere for an hour or two, obviously to conduct negotiations... Pelageya did not see the cabman, and when his name was mentioned she flushed up and cried:

"May he be thrice damned! As though I should be thinking of him! Tfoo!"

In the evening mamma went into the kitchen, while nurse and Pelageya were zealously mincing something, and said:

"You can marry him, of course--that's your business--but I must tell you, Pelageya, that he cannot live here... You know I don't like to have anyone sitting in the kitchen. Mind now, remember... And I can't let you sleep out."

"Goodness knows! What an idea, mistress!" shrieked the cook. "Why do you keep throwing him up at me? Plague take him! He's a regular curse, confound him!..."

Glancing one Sunday morning into the kitchen, Grisha was struck dumb with amazement. The kitchen was crammed full of people. Here were cooks from the whole courtyard, the porter, two policemen, a non-commissioned officer with good-conduct stripes, and the boy Filka... This Filka was generally hanging about the laundry playing with the dogs; now he was combed and washed, and was holding an ikon in a tinfoil setting. Pelageya was standing in the middle of the kitchen in a new cotton dress, with a flower on her head. Beside her stood the cabman. The happy pair were red in the face and perspiring and blinking with embarrassment.

"Well... I fancy it is time," said the non-commissioned officer, after a prolonged silence.

Pelageya's face worked all over and she began blubbering...

The soldier took a big loaf from the table, stood beside nurse, and began blessing the couple. The cabman went up to the soldier, flopped down on his knees, and gave a smacking kiss on his hand. He did the same before nurse. Pelageya followed him mechanically, and she too bowed down to the ground. At last the outer door was opened, there was a whiff of white mist, and the whole party flocked noisily out of the kitchen into the yard.

"Poor thing, poor thing," thought Grisha, hearing the sobs of the cook. "Where have they taken her? Why don't papa and mamma protect her?"

After the wedding there was singing and concertina-playing in the laundry till late evening. Mamma was cross all the evening because nurse smelt of vodka, and owing to the wedding there was no one to heat the samovar. Pelageya had not come back by the time Grisha went to bed.

"The poor thing is crying somewhere in the dark!" he thought. "While the cabman is saying to her 'shut up!'"

Next morning the cook was in the kitchen again. The cabman came in for a minute. He thanked mamma, and glancing sternly at Pelageya, said:

"Will you look after her, madam? Be a father and a mother to her. And you, too, Aksinya Stepanovna, do not forsake her, see that everything is as it should be... without any nonsense... And also, madam, if you would kindly advance me five roubles of her wages. I have got to buy a new horse-collar."

Again a problem for Grisha: Pelageya was living in freedom, doing as she liked, and not having to account to anyone for her actions, and all at once, for no sort of reason, a stranger turns up, who has somehow acquired rights over her conduct and her property! Grisha was distressed. He longed passionately, almost to tears, to comfort this victim, as he supposed, of man's injustice. Picking out the very biggest apple in the store-room he stole into the kitchen, slipped it into Pelageya's hand, and darted headlong away.

Sleepy

Night. Varka, the little nurse, a girl of thirteen, is rocking the cradle in which the baby is lying, and humming hardly audibly:

"Hush-a-bye, my baby wee,
While I sing a song for thee."

A little green lamp is burning before the ikon; there is a string stretched from one end of the room to the other, on which baby-clothes and a pair of big black trousers are hanging. There is a big patch of green on the ceiling from the ikon lamp, and the baby-clothes and the trousers throw long shadows on the stove, on the cradle, and on Varka... When the lamp begins to flicker, the green patch and the shadows come to life, and are set in motion, as though by the wind. It is stuffy. There is a smell of cabbage soup, and of the inside of a boot-shop.

The baby's crying. For a long while he has been hoarse and exhausted with crying; but he still goes on screaming, and there is no knowing when he will stop. And Varka is sleepy. Her eyes are glued together, her head droops, her neck aches. She cannot move her eyelids or her lips, and she feels as though her face is dried and wooden, as though her head has become as small as the head of a pin.

"Hush-a-bye, my baby wee," she hums, "while I cook the groats for thee..."

A cricket is churring in the stove. Through the door in the next room the master and the apprentice Afanasy are snoring... The cradle creaks plaintively, Varka murmurs--and it all blends into that soothing music of the night to which it is so sweet to listen, when one is lying in bed. Now that music is merely irritating and oppressive, because it goads her to sleep, and she must not sleep; if Varka--God forbid!--should fall asleep, her master and mistress would beat her.

The lamp flickers. The patch of green and the shadows are set in motion, forcing themselves on Varka's fixed, half-open eyes, and in her half slumbering brain are fashioned into misty visions. She sees dark clouds chasing one another over the sky, and screaming like the baby. But then the wind blows, the clouds are gone, and Varka sees a broad high road covered with liquid mud; along the high road stretch files of wagons, while people with wallets on their backs are trudging along and shadows flit backwards and forwards; on both sides she can see forests through the cold harsh mist. All at once the people with their wallets and their shadows fall on the ground in the liquid mud. "What is that for?" Varka asks. "To sleep, to sleep!" they answer her. And they fall sound asleep, and sleep sweetly, while crows and magpies sit on the telegraph wires, scream like the baby, and try to wake them.

"Hush-a-bye, my baby wee, and I will sing a song to thee," murmurs Varka, and now she sees herself in a dark stuffy hut.

Her dead father, Yefim Stepanov, is tossing from side to side on the floor. She does not see him, but she hears him moaning and rolling on the floor from pain. "His guts have burst," as he says; the pain is so violent that he cannot utter a single word, and can only draw in his breath and clack his teeth like the rattling of a drum:

"Boo--boo--boo--boo..."

Her mother, Pelageya, has run to the master's house to say that Yefim is dying. She has been gone a long time, and ought to be back. Varka lies awake on the stove, and hears her father's "boo--boo--boo." And then she hears someone has driven up to the hut. It is a young doctor from the town, who has been sent from the big house where he is staying on a visit. The doctor comes into the hut; he cannot be seen in the darkness, but he can be heard coughing and rattling the door.

"Light a candle," he says.

"Boo--boo--boo," answers Yefim.

Pelageya rushes to the stove and begins looking for the broken pot with the matches. A minute passes in silence. The doctor, feeling in his pocket, lights a match.

"In a minute, sir, in a minute," says Pelageya. She rushes out of the hut, and soon afterwards comes back with a bit of candle.

Yefim's cheeks are rosy and his eyes are shining, and there is a peculiar keenness in his glance, as though he were seeing right through the hut and the doctor.

"Come, what is it? What are you thinking about?" says the doctor, bending down to him. "Aha! have you had this long?"

"What? Dying, your honour, my hour has come... I am not to stay among the living."

"Don't talk nonsense! We will cure you!"

"That's as you please, your honour, we humbly thank you, only we understand... Since death has come, there it is."

The doctor spends a quarter of an hour over Yefim, then he gets up and says:

"I can do nothing. You must go into the hospital, there they will operate on you. Go at once... You must go! It's rather late, they will all be asleep in the hospital, but that doesn't matter, I will give you a note. Do you hear?"

"Kind sir, but what can he go in?" says Pelageya. "We have no horse."

"Never mind. I'll ask your master, he'll let you have a horse."

The doctor goes away, the candle goes out, and again there is the sound of "boo--boo--boo." Half an hour later someone drives up to the hut. A cart has been sent to take Yefim to the hospital. He gets ready and goes...

But now it is a clear bright morning. Pelageya is not at home; she has gone to the hospital to find what is being done to Yefim. Somewhere there is a baby crying, and Varka hears someone singing with her own voice:

"Hush-a-bye, my baby wee, I will sing a song to thee."

Pelageya comes back; she crosses herself and whispers:

"They put him to rights in the night, but towards morning he gave up his soul to God... The Kingdom of Heaven be his and peace everlasting... They say he was taken too late... He ought to have gone sooner..."

Varka goes out into the road and cries there, but all at once someone hits her on the back of her head so hard that her forehead knocks against a birch tree. She raises her eyes, and sees facing her, her master, the shoemaker.

"What are you about, you scabby slut?" he says. "The child is crying, and you are asleep!"

He gives her a sharp slap behind the ear, and she shakes her head, rocks the cradle, and murmurs her song. The green patch and the shadows from the trousers and the baby-clothes move up and down, nod to her, and soon take possession of her brain again. Again she sees the high road covered with liquid mud. The people with wallets on their backs and the shadows have lain down and are fast asleep. Looking at them, Varka has a passionate longing for sleep; she would lie down with enjoyment, but her mother Pelageya is walking beside her, hurrying her on. They are hastening together to the town to find situations.

"Give alms, for Christ's sake!" her mother begs of the people they meet. "Show us the Divine Mercy, kind-hearted gentlefolk!"

"Give the baby here!" a familiar voice answers. "Give the baby here!" the same voice repeats, this time harshly and angrily. "Are you asleep, you wretched girl?"

Varka jumps up, and looking round grasps what is the matter: there is no high road, no Pelageya, no people meeting them, there is only her mistress, who has come to feed the baby, and is standing in the middle of the room. While the stout, broad-shouldered woman nurses the child and soothes it, Varka stands looking at her and waiting till she has done. And outside the windows the air is already turning blue, the shadows and the green patch on the ceiling are visibly growing pale, it will soon be morning.

"Take him," says her mistress, buttoning up her chemise over her bosom; "he is crying. He must be bewitched."

Varka takes the baby, puts him in the cradle and begins rocking it again. The green patch and the shadows gradually disappear, and now there is nothing to force itself on her eyes and cloud her brain. But she is as sleepy as before, fearfully sleepy! Varka lays her head on the edge of the cradle, and rocks her whole body to overcome her sleepiness, but yet her eyes are glued together, and her head is heavy.

"Varka, heat the stove!" she hears the master's voice through the door.

So it is time to get up and set to work. Varka leaves the cradle, and runs to the shed for firewood. She is glad. When one moves and runs about, one is not so sleepy as when one is sitting down. She brings the wood, heats the stove, and feels that her wooden face is getting supple again, and that her thoughts are growing clearer.

"Varka, set the samovar!" shouts her mistress.

Varka splits a piece of wood, but has scarcely time to light the splinters and put them in the samovar, when she hears a fresh order:

"Varka, clean the master's galoshes!"

She sits down on the floor, cleans the galoshes, and thinks how nice it would be to put her head into a big deep galosh, and have a little nap in it... And all at once the galosh grows, swells, fills up the whole room. Varka drops the brush, but at once shakes her head, opens her eyes wide, and tries to look at things so that they may not grow big and move before her eyes.

"Varka, wash the steps outside; I am ashamed for the customers to see them!"

Varka washes the steps, sweeps and dusts the rooms, then heats another stove and runs to the shop. There is a great deal of work: she hasn't one minute free.

But nothing is so hard as standing in the same place at the kitchen table peeling potatoes. Her head droops over the table, the potatoes dance before her eyes, the knife tumbles out of her hand while her fat, angry mistress is moving about near her with her sleeves tucked up, talking so loud that it makes a ringing in Varka's ears. It is agonising, too, to wait at dinner, to wash, to sew, there are minutes when she longs to flop on to the floor regardless of everything, and to sleep.

The day passes. Seeing the windows getting dark, Varka presses her temples that feel as though they were made of wood, and smiles, though she does not know why. The dusk of evening caresses her eyes that will hardly keep open, and promises her sound sleep soon. In the evening visitors come.

"Varka, set the samovar!" shouts her mistress. The samovar is a little one, and before the visitors have drunk all the tea they want, she has to heat it five times. After tea Varka stands for a whole hour on the same spot, looking at the visitors, and waiting for orders.

"Varka, run and buy three bottles of beer!"

She starts off, and tries to run as quickly as she can, to drive away sleep.

"Varka, fetch some vodka! Varka, where's the corkscrew? Varka, clean a herring!"

But now, at last, the visitors have gone; the lights are put out, the master and mistress go to bed.

"Varka, rock the baby!" she hears the last order.

The cricket churrs in the stove; the green patch on the ceiling and the shadows from the trousers and the baby-clothes force themselves on Varka's half-opened eyes again, wink at her and cloud her mind.

"Hush-a-bye, my baby wee," she murmurs, "and I will sing a song to thee."

And the baby screams, and is worn out with screaming. Again Varka sees the muddy high road, the people with wallets, her mother Pelageya, her father Yefim. She understands everything, she recognises everyone, but through her half sleep she cannot understand the force which binds her, hand and foot, weighs upon her, and prevents her from living. She looks round, searches for that force that she may escape from it, but she cannot find it. At last, tired to death, she does her very utmost, strains her eyes, looks up at the flickering green patch, and listening to the screaming, finds the foe who will not let her live.

That foe is the baby.

She laughs. It seems strange to her that she has failed to grasp such a simple thing before. The green patch, the shadows, and the cricket seem to laugh and wonder too.

The hallucination takes possession of Varka. She gets up from her stool, and with a broad smile on her face and wide unblinking eyes, she walks up and down the room. She feels pleased and tickled at the thought that she will be rid directly of the baby that binds her hand and foot... Kill the baby and then sleep, sleep, sleep...

Laughing and winking and shaking her fingers at the green patch, Varka steals up to the cradle and bends over the baby. When she has strangled him, she quickly lies down on the floor, laughs with delight that she can sleep, and in a minute is sleeping as sound as the dead.

Children

Papa and mamma and Aunt Nadya are not at home. They have gone to a christening party at the house of that old officer who rides on a little grey horse. While waiting for them to come home, Grisha, Anya, Alyosha, Sonya, and the cook's son, Andrey, are sitting at the table in the dining-room, playing at loto. To tell the truth, it is bedtime, but how can one go to sleep without hearing from mamma what the baby was like at the christening, and what they had for supper? The table, lighted by a hanging lamp, is dotted with numbers, nutshells, scraps of paper, and little bits of glass. Two cards lie in front of each player, and a heap of bits of glass for covering the numbers. In the middle of the table is a white saucer with five kopecks in it. Beside the saucer, a half-eaten apple, a pair of scissors, and a plate on which they have been told to put their nutshells. The children are playing for money. The stake is a kopeck. The rule is: if anyone cheats, he is turned out at once. There is no one in the dining-room but the players, and nurse, Agafya Ivanovna, is in the kitchen, showing the cook how to cut a pattern, while their elder brother, Vasya, a schoolboy in the fifth class, is lying on the sofa in the drawing-room, feeling bored.

They are playing with zest. The greatest excitement is expressed on the face of Grisha. He is a small boy of nine, with a head cropped so that the bare skin shows through, chubby cheeks, and thick lips like a negro's. He is already in the preparatory class, and so is regarded as grown up, and the cleverest. He is playing entirely for the sake of the money. If there had been no kopecks in the saucer, he would have been asleep long ago. His brown eyes stray uneasily and jealously over the other players' cards. The fear that he may not win, envy, and the financial combinations of which his cropped head is full, will not let him sit still and concentrate his mind. He fidgets as though he were sitting on thorns. When he wins, he snatches up the money greedily, and instantly puts it in his pocket. His sister, Anya, a girl of eight, with a sharp chin and clever shining eyes, is also afraid that someone else may win. She flushes and turns pale, and watches the players keenly. The kopecks do not interest her. Success in the game is for her a question of vanity. The other sister, Sonya, a child of six with a curly head, and a complexion such as is seen only in very healthy children, expensive dolls, and the faces on bonbon boxes, is playing loto for the process of the game itself. There is bliss all over her face. Whoever wins, she laughs and claps her hands. Alyosha, a chubby, spherical little figure, gasps, breathes hard through his nose, and stares open-eyed at the cards. He is moved neither by covetousness nor vanity. So long as he is not driven out of the room, or sent to bed, he is thankful. He looks phlegmatic, but at heart he is rather a little beast. He is not there so much for the sake of the loto, as for the sake of the misunderstandings which are inevitable in the game. He is greatly delighted if one hits another, or calls him names. He ought to have run off somewhere long ago, but he won't leave the table for a minute, for fear they should steal his counters or his kopecks. As he can only count the units and numbers which end in nought, Anya covers his numbers for him. The fifth player, the cook's son, Andrey, a dark-skinned and sickly looking boy in a cotton shirt, with a copper cross on his breast, stands motionless, looking dreamily at the numbers. He takes no interest in winning, or in the success of the others, because he is entirely engrossed by the arithmetic of the game, and its far from complex theory; "How many numbers there are in the world," he is thinking, "and how is it they don't get mixed up?"

They all shout out the numbers in turn, except Sonya and Alyosha. To vary the monotony, they have invented in the course of time a number of synonyms and comic nicknames. Seven, for instance, is called the "ovenrake," eleven the "sticks," seventy-seven "Semyon

Semyonitch," ninety "grandfather," and so on. The game is going merrily.

"Thirty-two," cries Grisha, drawing the little yellow cylinders out of his father's cap. "Seventeen! Ovenrake! Twenty-eight! Lay them straight..."

Anya sees that Andrey has let twenty-eight slip. At any other time she would have pointed it out to him, but now when her vanity lies in the saucer with the kopecks, she is triumphant.

"Twenty-three!" Grisha goes on, "Semyon Semyonitch! Nine!"

"A beetle, a beetle," cries Sonya, pointing to a beetle running across the table. "Aie!"

"Don't kill it," says Alyosha, in his deep bass, "perhaps it's got children..."

Sonya follows the black beetle with her eyes and wonders about its children: what tiny little beetles they must be!

"Forty-three! One!" Grisha goes on, unhappy at the thought that Anya has already made two fours. "Six!"

"Game! I have got the game!" cries Sonya, rolling her eyes coquettishly and giggling.

The players' countenances lengthen.

"Must make sure!" says Grisha, looking with hatred at Sonya.

Exercising his rights as a big boy, and the cleverest, Grisha takes upon himself to decide. What he wants, that they do. Sonya's reckoning is slowly and carefully verified, and to the great regret of her fellow players, it appears that she has not cheated. Another game is begun.

"I did see something yesterday!" says Anya, as though to herself. "Filipp Filippitch turned his eyelids inside out somehow and his eyes looked red and dreadful, like an evil spirit's."

"I saw it too," says Grisha. "Eight! And a boy at our school can move his ears. Twenty-seven!"

Andrey looks up at Grisha, meditates, and says:

"I can move my ears too..."

"Well then, move them."

Andrey moves his eyes, his lips, and his fingers, and fancies that his ears are moving too. Everyone laughs.

"He is a horrid man, that Filipp Filippitch," sighs Sonya. "He came into our nursery yesterday, and I had nothing on but my chemise... And I felt so improper!"

"Game!" Grisha cries suddenly, snatching the money from the saucer. "I've got the game! You can look and see if you like."

The cook's son looks up and turns pale.

"Then I can't go on playing any more," he whispers.

"Why not?"

"Because... because I have got no more money."

"You can't play without money," says Grisha.

Andrey ransacks his pockets once more to make sure. Finding nothing in them but crumbs and a bitten pencil, he drops the corners of his mouth and begins blinking miserably. He is on the point of crying...

"I'll put it down for you!" says Sonya, unable to endure his look of agony. "Only mind you must pay me back afterwards."

The money is brought and the game goes on.

"I believe they are ringing somewhere," says Anya, opening her eyes wide.

They all leave off playing and gaze open-mouthed at the dark window. The reflection of the lamp glimmers in the darkness.

"It was your fancy."

"At night they only ring in the cemetery," says Andrey.

"And what do they ring there for?"

"To prevent robbers from breaking into the church. They are afraid of the bells."

"And what do robbers break into the church for?" asks Sonya.

"Everyone knows what for: to kill the watchmen."

A minute passes in silence. They all look at one another, shudder, and go on playing. This time Andrey wins.

"He has cheated," Alyosha booms out, apropos of nothing.

"What a lie, I haven't cheated."

Andrey turns pale, his mouth works, and he gives Alyosha a slap on the head! Alyosha glares angrily, jumps up, and with one knee on the table, slaps Andrey on the cheek! Each gives the other a second blow, and both howl. Sonya, feeling such horrors too much for her, begins crying too, and the dining-room resounds with lamentations on various notes. But do not imagine that is the end of the game. Before five minutes are over, the children are laughing and talking peaceably again. Their faces are tear-stained, but that does not prevent them from smiling; Alyosha is positively blissful, there has been a squabble!

Vasya, the fifth form schoolboy, walks into the dining-room. He looks sleepy and disillusioned.

"This is revolting!" he thinks, seeing Grisha feel in his pockets in which the kopecks are jingling. "How can they give children money? And how can they let them play games of chance? A nice way to bring them up, I must say! It's revolting!"

But the children's play is so tempting that he feels an inclination to join them and to try his luck.

"Wait a minute and I'll sit down to a game," he says.

"Put down a kopeck!"

"In a minute," he says, fumbling in his pockets. "I haven't a kopeck, but here is a rouble. I'll stake a rouble."

"No, no, no... You must put down a kopeck."

"You stupids. A rouble is worth more than a kopeck anyway," the schoolboy explains. "Whoever wins can give me change."

"No, please! Go away!"

The fifth form schoolboy shrugs his shoulders, and goes into the kitchen to get change from the servants. It appears there is not a single kopeck in the kitchen.

"In that case, you give me change," he urges Grisha, coming back from the kitchen. "I'll pay you for the change. Won't you? Come, give me ten kopecks for a rouble."

Grisha looks suspiciously at Vasya, wondering whether it isn't some trick, a swindle.

"I won't," he says, holding his pockets.

Vasya begins to get cross, and abuses them, calling them idiots and blockheads.

"I'll put down a stake for you, Vasya!" says Sonya. "Sit down." He sits down and lays two cards before him. Anya begins counting the numbers.

"I've dropped a kopeck!" Grisha announces suddenly, in an agitated voice. "Wait!"

He takes the lamp, and creeps under the table to look for the kopeck. They clutch at nutshells and all sorts of nastiness, knock their heads together, but do not find the kopeck. They begin looking again, and look till Vasya takes the lamp out of Grisha's hands and puts it in its place. Grisha goes on looking in the dark. But at last the kopeck is found. The players sit down at the table and mean to go on playing.

"Sonya is asleep!" Alyosha announces.

Sonya, with her curly head lying on her arms, is in a sweet, sound, tranquil sleep, as though she had been asleep for an hour. She has fallen asleep by accident, while the others were looking for the kopeck.

"Come along, lie on mamma's bed!" says Anya, leading her away from the table. "Come along!"

They all troop out with her, and five minutes later mamma's bed presents a curious spectacle. Sonya is asleep. Alyosha is snoring beside her. With their heads to the others' feet, sleep Grisha and Anya. The cook's son, Andrey too, has managed to snuggle in beside them. Near them lie the kopecks, that have lost their power till the next game. Good-night!

Grisha

Grisha, a chubby little boy, born two years and eight months ago, is walking on the boulevard with his nurse. He is wearing a long, wadded pelisse, a scarf, a big cap with a fluffy pom-pom, and warm over-boots. He feels hot and stifled, and now, too, the rollicking April sunshine is beating straight in his face, and making his eyelids tingle.

The whole of his clumsy, timidly and uncertainly stepping little figure expresses the utmost bewilderment.

Hitherto Grisha has known only a rectangular world, where in one corner stands his bed, in the other nurse's trunk, in the third a chair, while in the fourth there is a little lamp burning. If one looks under the bed, one sees a doll with a broken arm and a drum; and behind nurse's trunk, there are a great many things of all sorts: cotton reels, boxes without lids, and a broken Jack-a-dandy. In that world, besides nurse and Grisha, there are often mamma and the cat. Mamma is like a doll, and puss is like papa's fur-coat, only the coat hasn't got eyes and a tail. From the world which is called the nursery a door leads to a great expanse where they have dinner and tea. There stands Grisha's chair on high legs, and on the wall hangs a clock which exists to swing its pendulum and chime. From the dining-room, one can go into a room where there are red arm-chairs. Here, there is a dark patch on the carpet, concerning which fingers are still shaken at Grisha. Beyond that room is still another, to which one is not admitted, and where one sees glimpses of papa--an extremely enigmatical person! Nurse and mamma are comprehensible: they dress Grisha, feed him, and put him to bed, but what papa exists for is unknown. There is another enigmatical person, auntie, who presented Grisha with a drum. She appears and disappears. Where does she disappear to? Grisha has more than once looked under the bed, behind the trunk, and under the sofa, but she was not there.

In this new world, where the sun hurts one's eyes, there are so many papas and mammas and aunties, that there is no knowing to whom to run. But what is stranger and more absurd than anything is the horses. Grisha gazes at their moving legs, and can make nothing of it. He looks at his nurse for her to solve the mystery, but she does not speak.

All at once he hears a fearful tramping... A crowd of soldiers, with red faces and bath brooms under their arms, move in step along the boulevard straight upon him. Grisha turns cold all over with terror, and looks inquiringly at nurse to know whether it is dangerous. But nurse neither weeps nor runs away, so there is no danger. Grisha looks after the soldiers, and begins to move his feet in step with them himself.

Two big cats with long faces run after each other across the boulevard, with their tongues out, and their tails in the air. Grisha thinks that he must run too, and runs after the cats.

"Stop!" cries nurse, seizing him roughly by the shoulder. "Where are you off to? Haven't you been told not to be naughty?"

Here there is a nurse sitting holding a tray of oranges. Grisha passes by her, and, without saying anything, takes an orange.

"What are you doing that for?" cries the companion of his travels, slapping his hand and snatching away the orange. "Silly!"

Now Grisha would have liked to pick up a bit of glass that was lying at his feet and gleaming like a lamp, but he is afraid that his hand will be slapped again.

"My respects to you!" Grisha hears suddenly, almost above his ear, a loud thick voice, and he sees a tall man with bright buttons.

To his great delight, this man gives nurse his hand, stops, and begins talking to her. The brightness of the sun, the noise of the carriages, the horses, the bright buttons are all so impressively new and not dreadful, that Grisha's soul is filled with a feeling of enjoyment and he begins to laugh.

"Come along! Come along!" he cries to the man with the bright buttons, tugging at his coattails.

"Come along where?" asks the man.

"Come along!" Grisha insists.

He wants to say that it would be just as well to take with them papa, mamma, and the cat, but his tongue does not say what he wants to.

A little later, nurse turns out of the boulevard, and leads Grisha into a big courtyard where there is still snow; and the man with the bright buttons comes with them too. They carefully avoid the lumps of snow and the puddles, then, by a dark and dirty staircase, they go into a room. Here there is a great deal of smoke, there is a smell of roast meat, and a woman is standing by the stove frying cutlets. The cook and the nurse kiss each other, and sit down on the bench together with the man, and begin talking in a low voice. Grisha, wrapped up as he is, feels insufferably hot and stifled.

"Why is this?" he wonders, looking about him.

He sees the dark ceiling, the oven fork with two horns, the stove which looks like a great black hole.

"Mam-ma," he drawls.

"Come, come, come!" cries the nurse. "Wait a bit!"

The cook puts a bottle on the table, two wine-glasses, and a pie. The two women and the man with the bright buttons clink glasses and empty them several times, and, the man puts his arm round first the cook and then the nurse. And then all three begin singing in an undertone.

Grisha stretches out his hand towards the pie, and they give him a piece of it. He eats it and watches nurse drinking... He wants to drink too.

"Give me some, nurse!" he begs.

The cook gives him a sip out of her glass. He rolls his eyes, blinks, coughs, and waves his hands for a long time afterwards, while the cook looks at him and laughs.

When he gets home Grisha begins to tell mamma, the walls, and the bed where he has been, and what he has seen. He talks not so much with his tongue, as with his face and his hands. He shows how the sun shines, how the horses run, how the terrible stove looks, and how the cook drinks...

In the evening he cannot get to sleep. The soldiers with the brooms, the big cats, the horses, the bit of glass, the tray of oranges, the bright buttons, all gathered together, weigh on his brain. He tosses from side to side, babbles, and, at last, unable to endure his excitement, begins crying.

"You are feverish," says mamma, putting her open hand on his forehead. "What can have caused it?

"Stove!" wails Grisha. "Go away, stove!"

"He must have eaten too much..." mamma decides.

And Grisha, shattered by the impressions of the new life he has just experienced, receives a spoonful of castor-oil from mamma.

Oysters

I need no great effort of memory to recall, in every detail, the rainy autumn evening when I stood with my father in one of the more frequented streets of Moscow, and felt that I was gradually being overcome by a strange illness. I had no pain at all, but my legs were giving way under me, the words stuck in my throat, my head slipped weakly on one side... It seemed as though, in a moment, I must fall down and lose consciousness.

If I had been taken into a hospital at that minute, the doctors would have had to write over my bed: Fames , a disease which is not in the manuals of medicine.

Beside me on the pavement stood my father in a shabby summer overcoat and a serge cap, from which a bit of white wadding was sticking out. On his feet he had big heavy galoshes. Afraid, vain man, that people would see that his feet were bare under his galoshes, he had drawn the tops of some old boots up round the calves of his legs.

This poor, foolish, queer creature, whom I loved the more warmly the more ragged and dirty his smart summer overcoat became, had come to Moscow, five months before, to look for a job as copying-clerk. For those five months he had been trudging about Moscow looking for work, and it was only on that day that he had brought himself to go into the street to beg for alms.

Before us was a big house of three storeys, adorned with a blue signboard with the word "Restaurant" on it. My head was drooping feebly backwards and on one side, and I could not help looking upwards at the lighted windows of the restaurant. Human figures were flitting about at the windows. I could see the right side of the orchestrion, two oleo graphs, hanging lamps... Staring into one window, I saw a patch of white. The patch was motionless, and its rectangular outlines stood out sharply against the dark, brown background. I looked intently and made out of the patch a white placard on the wall. Something was written on it, but what it was, I could not see...

For half an hour I kept my eyes on the placard. Its white attracted my eyes, and, as it were, hypnotised my brain. I tried to read it, but my efforts were in vain.

At last the strange disease got the upper hand.

The rumble of the carriages began to seem like thunder, in the stench of the street I distinguished a thousand smells. The restaurant lights and the lamps dazzled my eyes like lightning. My five senses were overstrained and sensitive beyond the normal. I began to see what I had not seen before.

"Oysters..." I made out on the placard.

A strange word! I had lived in the world eight years and three months, but had never come across that word. What did it mean? Surely it was not the name of the restaurant-keeper? But signboards with names on them always hang outside, not on the walls indoors!

"Papa, what does 'oysters' mean?" I asked in a husky voice, making an effort to turn my face towards my father.

My father did not hear. He was keeping a watch on the movements of the crowd, and following every passer-by with his eyes... From his eyes I saw that he wanted to say something to the passers-by, but the fatal word hung like a heavy weight on his trembling lips and could not be flung off. He even took a step after one passer-by and touched him on the sleeve, but when he turned round, he said, "I beg your pardon," was overcome with confusion, and staggered back.

"Papa, what does 'oysters' mean?" I repeated.

"It is an animal... that lives in the sea."

I instantly pictured to myself this unknown marine animal... I thought it must be something midway between a fish and a crab. As it was from the sea they made of it, of course, a very nice hot fish soup with savoury pepper and laurel leaves, or broth with vinegar and fricassee of fish and cabbage, or crayfish sauce, or served it cold with horse-radish... I vividly imagined it being brought from the market, quickly cleaned, quickly put in the pot, quickly, quickly, for everyone was hungry... awfully hungry! From the kitchen rose the smell of hot fish and crayfish soup.

I felt that this smell was tickling my palate and nostrils, that it was gradually taking possession of my whole body... The restaurant, my father, the white placard, my sleeves were all smelling of it, smelling so strongly that I began to chew. I moved my jaws and swallowed as though I really had a piece of this marine animal in my mouth...

My legs gave way from the blissful sensation I was feeling, and I clutched at my father's arm to keep myself from falling, and leant against his wet summer overcoat. My father was trembling and shivering. He was cold...

"Papa, are oysters a Lenten dish?" I asked.

"They are eaten alive..." said my father. "They are in shells like tortoises, but... in two halves."

The delicious smell instantly left off affecting me, and the illusion vanished... Now I understood it all!

"How nasty," I whispered, "how nasty!"

So that's what "oysters" meant! I imagined to myself a creature like a frog. A frog sitting in a shell, peeping out from it with big, glittering eyes, and moving its revolting jaws. I imagined this creature in a shell with claws, glittering eyes, and a slimy skin, being brought from the market... The children would all hide while the cook, frowning with an air of disgust, would take the creature by its claw, put it on a plate, and carry it into the dining-room. The grown-ups would take it and eat it, eat it alive with its eyes, its teeth, its legs! While it squeaked and tried to bite their lips...

I frowned, but... but why did my teeth move as though I were munching? The creature was loathsome, disgusting, terrible, but I ate it, ate it greedily, afraid of distinguishing its taste or smell. As soon as I had eaten one, I saw the glittering eyes of a second, a third... I ate them too... At last I ate the table-napkin, the plate, my father's galoshes, the white placard... I ate everything that caught my eye, because I felt that nothing but eating would take away my illness. The oysters had a terrible look in their eyes and were loathsome. I shuddered at the thought of them, but I wanted to eat! To eat!

"Oysters! Give me some oysters!" was the cry that broke from me and I stretched out my hand.

"Help us, gentlemen!" I heard at that moment my father say, in a hollow and shaking voice. "I am ashamed to ask but--my God!--I can bear no more!"

"Oysters!" I cried, pulling my father by the skirts of his coat.

"Do you mean to say you eat oysters? A little chap like you!" I heard laughter close to me.

Two gentlemen in top hats were standing before us, looking into my face and laughing.

"Do you really eat oysters, youngster? That's interesting! How do you eat them?"

I remember that a strong hand dragged me into the lighted restaurant. A minute later there was a crowd round me, watching me with curiosity and amusement. I sat at a table and ate something slimy, salt with a flavour of dampness and mouldiness. I ate greedily without chewing, without looking and trying to discover what I was eating. I fancied that if I opened my eyes I should see glittering eyes, claws, and sharp teeth.

All at once I began biting something hard, there was a sound of a scrunching.

"Ha, ha! He is eating the shells," laughed the crowd. "Little silly, do you suppose you can eat that?"

After that I remember a terrible thirst. I was lying in my bed, and could not sleep for heartburn and the strange taste in my parched mouth. My father was walking up and down, gesticulating with his hands.

"I believe I have caught cold," he was muttering. "I've a feeling in my head as though someone were sitting on it... Perhaps it is because I have not... er... eaten anything to-day... I really am a queer, stupid creature... I saw those gentlemen pay ten roubles for the oysters. Why didn't I go up to them and ask them... to lend me something? They would have given something."

Towards morning, I fell asleep and dreamt of a frog sitting in a shell, moving its eyes. At midday I was awakened by thirst, and looked for my father: he was still walking up and down and gesticulating.

A Classical Student

Before setting off for his examination in Greek, Vanya kissed all the holy images. His stomach felt as though it were upside down; there was a chill at his heart, while the heart itself throbbed and stood still with terror before the unknown. What would he get that day? A three or a two? Six times he went to his mother for her blessing, and, as he went out, asked his aunt to pray for him. On the way to school he gave a beggar two kopecks, in the hope that those two kopecks would atone for his ignorance, and that, please God, he would not get the numerals with those awful forties and eighties.

He came back from the high school late, between four and five. He came in, and noiselessly lay down on his bed. His thin face was pale. There were dark rings round his red eyes.

"Well, how did you get on? How were you marked?" asked his mother, going to his bedside.

Vanya blinked, twisted his mouth, and burst into tears. His mother turned pale, let her mouth fall open, and clasped her hands. The breeches she was mending dropped out of her hands.

"What are you crying for? You've failed, then?" she asked.

"I am plucked... I got a two."

"I knew it would be so! I had a presentiment of it," said his mother. "Merciful God! How is it you have not passed? What is the reason of it? What subject have you failed in?"

"In Greek... Mother, I... They asked me the future of phero , and I... instead of saying oisomai said opsomai . Then... then there isn't an accent, if the last syllable is long, and I... I got flustered... I forgot that the alpha was long in it... I went and put in the accent. Then Artaxerxov told me to give the list of the enclitic particles... I did, and I accidentally mixed in a pronoun... and made a mistake... and so he gave me a two... I am a miserable person... I was working all night... I've been getting up at four o'clock all this week..."

"No, it's not you but I who am miserable, you wretched boy! It's I that am miserable! You've worn me to a threadpaper, you Herod, you torment, you bane of my life! I pay for you, you good-for-nothing rubbish; I've bent my back toiling for you, I'm worried to death, and, I may say, I am unhappy, and what do you care? How do you work?"

"I... I do work. All night... You've seen it yourself."

"I prayed to God to take me, but He won't take me, a sinful woman... You torment! Other people have children like everyone else, and I've one only and no sense, no comfort out of him. Beat you? I'd beat you, but where am I to find the strength? Mother of God, where am I to find the strength?"

The mamma hid her face in the folds of her blouse and broke into sobs. Vanya wriggled with anguish and pressed his forehead against the wall. The aunt came in.

"So that's how it is... Just what I expected," she said, at once guessing what was wrong, turning pale and clasping her hands.

"I've been depressed all the morning... There's trouble coming, I thought... and here it's come..."

"The villain, the torment!"

"Why are you swearing at him?" cried the aunt, nervously pulling her coffee-coloured kerchief off her head and turning upon the mother. "It's not his fault! It's your fault! You are to blame! Why did you send him to that high school? You are a fine lady! You want to be a lady? A-a-ah! I dare say, as though you'll turn into gentry!

But if you had sent him, as I told you, into business... to an office, like my Kuzya... here is Kuzya getting five hundred a year... Five hundred roubles is worth having, isn't it? And you are wearing yourself out, and wearing the boy out with this studying, plague take it! He is thin, he coughs... just look at him! He's thirteen, and he looks no more than ten."

"No, Nastenka, no, my dear! I haven't thrashed him enough, the torment! He ought to have been thrashed, that's what it is! Ugh... Jesuit, Mahomet, torment!" she shook her fist at her son. "You want a flogging, but I haven't the strength. They told me years ago when he was little, 'Whip him, whip him!' I didn't heed them, sinful woman as I am. And now I am suffering for it. You wait a bit! I'll flay you! Wait a bit..."

The mamma shook her wet fist, and went weeping into her lodger's room. The lodger, Yevtihy Kuzmitch Kuporossov, was sitting at his table, reading "Dancing Self-taught." Yevtihy Kuzmitch was a man of intelligence and education. He spoke through his nose, washed with a soap the smell of which made everyone in the house sneeze, ate meat on fast days, and was on the look-out for a bride of refined education, and so was considered the cleverest of the lodgers. He sang tenor.

"My good friend," began the mamma, dissolving into tears. "If you would have the generosity--thrash my boy for me... Do me the favour! He's failed in his examination, the nuisance of a boy! Would you believe it, he's failed! I can't punish him, through the weakness of my ill-health... Thrash him for me, if you would be so obliging and considerate, Yevtihy Kuzmitch! Have regard for a sick woman!"

Kuporossov frowned and heaved a deep sigh through his nose. He thought a little, drummed on the table with his fingers, and sighing once more, went to Vanya.

"You are being taught, so to say," he began, "being educated, being given a chance, you revolting young person! Why have you done it?"

He talked for a long time, made a regular speech. He alluded to science, to light, and to darkness.

"Yes, young person."

When he had finished his speech, he took off his belt and took Vanya by the hand.

"It's the only way to deal with you," he said. Vanya knelt down submissively and thrust his head between the lodger's knees. His prominent pink ears moved up and down against the lodger's new serge trousers, with brown stripes on the outer seams.

Vanya did not utter a single sound. At the family council in the evening, it was decided to send him into business.

Vanka

Vanka Zhukov, a boy of nine, who had been for three months apprenticed to Alyahin the shoemaker, was sitting up on Christmas Eve. Waiting till his master and mistress and their workmen had gone to the midnight service, he took out of his master's cupboard a bottle of ink and a pen with a rusty nib, and, spreading out a crumpled sheet of paper in front of him, began writing. Before forming the first letter he several times looked round fearfully at the door and the windows, stole a glance at the dark ikon, on both sides of which stretched shelves full of lasts, and heaved a broken sigh. The paper lay on the bench while he knelt before it.

"Dear grandfather, Konstantin Makaritch," he wrote, "I am writing you a letter. I wish you a happy Christmas, and all blessings from God Almighty. I have neither father nor mother, you are the only one left me."

Vanka raised his eyes to the dark ikon on which the light of his candle was reflected, and vividly recalled his grandfather, Konstantin Makaritch, who was night watchman to a family called Zhivarev. He was a thin but extraordinarily nimble and lively little old man of sixty-five, with an everlastingly laughing face and drunken eyes. By day he slept in the servants' kitchen, or made jokes with the cooks; at night, wrapped in an ample sheepskin, he walked round the grounds and tapped with his little mallet. Old Kashtanka and Eel, so-called on account of his dark colour and his long body like a weasel's, followed him with hanging heads. This Eel was exceptionally polite and affectionate, and looked with equal kindness on strangers and his own masters, but had not a very good reputation. Under his politeness and meekness was hidden the most Jesuitical cunning. No one knew better how to creep up on occasion and snap at one's legs, to slip into the store-room, or steal a hen from a peasant. His hind legs had been nearly pulled off more than once, twice he had been hanged, every week he was thrashed till he was half dead, but he always revived.

At this moment grandfather was, no doubt, standing at the gate, screwing up his eyes at the red windows of the church, stamping with his high felt boots, and joking with the servants. His little mallet was hanging on his belt. He was clasping his hands, shrugging with the cold, and, with an aged chuckle, pinching first the housemaid, then the cook.

"How about a pinch of snuff?" he was saying, offering the women his snuff-box.

The women would take a sniff and sneeze. Grandfather would be indescribably delighted, go off into a merry chuckle, and cry:

"Tear it off, it has frozen on!"

They give the dogs a sniff of snuff too. Kashtanka sneezes, wriggles her head, and walks away offended. Eel does not sneeze, from politeness, but wags his tail. And the weather is glorious. The air is still, fresh, and transparent. The night is dark, but one can see the whole village with its white roofs and coils of smoke coming from the chimneys, the trees silvered with hoar frost, the snowdrifts. The whole sky spangled with gay twinkling stars, and the Milky Way is as distinct as though it had been washed and rubbed with snow for a holiday...

Vanka sighed, dipped his pen, and went on writing:

"And yesterday I had a wigging. The master pulled me out into the yard by my hair, and whacked me with a boot-stretcher because I accidentally fell asleep while I was rocking their brat in the cradle. And a week ago the mistress told me to clean a herring, and I began from the tail end, and she took the herring and thrust its head in my face. The workmen laugh at me and send me to the tavern for vodka, and tell me to steal the master's cucumbers for them, and the master beats me with anything that comes to hand. And there is nothing to eat. In the morning they give me bread, for dinner, porridge, and in the evening, bread again; but as for tea, or soup, the master and mistress gobble it all up themselves. And I am put to sleep in the passage, and when their wretched brat cries I get no sleep at all, but have to rock the cradle. Dear grandfather, show the divine mercy, take me away from here, home to the village. It's more than I can bear. I bow down to your feet, and will pray to God for you for ever, take me away from here or I shall die."

Vanka's mouth worked, he rubbed his eyes with his black fist, and gave a sob.

"I will powder your snuff for you," he went on. "I will pray for you, and if I do anything you can thrash me like Sidor's goat. And if you think I've no job, then I will beg the steward for Christ's sake to let me clean his boots, or I'll go for a shepherd-boy instead of Fedka. Dear grandfather, it is more than I can bear, it's simply no life at all. I wanted to run away to the village, but I have no boots, and I am afraid of the frost. When I grow up big I will take care of you for this, and not let anyone annoy you, and when you die I will pray for the rest of your soul, just as for my mammy's."

"Moscow is a big town. It's all gentlemen's houses, and there are lots of horses, but there are no sheep, and the dogs are not spiteful. The lads here don't go out with the star, and they don't let anyone go into the choir, and once I saw in a shop window fishing-hooks for sale, fitted ready with the line and for all sorts of fish, awfully good ones, there was even one hook that would hold a forty-pound sheat-fish. And I have seen shops where there are guns of all sorts, after the pattern of the master's guns at home, so that I shouldn't wonder if they are a hundred roubles each... And in the butchers' shops there are grouse and woodcocks and fish and hares, but the shopmen don't say where they shoot them."

"Dear grandfather, when they have the Christmas tree at the big house, get me a gilt walnut, and put it away in the green trunk. Ask the young lady Olga Ignatyevna, say it's for Vanka."

Vanka gave a tremulous sigh, and again stared at the window. He remembered how his grandfather always went into the forest to get the Christmas tree for his master's family, and took his grandson with him. It was a merry time! Grandfather made a noise in his throat, the forest crackled with the frost, and looking at them Vanka chortled too. Before chopping down the Christmas tree, grandfather would smoke a pipe, slowly take a pinch of snuff, and laugh at frozen Vanka... The young fir trees, covered with hoar frost, stood motionless, waiting to see which of them was to die. Wherever one looked, a hare flew like an arrow over the snowdrifts... Grandfather could not refrain from shouting: "Hold him, hold him... hold him! Ah, the bob-tailed devil!"

When he had cut down the Christmas tree, grandfather used to drag it to the big house, and there set to work to decorate it... The young lady, who was Vanka's favourite, Olga Ignatyevna, was the busiest of all. When Vanka's mother Pelageya was alive, and a servant in the big house, Olga Ignatyevna used to give him goodies, and having nothing better to do, taught him to read and write, to count up to a hundred, and even to dance a quadrille. When Pelageya died, Vanka had been transferred to the servants' kitchen to be with his grandfather, and from the kitchen to the shoemaker's in Moscow.

"Do come, dear grandfather," Vanka went on with his letter. "For Christ's sake, I beg you, take me away. Have pity on an unhappy orphan like me; here everyone knocks me about, and I am fearfully hungry; I can't tell you what misery it is, I am always crying. And the other day the master hit me on the head with a last, so that I fell down. My life is wretched, worse than any dog's... I send greetings to Alyona, one-eyed Yegorka, and the coachman, and don't give my concertina to anyone. I remain, your grandson, Ivan Zhukov. Dear grandfather, do come."

Vanka folded the sheet of writing-paper twice, and put it into an envelope he had bought the day before for a kopeck... After thinking a little, he dipped the pen and wrote the address:

To grandfather in the village.

Then he scratched his head, thought a little, and added: Konstantin Makaritch. Glad that he had not been prevented from writing, he put on his cap and, without putting on his little greatcoat, ran out into the street as he was in his shirt...

The shopmen at the butcher's, whom he had questioned the day before, told him that letters were put in post-boxes, and from the boxes were carried about all over the earth in mailcarts with drunken drivers and ringing bells. Vanka ran to the nearest post-box, and thrust the precious letter in the slit...

An hour later, lulled by sweet hopes, he was sound asleep... He dreamed of the stove. On the stove was sitting his grandfather, swinging his bare legs, and reading the letter to the cooks...

By the stove was Eel, wagging his tail.

An Incident

Morning. Brilliant sunshine is piercing through the frozen lacework on the window-panes into the nursery. Vanya, a boy of six, with a cropped head and a nose like a button, and his sister Nina, a short, chubby, curly-headed girl of four, wake up and look crossly at each other through the bars of their cots.

"Oo-oo-oo! naughty children!" grumbles their nurse. "Good people have had their breakfast already, while you can't get your eyes open."

The sunbeams frolic over the rugs, the walls, and nurse's skirts, and seem inviting the children to join in their play, but they take no notice. They have woken up in a bad humour. Nina pouts, makes a grimace, and begins to whine:

"Brea-eakfast, nurse, breakfast!"

Vanya knits his brows and ponders what to pitch upon to howl over. He has already begun screwing up his eyes and opening his mouth, but at that instant the voice of mamma reaches them from the drawing-room, saying: "Don't forget to give the cat her milk, she has a family now!"

The children's puckered countenances grow smooth again as they look at each other in astonishment. Then both at once begin shouting, jump out of their cots, and filling the air with piercing shrieks, run barefoot, in their nightgowns, to the kitchen.

"The cat has puppies!" they cry. "The cat has got puppies!"

Under the bench in the kitchen there stands a small box, the one in which Stepan brings coal when he lights the fire. The cat is peeping out of the box. There is an expression of extreme exhaustion on her grey face; her green eyes, with their narrow black pupils, have a languid, sentimental look. From her face it is clear that the only thing lacking to complete her happiness is the presence in the box of "him," the father of her children, to whom she had abandoned herself so recklessly! She wants to mew, and opens her mouth wide, but nothing but a hiss comes from her throat; the squealing of the kittens is audible.

The children squat on their heels before the box, and, motionless, holding their breath, gaze at the cat... They are surprised, impressed, and do not hear nurse grumbling as she pursues them. The most genuine delight shines in the eyes of both.

Domestic animals play a scarcely noticed but undoubtedly beneficial part in the education and life of children. Which of us does not remember powerful but magnanimous dogs, lazy lapdogs, birds dying in captivity, dull-witted but haughty turkeys, mild old tabby cats, who forgave us when we trod on their tails for fun and caused them agonising pain? I even fancy, sometimes, that the patience, the fidelity, the readiness to forgive, and the sincerity which are characteristic of our domestic animals have a far stronger and more definite effect on the mind of a child than the long exhortations of some dry, pale Karl Karlovitch, or the misty expositions of a governess, trying to prove to children that water is made up of hydrogen and oxygen.

"What little things!" says Nina, opening her eyes wide and going off into a joyous laugh. "They are like mice!"

"One, two, three," Vanya counts. "Three kittens. So there is one for you, one for me, and one for somebody else, too."

"Murrm... murrm..." purrs the mother, flattered by their attention. "Murrm."

After gazing at the kittens, the children take them from under the cat, and begin squeezing them in their hands, then, not satisfied with this, they put them in the skirts of their nightgowns, and run into the other rooms.

"Mamma, the cat has got pups!" they shout.

Mamma is sitting in the drawing-room with some unknown gentleman. Seeing the children unwashed, undressed, with their nightgowns held up high, she is embarrassed, and looks at them severely.

"Let your nightgowns down, disgraceful children," she says. "Go out of the room, or I will punish you."

But the children do not notice either mamma's threats or the presence of a stranger. They put the kittens down on the carpet, and go off into deafening squeals. The mother walks round them, mewing imploringly. When, a little afterwards, the children are dragged off to the nursery, dressed, made to say their prayers, and given their breakfast, they are full of a passionate desire to get away from these prosaic duties as quickly as possible, and to run to the kitchen again.

Their habitual pursuits and games are thrown completely into the background.

The kittens throw everything into the shade by making their appearance in the world, and supply the great sensation of the day. If Nina or Vanya had been offered forty pounds of sweets or ten thousand kopecks for each kitten, they would have rejected such a barter without the slightest hesitation. In spite of the heated protests of the nurse and the cook, the children persist in sitting by the cat's box in the kitchen, busy with the kittens till dinner-time. Their faces are earnest and concentrated and express anxiety. They are worried not so much by the present as by the future of the kittens. They decide that one kitten shall remain at home with the old cat to be a comfort to her mother, while the second shall go to their summer villa, and the third shall live in the cellar, where there are ever so many rats.

"But why don't they look at us?" Nina wondered. "Their eyes are blind like the beggars."

Vanya, too, is perturbed by this question. He tries to open one kitten's eyes, and spends a long time puffing and breathing hard over it, but his operation is unsuccessful. They are a good deal troubled, too, by the circumstance that the kittens obstinately refuse the milk and the meat that is offered to them. Everything that is put before their little noses is eaten by their grey mamma.

"Let's build the kittens little houses," Vanya suggests. "They shall live in different houses, and the cat shall come and pay them visits..."

Cardboard hat-boxes are put in the different corners of the kitchen and the kittens are installed in them. But this division turns out to be premature; the cat, still wearing an imploring and sentimental expression on her face, goes the round of all the hat-boxes, and carries off her children to their original position.

"The cat's their mother," observed Vanya, "but who is their father?"

"Yes, who is their father?" repeats Nina.

"They must have a father."

Vanya and Nina are a long time deciding who is to be the kittens' father, and, in the end, their choice falls on a big dark-red horse without a tail, which is lying in the store-cupboard under the stairs, together with other relics of toys that have outlived their day. They drag him up out of the store-cupboard and stand him by the box.

"Mind now!" they admonish him, "stand here and see they behave themselves properly."

All this is said and done in the gravest way, with an expression of anxiety on their faces. Vanya and Nina refuse to recognise the existence of any world but the box of kittens. Their joy knows no bounds. But they have to pass through bitter, agonising moments, too.

Just before dinner, Vanya is sitting in his father's study, gazing dreamily at the table. A kitten is moving about by the lamp, on stamped note paper. Vanya is watching its movements, and thrusting first a pencil, then a match into its little mouth... All at once, as though he has sprung out of the floor, his father is beside the table.

"What's this?" Vanya hears, in an angry voice.

"It's... it's the kitty, papa..."

"I'll give it you; look what you have done, you naughty boy! You've dirtied all my paper!"

To Vanya's great surprise his papa does not share his partiality for the kittens, and, instead of being moved to enthusiasm and delight, he pulls Vanya's ear and shouts:

"Stepan, take away this horrid thing."

At dinner, too, there is a scene... During the second course there is suddenly the sound of a shrill mew. They begin to investigate its origin, and discover a kitten under Nina's pinafore.

"Nina, leave the table!" cries her father angrily. "Throw the kittens in the cesspool! I won't have the nasty things in the house!..."

Vanya and Nina are horrified. Death in the cesspool, apart from its cruelty, threatens to rob the cat and the wooden horse of their children, to lay waste the cat's box, to destroy their plans for the future, that fair future in which one cat will be a comfort to its old mother, another will live in the country, while the third will catch rats in the cellar. The children begin to cry and entreat that the kittens may be spared. Their father consents, but on the condition that the children do not go into the kitchen and touch the kittens.

After dinner, Vanya and Nina slouch about the rooms, feeling depressed. The prohibition of visits to the kitchen has reduced them to dejection. They refuse sweets, are naughty, and are rude to their mother. When their uncle Petrusha comes in the evening, they draw him aside, and complain to him of their father, who wanted to throw the kittens into the cesspool.

"Uncle Petrusha, tell mamma to have the kittens taken to the nursery," the children beg their uncle, "do-o tell her."

"There, there... very well," says their uncle, waving them off. "All right."

Uncle Petrusha does not usually come alone. He is accompanied by Nero, a big black dog of Danish breed, with drooping ears, and a tail as hard as a stick. The dog is silent, morose, and full of a sense of his own dignity. He takes not the slightest notice of the children, and when he passes them hits them with his tail as though they were chairs. The children hate him from the bottom of their hearts, but on this occasion, practical considerations override sentiment.

"I say, Nina," says Vanya, opening his eyes wide. "Let Nero be their father, instead of the horse! The horse is dead and he is alive, you see."

They are waiting the whole evening for the moment when papa will sit down to his cards and it will be possible to take Nero to the kitchen without being observed... At last, papa sits down to cards, mamma is busy with the samovar and not noticing the children...

The happy moment arrives.

"Come along!" Vanya whispers to his sister.

But, at that moment, Stepan comes in and, with a snigger, announces:

"Nero has eaten the kittens, madam."

Nina and Vanya turn pale and look at Stepan with horror.

"He really has..." laughs the footman, "he went to the box and gobbled them up."

The children expect that all the people in the house will be aghast and fall upon the miscreant Nero. But they all sit calmly in their seats, and only express surprise at the appetite of the huge dog. Papa and mamma laugh. Nero walks about by the table, wags his tail, and licks his lips complacently... the cat is the only one who is uneasy. With her tail in the air she walks about the rooms, looking suspiciously at people and mewing plaintively.

"Children, it's past nine," cries mamma, "it's bedtime."

Vanya and Nina go to bed, shed tears, and spend a long time thinking about the injured cat, and the cruel, insolent, and unpunished Nero.

A Day in the Country

Between eight and nine o'clock in the morning.

A dark leaden-coloured mass is creeping over the sky towards the sun. Red zigzags of lightning gleam here and there across it. There is a sound of far-away rumbling. A warm wind frolics over the grass, bends the trees, and stirs up the dust. In a minute there will be a spurt of May rain and a real storm will begin.

Fyokla, a little beggar-girl of six, is running through the village, looking for Terenty the cobbler. The white-haired, barefoot child is pale. Her eyes are wide-open, her lips are trembling.

"Uncle, where is Terenty?" she asks every one she meets. No one answers. They are all preoccupied with the approaching storm and take refuge in their huts. At last she meets Silanty Silitch, the sacristan, Terenty's bosom friend. He is coming along, staggering from the wind.

"Uncle, where is Terenty?"

"At the kitchen-gardens," answers Silanty.

The beggar-girl runs behind the huts to the kitchen-gardens and there finds Terenty; the tall old man with a thin, pock-marked face, very long legs, and bare feet, dressed in a woman's tattered jacket, is standing near the vegetable plots, looking with drowsy, drunken eyes at the dark storm-cloud. On his long crane-like legs he sways in the wind like a starling-cote.

"Uncle Terenty!" the white-headed beggar-girl addresses him. "Uncle, darling!"

Terenty bends down to Fyokla, and his grim, drunken face is overspread with a smile, such as come into people's faces when they look at something little, foolish, and absurd, but warmly loved.

"Ah! servant of God, Fyokia," he says, lisping tenderly, "where have you come from?"

"Uncle Terenty," says Fyokia, with a sob, tugging at the lapel of the cobbler's coat. "Brother Danilka has had an accident! Come along!"

"What sort of accident? Ough, what thunder! Holy, holy, holy... What sort of accident?"

"In the count's copse Danilka stuck his hand into a hole in a tree, and he can't get it out. Come along, uncle, do be kind and pull his hand out!"

"How was it he put his hand in? What for?"

"He wanted to get a cuckoo's egg out of the hole for me."

"The day has hardly begun and already you are in trouble..." Terenty shook his head and spat deliberately. "Well, what am I to do with you now? I must come... I must, may the wolf gobble you up, you naughty children! Come, little orphan!"

Terenty comes out of the kitchen-garden and, lifting high his long legs, begins striding down the village street. He walks quickly without stopping or looking from side to side, as though he were shoved from behind or afraid of pursuit. Fyokla can hardly keep up with him.

They come out of the village and turn along the dusty road towards the count's copse that lies dark blue in the distance. It is about a mile and a half away. The clouds have by now covered the sun, and soon afterwards there is not a speck of blue left in the sky. It grows dark.

"Holy, holy, holy..." whispers Fyokla, hurrying after Terenty. The first rain-drops, big and heavy, lie, dark dots on the dusty road. A big drop falls on Fyokla's cheek and glides like a tear down her chin.

"The rain has begun," mutters the cobbler, kicking up the dust with his bare, bony feet. "That's fine, Fyokla, old girl. The grass and the trees are fed by the rain, as we are by bread. And as for the thunder, don't you be frightened, little orphan. Why should it kill a little thing like you?"

As soon as the rain begins, the wind drops. The only sound is the patter of rain dropping like fine shot on the young rye and the parched road.

"We shall get soaked, Fyolka," mutters Terenty. "There won't be a dry spot left on us... Ho-ho, my girl! It's run down my neck! But don't be frightened, silly... The grass will be dry again, the earth will be dry again, and we shall be dry again. There is the same sun for us all."

A flash of lightning, some fourteen feet long, gleams above their heads. There is a loud peal of thunder, and it seems to Fyokla that something big, heavy, and round is rolling over the sky and tearing it open, exactly over her head.

"Holy, holy, holy..." says Terenty, crossing himself. "Don't be afraid, little orphan! It is not from spite that it thunders."

Terenty's and Fyokla's feet are covered with lumps of heavy, wet clay. It is slippery and difficult to walk, but Terenty strides on more and more rapidly. The weak little beggar-girl is breathless and ready to drop.

But at last they go into the count's copse. The washed trees, stirred by a gust of wind, drop a perfect waterfall upon them. Terenty stumbles over stumps and begins to slacken his pace.

"Whereabouts is Danilka?" he asks. "Lead me to him."

Fyokla leads him into a thicket, and, after going a quarter of a mile, points to Danilka. Her brother, a little fellow of eight, with hair as red as ochre and a pale sickly face, stands leaning against a tree, and, with his head on one side, looking sideways at the sky. In one hand he holds his shabby old cap, the other is hidden in an old lime tree. The boy is gazing at the stormy sky, and apparently not thinking of his trouble. Hearing footsteps and seeing the cobbler he gives a sickly smile and says:

"A terrible lot of thunder, Terenty... I've never heard so much thunder in all my life."

"And where is your hand?"

"In the hole... Pull it out, please, Terenty!"

The wood had broken at the edge of the hole and jammed Danilka's hand: he could push it farther in, but could not pull it out. Terenty snaps off the broken piece, and the boy's hand, red and crushed, is released.

"It's terrible how it's thundering," the boy says again, rubbing his hand. "What makes it thunder, Terenty?"

"One cloud runs against the other," answers the cobbler. The party come out of the copse, and walk along the edge of it towards the darkened road. The thunder gradually abates, and its rumbling is heard far away beyond the village.

"The ducks flew by here the other day, Terenty," says Danilka, still rubbing his hand. "They must be nesting in the Gniliya Zaimishtcha marshes... Fyolka, would you like me to show you a nightingale's nest?"

"Don't touch it, you might disturb them," says Terenty, wringing the water out of his cap. "The nightingale is a singing-bird, without sin. He has had a voice given him in his throat, to praise God and gladden the heart of man. It's a sin to disturb him."

"What about the sparrow?"

"The sparrow doesn't matter, he's a bad, spiteful bird. He is like a pickpocket in his ways. He doesn't like man to be happy. When Christ was crucified it was the sparrow brought nails to the Jews, and called 'alive! alive!'"

A bright patch of blue appears in the sky.

"Look!" says Terenty. "An ant-heap burst open by the rain! They've been flooded, the rogues!"

They bend over the ant-heap. The downpour has damaged it; the insects are scurrying to and fro in the mud, agitated, and busily trying to carry away their drowned companions.

"You needn't be in such a taking, you won't die of it!" says Terenty, grinning. "As soon as the sun warms you, you'll come to your senses again... It's a lesson to you, you stupids. You won't settle on low ground another time."

They go on.

"And here are some bees," cries Danilka, pointing to the branch of a young oak tree.

The drenched and chilled bees are huddled together on the branch. There are so many of them that neither bark nor leaf can be seen. Many of them are settled on one another.

"That's a swarm of bees," Terenty informs them. "They were flying looking for a home, and when the rain came down upon them they settled. If a swarm is flying, you need only sprinkle water on them to make them settle. Now if, say, you wanted to take the swarm, you would bend the branch with them into a sack and shake it, and they all fall in."

Little Fyokla suddenly frowns and rubs her neck vigorously. Her brother looks at her neck, and sees a big swelling on it.

"Hey-hey!" laughs the cobbler. "Do you know where you got that from, Fyokia, old girl? There are Spanish flies on some tree in the wood. The rain has trickled off them, and a drop has fallen on your neck --that's what has made the swelling."

The sun appears from behind the clouds and floods the wood, the fields, and the three friends with its warm light. The dark menacing cloud has gone far away and taken the storm with it. The air is warm and fragrant. There is a scent of bird-cherry, meadowsweet, and lilies-of-the-valley.

"That herb is given when your nose bleeds," says Terenty, pointing to a woolly-looking flower. "It does good."

They hear a whistle and a rumble, but not such a rumble as the storm-clouds carried away. A goods train races by before the eyes of Terenty, Danilka, and Fyokla. The engine, panting and puffing out black smoke, drags more than twenty vans after it. Its power is tremendous. The children are interested to know how an engine, not alive and without the help of horses, can move and drag such weights, and Terenty undertakes to explain it to them:

"It's all the steam's doing, children... The steam does the work... You see, it shoves under that thing near the wheels, and it... you see... it works..."

They cross the railway line, and, going down from the embankment, walk towards the river. They walk not with any object, but just at random, and talk all the way... Danilka asks questions, Terenty answers them...

Terenty answers all his questions, and there is no secret in Nature which baffles him. He knows everything. Thus, for example, he knows the names of all the wild flowers, animals, and stones. He knows what herbs cure diseases, he has no difficulty in telling the age of a horse or a cow. Looking at the sunset, at the moon, or the birds, he can tell what sort of weather it will be next day. And indeed, it is not only Terenty who is so wise. Silanty Silitch, the innkeeper, the market-gardener, the shepherd, and all the villagers, generally speaking, know as much as he does. These people have learned not from books, but in the fields, in the wood, on the river bank. Their teachers have been the birds themselves, when they sang to them, the sun when it left a glow of crimson behind it at setting, the very trees, and wild herbs.

Danilka looks at Terenty and greedily drinks in every word. In spring, before one is weary of the warmth and the monotonous green of the fields, when everything is fresh and full of fragrance, who would not want to hear about the golden may-beetles, about the cranes, about the gurgling streams, and the corn mounting into ear?

The two of them, the cobbler and the orphan, walk about the fields, talk unceasingly, and are not weary. They could wander about the world endlessly. They walk, and in their talk of the beauty of the earth do not notice the frail little beggar-girl tripping after them. She is breathless and moves with a lagging step. There are tears in her eyes; she would be glad to stop these inexhaustible wanderers, but to whom and where can she go? She has no home or people of her own; whether she likes it or not, she must walk and listen to their talk.

Towards midday, all three sit down on the river bank. Danilka takes out of his bag a piece of bread, soaked and reduced to a mash, and they begin to eat. Terenty says a prayer when he has eaten the bread, then stretches himself on the sandy bank and falls asleep. While he is asleep, the boy gazes at the water, pondering. He has many different things to think of. He has just seen the storm, the bees, the ants, the train. Now, before his eyes, fishes are whisking about. Some are two inches long and more, others are no bigger than one's nail. A viper, with its head held high, is swimming from one bank to the other.

Only towards the evening our wanderers return to the village. The children go for the night to a deserted barn, where the corn of the commune used to be kept, while Terenty, leaving them, goes to the tavern. The children lie huddled together on the straw, dozing.

The boy does not sleep. He gazes into the darkness, and it seems to him that he is seeing all that he has seen in the day: the storm-clouds, the bright sunshine, the birds, the fish, lanky Terenty. The number of his impressions, together with exhaustion and hunger, are too much for him; he is as hot as though he were on fire, and tosses from, side to side. He longs to tell someone all that is haunting him now in the darkness and agitating his soul, but there is no one to tell. Fyokla is too little and could not understand.

"I'll tell Terenty to-morrow," thinks the boy.

The children fall asleep thinking of the homeless cobbler, and, in the night, Terenty comes to them, makes the sign of the cross over them, and puts bread under their heads. And no one sees his love. It is seen only by the moon which floats in the sky and peeps caressingly through the holes in the wall of the deserted barn.

Boys

"Volodya's come!" someone shouted in the yard.

"Master Volodya's here!" bawled Natalya the cook, running into the dining-room. "Oh, my goodness!"

The whole Korolyov family, who had been expecting their Volodya from hour to hour, rushed to the windows. At the front door stood a wide sledge, with three white horses in a cloud of steam. The sledge was empty, for Volodya was already in the hall, untying his hood with red and chilly fingers. His school overcoat, his cap, his snowboots, and the hair on his temples were all white with frost, and his whole figure from head to foot diffused such a pleasant, fresh smell of the snow that the very sight of him made one want to shiver and say "brrr!"

His mother and aunt ran to kiss and hug him. Natalya plumped down at his feet and began pulling off his snowboots, his sisters shrieked with delight, the doors creaked and banged, and Volodya's father, in his waistcoat and shirt-sleeves, ran out into the hall with scissors in his hand, and cried out in alarm:

"We were expecting you all yesterday? Did you come all right? Had a good journey? Mercy on us! you might let him say 'how do you do' to his father! I am his father after all!"

"Bow-wow!" barked the huge black dog, Milord, in a deep bass, tapping with his tail on the walls and furniture.

For two minutes there was nothing but a general hubbub of joy. After the first outburst of delight was over the Korolyovs noticed that there was, besides their Volodya, another small person in the hall, wrapped up in scarves and shawls and white with frost. He was standing perfectly still in a corner, in the shadow of a big fox-lined overcoat.

"Volodya darling, who is it?" asked his mother, in a whisper.

"Oh!" cried Volodya. "This is--let me introduce my friend Lentilov, a schoolfellow in the second class... I have brought him to stay with us."

"Delighted to hear it! You are very welcome," the father said cordially. "Excuse me, I've been at work without my coat... Please come in! Natalya, help Mr. Lentilov off with his things. Mercy on us, do turn that dog out! He is unendurable!"

A few minutes later, Volodya and his friend Lentilov, somewhat dazed by their noisy welcome, and still red from the outside cold, were sitting down to tea. The winter sun, making its way through the snow and the frozen tracery on the window-panes, gleamed on the samovar, and plunged its pure rays in the tea-basin. The room was warm, and the boys felt as though the warmth and the frost were struggling together with a tingling sensation in their bodies.

"Well, Christmas will soon be here," the father said in a pleasant sing-song voice, rolling a cigarette of dark reddish tobacco. "It doesn't seem long since the summer, when mamma was crying at your going... and here you are back again... Time flies, my boy. Before you have time to cry out, old age is upon you. Mr. Lentilov, take some more, please help yourself! We don't stand on ceremony!"

Volodya's three sisters, Katya, Sonya, and Masha (the eldest was eleven), sat at the table and never took their eyes off the newcomer.

Lentilov was of the same height and age as Volodya, but not as round-faced and fair-skinned. He was thin, dark, and freckled; his hair stood up like a brush, his eyes were small, and his lips were thick. He was, in fact, distinctly ugly, and if he had not been wearing the school uniform, he might have been taken for the son of a cook. He seemed morose, did not speak, and never once smiled. The little girls, staring at him, immediately came to the conclusion that he must be a very clever and learned person. He seemed to be thinking about something all the time, and was so absorbed in his own thoughts, that, whenever he was spoken to, he started, threw his head back, and asked to have the question repeated.

The little girls noticed that Volodya, who had always been so merry and talkative, also said very little, did not smile at all, and hardly seemed to be glad to be home. All the time they were at tea he only once addressed his sisters, and then he said something so strange. He pointed to the samovar and said:

"In California they don't drink tea, but gin."

He, too, seemed absorbed in his own thoughts, and, to judge by the looks that passed between him and his friend Lentilov, their thoughts were the same.

After tea, they all went into the nursery. The girls and their father took up the work that had been interrupted by the arrival of the boys. They were making flowers and frills for the Christmas tree out of paper of different colours. It was an attractive and noisy occupation. Every fresh flower was greeted by the little girls with shrieks of delight, even of awe, as though the flower had dropped straight from heaven; their father was in ecstasies too, and every now and then he threw the scissors on the floor, in vexation at their bluntness. Their mother kept running into the nursery with an anxious face, asking:

"Who has taken my scissors? Ivan Nikolaitch, have you taken my scissors again?"

"Mercy on us! I'm not even allowed a pair of scissors!" their father would respond in a lachrymose voice, and, flinging himself back in his chair, he would pretend to be a deeply injured man; but a minute later, he would be in ecstasies again.

On his former holidays Volodya, too, had taken part in the preparations for the Christmas tree, or had been running in the yard to look at the snow mountain that the watchman and the shepherd were building. But this time Volodya and Lentilov took no notice whatever of the coloured paper, and did not once go into the stable. They sat in the window and began whispering to one another; then they opened an atlas and looked carefully at a map.

"First to Perm..." Lentilov said, in an undertone, "from there to Tiumen, then Tomsk... then... then... Kamchatka. There the Samoyedes take one over Behring's Straits in boats... And then we are in America... There are lots of furry animals there..."

"And California?" asked Volodya.

"California is lower down... We've only to get to America and California is not far off... And one can get a living by hunting and plunder."

All day long Lentilov avoided the little girls, and seemed to look at them with suspicion. In the evening he happened to be left alone with them for five minutes or so. It was awkward to be silent.

He cleared his throat morosely, rubbed his left hand against his right, looked sullenly at Katya and asked:

"Have you read Mayne Reid?"

"No, I haven't... I say, can you skate?"

Absorbed in his own reflections, Lentilov made no reply to this question; he simply puffed out his cheeks, and gave a long sigh as though he were very hot. He looked up at Katya once more and said:

"When a herd of bisons stampedes across the prairie the earth trembles, and the frightened mustangs kick and neigh."

He smiled impressively and added:

"And the Indians attack the trains, too. But worst of all are the mosquitoes and the termites."

"Why, what's that?"

"They're something like ants, but with wings. They bite fearfully. Do you know who I am?"

"Mr. Lentilov."

"No, I am Montehomo, the Hawk's Claw, Chief of the Ever Victorious."

Masha, the youngest, looked at him, then into the darkness out of window and said, wondering:

"And we had lentils for supper yesterday."

Lentilov's incomprehensible utterances, and the way he was always whispering with Volodya, and the way Volodya seemed now to be always thinking about something instead of playing... all this was strange and mysterious. And the two elder girls, Katya and Sonya, began to keep a sharp look-out on the boys. At night, when the boys had gone to bed, the girls crept to their bedroom door, and listened to what they were saying. Ah, what they discovered! The boys were planning to run away to America to dig for gold: they had everything ready for the journey, a pistol, two knives, biscuits, a burning glass to serve instead of matches, a compass, and four roubles in cash. They learned that the boys would have to walk some thousands of miles, and would have to fight tigers and savages on the road: then they would get gold and ivory, slay their enemies, become pirates, drink gin, and finally marry beautiful maidens, and make a plantation.

The boys interrupted each other in their excitement. Throughout the conversation, Lentilov called himself "Montehomo, the Hawk's Claw," and Volodya was "my pale-face brother!"

"Mind you don't tell mamma," said Katya, as they went back to bed. "Volodya will bring us gold and ivory from America, but if you tell mamma he won't be allowed to go."

The day before Christmas Eve, Lentilov spent the whole day poring over the map of Asia and making notes, while Volodya, with a languid and swollen face that looked as though it had been stung by a bee, walked about the rooms and ate nothing. And once he stood still before the holy image in the nursery, crossed himself, and said:

"Lord, forgive me a sinner; Lord, have pity on my poor unhappy mamma!"

In the evening he burst out crying. On saying good-night he gave his father a long hug, and then hugged his mother and sisters. Katya and Sonya knew what was the matter, but little Masha was puzzled, completely puzzled. Every time she looked at Lentilov she grew thoughtful and said with a sigh:

"When Lent comes, nurse says we shall have to eat peas and lentils."

Early in the morning of Christmas Eve, Katya and Sonya slipped quietly out of bed, and went to find out how the boys meant to run away to America. They crept to their door.

"Then you don't mean to go?" Lentilov was saying angrily. "Speak out: aren't you going?"

"Oh dear," Volodya wept softly. "How can I go? I feel so unhappy about mamma."

"My pale-face brother, I pray you, let us set off. You declared you were going, you egged me on, and now the time comes, you funk it!"

"I... I... I'm not funking it, but I... I... I'm sorry for mamma."

"Say once and for all, are you going or are you not?"

"I am going, only... wait a little... I want to be at home a little."

"In that case I will go by myself," Lentilov declared. "I can get on without you. And you wanted to hunt tigers and fight! Since that's how it is, give me back my cartridges!"

At this Volodya cried so bitterly that his sisters could not help crying too. Silence followed.

"So you are not coming?" Lentilov began again.

"I... I... I am coming!"

"Well, put on your things, then."

And Lentilov tried to cheer Volodya up by singing the praises of America, growling like a tiger, pretending to be a steamer, scolding him, and promising to give him all the ivory and lions' and tigers' skins.

And this thin, dark boy, with his freckles and his bristling shock of hair, impressed the little girls as an extraordinary remarkable person. He was a hero, a determined character, who knew no fear, and he growled so ferociously, that, standing at the door, they really might imagine there was a tiger or lion inside. When the little girls went back to their room and dressed, Katya's eyes were full of tears, and she said:

"Oh, I feel so frightened!"

Everything was as usual till two o'clock, when they sat down to dinner. Then it appeared that the boys were not in the house. They sent to the servants' quarters, to the stables, to the bailiff's cottage. They were not to be found. They sent into the village-- they were not there.

At tea, too, the boys were still absent, and by supper-time Volodya's mother was dreadfully uneasy, and even shed tears.

Late in the evening they sent again to the village, they searched everywhere, and walked along the river bank with lanterns. Heavens! what a fuss there was!

Next day the police officer came, and a paper of some sort was written out in the dining-room. Their mother cried...

All of a sudden a sledge stopped at the door, with three white horses in a cloud of steam.

"Volodya's come," someone shouted in the yard.

"Master Volodya's here!" bawled Natalya, running into the dining-room. And Milord barked his deep bass, "bow-wow."

It seemed that the boys had been stopped in the Arcade, where they had gone from shop to shop asking where they could get gunpowder.

Volodya burst into sobs as soon as he came into the hall, and flung himself on his mother's neck. The little girls, trembling, wondered with terror what would happen next. They saw their father take Volodya and Lentilov into his study, and there he talked to them a long while.

"Is this a proper thing to do?" their father said to them. "I only pray they won't hear of it at school, you would both be expelled. You ought to be ashamed, Mr. Lentilov, really. It's not at all the thing to do! You began it, and I hope you will be punished by your parents. How could you? Where did you spend the night?"

"At the station," Lentilov answered proudly.

Then Volodya went to bed, and had a compress, steeped in vinegar, on his forehead.

A telegram was sent off, and next day a lady, Lentilov's mother, made her appearance and bore off her son.

Lentilov looked morose and haughty to the end, and he did not utter a single word at taking leave of the little girls. But he took Katya's book and wrote in it as a souvenir: "Montehomo, the Hawk's Claw, Chief of the Ever Victorious."

Shrove Tuesday

"Pavel Vassilitch!" cries Pelageya Ivanovna, waking her husband. "Pavel Vassilitch! You might go and help Styopa with his lessons, he is sitting crying over his book. He can't understand something again!"

Pavel Vassilitch gets up, makes the sign of the cross over his mouth as he yawns, and says softly: "In a minute, my love!"

The cat who has been asleep beside him gets up too, straightens out its tail, arches its spine, and half-shuts its eyes. There is stillness... Mice can be heard scurrying behind the wall-paper. Putting on his boots and his dressing-gown, Pavel Vassilitch, crumpled and frowning from sleepiness, comes out of his bedroom into the dining-room; on his entrance another cat, engaged in sniffing a marinade of fish in the window, jumps down to the floor, and hides behind the cupboard.

"Who asked you to sniff that!" he says angrily, covering the fish with a sheet of newspaper. "You are a pig to do that, not a cat..."

From the dining-room there is a door leading into the nursery. There, at a table covered with stains and deep scratches, sits Styopa, a high-school boy in the second class, with a peevish expression of face and tear-stained eyes. With his knees raised almost to his chin, and his hands clasped round them, he is swaying to and fro like a Chinese idol and looking crossly at a sum book.

"Are you working?" asks Pavel Vassilitch, sitting down to the table and yawning. "Yes, my boy... We have enjoyed ourselves, slept, and eaten pancakes, and to-morrow comes Lenten fare, repentance, and going to work. Every period of time has its limits. Why are your eyes so red? Are you sick of learning your lessons? To be sure, after pancakes, lessons are nasty to swallow. That's about it."

"What are you laughing at the child for?" Pelageya Ivanovna calls from the next room. "You had better show him instead of laughing at him. He'll get a one again to-morrow, and make me miserable."

"What is it you don't understand?" Pavel Vassilitch asks Styopa.

"Why this... division of fractions," the boy answers crossly. "The division of fractions by fractions..."

"H'm... queer boy! What is there in it? There's nothing to understand in it. Learn the rules, and that's all... To divide a fraction by a fraction you must multiply the numerator of the first fraction by the denominator of the second, and that will be the numerator of the quotient... In this case, the numerator of the first fraction..."

"I know that without your telling me," Styopa interrupts him, flicking a walnut shell off the table. "Show me the proof."

"The proof? Very well, give me a pencil. Listen... Suppose we want to divide seven eighths by two fifths. Well, the point of it is, my boy, that it's required to divide these fractions by each other... Have they set the samovar?"

"I don't know."

"It's time for tea... It's past seven. Well, now listen. We will look at it like this... Suppose we want to divide seven eighths not by two fifths but by two, that is, by the numerator only. We divide it, what do we get?"

"Seven sixteenths."

"Right. Bravo! Well, the trick of it is, my boy, that if we... so if we have divided it by two then... Wait a bit, I am getting muddled. I remember when I was at school, the teacher of arithmetic was called Sigismund Urbanitch, a Pole. He used to get into a muddle over every lesson. He would begin explaining some theory, get in a tangle, and turn crimson all over and race up and down the class-room as though someone were sticking an awl in his back, then he would blow his nose half a dozen times and begin to cry. But you know we were magnanimous to him, we pretended not to see it. 'What is it, Sigismund Urbanitch?' we used to ask him. 'Have you got toothache?'

And what a set of young ruffians, regular cut-throats, we were, but yet we were magnanimous, you know! There weren't any boys like you in my day, they were all great hulking fellows, great strapping louts, one taller than another. For instance, in our third class, there was Mamahin. My goodness, he was a solid chap! You know, a regular maypole, seven feet high. When he moved, the floor shook; when he brought his great fist down on your back, he would knock the breath out of your body! Not only we boys, but even the teachers were afraid of him. So this Mamahin used to..."

Pelageya Ivanovna's footsteps are heard through the door. Pavel Vassilitch winks towards the door and says:

"There's mother coming. Let's get to work. Well, so you see, my boy," he says, raising his voice. "This fraction has to be multiplied by that one. Well, and to do that you have to take the numerator of the first fraction..."

"Come to tea!" cries Pelageya Ivanovna. Pavel Vassilitch and his son abandon arithmetic and go in to tea. Pelageya Ivanovna is already sitting at the table with an aunt who never speaks, another aunt who is deaf and dumb, and Granny Markovna, a midwife who had helped Styopa into the world. The samovar is hissing and puffing out steam which throws flickering shadows on the ceiling. The cats come in from the entry sleepy and melancholy with their tails in the air...

"Have some jam with your tea, Markovna," says Pelageya Ivanovna, addressing the midwife. "To-morrow the great fast begins. Eat well to-day."

Markovna takes a heaped spoonful of jam hesitatingly as though it were a powder, raises it to her lips, and with a sidelong look at Pavel Vassilitch, eats it; at once her face is overspread with a sweet smile, as sweet as the jam itself.

"The jam is particularly good," she says. "Did you make it yourself, Pelageya Ivanovna, ma'am?"

"Yes. Who else is there to do it? I do everything myself. Styopotchka, have I given you your tea too weak? Ah, you have drunk it already.

Pass your cup, my angel; let me give you some more."

"So this Mamahin, my boy, could not bear the French master,"
Pavel Vassilitch goes on, addressing his son. "'I am a nobleman,' he
used to shout, 'and I won't allow a Frenchman to lord it over me! We
beat the French in 1812!' Well, of course they used to thrash him for
it... thrash him dre-ead-fully, and sometimes when he saw they were
meaning to thrash him, he would jump out of window, and off he
would go! Then for five or six days afterwards he would not show
himself at the school. His mother would come to the head-master and
beg him for God's sake: 'Be so kind, sir, as to find my Mishka, and flog
him, the rascal!' And the head-master would say to her: 'Upon my
word, madam, our five porters aren't a match for him!'"

"Good heavens, to think of such ruffians being born," whispers
Pelageya Ivanovna, looking at her husband in horror. "What a trial for
the poor mother!"

A silence follows. Styopa yawns loudly, and scrutinises the
Chinaman on the tea-caddy whom he has seen a thousand times
already. Markovna and the two aunts sip tea carefully out of their
saucers. The air is still and stifling from the stove... Faces and gestures
betray the sloth and repletion that comes when the stomach is full,
and yet one must go on eating. The samovar, the cups, and the tablecloth are cleared away, but still the family sits on at the table... Pelageya
Ivanovna is continually jumping up and, with an expression of alarm
on her face, running off into the kitchen, to talk to the cook about the
supper. The two aunts go on sitting in the same position immovably,
with their arms folded across their bosoms and doze, staring with
their pewtery little eyes at the lamp. Markovna hiccups every minute
and asks:

"Why is it I have the hiccups? I don't think I have eaten anything
to account for it... nor drunk anything either... Hic!"

Pavel Vassilitch and Styopa sit side by side, with their heads
touching, and, bending over the table, examine a volume of the "Neva"
for 1878.

"'The monument of Leonardo da Vinci, facing the gallery of Victor Emmanuel at Milan.' I say!... After the style of a triumphal arch... A cavalier with his lady... And there are little men in the distance..."

"That little man is like a schoolfellow of mine called Niskubin," says Styopa.

"Turn over... 'The proboscis of the common house-fly seen under the microscope.' So that's a proboscis! I say--a fly. Whatever would a bug look like under a microscope, my boy? Wouldn't it be horrid!"

The old-fashioned clock in the drawing-room does not strike, but coughs ten times huskily as though it had a cold. The cook, Anna, comes into the dining-room, and plumps down at the master's feet.

"Forgive me, for Christ's sake, Pavel Vassilitch!" she says, getting up, flushed all over.

"You forgive me, too, for Christ's sake," Pavel Vassilitch responds unconcernedly.

In the same manner, Anna goes up to the other members of the family, plumps down at their feet, and begs forgiveness. She only misses out Markovna to whom, not being one of the gentry, she does not feel it necessary to bow down.

Another half-hour passes in stillness and tranquillity. The "Neva" is by now lying on the sofa, and Pavel Vassilitch, holding up his finger, repeats by heart some Latin verses he has learned in his childhood. Styopa stares at the finger with the wedding ring, listens to the unintelligible words, and dozes; he rubs his eyelids with his fists, and they shut all the tighter.

"I am going to bed..." he says, stretching and yawning.

"What, to bed?" says Pelageya Ivanovna. "What about supper before the fast?"

"I don't want any."

"Are you crazy?" says his mother in alarm. "How can you go without your supper before the fast? You'll have nothing but Lenten food all through the fast!"

Pavel Vassilitch is scared too.

"Yes, yes, my boy," he says. "For seven weeks mother will give you nothing but Lenten food. You can't miss the last supper before the fast."

"Oh dear, I am sleepy," says Styopa peevishly.

"Since that is how it is, lay the supper quickly," Pavel Vassilitch cries in a fluster. "Anna, why are you sitting there, silly? Make haste and lay the table."

Pelageya Ivanovna clasps her hands and runs into the kitchen with an expression as though the house were on fire.

"Make haste, make haste," is heard all over the house. "Styopotchka is sleepy. Anna! Oh dear me, what is one to do? Make haste."

Five minutes later the table is laid. Again the cats, arching their spines, and stretching themselves with their tails in the air, come into the dining-room... The family begin supper... No one is hungry, everyone's stomach is overfull, but yet they must eat.

The Old House

(A Story told by a Houseowner)

The old house had to be pulled down that a new one might be built in its place. I led the architect through the empty rooms, and between our business talk told him various stories. The tattered wallpapers, the dingy windows, the dark stoves, all bore the traces of recent habitation and evoked memories. On that staircase, for instance, drunken men were once carrying down a dead body when they stumbled and flew headlong downstairs together with the coffin; the living were badly bruised, while the dead man looked very serious, as though nothing had happened, and shook his head when they lifted him up from the ground and put him back in the coffin. You see those three doors in a row: in there lived young ladies who were always receiving visitors, and so were better dressed than any other lodgers, and could pay their rent regularly. The door at the end of the corridor leads to the wash-house, where by day they washed clothes and at night made an uproar and drank beer. And in that flat of three rooms everything is saturated with bacteria and bacilli. It's not nice there. Many lodgers have died there, and I can positively assert that that flat was at some time cursed by someone, and that together with its human lodgers there was always another lodger, unseen, living in it. I remember particularly the fate of one family. Picture to yourself an ordinary man, not remarkable in any way, with a wife, a mother, and four children. His name was Putohin; he was a copying clerk at a notary's, and received thirty-five roubles a month. He was a sober, religious, serious man. When he brought me his rent for the flat he always apologised for being badly dressed; apologised for being five days late, and when I gave him a receipt he would smile good-humouredly and say: "Oh yes, there's that too, I don't like those receipts." He lived poorly but decently. In that middle room, the grandmother used to be with the four children; there they used to cook, sleep, receive their visitors, and even dance. This was Putohin's own room; he had a table in it, at which he used to work doing private jobs, copying parts for the theatre, advertisements, and so on. This room on the right was let to his lodger, Yegoritch, a locksmith--a steady fellow, but given to drink; he was always too hot, and so used to go about in his waistcoat and barefoot. Yegoritch used to mend locks, pistols, children's bicycles, would not refuse to mend cheap clocks and make skates for a quarter-rouble, but he despised that work, and looked on himself as a specialist in musical instruments. Amongst the litter of steel and iron on his table there was always to be seen a concertina with a broken key, or a trumpet with its sides bent in. He paid Putohin two and a half roubles for his room; he was always at his work-table, and only came out to thrust some piece of iron into the stove.

On the rare occasions when I went into that flat in the evening, this was always the picture I came upon: Putohin would be sitting at his little table, copying something; his mother and his wife, a thin woman with an exhausted-looking face, were sitting near the lamp, sewing; Yegoritch would be making a rasping sound with his file. And the hot, still smouldering embers in the stove filled the room with heat and fumes; the heavy air smelt of cabbage soup, swaddling-clothes, and Yegoritch. It was poor and stuffy, but the working-class faces, the children's little drawers hung up along by the stove, Yegoritch's bits of iron had yet an air of peace, friendliness, content... In the corridor outside the children raced about with well-combed heads, merry and profoundly convinced that everything was satisfactory in this world, and would be so endlessly, that one had only to say one's prayers every morning and at bedtime.

Now imagine in the midst of that same room, two paces from the stove, the coffin in which Putohin's wife is lying. There is no husband whose wife will live for ever, but there was something special about this death. When, during the requiem service, I glanced at the husband's grave face, at his stern eyes, I thought: "Oho, brother!"

It seemed to me that he himself, his children, the grandmother and Yegoritch, were already marked down by that unseen being which lived with them in that flat. I am a thoroughly superstitious man, perhaps, because I am a houseowner and for forty years have had to do with lodgers. I believe if you don't win at cards from the beginning you will go on losing to the end; when fate wants to wipe you and your family off the face of the earth, it remains inexorable in its persecution, and the first misfortune is commonly only the first of a long series... Misfortunes are like stones. One stone has only to drop from a high cliff for others to be set rolling after it. In short, as I came away from the requiem service at Putohin's, I believed that he and his family were in a bad way.

And, in fact, a week afterwards the notary quite unexpectedly dismissed Putohin, and engaged a young lady in his place. And would you believe it, Putohin was not so much put out at the loss of his job as at being superseded by a young lady and not by a man. Why a young lady? He so resented this that on his return home he thrashed his children, swore at his mother, and got drunk. Yegoritch got drunk, too, to keep him company.

Putohin brought me the rent, but did not apologise this time, though it was eighteen days overdue, and said nothing when he took the receipt from me. The following month the rent was brought by his mother; she only brought me half, and promised to bring the remainder a week later. The third month, I did not get a farthing, and the porter complained to me that the lodgers in No. 23 were "not behaving like gentlemen."

These were ominous symptoms.

Picture this scene. A sombre Petersburg morning looks in at the dingy windows. By the stove, the granny is pouring out the children's tea. Only the eldest, Vassya, drinks out of a glass, for the others the tea is poured out into saucers. Yegoritch is squatting on his heels before the stove, thrusting a bit of iron into the fire. His head is heavy and his eyes are lustreless from yesterday's drinking-bout; he sighs and groans, trembles and coughs.

"He has quite put me off the right way, the devil," he grumbles; "he drinks himself and leads others into sin."

Putohin sits in his room, on the bedstead from which the bedclothes and the pillows have long ago disappeared, and with his hands straying in his hair looks blankly at the floor at his feet. He is tattered, unkempt, and ill.

"Drink it up, make haste or you will be late for school," the old woman urges on Vassya, "and it's time for me, too, to go and scrub the floors for the Jews..."

The old woman is the only one in the flat who does not lose heart. She thinks of old times, and goes out to hard dirty work. On Fridays she scrubs the floors for the Jews at the crockery shop, on Saturdays she goes out washing for shopkeepers, and on Sundays she is racing about the town from morning to night, trying to find ladies who will help her. Every day she has work of some sort; she washes and scrubs, and is by turns a midwife, a matchmaker, or a beggar. It is true she, too, is not disinclined to drown her sorrows, but even when she has had a drop she does not forget her duties. In Russia there are many such tough old women, and how much of its welfare rests upon them!

When he has finished his tea, Vassya packs up his books in a satchel and goes behind the stove; his greatcoat ought to be hanging there beside his granny's clothes. A minute later he comes out from behind the stove and asks:

"Where is my greatcoat?"

The grandmother and the other children look for the greatcoat together, they waste a long time in looking for it, but the greatcoat has utterly vanished. Where is it? The grandmother and Vassya are pale and frightened. Even Yegoritch is surprised. Putohin is the only one who does not move. Though he is quick to notice anything irregular or disorderly, this time he makes a pretence of hearing and seeing nothing. That is suspicious.

"He's sold it for drink," Yegoritch declares.

Putohin says nothing, so it is the truth. Vassya is overcome with horror. His greatcoat, his splendid greatcoat, made of his dead mother's cloth dress, with a splendid calico lining, gone for drink at the tavern! And with the greatcoat is gone too, of course, the blue pencil that lay in the pocket, and the note-book with " Nota bene " in gold letters on it! There's another pencil with india-rubber stuck into the note-book, and, besides that, there are transfer pictures lying in it.

Vassya would like to cry, but to cry is impossible. If his father, who has a headache, heard crying he would shout, stamp with his feet, and begin fighting, and after drinking he fights horribly. Granny would stand up for Vassya, and his father would strike granny too; it would end in Yegoritch getting mixed up in it too, clutching at his father and falling on the floor with him. The two would roll on the floor, struggling together and gasping with drunken animal fury, and granny would cry, the children would scream, the neighbours would send for the porter. No, better not cry.

Because he mustn't cry, or give vent to his indignation aloud, Vassya moans, wrings his hands and moves his legs convulsively, or biting his sleeve shakes it with his teeth as a dog does a hare. His eyes are frantic, and his face is distorted with despair. Looking at him, his granny all at once takes the shawl off her head, and she too makes queer movements with her arms and legs in silence, with her eyes fixed on a point in the distance. And at that moment I believe there is a definite certainty in the minds of the boy and the old woman that their life is ruined, that there is no hope...

Putohin hears no crying, but he can see it all from his room. When, half an hour later, Vassya sets off to school, wrapped in his grandmother's shawl, he goes out with a face I will not undertake to describe, and walks after him. He longs to call the boy, to comfort him, to beg his forgiveness, to promise him on his word of honour, to call his dead mother to witness, but instead of words, sobs break from him. It is a grey, cold morning. When he reaches the town school Vassya untwists his granny's shawl, and goes into the school with nothing over his jacket for fear the boys should say he looks like a woman. And when he gets home Putohin sobs, mutters some incoherent words, bows down to the ground before his mother and Yegoritch, and the locksmith's table. Then, recovering himself a little, he runs to me and begs me breathlessly, for God's sake, to find him some job. I give him hopes, of course.

"At last I am myself again," he said. "It's high time, indeed, to come to my senses. I've made a beast of myself, and now it's over."

He is delighted and thanks me, while I, who have studied these gentry thoroughly during the years I have owned the house, look at him, and am tempted to say:

"It's too late, dear fellow! You are a dead man already."

From me, Putohin runs to the town school. There he paces up and down, waiting till his boy comes out.

"I say, Vassya," he says joyfully, when the boy at last comes out, "I have just been promised a job. Wait a bit, I will buy you a splendid fur-coat... I'll send you to the high school! Do you understand? To the high school! I'll make a gentleman of you! And I won't drink any more. On my honour I won't."

And he has intense faith in the bright future. But the evening comes on. The old woman, coming back from the Jews with twenty kopecks, exhausted and aching all over, sets to work to wash the children's clothes. Vassya is sitting doing a sum. Yegoritch is not working. Thanks to Putohin he has got into the way of drinking, and is feeling at the moment an overwhelming desire for drink. It's hot and stuffy in the room. Steam rises in clouds from the tub where the old woman is washing.

"Are we going?" Yegoritch asks surlily.

My lodger does not answer. After his excitement he feels insufferably dreary. He struggles with the desire to drink, with acute depression and... and, of course, depression gets the best of it. It is a familiar story.

Towards night, Yegoritch and Putohin go out, and in the morning Vassya cannot find granny's shawl.

That is the drama that took place in that flat. After selling the shawl for drink, Putohin did not come home again. Where he disappeared to I don't know. After he disappeared, the old woman first got drunk, then took to her bed. She was taken to the hospital, the younger children were fetched by relations of some sort, and Vassya went into the wash-house here. In the day-time he handed the irons, and at night fetched the beer. When he was turned out of the wash-house he went into the service of one of the young ladies, used to run about at night on errands of some sort, and began to be spoken of as "a dangerous customer."

What has happened to him since I don't know.

And in this room here a street musician lived for ten years. When he died they found twenty thousand roubles in his feather bed.

In Passion Week

"Go along, they are ringing already; and mind, don't be naughty in church or God will punish you."

My mother thrusts a few copper coins upon me, and, instantly forgetting about me, runs into the kitchen with an iron that needs reheating. I know well that after confession I shall not be allowed to eat or drink, and so, before leaving the house, I force myself to eat a crust of white bread, and to drink two glasses of water. It is quite spring in the street. The roads are all covered with brownish slush, in which future paths are already beginning to show; the roofs and side-walks are dry; the fresh young green is piercing through the rotting grass of last year, under the fences. In the gutters there is the merry gurgling and foaming of dirty water, in which the sunbeams do not disdain to bathe. Chips, straws, the husks of sunflower seeds are carried rapidly along in the water, whirling round and sticking in the dirty foam. Where, where are those chips swimming to? It may well be that from the gutter they may pass into the river, from the river into the sea, and from the sea into the ocean. I try to imagine to myself that long terrible journey, but my fancy stops short before reaching the sea.

A cabman drives by. He clicks to his horse, tugs at the reins, and does not see that two street urchins are hanging on the back of his cab. I should like to join them, but think of confession, and the street urchins begin to seem to me great sinners.

"They will be asked on the day of judgment: 'Why did you play pranks and deceive the poor cabman?'" I think. "They will begin to defend themselves, but evil spirits will seize them, and drag them to fire everlasting. But if they obey their parents, and give the beggars a kopeck each, or a roll, God will have pity on them, and will let them into Paradise."

The church porch is dry and bathed in sunshine. There is not a soul in it. I open the door irresolutely and go into the church. Here, in the twilight which seems to me thick and gloomy as at no other time, I am overcome by the sense of sinfulness and insignificance. What strikes the eye first of all is a huge crucifix, and on one side of it the Mother of God, and on the other, St. John the Divine. The candelabra and the candlestands are draped in black mourning covers, the lamps glimmer dimly and faintly, and the sun seems intentionally to pass by the church windows. The Mother of God and the beloved disciple of Jesus Christ, depicted in profile, gaze in silence at the insufferable agony and do not observe my presence; I feel that to them I am alien, superfluous, unnoticed, that I can be no help to them by word or deed, that I am a loathsome, dishonest boy, only capable of mischief, rudeness, and tale-bearing. I think of all the people I know, and they all seem to me petty, stupid, and wicked, and incapable of bringing one drop of relief to that intolerable sorrow which I now behold.

The twilight of the church grows darker and more gloomy. And the Mother of God and St. John look lonely and forlorn to me.

Prokofy Ignatitch, a veteran soldier, the church verger's assistant, is standing behind the candle cupboard. Raising his eyebrows and stroking his beard he explains in a half-whisper to an old woman: "Matins will be in the evening to-day, directly after vespers. And they will ring for the 'hours' to-morrow between seven and eight. Do you understand? Between seven and eight."

Between the two broad columns on the right, where the chapel of Varvara the Martyr begins, those who are going to confess stand beside the screen, awaiting their turn. And Mitka is there too-- a ragged boy with his head hideously cropped, with ears that jut out, and little spiteful eyes. He is the son of Nastasya the charwoman, and is a bully and a ruffian who snatches apples from the women's baskets, and has more than once carried off my knuckle-bones. He looks at me angrily, and I fancy takes a spiteful pleasure in the fact that he, not I, will first go behind the screen. I feel boiling over with resentment, I try not to look at him, and, at the bottom of my heart, I am vexed that this wretched boy's sins will soon be forgiven.

In front of him stands a grandly dressed, beautiful lady, wearing a hat with a white feather. She is noticeably agitated, is waiting in strained suspense, and one of her cheeks is flushed red with excitement.

I wait for five minutes, for ten... A well-dressed young man with a long thin neck, and rubber galoshes, comes out from behind the screen. I begin dreaming how, when I am grown up, I will buy galoshes exactly like them. I certainly will! The lady shudders and goes behind the screen. It is her turn.

In the crack, between the two panels of the screen, I can see the lady go up to the lectern and bow down to the ground, then get up, and, without looking at the priest, bow her head in anticipation. The priest stands with his back to the screen, and so I can only see his grey curly head, the chain of the cross on his chest, and his broad back. His face is not visible. Heaving a sigh, and not looking at the lady, he begins speaking rapidly, shaking his head, alternately raising and dropping his whispering voice. The lady listens meekly as though conscious of guilt, answers meekly, and looks at the floor.

"In what way can she be sinful?" I wonder, looking reverently at her gentle, beautiful face. "God forgive her sins, God send her happiness." But now the priest covers her head with the stole. "And I, unworthy priest..." I hear his voice, "...by His power given unto me, do forgive and absolve thee from all thy sins..."

The lady bows down to the ground, kisses the cross, and comes back. Both her cheeks are flushed now, but her face is calm and serene and cheerful.

"She is happy now," I think to myself, looking first at her and then at the priest who had forgiven her sins. "But how happy the man must be who has the right to forgive sins!"

Now it is Mitka's turn, but a feeling of hatred for that young ruffian suddenly boils up in me. I want to go behind the screen before him, I want to be the first. Noticing my movement he hits me on the head with his candle, I respond by doing the same, and, for half a minute, there is a sound of panting, and, as it were, of someone breaking candles... We are separated. My foe goes timidly up to the lectern, and bows down to the floor without bending his knees, but I do not see what happens after that; the thought that my turn is coming after Mitka's makes everything grow blurred and confused before my eyes; Mitka's protruding ears grow large, and melt into his dark head, the priest sways, the floor seems to be undulating...

The priest's voice is audible: "And I, unworthy priest..."

Now I too move behind the screen. I do not feel the ground under my feet, it is as though I were walking on air... I go up to the lectern which is taller than I am. For a minute I have a glimpse of the indifferent, exhausted face of the priest. But after that I see nothing but his sleeve with its blue lining, the cross, and the edge of the lectern. I am conscious of the close proximity of the priest, the smell of his cassock; I hear his stern voice, and my cheek turned towards him begins to burn... I am so troubled that I miss a great deal that he says, but I answer his questions sincerely in an unnatural voice, not my own. I think of the forlorn figures of the Holy Mother and St. John the Divine, the crucifix, my mother, and I want to cry and beg forgiveness.

"What is your name?" the priest asks me, covering my head with the soft stole.

How light-hearted I am now, with joy in my soul!

I have no sins now, I am holy, I have the right to enter Paradise! I fancy that I already smell like the cassock. I go from behind the screen to the deacon to enter my name, and sniff at my sleeves. The dusk of the church no longer seems gloomy, and I look indifferently, without malice, at Mitka.

"What is your name?" the deacon asks.

"Fedya."

"And your name from your father?"

"I don't know."

"What is your papa's name?"

"Ivan Petrovitch."

"And your surname?"

I make no answer.

"How old are you?"

"Nearly nine."

When I get home I go to bed quickly, that I may not see them eating supper; and, shutting my eyes, dream of how fine it would be to endure martyrdom at the hands of some Herod or Dioskorus, to live in the desert, and, like St. Serafim, feed the bears, live in a cell, and eat nothing but holy bread, give my property to the poor, go on a pilgrimage to Kiev. I hear them laying the table in the dining-room--they are going to have supper, they will eat salad, cabbage pies, fried and baked fish. How hungry I am! I would consent to endure any martyrdom, to live in the desert without my mother, to feed bears out of my own hands, if only I might first eat just one cabbage pie!

"Lord, purify me a sinner," I pray, covering my head over. "Guardian angel, save me from the unclean spirit."

The next day, Thursday, I wake up with my heart as pure and clean as a fine spring day. I go gaily and boldly into the church, feeling that I am a communicant, that I have a splendid and expensive shirt on, made out of a silk dress left by my grandmother. In the church everything has an air of joy, happiness, and spring. The faces of the Mother of God and St. John the Divine are not so sorrowful as yesterday. The faces of the communicants are radiant with hope, and it seems as though all the past is forgotten, all is forgiven. Mitka, too, has combed his hair, and is dressed in his best. I look gaily at his protruding ears, and to show that I have nothing against him, I say:

"You look nice to-day, and if your hair did not stand up so, and you weren't so poorly dressed, everybody would think that your mother was not a washerwoman but a lady. Come to me at Easter, we will play knuckle-bones."

Mitka looks at me mistrustfully, and shakes his fist at me on the sly.

And the lady I saw yesterday looks lovely. She is wearing a light blue dress, and a big sparkling brooch in the shape of a horse-shoe. I admire her, and think that, when I am grown-up, I will certainly marry a woman like that, but remembering that getting married is shameful, I leave off thinking about it, and go into the choir where the deacon is already reading the "hours."

Whitebrow

A hungry she-wolf got up to go hunting. Her cubs, all three of them, were sound asleep, huddled in a heap and keeping each other warm. She licked them and went off.

It was already March, a month of spring, but at night the trees snapped with the cold, as they do in December, and one could hardly put one's tongue out without its being nipped. The wolf-mother was in delicate health and nervous; she started at the slightest sound, and kept hoping that no one would hurt the little ones at home while she was away. The smell of the tracks of men and horses, logs, piles of faggots, and the dark road with horse-dung on it frightened her; it seemed to her that men were standing behind the trees in the darkness, and that dogs were howling somewhere beyond the forest.

She was no longer young and her scent had grown feebler, so that it sometimes happened that she took the track of a fox for that of a dog, and even at times lost her way, a thing that had never been in her youth. Owing to the weakness of her health she no longer hunted calves and big sheep as she had in old days, and kept her distance now from mares with colts; she fed on nothing but carrion; fresh meat she tasted very rarely, only in the spring when she would come upon a hare and take away her young, or make her way into a peasant's stall where there were lambs.

Some three miles from her lair there stood a winter hut on the posting road. There lived the keeper Ignat, an old man of seventy, who was always coughing and talking to himself; at night he was usually asleep, and by day he wandered about the forest with a single-barrelled gun, whistling to the hares. He must have worked among machinery in early days, for before he stood still he always shouted to himself: "Stop the machine!" and before going on: "Full speed!" He had a huge black dog of indeterminate breed, called Arapka. When it ran too far ahead he used to shout to it: "Reverse action!" Sometimes he used to sing, and as he did so staggered violently, and often fell down (the wolf thought the wind blew him over), and shouted: "Run off the rails!"

The wolf remembered that, in the summer and autumn, a ram and two ewes were pasturing near the winter hut, and when she had run by not so long ago she fancied that she had heard bleating in the stall. And now, as she got near the place, she reflected that it was already March, and, by that time, there would certainly be lambs in the stall. She was tormented by hunger, she thought with what greediness she would eat a lamb, and these thoughts made her teeth snap, and her eyes glitter in the darkness like two sparks of light.

Ignat's hut, his barn, cattle-stall, and well were surrounded by high snowdrifts. All was still. Arapka was, most likely, asleep in the barn.

The wolf clambered over a snowdrift on to the stall, and began scratching away the thatched roof with her paws and her nose. The straw was rotten and decaying, so that the wolf almost fell through; all at once a smell of warm steam, of manure, and of sheep's milk floated straight to her nostrils. Down below, a lamb, feeling the cold, bleated softly. Leaping through the hole, the wolf fell with her four paws and chest on something soft and warm, probably a sheep, and at the same moment, something in the stall suddenly began whining, barking, and going off into a shrill little yap; the sheep huddled against the wall, and the wolf, frightened, snatched the first thing her teeth fastened on, and dashed away...

She ran at her utmost speed, while Arapka, who by now had scented the wolf, howled furiously, the frightened hens cackled, and Ignat, coming out into the porch, shouted: "Full speed! Blow the whistle!"

And he whistled like a steam-engine, and then shouted: "Ho-ho-ho-ho!" and all this noise was repeated by the forest echo. When, little by little, it all died away, the wolf somewhat recovered herself, and began to notice that the prey she held in her teeth and dragged along the snow was heavier and, as it were, harder than lambs usually were at that season; and it smelt somehow different, and uttered strange sounds... The wolf stopped and laid her burden on the snow, to rest and begin eating it, then all at once she leapt back in disgust. It was not a lamb, but a black puppy, with a big head and long legs, of a large breed, with a white patch on his brow, like Arapka's. Judging from his manners he was a simple, ignorant, yard-dog. He licked his crushed and wounded back, and, as though nothing was the matter, wagged his tail and barked at the wolf. She growled like a dog, and ran away from him. He ran after her. She looked round and snapped her teeth. He stopped in perplexity, and, probably deciding that she was playing with him, craned his head in the direction he had come from, and went off into a shrill, gleeful bark, as though inviting his mother Arapka to play with him and the wolf.

It was already getting light, and when the wolf reached her home in the thick aspen wood, each aspen tree could be seen distinctly, and the woodcocks were already awake, and the beautiful male birds often flew up, disturbed by the incautious gambols and barking of the puppy.

"Why does he run after me?" thought the wolf with annoyance. "I suppose he wants me to eat him."

She lived with her cubs in a shallow hole; three years before, a tall old pine tree had been torn up by the roots in a violent storm, and the hole had been formed by it. Now there were dead leaves and moss at the bottom, and around it lay bones and bullocks' horns, with which the little ones played. They were by now awake, and all three of them, very much alike, were standing in a row at the edge of their hole, looking at their returning mother, and wagging their tails. Seeing them, the puppy stopped a little way off, and stared at them for a very long time; seeing that they, too, were looking very attentively at him, he began barking angrily, as at strangers.

By now it was daylight and the sun had risen, the snow sparkled all around, but still the puppy stood a little way off and barked. The cubs sucked their mother, pressing her thin belly with their paws, while she gnawed a horse's bone, dry and white; she was tormented by hunger, her head ached from the dog's barking, and she felt inclined to fall on the uninvited guest and tear him to pieces.

At last the puppy was hoarse and exhausted; seeing they were not afraid of him, and not even attending to him, he began somewhat timidly approaching the cubs, alternately squatting down and bounding a few steps forward. Now, by daylight, it was easy to have a good look at him... His white forehead was big, and on it was a hump such as is only seen on very stupid dogs; he had little, blue, dingy-looking eyes, and the expression of his whole face was extremely stupid. When he reached the cubs he stretched out his broad paws, laid his head upon them, and began:

"Mnya, myna... nga--nga--nga... !"

The cubs did not understand what he meant, but they wagged their tails. Then the puppy gave one of the cubs a smack on its big head with his paw. The cub, too, gave him a smack on the head. The puppy stood sideways to him, and looked at him askance, wagging his tail, then dashed off, and ran round several times on the frozen snow. The cubs ran after him, he fell on his back and kicked up his legs, and all three of them fell upon him, squealing with delight, and began biting him, not to hurt but in play. The crows sat on the high pine tree, and looked down on their struggle, and were much troubled by it. They grew noisy and merry. The sun was hot, as though it were spring; and the woodcocks, continually flitting through the pine tree that had been blown down by the storm, looked as though made of emerald in the brilliant sunshine.

As a rule, wolf-mothers train their children to hunt by giving them prey to play with; and now watching the cubs chasing the puppy over the frozen snow and struggling with him, the mother thought:

"Let them learn."

When they had played long enough, the cubs went into the hole and lay down to sleep. The puppy howled a little from hunger, then he, too, stretched out in the sunshine. And when they woke up they began playing again.

All day long, and in the evening, the wolf-mother was thinking how the lamb had bleated in the cattle-shed the night before, and how it had smelt of sheep's milk, and she kept snapping her teeth from hunger, and never left off greedily gnawing the old bone, pretending to herself that it was the lamb. The cubs sucked their mother, and the puppy, who was hungry, ran round them and sniffed at the snow.

"I'll eat him..." the mother-wolf decided.

She went up to him, and he licked her nose and yapped at her, thinking that she wanted to play with him. In the past she had eaten dogs, but the dog smelt very doggy, and in the delicate state of her health she could not endure the smell; she felt disgusted and walked away...

Towards night it grew cold. The puppy felt depressed and went home.

When the wolf-cubs were fast asleep, their mother went out hunting again. As on the previous night she was alarmed at every sound, and she was frightened by the stumps, the logs, the dark juniper bushes, which stood out singly, and in the distance were like human beings. She ran on the ice-covered snow, keeping away from the road... All at once she caught a glimpse of something dark, far away on the road. She strained her eyes and ears: yes, something really was walking on in front, she could even hear the regular thud of footsteps. Surely not a badger? Cautiously holding her breath, and keeping always to one side, she overtook the dark patch, looked round, and recognised it. It was the puppy with the white brow, going with a slow, lingering step homewards.

"If only he doesn't hinder me again," thought the wolf, and ran quickly on ahead.

But the homestead was by now near. Again she clambered on to the cattle-shed by the snowdrift. The gap she had made yesterday had been already mended with straw, and two new rafters stretched across the roof. The wolf began rapidly working with her legs and nose, looking round to see whether the puppy were coming, but the smell of the warm steam and manure had hardly reached her nose before she heard a gleeful burst of barking behind her. It was the puppy. He leapt up to the wolf on the roof, then into the hole, and, feeling himself at home in the warmth, recognising his sheep, he barked louder than ever... Arapka woke up in the barn, and, scenting a wolf, howled, the hens began cackling, and by the time Ignat appeared in the porch with his single-barrelled gun the frightened wolf was already far away.

"Fuite!" whistled Ignat. "Fuite! Full steam ahead!"

He pulled the trigger--the gun missed fire; he pulled the trigger again--again it missed fire; he tried a third time--and a great blaze of flame flew out of the barrel and there was a deafening boom, boom. It kicked him violently on the shoulder, and, taking his gun in one hand and his axe in the other, he went to see what the noise was about.

A little later he went back to the hut.

"What was it?" a pilgrim, who was staying the night at the hut and had been awakened by the noise, asked in a husky voice.

"It's all right," answered Ignat. "Nothing of consequence. Our Whitebrow has taken to sleeping with the sheep in the warm. Only he hasn't the sense to go in at the door, but always tries to wriggle in by the roof. The other night he tore a hole in the roof and went off on the spree, the rascal, and now he has come back and scratched away the roof again."

"Stupid dog."

"Yes, there is a spring snapped in his brain. I do detest fools," sighed Ignat, clambering on to the stove. "Come, man of God, it's early yet to get up. Let us sleep full steam!..."

In the morning he called Whitebrow, smacked him hard about the ears, and then showing him a stick, kept repeating to him:

"Go in at the door! Go in at the door! Go in at the door!"

A Chameleon

The police superintendent Otchumyelov is walking across the market square wearing a new overcoat and carrying a parcel under his arm. A red-haired policeman strides after him with a sieve full of confiscated gooseberries in his hands. There is silence all around. Not a soul in the square... The open doors of the shops and taverns look out upon God's world disconsolately, like hungry mouths; there is not even a beggar near them.

"So you bite, you damned brute?" Otchumyelov hears suddenly. "Lads, don't let him go! Biting is prohibited nowadays! Hold him! ah... ah!"

There is the sound of a dog yelping. Otchumyelov looks in the direction of the sound and sees a dog, hopping on three legs and looking about her, run out of Pitchugin's timber-yard. A man in a starched cotton shirt, with his waistcoat unbuttoned, is chasing her. He runs after her, and throwing his body forward falls down and seizes the dog by her hind legs. Once more there is a yelping and a shout of "Don't let go!" Sleepy countenances are protruded from the shops, and soon a crowd, which seems to have sprung out of the earth, is gathered round the timber-yard.

"It looks like a row, your honour..." says the policeman.

Otchumyelov makes a half turn to the left and strides towards the crowd.

He sees the aforementioned man in the unbuttoned waistcoat standing close by the gate of the timber-yard, holding his right hand in the air and displaying a bleeding finger to the crowd. On his half-drunken face there is plainly written: "I'll pay you out, you rogue!" and indeed the very finger has the look of a flag of victory. In this man Otchumyelov recognises Hryukin, the goldsmith. The culprit who has caused the sensation, a white borzoy puppy with a sharp muzzle and a yellow patch on her back, is sitting on the ground with her fore-paws outstretched in the middle of the crowd, trembling all over. There is an expression of misery and terror in her tearful eyes.

"What's it all about?" Otchumyelov inquires, pushing his way through the crowd. "What are you here for? Why are you waving your finger... ? Who was it shouted?"

"I was walking along here, not interfering with anyone, your honour," Hryukin begins, coughing into his fist. "I was talking about firewood to Mitry Mitritch, when this low brute for no rhyme or reason bit my finger... You must excuse me, I am a working man... Mine is fine work. I must have damages, for I shan't be able to use this finger for a week, may be... It's not even the law, your honour, that one should put up with it from a beast... If everyone is going to be bitten, life won't be worth living..."

"H'm. Very good," says Otchumyelov sternly, coughing and raising his eyebrows. "Very good. Whose dog is it? I won't let this pass! I'll teach them to let their dogs run all over the place! It's time these gentry were looked after, if they won't obey the regulations! When he's fined, the blackguard, I'll teach him what it means to keep dogs and such stray cattle! I'll give him a lesson!... Yeldyrin," cries the superintendent, addressing the policeman, "find out whose dog this is and draw up a report! And the dog must be strangled. Without delay! It's sure to be mad... Whose dog is it, I ask?"

"I fancy it's General Zhigalov's," says someone in the crowd.

"General Zhigalov's, h'm... Help me off with my coat, Yeldyrin... it's frightfully hot! It must be a sign of rain... There's one thing I can't make out, how it came to bite you?" Otchumyelov turns to Hryukin. "Surely it couldn't reach your finger. It's a little dog, and you are a great hulking fellow! You must have scratched your finger with a nail, and then the idea struck you to get damages for it. We all know... your sort! I know you devils!"

"He put a cigarette in her face, your honour, for a joke, and she had the sense to snap at him... He is a nonsensical fellow, your honour!"

"That's a lie, Squinteye! You didn't see, so why tell lies about it? His honour is a wise gentleman, and will see who is telling lies and who is telling the truth, as in God's sight... And if I am lying let the court decide. It's written in the law... We are all equal nowadays. My own brother is in the gendarmes... let me tell you..."

"Don't argue!"

"No, that's not the General's dog," says the policeman, with profound conviction, "the General hasn't got one like that. His are mostly setters."

"Do you know that for a fact?"

"Yes, your honour."

"I know it, too. The General has valuable dogs, thoroughbred, and this is goodness knows what! No coat, no shape... A low creature. And to keep a dog like that!... where's the sense of it. If a dog like that were to turn up in Petersburg or Moscow, do you know what would happen? They would not worry about the law, they would strangle it in a twinkling! You've been injured, Hryukin, and we can't let the matter drop... We must give them a lesson! It is high time... !"

"Yet maybe it is the General's," says the policeman, thinking aloud. "It's not written on its face... I saw one like it the other day in his yard."

"It is the General's, that's certain!" says a voice in the crowd.

"H'm, help me on with my overcoat, Yeldyrin, my lad... the wind's getting up... I am cold... You take it to the General's, and inquire there. Say I found it and sent it. And tell them not to let it out into the street... It may be a valuable dog, and if every swine goes sticking a cigar in its mouth, it will soon be ruined. A dog is a delicate animal... And you put your hand down, you blockhead. It's no use your displaying your fool of a finger. It's your own fault..."

"Here comes the General's cook, ask him... Hi, Prohor! Come here, my dear man! Look at this dog... Is it one of yours?"

"What an idea! We have never had one like that!"

"There's no need to waste time asking," says Otchumyelov. "It's a stray dog! There's no need to waste time talking about it... Since he says it's a stray dog, a stray dog it is... It must be destroyed, that's all about it."

"It is not our dog," Prohor goes on. "It belongs to the General's brother, who arrived the other day. Our master does not care for hounds. But his honour is fond of them..."

"You don't say his Excellency's brother is here? Vladimir Ivanitch?" inquires Otchumyelov, and his whole face beams with an ecstatic smile. "'Well, I never! And I didn't know! Has he come on a visit?

"Yes."

"Well, I never... He couldn't stay away from his brother... And there I didn't know! So this is his honour's dog? Delighted to hear it... Take it. It's not a bad pup... A lively creature... Snapped at this fellow's finger! Ha-ha-ha... Come, why are you shivering? Rrr... Rrrr... The rogue's angry... a nice little pup."

Prohor calls the dog, and walks away from the timber-yard with her. The crowd laughs at Hryukin.

"I'll make you smart yet!" Otchumyelov threatens him, and wrapping himself in his greatcoat, goes on his way across the square.

Who was to Blame?

As my uncle Pyotr Demyanitch, a lean, bilious collegiate councillor, exceedingly like a stale smoked fish with a stick through it, was getting ready to go to the high school, where he taught Latin, he noticed that the corner of his grammar was nibbled by mice.

"I say, Praskovya," he said, going into the kitchen and addressing the cook, "how is it we have got mice here? Upon my word! yesterday my top hat was nibbled, to-day they have disfigured my Latin grammar... At this rate they will soon begin eating my clothes!"

"What can I do? I did not bring them in!" answered Praskovya.

"We must do something! You had better get a cat, hadn't you?"

"I've got a cat, but what good is it?"

And Praskovya pointed to the corner where a white kitten, thin as a match, lay curled up asleep beside a broom.

"Why is it no good?" asked Pyotr Demyanitch.

"It's young yet, and foolish. It's not two months old yet."

"H'm... Then it must be trained. It had much better be learning instead of lying there."

Saying this, Pyotr Demyanitch sighed with a careworn air and went out of the kitchen. The kitten raised his head, looked lazily after him, and shut his eyes again.

The kitten lay awake thinking. Of what? Unacquainted with real life, having no store of accumulated impressions, his mental processes could only be instinctive, and he could but picture life in accordance with the conceptions that he had inherited, together with his flesh and blood, from his ancestors, the tigers (vide Darwin). His thoughts were of the nature of day-dreams. His feline imagination pictured something like the Arabian desert, over which flitted shadows closely resembling Praskovya, the stove, the broom. In the midst of the shadows there suddenly appeared a saucer of milk; the saucer began to grow paws, it began moving and displayed a tendency to run; the kitten made a bound, and with a thrill of blood-thirsty sensuality thrust his claws into it.

When the saucer had vanished into obscurity a piece of meat appeared, dropped by Praskovya; the meat ran away with a cowardly squeak, but the kitten made a bound and got his claws into it... Everything that rose before the imagination of the young dreamer had for its starting-point leaps, claws, and teeth... The soul of another is darkness, and a cat's soul more than most, but how near the visions just described are to the truth may be seen from the following fact: under the influence of his day-dreams the kitten suddenly leaped up, looked with flashing eyes at Praskovya, ruffled up his coat, and making one bound, thrust his claws into the cook's skirt. Obviously he was born a mouse catcher, a worthy son of his bloodthirsty ancestors. Fate had destined him to be the terror of cellars, store-rooms and cornbins, and had it not been for education... we will not anticipate, however.

On his way home from the high school, Pyotr Demyanitch went into a general shop and bought a mouse-trap for fifteen kopecks. At dinner he fixed a little bit of his rissole on the hook, and set the trap under the sofa, where there were heaps of the pupils' old exercise-books, which Praskovya used for various domestic purposes. At six o'clock in the evening, when the worthy Latin master was sitting at the table correcting his pupils' exercises, there was a sudden "klop!" so loud that my uncle started and dropped his pen. He went at once to the sofa and took out the trap. A neat little mouse, the size of a thimble, was sniffing the wires and trembling with fear.

"Aha," muttered Pyotr Demyanitch, and he looked at the mouse malignantly, as though he were about to give him a bad mark. "You are cau--aught, wretch! Wait a bit! I'll teach you to eat my grammar!"

Having gloated over his victim, Poytr Demyanitch put the mouse-trap on the floor and called:

"Praskovya, there's a mouse caught! Bring the kitten here!"

"I'm coming," responded Praskovya, and a minute later she came in with the descendant of tigers in her arms.

"Capital!" said Pyotr Demyanitch, rubbing his hands. "We will give him a lesson... Put him down opposite the mouse-trap... that's it... Let him sniff it and look at it... That's it..."

The kitten looked wonderingly at my uncle, at his arm-chair, sniffed the mouse-trap in bewilderment, then, frightened probably by the glaring lamplight and the attention directed to him, made a dash and ran in terror to the door.

"Stop!" shouted my uncle, seizing him by the tail, "stop, you rascal! He's afraid of a mouse, the idiot! Look! It's a mouse! Look! Well? Look, I tell you!"

Pyotr Demyanitch took the kitten by the scruff of the neck and pushed him with his nose against the mouse-trap.

"Look, you carrion! Take him and hold him, Praskovya... Hold him opposite the door of the trap... When I let the mouse out, you let him go instantly... Do you hear?... Instantly let go! Now!"

My uncle assumed a mysterious expression and lifted the door of the trap... The mouse came out irresolutely, sniffed the air, and flew like an arrow under the sofa... The kitten on being released darted under the table with his tail in the air.

"It has got away! got away!" cried Pyotr Demyanitch, looking ferocious. "Where is he, the scoundrel? Under the table? You wait..."

My uncle dragged the kitten from under the table and shook him in the air.

"Wretched little beast," he muttered, smacking him on the ear. "Take that, take that! Will you shirk it next time? Wr-r-r-etch..."

Next day Praskovya heard again the summons.

"Praskovya, there is a mouse caught! Bring the kitten here!"

After the outrage of the previous day the kitten had taken refuge under the stove and had not come out all night. When Praskovya pulled him out and, carrying him by the scruff of the neck into the study, set him down before the mouse-trap, he trembled all over and mewed piteously.

"Come, let him feel at home first," Pyotr Demyanitch commanded. "Let him look and sniff. Look and learn! Stop, plague take you!" he shouted, noticing that the kitten was backing away from the mouse-trap. "I'll thrash you! Hold him by the ear! That's it... Well now, set him down before the trap..."

My uncle slowly lifted the door of the trap... the mouse whisked under the very nose of the kitten, flung itself against Praskovya's hand and fled under the cupboard; the kitten, feeling himself free, took a desperate bound and retreated under the sofa.

"He's let another mouse go!" bawled Pyotr Demyanitch. "Do you call that a cat? Nasty little beast! Thrash him! thrash him by the mousetrap!"

When the third mouse had been caught, the kitten shivered all over at the sight of the mousetrap and its inmate, and scratched Praskovya's hand... After the fourth mouse my uncle flew into a rage, kicked the kitten, and said:

"Take the nasty thing away! Get rid of it! Chuck it away! It's no earthly use!"

A year passed, the thin, frail kitten had turned into a solid and sagacious tom-cat. One day he was on his way by the back yards to an amatory interview. He had just reached his destination when he suddenly heard a rustle, and thereupon caught sight of a mouse which ran from a water-trough towards a stable; my hero's hair stood on end, he arched his back, hissed, and trembling all over, took to ignominious flight.

Alas! sometimes I feel myself in the ludicrous position of the flying cat. Like the kitten, I had in my day the honour of being taught Latin by my uncle. Now, whenever I chance to see some work of classical antiquity, instead of being moved to eager enthusiasm, I begin recalling, ut consecutivum , the irregular verbs, the sallow grey face of my uncle, the ablative absolute... I turn pale, my hair stands up on my head, and, like the cat, I take to ignominious flight.

The Bird Market

There is a small square near the monastery of the Holy Birth which is called Trubnoy, or simply Truboy; there is a market there on Sundays. Hundreds of sheepskins, wadded coats, fur caps, and chimney-pot hats swarm there, like crabs in a sieve. There is the sound of the twitter of birds in all sorts of keys, recalling the spring. If the sun is shining, and there are no clouds in the sky, the singing of the birds and the smell of hay make a more vivid impression, and this reminder of spring sets one thinking and carries one's fancy far, far away. Along one side of the square there stands a string of waggons. The waggons are loaded, not with hay, not with cabbages, nor with beans, but with goldfinches, siskins, larks, blackbirds and thrushes, bluetits, bullfinches. All of them are hopping about in rough, home-made cages, twittering and looking with envy at the free sparrows. The goldfinches cost five kopecks, the siskins are rather more expensive, while the value of the other birds is quite indeterminate.

"How much is a lark?"

The seller himself does not know the value of a lark. He scratches his head and asks whatever comes into it, a rouble, or three kopecks, according to the purchaser. There are expensive birds too. A faded old blackbird, with most of its feathers plucked out of its tail, sits on a dirty perch. He is dignified, grave, and motionless as a retired general. He has waved his claw in resignation to his captivity long ago, and looks at the blue sky with indifference. Probably, owing to this indifference, he is considered a sagacious bird. He is not to be bought for less than forty kopecks. Schoolboys, workmen, young men in stylish greatcoats, and bird-fanciers in incredibly shabby caps, in ragged trousers that are turned up at the ankles, and look as though they had been gnawed by mice, crowd round the birds, splashing through the mud. The young people and the workmen are sold hens for cocks, young birds for old ones... They know very little about birds. But there is no deceiving the bird-fancier. He sees and understands his bird from a distance.

"There is no relying on that bird," a fancier will say, looking into a siskin's beak, and counting the feathers on its tail. "He sings now, it's true, but what of that? I sing in company too. No, my boy, shout, sing to me without company; sing in solitude, if you can... You give me that one yonder that sits and holds its tongue! Give me the quiet one! That one says nothing, so he thinks the more..."

Among the waggons of birds there are some full of other live creatures. Here you see hares, rabbits, hedgehogs, guinea-pigs, polecats. A hare sits sorrowfully nibbling the straw. The guinea-pigs shiver with cold, while the hedgehogs look out with curiosity from under their prickles at the public.

"I have read somewhere," says a post-office official in a faded overcoat, looking lovingly at the hare, and addressing no one in particular, "I have read that some learned man had a cat and a mouse and a falcon and a sparrow, who all ate out of one bowl."

"That's very possible, sir. The cat must have been beaten, and the falcon, I dare say, had all its tail pulled out. There's no great cleverness in that, sir. A friend of mine had a cat who, saving your presence, used to eat his cucumbers. He thrashed her with a big whip for a fortnight, till he taught her not to. A hare can learn to light matches if you beat it. Does that surprise you? It's very simple! It takes the match in its mouth and strikes it. An animal is like a man. A man's made wiser by beating, and it's the same with a beast."

Men in long, full-skirted coats move backwards and forwards in the crowd with cocks and ducks under their arms. The fowls are all lean and hungry. Chickens poke their ugly, mangy-looking heads out of their cages and peck at something in the mud. Boys with pigeons stare into your face and try to detect in you a pigeon-fancier.

"Yes, indeed! It's no use talking to you," someone shouts angrily. "You should look before you speak! Do you call this a pigeon? It is an eagle, not a pigeon!"

A tall thin man, with a shaven upper lip and side whiskers, who looks like a sick and drunken footman, is selling a snow-white lap-dog. The old lap-dog whines.

"She told me to sell the nasty thing," says the footman, with a contemptuous snigger. "She is bankrupt in her old age, has nothing to eat, and here now is selling her dogs and cats. She cries, and kisses them on their filthy snouts. And then she is so hard up that she sells them. 'Pon my soul, it is a fact! Buy it, gentlemen! The money is wanted for coffee."

But no one laughs. A boy who is standing by screws up one eye and looks at him gravely with compassion.

The most interesting of all is the fish section. Some dozen peasants are sitting in a row. Before each of them is a pail, and in each pail there is a veritable little hell. There, in the thick, greenish water are swarms of little carp, eels, small fry, water-snails, frogs, and newts. Big water-beetles with broken legs scurry over the small surface, clambering on the carp, and jumping over the frogs. The creatures have a strong hold on life. The frogs climb on the beetles, the newts on the frogs. The dark green tench, as more expensive fish, enjoy an exceptional position; they are kept in a special jar where they can't swim, but still they are not so cramped...

"The carp is a grand fish! The carp's the fish to keep, your honour, plague take him! You can keep him for a year in a pail and he'll live! It's a week since I caught these very fish. I caught them, sir, in Pererva, and have come from there on foot. The carp are two kopecks each, the eels are three, and the minnows are ten kopecks the dozen, plague take them! Five kopecks' worth of minnows, sir? Won't you take some worms?"

The seller thrusts his coarse rough fingers into the pail and pulls out of it a soft minnow, or a little carp, the size of a nail. Fishing lines, hooks, and tackle are laid out near the pails, and pond-worms glow with a crimson light in the sun.

An old fancier in a fur cap, iron-rimmed spectacles, and galoshes that look like two dread-noughts, walks about by the waggons of birds and pails of fish. He is, as they call him here, "a type." He hasn't a farthing to bless himself with, but in spite of that he haggles, gets excited, and pesters purchasers with advice. He has thoroughly examined all the hares, pigeons, and fish; examined them in every detail, fixed the kind, the age, and the price of each one of them a good hour ago. He is as interested as a child in the goldfinches, the carp, and the minnows. Talk to him, for instance, about thrushes, and the queer old fellow will tell you things you could not find in any book. He will tell you them with enthusiasm, with passion, and will scold you too for your ignorance. Of goldfinches and bullfinches he is ready to talk endlessly, opening his eyes wide and gesticulating violently with his hands. He is only to be met here at the market in the cold weather; in the summer he is somewhere in the country, catching quails with a bird-call and angling for fish.

And here is another "type," a very tall, very thin, close-shaven gentleman in dark spectacles, wearing a cap with a cockade, and looking like a scrivener of by-gone days. He is a fancier; he is a man of decent position, a teacher in a high school, and that is well known to the habitues of the market, and they treat him with respect, greet him with bows, and have even invented for him a special title: "Your Scholarship." At Suharev market he rummages among the books, and at Trubnoy looks out for good pigeons.

"Please, sir!" the pigeon-sellers shout to him, "Mr. Schoolmaster, your Scholarship, take notice of my tumblers! your Scholarship!"

"Your Scholarship!" is shouted at him from every side.

"Your Scholarship!" an urchin repeats somewhere on the boulevard.

And his "Scholarship," apparently quite accustomed to his title, grave and severe, takes a pigeon in both hands, and lifting it above his head, begins examining it, and as he does so frowns and looks graver than ever, like a conspirator.

And Trubnoy Square, that little bit of Moscow where animals are so tenderly loved, and where they are so tortured, lives its little life, grows noisy and excited, and the business-like or pious people who pass by along the boulevard cannot make out what has brought this crowd of people, this medley of caps, fur hats, and chimney-pots together; what they are talking about there, what they are buying and selling.

Art

A gloomy winter morning.

On the smooth and glittering surface of the river Bystryanka, sprinkled here and there with snow, stand two peasants, scrubby little Seryozhka and the church beadle, Matvey. Seryozhka, a short-legged, ragged, mangy-looking fellow of thirty, stares angrily at the ice. Tufts of wool hang from his shaggy sheepskin like a mangy dog. In his hands he holds a compass made of two pointed sticks. Matvey, a fine-looking old man in a new sheepskin and high felt boots, looks with mild blue eyes upwards where on the high sloping bank a village nestles picturesquely. In his hands there is a heavy crowbar.

"Well, are we going to stand like this till evening with our arms folded?" says Seryozhka, breaking the silence and turning his angry eyes on Matvey. "Have you come here to stand about, old fool, or to work?"

"Well, you... er... show me..." Matvey mutters, blinking mildly.

"Show you... It's always me: me to show you, and me to do it. They have no sense of their own! Mark it out with the compasses, that's what's wanted! You can't break the ice without marking it out. Mark it! Take the compass."

Matvey takes the compasses from Seryozhka's hands, and, shuffling heavily on the same spot and jerking with his elbows in all directions, he begins awkwardly trying to describe a circle on the ice. Seryozhka screws up his eyes contemptuously and obviously enjoys his awkwardness and incompetence.

"Eh-eh-eh!" he mutters angrily. "Even that you can't do! The fact is you are a stupid peasant, a wooden-head! You ought to be grazing geese and not making a Jordan! Give the compasses here! Give them here, I say!"

Seryozhka snatches the compasses out of the hands of the perspiring Matvey, and in an instant, jauntily twirling round on one heel, he describes a circle on the ice. The outline of the new Jordan is ready now, all that is left to do is to break the ice...

But before proceeding to the work Seryozhka spends a long time in airs and graces, whims and reproaches...

"I am not obliged to work for you! You are employed in the church, you do it!"

He obviously enjoys the peculiar position in which he has been placed by the fate that has bestowed on him the rare talent of surprising the whole parish once a year by his art. Poor mild Matvey has to listen to many venomous and contemptuous words from him. Seryozhka sets to work with vexation, with anger. He is lazy. He has hardly described the circle when he is already itching to go up to the village to drink tea, lounge about, and babble...

"I'll be back directly," he says, lighting his cigarette, "and meanwhile you had better bring something to sit on and sweep up, instead of standing there counting the crows."

Matvey is left alone. The air is grey and harsh but still. The white church peeps out genially from behind the huts scattered on the river bank. Jackdaws are incessantly circling round its golden crosses. On one side of the village where the river bank breaks off and is steep a hobbled horse is standing at the very edge, motionless as a stone, probably asleep or deep in thought.

Matvey, too, stands motionless as a statue, waiting patiently. The dreamily brooding look of the river, the circling of the jackdaws, and the sight of the horse make him drowsy. One hour passes, a second, and still Seryozhka does not come. The river has long been swept and a box brought to sit on, but the drunken fellow does not appear. Matvey waits and merely yawns. The feeling of boredom is one of which he knows nothing. If he were told to stand on the river for a day, a month, or a year he would stand there.

At last Seryozhka comes into sight from behind the huts. He walks with a lurching gait, scarcely moving. He is too lazy to go the long way round, and he comes not by the road, but prefers a short cut in a straight line down the bank, and sticks in the snow, hangs on to the bushes, slides on his back as he comes--and all this slowly, with pauses.

"What are you about?" he cries, falling on Matvey at once. "Why are you standing there doing nothing! When are you going to break the ice?"

Matvey crosses himself, takes the crowbar in both hands, and begins breaking the ice, carefully keeping to the circle that has been drawn. Seryozhka sits down on the box and watches the heavy clumsy movements of his assistant.

"Easy at the edges! Easy there!" he commands. "If you can't do it properly, you shouldn't undertake it, once you have undertaken it you should do it. You!"

A crowd collects on the top of the bank. At the sight of the spectators Seryozhka becomes even more excited.

"I declare I am not going to do it..." he says, lighting a stinking cigarette and spitting on the ground. "I should like to see how you get on without me. Last year at Kostyukovo, Styopka Gulkov undertook to make a Jordan as I do. And what did it amount to--it was a laughing-stock. The Kostyukovo folks came to ours --crowds and crowds of them! The people flocked from all the villages."

"Because except for ours there is nowhere a proper Jordan..."

"Work, there is no time for talking... Yes, old man... you won't find another Jordan like it in the whole province. The soldiers say you would look in vain, they are not so good even in the towns. Easy, easy!"

Matvey puffs and groans. The work is not easy. The ice is firm and thick; and he has to break it and at once take the pieces away that the open space may not be blocked up.

But, hard as the work is and senseless as Seryozhka's commands are, by three o'clock there is a large circle of dark water in the Bystryanka.

"It was better last year," says Seryozhka angrily. "You can't do even that! Ah, dummy! To keep such fools in the temple of God! Go and bring a board to make the pegs! Bring the ring, you crow! And er... get some bread somewhere... and some cucumbers, or something."

Matvey goes off and soon afterwards comes back, carrying on his shoulders an immense wooden ring which had been painted in previous years in patterns of various colours. In the centre of the ring is a red cross, at the circumference holes for the pegs. Seryozhka takes the ring and covers the hole in the ice with it.

"Just right... it fits... We have only to renew the paint and it will be first-rate... Come, why are you standing still? Make the lectern. Or--er--go and get logs to make the cross..."

Matvey, who has not tasted food or drink all day, trudges up the hill again. Lazy as Seryozhka is, he makes the pegs with his own hands. He knows that those pegs have a miraculous power: whoever gets hold of a peg after the blessing of the water will be lucky for the whole year. Such work is really worth doing.

But the real work begins the following day. Then Seryozhka displays himself before the ignorant Matvey in all the greatness of his talent. There is no end to his babble, his fault-finding, his whims and fancies. If Matvey nails two big pieces of wood to make a cross, he is dissatisfied and tells him to do it again. If Matvey stands still, Seryozhka asks him angrily why he does not go; if he moves, Seryozhka shouts to him not to go away but to do his work. He is not satisfied with his tools, with the weather, or with his own talent; nothing pleases him.

Matvey saws out a great piece of ice for a lectern.

"Why have you broken off the corner?" cries Seryozhka, and glares at him furiously. "Why have you broken off the corner? I ask you."

"Forgive me, for Christ's sake."

"Do it over again!"

Matvey saws again... and there is no end to his sufferings. A lectern is to stand by the hole in the ice that is covered by the painted ring; on the lectern is to be carved the cross and the open gospel. But that is not all. Behind the lectern there is to be a high cross to be seen by all the crowd and to glitter in the sun as though sprinkled with diamonds and rubies. On the cross is to be a dove carved out of ice. The path from the church to the Jordan is to be strewn with branches of fir and juniper. All this is their task.

First of all Seryozhka sets to work on the lectern. He works with a file, a chisel, and an awl. He is perfectly successful in the cross on the lectern, the gospel, and the drapery that hangs down from the lectern. Then he begins on the dove. While he is trying to carve an expression of meekness and humility on the face of the dove, Matvey, lumbering about like a bear, is coating with ice the cross he has made of wood. He takes the cross and dips it in the hole. Waiting till the water has frozen on the cross he dips it in a second time, and so on till the cross is covered with a thick layer of ice. It is a difficult job, calling for a great deal of strength and patience.

But now the delicate work is finished. Seryozhka races about the village like one possessed. He swears and vows he will go at once to the river and smash all his work. He is looking for suitable paints.

His pockets are full of ochre, dark blue, red lead, and verdigris; without paying a farthing he rushes headlong from one shop to another. The shop is next door to the tavern. Here he has a drink; with a wave of his hand he darts off without paying. At one hut he gets beetroot leaves, at another an onion skin, out of which he makes a yellow colour. He swears, shoves, threatens, and not a soul murmurs! They all smile at him, they sympathise with him, call him Sergey Nikititch; they all feel that his art is not his personal affair but something that concerns them all, the whole people. One creates, the others help him. Seryozhka in himself is a nonentity, a sluggard, a drunkard, and a wastrel, but when he has his red lead or compasses in his hand he is at once something higher, a servant of God.

Epiphany morning comes. The precincts of the church and both banks of the river for a long distance are swarming with people. Everything that makes up the Jordan is scrupulously concealed under new mats. Seryozhka is meekly moving about near the mats, trying to control his emotion. He sees thousands of people. There are many here from other parishes; these people have come many a mile on foot through the frost and the snow merely to see his celebrated Jordan. Matvey, who had finished his coarse, rough work, is by now back in the church, there is no sight, no sound of him; he is already forgotten... The weather is lovely... There is not a cloud in the sky. The sunshine is dazzling.

The church bells ring out on the hill... Thousands of heads are bared, thousands of hands are moving, there are thousands of signs of the cross!

And Seryozhka does not know what to do with himself for impatience. But now they are ringing the bells for the Sacrament; then half an hour later a certain agitation is perceptible in the belfry and among the people. Banners are borne out of the church one after the other, while the bells peal in joyous haste. Seryozhka, trembling, pulls away the mat... and the people behold something extraordinary. The lectern, the wooden ring, the pegs, and the cross in the ice are iridescent with thousands of colors. The cross and the dove glitter so dazzlingly that it hurts the eyes to look at them. Merciful God, how fine it is! A murmur of wonder and delight runs through the crowd; the bells peal more loudly still, the day grows brighter; the banners oscillate and move over the crowd as over the waves. The procession, glittering with the settings of the ikons and the vestments of the clergy, comes slowly down the road and turns towards the Jordan. Hands are waved to the belfry for the ringing to cease, and the blessing of the water begins. The priests conduct the service slowly, deliberately, evidently trying to prolong the ceremony and the joy of praying all gathered together. There is perfect stillness.

But now they plunge the cross in, and the air echoes with an extraordinary din. Guns are fired, the bells peal furiously, loud exclamations of delight, shouts, and a rush to get the pegs. Seryozhka listens to this uproar, sees thousands of eyes fixed upon him, and the lazy fellow's soul is filled with a sense of glory and triumph.

The Swedish Match

(The Story of a Crime)

I

On the morning of October 6, 1885, a well-dressed young man presented himself at the office of the police superintendent of the 2nd division of the S. district, and announced that his employer, a retired cornet of the guards, called Mark Ivanovitch Klyauzov, had been murdered. The young man was pale and extremely agitated as he made this announcement. His hands trembled and there was a look of horror in his eyes.

"To whom have I the honour of speaking?" the superintendent asked him.

"Psyekov, Klyauzov's steward. Agricultural and engineering expert."

The police superintendent, on reaching the spot with Psyekov and the necessary witnesses, found the position as follows.

Masses of people were crowding about the lodge in which Klyauzov lived. The news of the event had flown round the neighbourhood with the rapidity of lightning, and, thanks to its being a holiday, the people were flocking to the lodge from all the neighbouring villages. There was a regular hubbub of talk. Pale and tearful faces were to be seen here and there. The door into Klyauzov's bedroom was found to be locked. The key was in the lock on the inside.

"Evidently the criminals made their way in by the window" Psyekov observed, as they examined the door.

They went into the garden into which the bedroom window looked. The window had a gloomy, ominous air. It was covered by a faded green curtain. One corner of the curtain was slightly turned back, which made it possible to peep into the bedroom.

"Has anyone of you looked in at the window?" inquired the superintendent.

"No, your honour," said Yefrem, the gardener, a little, grey-haired old man with the face of a veteran non-commissioned officer. "No one feels like looking when they are shaking in every limb!"

"Ech, Mark Ivanitch! Mark Ivanitch!" sighed the superintendent, as he looked at the window. "I told you that you would come to a bad end! I told you, poor dear--you wouldn't listen! Dissipation leads to no good!"

"It's thanks to Yefrem," said Psyekov. "We should never have guessed it but for him. It was he who first thought that something was wrong. He came to me this morning and said: 'Why is it our master hasn't waked up for so long? He hasn't been out of his bedroom for a whole week! When he said that to me I was struck all of a heap... The thought flashed through my mind at once. He hasn't made an appearance since Saturday of last week, and to-day's Sunday. Seven days is no joke!"

"Yes, poor man," the superintendent sighed again. "A clever fellow, well-educated, and so good-hearted. There was no one like him, one may say, in company. But a rake; the kingdom of heaven be his! I'm not surprised at anything with him! Stepan," he said, addressing one of the witnesses, "ride off this minute to my house and send Andryushka to the police captain's, let him report to him. Say Mark Ivanitch has been murdered! Yes, and run to the inspector--why should he sit in comfort doing nothing? Let him come here. And you go yourself as fast as you can to the examining magistrate, Nikolay Yermolaitch, and tell him to come here. Wait a bit, I will write him a note."

The police superintendent stationed watchmen round the lodge, and went off to the steward's to have tea. Ten minutes later he was sitting on a stool, carefully nibbling lumps of sugar, and sipping tea as hot as a red-hot coal.

"There it is!..." he said to Psyekov, "there it is!... a gentleman, and a well-to-do one, too... a favourite of the gods, one may say, to use Pushkin's expression, and what has he made of it? Nothing! He gave himself up to drinking and debauchery, and... here now... he has been murdered!"

Two hours later the examining magistrate drove up. Nikolay Yermolaitch Tchubikov (that was the magistrate's name), a tall, thickset old man of sixty, had been hard at work for a quarter of a century. He was known to the whole district as an honest, intelligent, energetic man, devoted to his work. His invariable companion, assistant, and secretary, a tall young man of six and twenty, called Dyukovsky, arrived on the scene of action with him.

"Is it possible, gentlemen?" Tchubikov began, going into Psyekov's room and rapidly shaking hands with everyone. "Is it possible? Mark Ivanitch? Murdered? No, it's impossible! Imposs-i-ble!"

"There it is," sighed the superintendent

"Merciful heavens! Why I saw him only last Friday. At the fair at Tarabankovo! Saving your presence, I drank a glass of vodka with him!"

"There it is," the superintendent sighed once more.

They heaved sighs, expressed their horror, drank a glass of tea each, and went to the lodge.

"Make way!" the police inspector shouted to the crowd.

On going into the lodge the examining magistrate first of all set to work to inspect the door into the bedroom. The door turned out to be made of deal, painted yellow, and not to have been tampered with. No special traces that might have served as evidence could be found. They proceeded to break open the door.

"I beg you, gentlemen, who are not concerned, to retire," said the examining magistrate, when, after long banging and cracking, the door yielded to the axe and the chisel. "I ask this in the interests of the investigation... Inspector, admit no one!"

Tchubikov, his assistant, and the police superintendent opened the door and hesitatingly, one after the other, walked into the room. The following spectacle met their eyes. In the solitary window stood a big wooden bedstead with an immense feather bed on it. On the rumpled feather bed lay a creased and crumpled quilt. A pillow, in a cotton pillow case--also much creased, was on the floor. On a little table beside the bed lay a silver watch, and silver coins to the value of twenty kopecks. Some sulphur matches lay there too. Except the bed, the table, and a solitary chair, there was no furniture in the room. Looking under the bed, the superintendent saw two dozen empty bottles, an old straw hat, and a jar of vodka. Under the table lay one boot, covered with dust. Taking a look round the room, Tchubikov frowned and flushed crimson.

"The blackguards!" he muttered, clenching his fists.

"And where is Mark Ivanitch?" Dyukovsky asked quietly.

"I beg you not to put your spoke in," Tchubikov answered roughly. "Kindly examine the floor. This is the second case in my experience, Yevgraf Kuzmitch," he added to the police superintendent, dropping his voice. "In 1870 I had a similar case. But no doubt you remember it... The murder of the merchant Portretov. It was just the same. The blackguards murdered him, and dragged the dead body out of the window."

Tchubikov went to the window, drew the curtain aside, and cautiously pushed the window. The window opened.

"It opens, so it was not fastened... H'm there are traces on the window-sill. Do you see? Here is the trace of a knee... Some one climbed out... We shall have to inspect the window thoroughly."

"There is nothing special to be observed on the floor," said Dyukovsky. "No stains, nor scratches. The only thing I have found is a used Swedish match. Here it is. As far as I remember, Mark Ivanitch didn't smoke; in a general way he used sulphur ones, never Swedish matches. This match may serve as a clue..."

"Oh, hold your tongue, please!" cried Tchubikov, with a wave of his hand. "He keeps on about his match! I can't stand these excitable people! Instead of looking for matches, you had better examine the bed!"

On inspecting the bed, Dyukovsky reported:

"There are no stains of blood or of anything else... Nor are there any fresh rents. On the pillow there are traces of teeth. A liquid, having the smell of beer and also the taste of it, has been spilt on the quilt... The general appearance of the bed gives grounds for supposing there has been a struggle."

"I know there was a struggle without your telling me! No one asked you whether there was a struggle. Instead of looking out for a struggle you had better be..."

"One boot is here, the other one is not on the scene."

"Well, what of that?"

"Why, they must have strangled him while he was taking off his boots. He hadn't time to take the second boot off when..."

"He's off again!... And how do you know that he was strangled?"

"There are marks of teeth on the pillow. The pillow itself is very much crumpled, and has been flung to a distance of six feet from the bed."

"He argues, the chatterbox! We had better go into the garden. You had better look in the garden instead of rummaging about here... I can do that without your help."

When they went out into the garden their first task was the inspection of the grass. The grass had been trampled down under the windows. The clump of burdock against the wall under the window turned out to have been trodden on too. Dyukovsky succeeded in finding on it some broken shoots, and a little bit of wadding. On the topmost burrs, some fine threads of dark blue wool were found.

208

"What was the colour of his last suit? Dyukovsky asked Psyekov.

"It was yellow, made of canvas."

"Capital! Then it was they who were in dark blue..."

Some of the burrs were cut off and carefully wrapped up in paper. At that moment Artsybashev-Svistakovsky, the police captain, and Tyutyuev, the doctor, arrived. The police captain greeted the others, and at once proceeded to satisfy his curiosity; the doctor, a tall and extremely lean man with sunken eyes, a long nose, and a sharp chin, greeting no one and asking no questions, sat down on a stump, heaved a sigh and said:

"The Serbians are in a turmoil again! I can't make out what they want! Ah, Austria, Austria! It's your doing!"

The inspection of the window from outside yielded absolutely no result; the inspection of the grass and surrounding bushes furnished many valuable clues. Dyukovsky succeeded, for instance, in detecting a long, dark streak in the grass, consisting of stains, and stretching from the window for a good many yards into the garden. The streak ended under one of the lilac bushes in a big, brownish stain. Under the same bush was found a boot, which turned out to be the fellow to the one found in the bedroom.

"This is an old stain of blood," said Dyukovsky, examining the stain.

At the word "blood," the doctor got up and lazily took a cursory glance at the stain.

"Yes, it's blood," he muttered.

"Then he wasn't strangled since there's blood," said Tchubikov, looking malignantly at Dyukovsky.

"He was strangled in the bedroom, and here, afraid he would come to, they stabbed him with something sharp. The stain under the bush shows that he lay there for a comparatively long time, while they were trying to find some way of carrying him, or something to carry him on out of the garden."

"Well, and the boot?"

"That boot bears out my contention that he was murdered while he was taking off his boots before going to bed. He had taken off one boot, the other, that is, this boot he had only managed to get half off. While he was being dragged and shaken the boot that was only half on came off of itself..."

"What powers of deduction! Just look at him!" Tchubikov jeered. "He brings it all out so pat! And when will you learn not to put your theories forward? You had better take a little of the grass for analysis instead of arguing!"

After making the inspection and taking a plan of the locality they went off to the steward's to write a report and have lunch. At lunch they talked.

"Watch, money, and everything else... are untouched," Tchubikov began the conversation. "It is as clear as twice two makes four that the murder was committed not for mercenary motives."

"It was committed by a man of the educated class," Dyukovsky put in.

"From what do you draw that conclusion?"

"I base it on the Swedish match which the peasants about here have not learned to use yet. Such matches are only used by landowners and not by all of them. He was murdered, by the way, not by one but by three, at least: two held him while the third strangled him. Klyauzov was strong and the murderers must have known that."

"What use would his strength be to him, supposing he were asleep?"

"The murderers came upon him as he was taking off his boots. He was taking off his boots, so he was not asleep."

"It's no good making things up! You had better eat your lunch!"

"To my thinking, your honour," said Yefrem, the gardener, as he set the samovar on the table, "this vile deed was the work of no other than Nikolashka."

"Quite possible," said Psyekov.

"Who's this Nikolashka?"

"The master's valet, your honour," answered Yefrem. "Who else should it be if not he? He's a ruffian, your honour! A drunkard, and such a dissipated fellow! May the Queen of Heaven never bring the like again! He always used to fetch vodka for the master, he always used to put the master to bed... Who should it be if not he? And what's more, I venture to bring to your notice, your honour, he boasted once in a tavern, the rascal, that he would murder his master. It's all on account of Akulka, on account of a woman... He had a soldier's wife... The master took a fancy to her and got intimate with her, and he... was angered by it, to be sure. He's lolling about in the kitchen now, drunk. He's crying... making out he is grieving over the master..."

"And anyone might be angry over Akulka, certainly," said Psyekov. "She is a soldier's wife, a peasant woman, but... Mark Ivanitch might well call her Nana. There is something in her that does suggest Nana... fascinating..."

"I have seen her... I know..." said the examining magistrate, blowing his nose in a red handkerchief.

Dyukovsky blushed and dropped his eyes. The police superintendent drummed on his saucer with his fingers. The police captain coughed and rummaged in his portfolio for something. On the doctor alone the mention of Akulka and Nana appeared to produce no impression. Tchubikov ordered Nikolashka to be fetched. Nikolashka, a lanky young man with a long pock-marked nose and a hollow chest, wearing a reefer jacket that had been his master's, came into Psyekov's room and bowed down to the ground before Tchubikov. His face looked sleepy and showed traces of tears. He was drunk and could hardly stand up.

"Where is your master?" Tchubikov asked him.

"He's murdered, your honour."

As he said this Nikolashka blinked and began to cry.

"We know that he is murdered. But where is he now? Where is his body?"

"They say it was dragged out of window and buried in the garden."

"H'm... the results of the investigation are already known in the kitchen then... That's bad. My good fellow, where were you on the night when your master was killed? On Saturday, that is?"

Nikolashka raised his head, craned his neck, and pondered.

"I can't say, your honour," he said. "I was drunk and I don't remember."

"An alibi!" whispered Dyukovsky, grinning and rubbing his hands.

"Ah! And why is it there's blood under your master's window!"

Nikolashka flung up his head and pondered.

"Think a little quicker," said the police captain.

"In a minute. That blood's from a trifling matter, your honour. I killed a hen; I cut her throat very simply in the usual way, and she fluttered out of my hands and took and ran off...That's what the blood's from."

Yefrem testified that Nikolashka really did kill a hen every evening and killed it in all sorts of places, and no one had seen the half-killed hen running about the garden, though of course it could not be positively denied that it had done so.

"An alibi," laughed Dyukovsky, "and what an idiotic alibi."

"Have you had relations with Akulka?"

"Yes, I have sinned."

"And your master carried her off from you?"

"No, not at all. It was this gentleman here, Mr. Psyekov, Ivan Mihalitch, who enticed her from me, and the master took her from Ivan Mihalitch. That's how it was."

Psyekov looked confused and began rubbing his left eye. Dyukovsky fastened his eyes upon him, detected his confusion, and started. He saw on the steward's legs dark blue trousers which he had not previously noticed. The trousers reminded him of the blue threads found on the burdock. Tchubikov in his turn glanced suspiciously at Psyekov.

"You can go!" he said to Nikolashka. "And now allow me to put one question to you, Mr. Psyekov. You were here, of course, on the Saturday of last week?

"Yes, at ten o'clock I had supper with Mark Ivanitch."

"And afterwards?"

Psyekov was confused, and got up from the table.

"Afterwards... afterwards... I really don't remember," he muttered. "I had drunk a good deal on that occasion... I can't remember where and when I went to bed... Why do you all look at me like that? As though I had murdered him!"

"Where did you wake up?"

"I woke up in the servants' kitchen on the stove... They can all confirm that. How I got on to the stove I can't say..."

"Don't disturb yourself... Do you know Akulina?"

"Oh well, not particularly."

"Did she leave you for Klyauzov?"

"Yes... Yefrem, bring some more mushrooms! Will you have some tea, Yevgraf Kuzmitch?"

There followed an oppressive, painful silence that lasted for some five minutes. Dyukovsky held his tongue, and kept his piercing eyes on Psyekov's face, which gradually turned pale. The silence was broken by Tchubikov.

"We must go to the big house," he said, "and speak to the deceased's sister, Marya Ivanovna. She may give us some evidence."

Tchubikov and his assistant thanked Psyekov for the lunch, then went off to the big house. They found Klyauzov's sister, a maiden lady of five and forty, on her knees before a high family shrine of ikons. When she saw portfolios and caps adorned with cockades in her visitors' hands, she turned pale.

"First of all, I must offer an apology for disturbing your devotions, so to say," the gallant Tchubikov began with a scrape. "We have come to you with a request. You have heard, of course, already... There is a suspicion that your brother has somehow been murdered. God's will, you know... Death no one can escape, neither Tsar nor ploughman. Can you not assist us with some fact, something that will throw light?"

"Oh, do not ask me!" said Marya Ivanovna, turning whiter still, and hiding her face in her hands. "I can tell you nothing! Nothing! I implore you! I can say nothing... What can I do? Oh, no, no... not a word... of my brother! I would rather die than speak!"

Marya Ivanovna burst into tears and went away into another room. The officials looked at each other, shrugged their shoulders, and beat a retreat.

"A devil of a woman!" said Dyukovsky, swearing as they went out of the big house. "Apparently she knows something and is concealing it. And there is something peculiar in the maid-servant's expression too... You wait a bit, you devils! We will get to the bottom of it all!"

In the evening, Tchubikov and his assistant were driving home by the light of a pale-faced moon; they sat in their waggonette, summing up in their minds the incidents of the day. Both were exhausted and sat silent. Tchubikov never liked talking on the road. In spite of his talkativeness, Dyukovsky held his tongue in deference to the old man. Towards the end of the journey, however, the young man could endure the silence no longer, and began:

"That Nikolashka has had a hand in the business," he said, " non dubitandum est . One can see from his mug too what sort of a chap he is... His alibi gives him away hand and foot. There is no doubt either that he was not the instigator of the crime. He was only the stupid hired tool. Do you agree? The discreet Psyekov plays a not unimportant part in the affair too. His blue trousers, his embarrassment, his lying on the stove from fright after the murder, his alibi, and Akulka."

"Keep it up, you're in your glory! According to you, if a man knows Akulka he is the murderer. Ah, you hot-head! You ought to be sucking your bottle instead of investigating cases! You used to be running after Akulka too, does that mean that you had a hand in this business?"

"Akulka was a cook in your house for a month, too, but... I don't say anything. On that Saturday night I was playing cards with you, I saw you, or I should be after you too. The woman is not the point, my good sir. The point is the nasty, disgusting, mean feeling... The discreet young man did not like to be cut out, do you see. Vanity, do you see... He longed to be revenged. Then... His thick lips are a strong indication of sensuality. Do you remember how he smacked his lips when he compared Akulka to Nana? That he is burning with passion, the scoundrel, is beyond doubt! And so you have wounded vanity and unsatisfied passion. That's enough to lead to murder. Two of them are in our hands, but who is the third? Nikolashka and Psyekov held him. Who was it smothered him? Psyekov is timid, easily embarrassed, altogether a coward. People like Nikolashka are not equal to smothering with a pillow, they set to work with an axe or a mallet... Some third person must have smothered him, but who?"

Dyukovsky pulled his cap over his eyes, and pondered. He was silent till the waggonette had driven up to the examining magistrate's house.

"Eureka!" he said, as he went into the house, and took off his overcoat. "Eureka, Nikolay Yermolaitch! I can't understand how it is it didn't occur to me before. Do you know who the third is?"

"Do leave off, please! There's supper ready. Sit down to supper!"

Tchubikov and Dyukovsky sat down to supper. Dyukovsky poured himself out a wine-glassful of vodka, got up, stretched, and with sparkling eyes, said:

"Let me tell you then that the third person who collaborated with the scoundrel Psyekov and smothered him was a woman! Yes! I am speaking of the murdered man's sister, Marya Ivanovna!"

Tchubikov coughed over his vodka and fastened his eyes on Dyukovsky.

"Are you... not quite right? Is your head... not quite right? Does it ache?"

"I am quite well. Very good, suppose I have gone out of my mind, but how do you explain her confusion on our arrival? How do you explain her refusal to give information? Admitting that is trivial--very good! All right!--but think of the terms they were on! She detested her brother! She is an Old Believer, he was a profligate, a godless fellow... that is what has bred hatred between them! They say he succeeded in persuading her that he was an angel of Satan! He used to practise spiritualism in her presence!"

"Well, what then?"

"Don't you understand? She's an Old Believer, she murdered him through fanaticism! She has not merely slain a wicked man, a profligate, she has freed the world from Antichrist--and that she fancies is her merit, her religious achievement! Ah, you don't know these old maids, these Old Believers! You should read Dostoevsky! And what does Lyeskov say... and Petchersky! It's she, it's she, I'll stake my life on it. She smothered him! Oh, the fiendish woman! Wasn't she, perhaps, standing before the ikons when we went in to put us off the scent? 'I'll stand up and say my prayers,' she said to herself, 'they will think I am calm and don't expect them.' That's the method of all novices in crime. Dear Nikolay Yermolaitch! My dear man! Do hand this case over to me! Let me go through with it to the end! My dear fellow! I have begun it, and I will carry it through to the end."

Tchubikov shook his head and frowned.

"I am equal to sifting difficult cases myself," he said. "And it's your place not to put yourself forward. Write what is dictated to you, that is your business!"

Dyukovsky flushed crimson, walked out, and slammed the door.

"A clever fellow, the rogue," Tchubikov muttered, looking after him. "Ve-ery clever! Only inappropriately hasty. I shall have to buy him a cigar-case at the fair for a present."

Next morning a lad with a big head and a hare lip came from Klyauzovka. He gave his name as the shepherd Danilko, and furnished a very interesting piece of information.

"I had had a drop," said he. "I stayed on till midnight at my crony's. As I was going home, being drunk, I got into the river for a bathe. I was bathing and what do I see! Two men coming along the dam carrying something black. 'Tyoo!' I shouted at them. They were scared, and cut along as fast as they could go into the Makarev kitchen-gardens. Strike me dead, if it wasn't the master they were carrying!"

Towards evening of the same day Psyekov and Nikolashka were arrested and taken under guard to the district town. In the town they were put in the prison tower.

II

Twelve days passed.

It was morning. The examining magistrate, Nikolay Yermolaitch, was sitting at a green table at home, looking through the papers, relating to the "Klyauzov case"; Dyukovsky was pacing up and down the room restlessly, like a wolf in a cage.

"You are convinced of the guilt of Nikolashka and Psyekov," he said, nervously pulling at his youthful beard. "Why is it you refuse to be convinced of the guilt of Marya Ivanovna? Haven't you evidence enough?"

"I don't say that I don't believe in it. I am convinced of it, but somehow I can't believe it... There is no real evidence. It's all theoretical, as it were... Fanaticism and one thing and another..."

"And you must have an axe and bloodstained sheets!... You lawyers! Well, I will prove it to you then! Do give up your slip-shod attitude to the psychological aspect of the case. Your Marya Ivanovna ought to be in Siberia! I'll prove it. If theoretical proof is not enough for you, I have something material... It will show you how right my theory is! Only let me go about a little!"

"What are you talking about?"

"The Swedish match! Have you forgotten? I haven't forgotten it! I'll find out who struck it in the murdered man's room! It was not struck by Nikolashka, nor by Psyekov, neither of whom turned out to have matches when searched, but a third person, that is Marya Ivanovna. And I will prove it!... Only let me drive about the district, make some inquiries..."

"Oh, very well, sit down... Let us proceed to the examination."

Dyukovsky sat down to the table, and thrust his long nose into the papers.

"Bring in Nikolay Tetchov!" cried the examining magistrate.

Nikolashka was brought in. He was pale and thin as a chip. He was trembling.

"Tetchov!" began Tchubikov. "In 1879 you were convicted of theft and condemned to a term of imprisonment. In 1882 you were condemned for theft a second time, and a second time sent to prison... We know all about it..."

A look of surprise came up into Nikolashka's face. The examining magistrate's omniscience amazed him, but soon wonder was replaced by an expression of extreme distress. He broke into sobs, and asked leave to go to wash, and calm himself. He was led out.

"Bring in Psyekov!" said the examining magistrate.

Psyekov was led in. The young man's face had greatly changed during those twelve days. He was thin, pale, and wasted. There was a look of apathy in his eyes.

"Sit down, Psyekov," said Tchubikov. "I hope that to-day you will be sensible and not persist in lying as on other occasions. All this time you have denied your participation in the murder of Klyauzov, in spite of the mass of evidence against you. It is senseless. Confession is some mitigation of guilt. To-day I am talking to you for the last time. If you don't confess to-day, to-morrow it will be too late. Come, tell us..."

"I know nothing, and I don't know your evidence," whispered Psyekov.

"That's useless! Well then, allow me to tell you how it happened. On Saturday evening, you were sitting in Klyauzov's bedroom drinking vodka and beer with him." (Dyukovsky riveted his eyes on Psyekov's face, and did not remove them during the whole monologue.) "Nikolay was waiting upon you. Between twelve and one Mark Ivanitch told you he wanted to go to bed. He always did go to bed at that time. While he was taking off his boots and giving you some instructions regarding the estate, Nikolay and you at a given signal seized your intoxicated master and flung him back upon the bed. One of you sat on his feet, the other on his head. At that moment the lady, you know who, in a black dress, who had arranged with you beforehand the part she would take in the crime, came in from the passage. She picked up the pillow, and proceeded to smother him with it. During the struggle, the light went out. The woman took a box of Swedish matches out of her pocket and lighted the candle. Isn't that right? I see from your face that what I say is true. Well, to proceed... Having smothered him, and being convinced that he had ceased to breathe, Nikolay and you dragged him out of window and put him down near the burdocks. Afraid that he might regain consciousness, you struck him with something sharp. Then you carried him, and laid him for some time under a lilac bush. After resting and considering a little, you carried him... lifted him over the hurdle... Then went along the road... Then comes the dam; near the dam you were frightened by a peasant. But what is the matter with you?"

Psyekov, white as a sheet, got up, staggering.

"I am suffocating!" he said. "Very well... So be it... Only I must go... Please."

Psyekov was led out.

"At last he has admitted it!" said Tchubikov, stretching at his ease. "He has given himself away! How neatly I caught him there."

"And he didn't deny the woman in black!" said Dyukovsky, laughing. "I am awfully worried over that Swedish match, though! I can't endure it any longer. Good-bye! I am going!"

Dyukovsky put on his cap and went off. Tchubikov began interrogating Akulka.

Akulka declared that she knew nothing about it...

"I have lived with you and with nobody else!" she said.

At six o'clock in the evening Dyukovsky returned. He was more excited than ever. His hands trembled so much that he could not unbutton his overcoat. His cheeks were burning. It was evident that he had not come back without news.

" Veni, vidi, vici! " he cried, dashing into Tchubikov's room and sinking into an arm-chair. "I vow on my honour, I begin to believe in my own genius. Listen, damnation take us! Listen and wonder, old friend! It's comic and it's sad. You have three in your grasp already... haven't you? I have found a fourth murderer, or rather murderess, for it is a woman! And what a woman! I would have given ten years of my life merely to touch her shoulders. But... listen. I drove to Klyauzovka and proceeded to describe a spiral round it. On the way I visited all the shopkeepers and innkeepers, asking for Swedish matches. Everywhere I was told 'No.' I have been on my round up to now. Twenty times I lost hope, and as many times regained it. I have been on the go all day long, and only an hour ago came upon what I was looking for. A couple of miles from here they gave me a packet of a dozen boxes of matches. One box was missing... I asked at once: 'Who bought that box?' 'So-and-so. She took a fancy to them... They crackle.' My dear fellow! Nikolay Yermolaitch! What can sometimes be done by a man who has been expelled from a seminary and studied Gaboriau is beyond all conception! From to-day I shall began to respect myself!... Ough... Well, let us go!"

"Go where?"

"To her, to the fourth... We must make haste, or... I shall explode with impatience! Do you know who she is? You will never guess. The young wife of our old police superintendent, Yevgraf Kuzmitch, Olga Petrovna; that's who it is! She bought that box of matches!"

"You... you... Are you out of your mind?"

"It's very natural! In the first place she smokes, and in the second she was head over ears in love with Klyauzov. He rejected her love for the sake of an Akulka. Revenge. I remember now, I once came upon them behind the screen in the kitchen. She was cursing him, while he was smoking her cigarette and puffing the smoke into her face. But do come along; make haste, for it is getting dark already... Let us go!"

"I have not gone so completely crazy yet as to disturb a respectable, honourable woman at night for the sake of a wretched boy!"

"Honourable, respectable... You are a rag then, not an examining magistrate! I have never ventured to abuse you, but now you force me to it! You rag! you old fogey! Come, dear Nikolay Yermolaitch, I entreat you!"

The examining magistrate waved his hand in refusal and spat in disgust.

"I beg you! I beg you, not for my own sake, but in the interests of justice! I beseech you, indeed! Do me a favour, if only for once in your life!"

Dyukovsky fell on his knees.

"Nikolay Yermolaitch, do be so good! Call me a scoundrel, a worthless wretch if I am in error about that woman! It is such a case, you know! It is a case! More like a novel than a case. The fame of it will be all over Russia. They will make you examining magistrate for particularly important cases! Do understand, you unreasonable old man!"

The examining magistrate frowned and irresolutely put out his hand towards his hat.

"Well, the devil take you!" he said, "let us go."

It was already dark when the examining magistrate's waggonette rolled up to the police superintendent's door.

"What brutes we are!" said Tchubikov, as he reached for the bell. "We are disturbing people."

"Never mind, never mind, don't be frightened. We will say that one of the springs has broken."

Tchubikov and Dyukovsky were met in the doorway by a tall, plump woman of three and twenty, with eyebrows as black as pitch and full red lips. It was Olga Petrovna herself.

"Ah, how very nice," she said, smiling all over her face. "You are just in time for supper. My Yevgraf Kuzmitch is not at home... He is staying at the priest's. But we can get on without him. Sit down. Have you come from an inquiry?"

"Yes... We have broken one of our springs, you know," began Tchubikov, going into the drawing-room and sitting down in an easy-chair.

"Take her by surprise at once and overwhelm her," Dyukovsky whispered to him.

"A spring .. . er... yes... We just drove up..."

"Overwhelm her, I tell you! She will guess if you go drawing it out."

"Oh, do as you like, but spare me," muttered Tchubikov, getting up and walking to the window. "I can't! You cooked the mess, you eat it!"

"Yes, the spring," Dyukovsky began, going up to the superintendent's wife and wrinkling his long nose. "We have not come in to... er-er-er... supper, nor to see Yevgraf Kuzmitch. We have come to ask you, madam, where is Mark Ivanovitch whom you have murdered?"

"What? What Mark Ivanovitch?" faltered the superintendent's wife, and her full face was suddenly in one instant suffused with crimson. "I... don't understand."

"I ask you in the name of the law! Where is Klyauzov? We know all about it!"

"Through whom?" the superintendent's wife asked slowly, unable to face Dyukovsky's eyes.

"Kindly inform us where he is!"

"But how did you find out? Who told you?"

"We know all about it. I insist in the name of the law."

The examining magistrate, encouraged by the lady's confusion, went up to her.

"Tell us and we will go away. Otherwise we..."

"What do you want with him?"

"What is the object of such questions, madam? We ask you for information. You are trembling, confused... Yes, he has been murdered, and if you will have it, murdered by you! Your accomplices have betrayed you!"

The police superintendent's wife turned pale.

"Come along," she said quietly, wringing her hands. "He is hidden in the bath-house. Only for God's sake, don't tell my husband! I implore you! It would be too much for him."

The superintendent's wife took a big key from the wall, and led her visitors through the kitchen and the passage into the yard. It was dark in the yard. There was a drizzle of fine rain. The superintendent's wife went on ahead. Tchubikov and Dyukovsky strode after her through the long grass, breathing in the smell of wild hemp and slops, which made a squelching sound under their feet. It was a big yard. Soon there were no more pools of slops, and their feet felt ploughed land. In the darkness they saw the silhouette of trees, and among the trees a little house with a crooked chimney.

"This is the bath-house," said the superintendent's wife, "but, I implore you, do not tell anyone."

Going up to the bath-house, Tchubikov and Dyukovsky saw a large padlock on the door.

"Get ready your candle-end and matches," Tchubikov whispered to his assistant.

The superintendent's wife unlocked the padlock and let the visitors into the bath-house. Dyukovsky struck a match and lighted up the entry. In the middle of it stood a table. On the table, beside a podgy little samovar, was a soup tureen with some cold cabbage-soup in it, and a dish with traces of some sauce on it.

"Go on!"

They went into the next room, the bath-room. There, too, was a table. On the table there stood a big dish of ham, a bottle of vodka, plates, knives and forks.

"But where is he... where's the murdered man?"

"He is on the top shelf," whispered the superintendent's wife, turning paler than ever and trembling.

Dyukovsky took the candle-end in his hand and climbed up to the upper shelf. There he saw a long, human body, lying motionless on a big feather bed. The body emitted a faint snore...

"They have made fools of us, damn it all!" Dyukovsky cried. "This is not he! It is some living blockhead lying here. Hi! who are you, damnation take you!"

The body drew in its breath with a whistling sound and moved. Dyukovsky prodded it with his elbow. It lifted up its arms, stretched, and raised its head.

"Who is that poking?" a hoarse, ponderous bass voice inquired. "What do you want?"

Dyukovsky held the candle-end to the face of the unknown and uttered a shriek. In the crimson nose, in the ruffled, uncombed hair, in the pitch-black moustaches of which one was jauntily twisted and pointed insolently towards the ceiling, he recognised Cornet Klyauzov.

"You... Mark... Ivanitch! Impossible!"

The examining magistrate looked up and was dumbfounded.

"It is I, yes... And it's you, Dyukovsky! What the devil do you want here? And whose ugly mug is that down there? Holy Saints, it's the examining magistrate! How in the world did you come here?"

Klyauzov hurriedly got down and embraced Tchubikov. Olga Petrovna whisked out of the door.

"However did you come? Let's have a drink!--dash it all! Tra-ta-ti-to-tom... Let's have a drink! Who brought you here, though? How did you get to know I was here? It doesn't matter, though! Have a drink!"

Klyauzov lighted the lamp and poured out three glasses of vodka.

"The fact is, I don't understand you," said the examining magistrate, throwing out his hands. "Is it you, or not you?"

"Stop that... Do you want to give me a sermon? Don't trouble yourself! Dyukovsky boy, drink up your vodka! Friends, let us pass the... What are you staring at... ? Drink!"

"All the same, I can't understand," said the examining magistrate, mechanically drinking his vodka. "Why are you here?"

"Why shouldn't I be here, if I am comfortable here?"

Klyauzov sipped his vodka and ate some ham.

"I am staying with the superintendent's wife, as you see. In the wilds among the ruins, like some house goblin. Drink! I felt sorry for her, you know, old man! I took pity on her, and, well, I am living here in the deserted bath-house, like a hermit... I am well fed. Next week I am thinking of moving on... I've had enough of it..."

"Inconceivable!" said Dyukovsky.

"What is there inconceivable in it?"

"Inconceivable! For God's sake, how did your boot get into the garden?"

"What boot?"

"We found one of your boots in the bedroom and the other in the garden."

"And what do you want to know that for? It is not your business. But do drink, dash it all. Since you have waked me up, you may as well drink! There's an interesting tale about that boot, my boy. I didn't want to come to Olga's. I didn't feel inclined, you know, I'd had a drop too much... She came under the window and began scolding me... You know how women... as a rule. Being drunk, I up and flung my boot at her. Ha-ha!... 'Don't scold,' I said. She clambered in at the window, lighted the lamp, and gave me a good drubbing, as I was drunk. I have plenty to eat here... Love, vodka, and good things! But where are you off to? Tchubikov, where are you off to?"

The examining magistrate spat on the floor and walked out of the bath-house. Dyukovsky followed him with his head hanging. Both got into the waggonette in silence and drove off. Never had the road seemed so long and dreary. Both were silent. Tchubikov was shaking with anger all the way. Dyukovsky hid his face in his collar as though he were afraid the darkness and the drizzling rain might read his shame on his face.

On getting home the examining magistrate found the doctor, Tyutyuev, there. The doctor was sitting at the table and heaving deep sighs as he turned over the pages of the Neva .

"The things that are going on in the world," he said, greeting the examining magistrate with a melancholy smile. "Austria is at it again... and Gladstone, too, in a way..."

Tchubikov flung his hat under the table and began to tremble.

"You devil of a skeleton! Don't bother me! I've told you a thousand times over, don't bother me with your politics! It's not the time for politics! And as for you," he turned upon Dyukovsky and shook his fist at him, "as for you... I'll never forget it, as long as I live!"

"But the Swedish match, you know! How could I tell..."

"Choke yourself with your match! Go away and don't irritate me, or goodness knows what I shall do to you. Don't let me set eyes on you."

Dyukovsky heaved a sigh, took his hat, and went out.

"I'll go and get drunk!" he decided, as he went out of the gate, and he sauntered dejectedly towards the tavern.

When the superintendent's wife got home from the bath-house she found her husband in the drawing-room.

"What did the examining magistrate come about?" asked her husband.

"He came to say that they had found Klyauzov. Only fancy, they found him staying with another man's wife."

"Ah, Mark Ivanitch, Mark Ivanitch!" sighed the police superintendent, turning up his eyes. "I told you that dissipation would lead to no good! I told you so--you wouldn't heed me!"

The Duel

I

It was eight o'clock in the morning--the time when the officers, the local officials, and the visitors usually took their morning dip in the sea after the hot, stifling night, and then went into the pavilion to drink tea or coffee. Ivan Andreitch Laevsky, a thin, fair young man of twenty-eight, wearing the cap of a clerk in the Ministry of Finance and with slippers on his feet, coming down to bathe, found a number of acquaintances on the beach, and among them his friend Samoylenko, the army doctor.

With his big cropped head, short neck, his red face, his big nose, his shaggy black eyebrows and grey whiskers, his stout puffy figure and his hoarse military bass, this Samoylenko made on every newcomer the unpleasant impression of a gruff bully; but two or three days after making his acquaintance, one began to think his face extraordinarily good-natured, kind, and even handsome. In spite of his clumsiness and rough manner, he was a peaceable man, of infinite kindliness and goodness of heart, always ready to be of use. He was on familiar terms with every one in the town, lent every one money, doctored every one, made matches, patched up quarrels, arranged picnics at which he cooked shashlik and an awfully good soup of grey mullets. He was always looking after other people's affairs and trying to interest some one on their behalf, and was always delighted about something. The general opinion about him was that he was without faults of character. He had only two weaknesses: he was ashamed of his own good nature, and tried to disguise it by a surly expression and an assumed gruffness; and he liked his assistants and his soldiers to call him "Your Excellency," although he was only a civil councillor.

"Answer one question for me, Alexandr Daviditch," Laevsky began, when both he and Samoylenko were in the water up to their shoulders. "Suppose you had loved a woman and had been living with her for two or three years, and then left off caring for her, as one does, and began to feel that you had nothing in common with her. How would you behave in that case?"

"It's very simple. 'You go where you please, madam'--and that would be the end of it."

"It's easy to say that! But if she has nowhere to go? A woman with no friends or relations, without a farthing, who can't work..."

"Well? Five hundred roubles down or an allowance of twenty-five roubles a month--and nothing more. It's very simple."

"Even supposing you have five hundred roubles and can pay twenty-five roubles a month, the woman I am speaking of is an educated woman and proud. Could you really bring yourself to offer her money? And how would you do it?"

Samoylenko was going to answer, but at that moment a big wave covered them both, then broke on the beach and rolled back noisily over the shingle. The friends got out and began dressing.

"Of course, it is difficult to live with a woman if you don't love her," said Samoylenko, shaking the sand out of his boots. "But one must look at the thing humanely, Vanya. If it were my case, I should never show a sign that I did not love her, and I should go on living with her till I died."

He was at once ashamed of his own words; he pulled himself up and said:

"But for aught I care, there might be no females at all. Let them all go to the devil!"

The friends dressed and went into the pavilion. There Samoylenko was quite at home, and even had a special cup and saucer. Every morning they brought him on a tray a cup of coffee, a tall cut glass of iced water, and a tiny glass of brandy. He would first drink the brandy, then the hot coffee, then the iced water, and this must have been very nice, for after drinking it his eyes looked moist with pleasure, he would stroke his whiskers with both hands, and say, looking at the sea:

"A wonderfully magnificent view!"

After a long night spent in cheerless, unprofitable thoughts which prevented him from sleeping, and seemed to intensify the darkness and sultriness of the night, Laevsky felt listless and shattered. He felt no better for the bathe and the coffee.

"Let us go on with our talk, Alexandr Daviditch," he said. "I won't make a secret of it; I'll speak to you openly as to a friend. Things are in a bad way with Nadyezhda Fyodorovna and me... a very bad way! Forgive me for forcing my private affairs upon you, but I must speak out."

Samoylenko, who had a misgiving of what he was going to speak about, dropped his eyes and drummed with his fingers on the table.

"I've lived with her for two years and have ceased to love her," Laevsky went on; "or, rather, I realised that I never had felt any love for her... These two years have been a mistake."

It was Laevsky's habit as he talked to gaze attentively at the pink palms of his hands, to bite his nails, or to pinch his cuffs. And he did so now.

"I know very well you can't help me," he said. "But I tell you, because unsuccessful and superfluous people like me find their salvation in talking. I have to generalise about everything I do. I'm bound to look for an explanation and justification of my absurd existence in somebody else's theories, in literary types--in the idea that we, upper-class Russians, are degenerating, for instance, and so on. Last night, for example, I comforted myself by thinking all the time: 'Ah, how true Tolstoy is, how mercilessly true!' And that did me good. Yes, really, brother, he is a great writer, say what you like!"

Samoylenko, who had never read Tolstoy and was intending to do so every day of his life, was a little embarrassed, and said:

"Yes, all other authors write from imagination, but he writes straight from nature."

"My God!" sighed Laevsky; "how distorted we all are by civilisation! I fell in love with a married woman and she with me... To begin with, we had kisses, and calm evenings, and vows, and Spencer, and ideals, and interests in common... What a deception! We really ran away from her husband, but we lied to ourselves and made out that we ran away from the emptiness of the life of the educated class. We pictured our future like this: to begin with, in the Caucasus, while we were getting to know the people and the place, I would put on the Government uniform and enter the service; then at our leisure we would pick out a plot of ground, would toil in the sweat of our brow, would have a vineyard and a field, and so on. If you were in my place, or that zoologist of yours, Von Koren, you might live with Nadyezhda Fyodorovna for thirty years, perhaps, and might leave your heirs a rich vineyard and three thousand acres of maize; but I felt like a bankrupt from the first day. In the town you have insufferable heat, boredom, and no society; if you go out into the country, you fancy poisonous spiders, scorpions, or snakes lurking under every stone and behind every bush, and beyond the fields--mountains and the desert. Alien people, an alien country, a wretched form of civilisation--all that is not so easy, brother, as walking on the Nevsky Prospect in one's fur coat, arm-in-arm with Nadyezhda Fyodorovna, dreaming of the sunny South. What is needed here is a life and death struggle, and I'm not a fighting man. A wretched neurasthenic, an idle gentleman... From the first day I knew that my dreams of a life of labour and of a vineyard were worthless. As for love, I ought to tell you that living with a woman who has read Spencer and has followed you to the ends of the earth is no more interesting than living with any Anfissa or Akulina. There's the same smell of ironing, of powder, and of medicines, the same curl-papers every morning, the same self-deception."

"You can't get on in the house without an iron," said Samoylenko, blushing at Laevsky's speaking to him so openly of a lady he knew. "You are out of humour to-day, Vanya, I notice. Nadyezhda Fyodorovna is a splendid woman, highly educated, and you are a man of the highest intellect. Of course, you are not married," Samoylenko went on, glancing round at the adjacent tables, "but that's not your fault; and besides... one ought to be above conventional prejudices and rise to the level of modern ideas. I believe in free love myself, yes... But to my thinking, once you have settled together, you ought to go on living together all your life."

"Without love?"

"I will tell you directly," said Samoylenko. "Eight years ago there was an old fellow, an agent, here--a man of very great intelligence. Well, he used to say that the great thing in married life was patience. Do you hear, Vanya? Not love, but patience. Love cannot last long. You have lived two years in love, and now evidently your married life has reached the period when, in order to preserve equilibrium, so to speak, you ought to exercise all your patience..."

"You believe in your old agent; to me his words are meaningless. Your old man could be a hypocrite; he could exercise himself in the virtue of patience, and, as he did so, look upon a person he did not love as an object indispensable for his moral exercises; but I have not yet fallen so low. If I want to exercise myself in patience, I will buy dumb-bells or a frisky horse, but I'll leave human beings alone."

Samoylenko asked for some white wine with ice. When they had drunk a glass each, Laevsky suddenly asked:

"Tell me, please, what is the meaning of softening of the brain?"

"How can I explain it to you?... It's a disease in which the brain becomes softer... as it were, dissolves."

"Is it curable?"

"Yes, if the disease is not neglected. Cold douches, blisters... Something internal, too."

"Oh!... Well, you see my position; I can't live with her: it is more than I can do. While I'm with you I can be philosophical about it and smile, but at home I lose heart completely; I am so utterly miserable, that if I were told, for instance, that I should have to live another month with her, I should blow out my brains. At the same time, parting with her is out of the question. She has no friends or relations; she cannot work, and neither she nor I have any money... What could become of her? To whom could she go? There is nothing one can think of... Come, tell me, what am I to do?"

"H'm!..." growled Samoylenko, not knowing what to answer. "Does she love you?"

"Yes, she loves me in so far as at her age and with her temperament she wants a man. It would be as difficult for her to do without me as to do without her powder or her curl-papers. I am for her an indispensable, integral part of her boudoir."

Samoylenko was embarrassed.

"You are out of humour to-day, Vanya," he said. "You must have had a bad night."

"Yes, I slept badly... Altogether, I feel horribly out of sorts, brother. My head feels empty; there's a sinking at my heart, a weakness... I must run away."

"Run where?"

"There, to the North. To the pines and the mushrooms, to people and ideas... I'd give half my life to bathe now in some little stream in the province of Moscow or Tula; to feel chilly, you know, and then to stroll for three hours even with the feeblest student, and to talk and talk endlessly... And the scent of the hay! Do you remember it? And in the evening, when one walks in the garden, sounds of the piano float from the house; one hears the train passing..."

Laevsky laughed with pleasure; tears came into his eyes, and to cover them, without getting up, he stretched across the next table for the matches.

"I have not been in Russia for eighteen years," said Samoylenko. "I've forgotten what it is like. To my mind, there is not a country more splendid than the Caucasus."

"Vereshtchagin has a picture in which some men condemned to death are languishing at the bottom of a very deep well. Your magnificent Caucasus strikes me as just like that well. If I were offered the choice of a chimney-sweep in Petersburg or a prince in the Caucasus, I should choose the job of chimney-sweep."

Laevsky grew pensive. Looking at his stooping figure, at his eyes fixed dreamily at one spot, at his pale, perspiring face and sunken temples, at his bitten nails, at the slipper which had dropped off his heel, displaying a badly darned sock, Samoylenko was moved to pity, and probably because Laevsky reminded him of a helpless child, he asked:

"Is your mother living?"

"Yes, but we are on bad terms. She could not forgive me for this affair."

Samoylenko was fond of his friend. He looked upon Laevsky as a good-natured fellow, a student, a man with no nonsense about him, with whom one could drink, and laugh, and talk without reserve. What he understood in him he disliked extremely. Laevsky drank a great deal and at unsuitable times; he played cards, despised his work, lived beyond his means, frequently made use of unseemly expressions in conversation, walked about the streets in his slippers, and quarrelled with Nadyezhda Fyodorovna before other people--and Samoylenko did not like this. But the fact that Laevsky had once been a student in the Faculty of Arts, subscribed to two fat reviews, often talked so cleverly that only a few people understood him, was living with a well-educated woman--all this Samoylenko did not understand, and he liked this and respected Laevsky, thinking him superior to himself.

"There is another point," said Laevsky, shaking his head. "Only it is between ourselves. I'm concealing it from Nadyezhda Fyodorovna for the time... Don't let it out before her... I got a letter the day before yesterday, telling me that her husband has died from softening of the brain."

"The Kingdom of Heaven be his!" sighed Samoylenko. "Why are you concealing it from her?"

"To show her that letter would be equivalent to 'Come to church to be married.' And we should first have to make our relations clear. When she understands that we can't go on living together, I will show her the letter. Then there will be no danger in it."

"Do you know what, Vanya," said Samoylenko, and a sad and imploring expression came into his face, as though he were going to ask him about something very touching and were afraid of being refused. "Marry her, my dear boy!"

"Why?"

"Do your duty to that splendid woman! Her husband is dead, and so Providence itself shows you what to do!"

"But do understand, you queer fellow, that it is impossible. To marry without love is as base and unworthy of a man as to perform mass without believing in it."

"But it's your duty to."

"Why is it my duty?" Laevsky asked irritably.

"Because you took her away from her husband and made yourself responsible for her."

"But now I tell you in plain Russian, I don't love her!"

"Well, if you've no love, show her proper respect, consider her wishes..."

"'Show her respect, consider her wishes,'" Laevsky mimicked him. "As though she were some Mother Superior!... You are a poor psychologist and physiologist if you think that living with a woman one can get off with nothing but respect and consideration. What a woman thinks most of is her bedroom."

"Vanya, Vanya!" said Samoylenko, overcome with confusion.

Anton Chekhov

"You are an elderly child, a theorist, while I am an old man in spite of my years, and practical, and we shall never understand one another. We had better drop this conversation. Mustapha!" Laevsky shouted to the waiter. "What's our bill?"

"No, no..." the doctor cried in dismay, clutching Laevsky's arm. "It is for me to pay. I ordered it. Make it out to me," he cried to Mustapha.

The friends got up and walked in silence along the sea-front. When they reached the boulevard, they stopped and shook hands at parting.

"You are awfully spoilt, my friend!" Samoylenko sighed. "Fate has sent you a young, beautiful, cultured woman, and you refuse the gift, while if God were to give me a crooked old woman, how pleased I should be if only she were kind and affectionate! I would live with her in my vineyard and..."

Samoylenko caught himself up and said:

"And she might get the samovar ready for me there, the old hag."

After parting with Laevsky he walked along the boulevard. When, bulky and majestic, with a stern expression on his face, he walked along the boulevard in his snow-white tunic and superbly polished boots, squaring his chest, decorated with the Vladimir cross on a ribbon, he was very much pleased with himself, and it seemed as though the whole world were looking at him with pleasure. Without turning his head, he looked to each side and thought that the boulevard was extremely well laid out; that the young cypress-trees, the eucalyptuses, and the ugly, anemic palm-trees were very handsome and would in time give abundant shade; that the Circassians were an honest and hospitable people.

"It's strange that Laevsky does not like the Caucasus," he thought, "very strange."

Five soldiers, carrying rifles, met him and saluted him. On the right side of the boulevard the wife of a local official was walking along the pavement with her son, a schoolboy.

235

"Good-morning, Marya Konstantinovna," Samoylenko shouted to her with a pleasant smile. "Have you been to bathe? Ha, ha, ha!... My respects to Nikodim Alexandritch!"

And he went on, still smiling pleasantly, but seeing an assistant of the military hospital coming towards him, he suddenly frowned, stopped him, and asked:

"Is there any one in the hospital?"

"No one, Your Excellency."

"Eh?"

"No one, Your Excellency."

"Very well, run along..."

Swaying majestically, he made for the lemonade stall, where sat a full-bosomed old Jewess, who gave herself out to be a Georgian, and said to her as loudly as though he were giving the word of command to a regiment:

"Be so good as to give me some soda-water!"

II

Laevsky's not loving Nadyezhda Fyodorovna showed itself chiefly in the fact that everything she said or did seemed to him a lie, or equivalent to a lie, and everything he read against women and love seemed to him to apply perfectly to himself, to Nadyezhda Fyodorovna and her husband. When he returned home, she was sitting at the window, dressed and with her hair done, and with a preoccupied face was drinking coffee and turning over the leaves of a fat magazine; and he thought the drinking of coffee was not such a remarkable event that she need put on a preoccupied expression over it, and that she had been wasting her time doing her hair in a fashionable style, as there was no one here to attract and no need to be attractive. And in the magazine he saw nothing but falsity. He thought she had dressed and done her hair so as to look handsomer, and was reading in order to seem clever.

"Will it be all right for me to go to bathe to-day?" she said.

"Why? There won't be an earthquake whether you go or not, I suppose..."

"No, I only ask in case the doctor should be vexed."

"Well, ask the doctor, then; I'm not a doctor."

On this occasion what displeased Laevsky most in Nadyezhda Fyodorovna was her white open neck and the little curls at the back of her head. And he remembered that when Anna Karenin got tired of her husband, what she disliked most of all was his ears, and thought: "How true it is, how true!"

Feeling weak and as though his head were perfectly empty, he went into his study, lay down on his sofa, and covered his face with a handkerchief that he might not be bothered by the flies. Despondent and oppressive thoughts always about the same thing trailed slowly across his brain like a long string of waggons on a gloomy autumn evening, and he sank into a state of drowsy oppression. It seemed to him that he had wronged Nadyezhda Fyodorovna and her husband, and that it was through his fault that her husband had died. It seemed to him that he had sinned against his own life, which he had ruined, against the world of lofty ideas, of learning, and of work, and he conceived that wonderful world as real and possible, not on this sea-front with hungry Turks and lazy mountaineers sauntering upon it, but there in the North, where there were operas, theatres, newspapers, and all kinds of intellectual activity. One could only there--not here-- be honest, intelligent, lofty, and pure. He accused himself of having no ideal, no guiding principle in life, though he had a dim understanding now what it meant. Two years before, when he fell in love with Nadyezhda Fyodorovna, it seemed to him that he had only to go with her as his wife to the Caucasus, and he would be saved from vulgarity and emptiness; in the same way now, he was convinced that he had only to part from Nadyezhda Fyodorovna and to go to Petersburg, and he would get everything he wanted.

"Run away," he muttered to himself, sitting up and biting his nails. "Run away!"

He pictured in his imagination how he would go aboard the steamer and then would have some lunch, would drink some cold beer, would talk on deck with ladies, then would get into the train at Sevastopol and set off. Hurrah for freedom! One station after another would flash by, the air would keep growing colder and keener, then the birches and the fir-trees, then Kursk, Moscow... In the restaurants cabbage soup, mutton with kasha, sturgeon, beer, no more Asiaticism, but Russia, real Russia. The passengers in the train would talk about trade, new singers, the Franco-Russian entente ; on all sides there would be the feeling of keen, cultured, intellectual, eager life... Hasten on, on! At last Nevsky Prospect, and Great Morskaya Street, and then Kovensky Place, where he used to live at one time when he was a student, the dear grey sky, the drizzling rain, the drenched cabmen...

"Ivan Andreitch!" some one called from the next room. "Are you at home?"

"I'm here," Laevsky responded. "What do you want?"

"Papers."

Laevsky got up languidly, feeling giddy, walked into the other room, yawning and shuffling with his slippers. There, at the open window that looked into the street, stood one of his young fellow-clerks, laying out some government documents on the window-sill.

"One minute, my dear fellow," Laevsky said softly, and he went to look for the ink; returning to the window, he signed the papers without looking at them, and said: "It's hot!"

"Yes. Are you coming to-day?"

"I don't think so... I'm not quite well. Tell Sheshkovsky that I will come and see him after dinner."

The clerk went away. Laevsky lay down on his sofa again and began thinking:

"And so I must weigh all the circumstances and reflect on them.

Before I go away from here I ought to pay up my debts. I owe about two thousand roubles. I have no money... Of course, that's not important; I shall pay part now, somehow, and I shall send the rest, later, from Petersburg. The chief point is Nadyezhda Fyodorovna... First of all we must define our relations... Yes."

A little later he was considering whether it would not be better to go to Samoylenko for advice.

"I might go," he thought, "but what use would there be in it? I shall only say something inappropriate about boudoirs, about women, about what is honest or dishonest. What's the use of talking about what is honest or dishonest, if I must make haste to save my life, if I am suffocating in this cursed slavery and am killing myself?... One must realise at last that to go on leading the life I do is something so base and so cruel that everything else seems petty and trivial beside it. To run away," he muttered, sitting down, "to run away."

The deserted seashore, the insatiable heat, and the monotony of the smoky lilac mountains, ever the same and silent, everlastingly solitary, overwhelmed him with depression, and, as it were, made him drowsy and sapped his energy. He was perhaps very clever, talented, remarkably honest; perhaps if the sea and the mountains had not closed him in on all sides, he might have become an excellent Zemstvo leader, a statesman, an orator, a political writer, a saint. Who knows? If so, was it not stupid to argue whether it were honest or dishonest when a gifted and useful man--an artist or musician, for instance--to escape from prison, breaks a wall and deceives his jailers? Anything is honest when a man is in such a position.

At two o'clock Laevsky and Nadyezhda Fyodorovna sat down to dinner. When the cook gave them rice and tomato soup, Laevsky said:

"The same thing every day. Why not have cabbage soup?"

"There are no cabbages."

"It's strange. Samoylenko has cabbage soup and Marya Konstantinovna has cabbage soup, and only I am obliged to eat this mawkish mess. We can't go on like this, darling."

As is common with the vast majority of husbands and wives, not a single dinner had in earlier days passed without scenes and fault-finding between Nadyezhda Fyodorovna and Laevsky; but ever since Laevsky had made up his mind that he did not love her, he had tried to give way to Nadyezhda Fyodorovna in everything, spoke to her gently and politely, smiled, and called her "darling."

"This soup tastes like liquorice," he said, smiling; he made an effort to control himself and seem amiable, but could not refrain from saying: "Nobody looks after the housekeeping... If you are too ill or busy with reading, let me look after the cooking."

In earlier days she would have said to him, "Do by all means," or, "I see you want to turn me into a cook"; but now she only looked at him timidly and flushed crimson.

"Well, how do you feel to-day?" he asked kindly.

"I am all right to-day. There is nothing but a little weakness."

"You must take care of yourself, darling. I am awfully anxious about you."

Nadyezhda Fyodorovna was ill in some way. Samoylenko said she had intermittent fever, and gave her quinine; the other doctor, Ustimovitch, a tall, lean, unsociable man, who used to sit at home in the daytime, and in the evenings walk slowly up and down on the sea-front coughing, with his hands folded behind him and a cane stretched along his back, was of opinion that she had a female complaint, and prescribed warm compresses. In old days, when Laevsky loved her, Nadyezhda Fyodorovna's illness had excited his pity and terror; now he saw falsity even in her illness. Her yellow, sleepy face, her lustreless eyes, her apathetic expression, and the yawning that always followed her attacks of fever, and the fact that during them she lay under a shawl and looked more like a boy than a woman, and that it was close and stuffy in her room--all this, in his opinion, destroyed the illusion and was an argument against love and marriage.

The next dish given him was spinach with hard-boiled eggs, while Nadyezhda Fyodorovna, as an invalid, had jelly and milk. When with a preoccupied face she touched the jelly with a spoon and then began languidly eating it, sipping milk, and he heard her swallowing, he was possessed by such an overwhelming aversion that it made his head tingle. He recognised that such a feeling would be an insult even to a dog, but he was angry, not with himself but with Nadyezhda Fyodorovna, for arousing such a feeling, and he understood why lovers sometimes murder their mistresses. He would not murder her, of course, but if he had been on a jury now, he would have acquitted the murderer.

"Merci, darling," he said after dinner, and kissed Nadyezhda Fyodorovna on the forehead.

Going back into his study, he spent five minutes in walking to and fro, looking at his boots; then he sat down on his sofa and muttered:

"Run away, run away! We must define the position and run away!"

He lay down on the sofa and recalled again that Nadyezhda Fyodorovna's husband had died, perhaps, by his fault.

"To blame a man for loving a woman, or ceasing to love a woman, is stupid," he persuaded himself, lying down and raising his legs in order to put on his high boots. "Love and hatred are not under our control. As for her husband, maybe I was in an indirect way one of the causes of his death; but again, is it my fault that I fell in love with his wife and she with me?"

Then he got up, and finding his cap, set off to the lodgings of his colleague, Sheshkovsky, where the Government clerks met every day to play vint and drink beer.

"My indecision reminds me of Hamlet," thought Laevsky on the way. "How truly Shakespeare describes it! Ah, how truly!"

III

For the sake of sociability and from sympathy for the hard plight of newcomers without families, who, as there was not an hotel in the town, had nowhere to dine, Dr. Samoylenko kept a sort of table d'hote. At this time there were only two men who habitually dined with him: a young zoologist called Von Koren, who had come for the summer to the Black Sea to study the embryology of the medusa, and a deacon called Pobyedov, who had only just left the seminary and been sent to the town to take the duty of the old deacon who had gone away for a cure. Each of them paid twelve roubles a month for their dinner and supper, and Samoylenko made them promise to turn up at two o'clock punctually.

Von Koren was usually the first to appear. He sat down in the drawing-room in silence, and taking an album from the table, began attentively scrutinising the faded photographs of unknown men in full trousers and top-hats, and ladies in crinolines and caps. Samoylenko only remembered a few of them by name, and of those whom he had forgotten he said with a sigh: "A very fine fellow, remarkably intelligent!" When he had finished with the album, Von Koren took a pistol from the whatnot, and screwing up his left eye, took deliberate aim at the portrait of Prince Vorontsov, or stood still at the looking-glass and gazed a long time at his swarthy face, his big forehead, and his black hair, which curled like a negro's, and his shirt of dull-coloured cotton with big flowers on it like a Persian rug, and the broad leather belt he wore instead of a waistcoat. The contemplation of his own image seemed to afford him almost more satisfaction than looking at photographs or playing with the pistols. He was very well satisfied with his face, and his becomingly clipped beard, and the broad shoulders, which were unmistakable evidence of his excellent health and physical strength. He was satisfied, too, with his stylish get-up, from the cravat, which matched the colour of his shirt, down to his brown boots.

While he was looking at the album and standing before the glass, at that moment, in the kitchen and in the passage near, Samoylenko, without his coat and waistcoat, with his neck bare, excited and bathed in perspiration, was bustling about the tables, mixing the salad, or making some sauce, or preparing meat, cucumbers, and onion for the cold soup, while he glared fiercely at the orderly who was helping him, and brandished first a knife and then a spoon at him.

"Give me the vinegar!" he said. "That's not the vinegar--it's the salad oil!" he shouted, stamping. "Where are you off to, you brute?"

"To get the butter, Your Excellency," answered the flustered orderly in a cracked voice.

"Make haste; it's in the cupboard! And tell Daria to put some fennel in the jar with the cucumbers! Fennel! Cover the cream up, gaping laggard, or the flies will get into it!"

And the whole house seemed resounding with his shouts. When it was ten or fifteen minutes to two the deacon would come in; he was a lanky young man of twenty-two, with long hair, with no beard and a hardly perceptible moustache. Going into the drawing-room, he crossed himself before the ikon, smiled, and held out his hand to Von Koren.

"Good-morning," the zoologist said coldly. "Where have you been?"

"I've been catching sea-gudgeon in the harbour."

"Oh, of course... Evidently, deacon, you will never be busy with work."

"Why not? Work is not like a bear; it doesn't run off into the woods," said the deacon, smiling and thrusting his hands into the very deep pockets of his white cassock.

"There's no one to whip you!" sighed the zoologist.

Another fifteen or twenty minutes passed and they were not called to dinner, and they could still hear the orderly running into the kitchen and back again, noisily treading with his boots, and Samoylenko shouting:

"Put it on the table! Where are your wits? Wash it first."

The famished deacon and Von Koren began tapping on the floor with their heels, expressing in this way their impatience like the audience at a theatre. At last the door opened and the harassed orderly announced that dinner was ready! In the dining-room they were met by Samoylenko, crimson in the face, wrathful, perspiring from the heat of the kitchen; he looked at them furiously, and with an expression of horror, took the lid off the soup tureen and helped each of them to a plateful; and only when he was convinced that they were eating it with relish and liked it, he gave a sigh of relief and settled himself in his deep arm-chair. His face looked blissful and his eyes grew moist... He deliberately poured himself out a glass of vodka and said:

"To the health of the younger generation."

After his conversation with Laevsky, from early morning till dinner Samoylenko had been conscious of a load at his heart, although he was in the best of humours; he felt sorry for Laevsky and wanted to help him. After drinking a glass of vodka before the soup, he heaved a sigh and said:

"I saw Vanya Laevsky to-day. He is having a hard time of it, poor fellow! The material side of life is not encouraging for him, and the worst of it is all this psychology is too much for him. I'm sorry for the lad."

"Well, that is a person I am not sorry for," said Von Koren. "If that charming individual were drowning, I would push him under with a stick and say, 'Drown, brother, drown away'..."

"That's untrue. You wouldn't do it."

"Why do you think that?" The zoologist shrugged his shoulders. "I'm just as capable of a good action as you are."

"Is drowning a man a good action?" asked the deacon, and he laughed.

"Laevsky? Yes."

"I think there is something amiss with the soup..." said Samoylenko, anxious to change the conversation.

"Laevsky is absolutely pernicious and is as dangerous to society as the cholera microbe," Von Koren went on. "To drown him would be a service."

"It does not do you credit to talk like that about your neighbour. Tell us: what do you hate him for?"

"Don't talk nonsense, doctor. To hate and despise a microbe is stupid, but to look upon everybody one meets without distinction as one's neighbour, whatever happens--thanks very much, that is equivalent to giving up criticism, renouncing a straightforward attitude to people, washing one's hands of responsibility, in fact! I consider your Laevsky a blackguard; I do not conceal it, and I am perfectly conscientious in treating him as such. Well, you look upon him as your neighbour--and you may kiss him if you like: you look upon him as your neighbour, and that means that your attitude to him is the same as to me and to the deacon; that is no attitude at all. You are equally indifferent to all."

"To call a man a blackguard!" muttered Samoylenko, frowning with distaste--"that is so wrong that I can't find words for it!"

"People are judged by their actions," Von Koren continued. "Now you decide, deacon... I am going to talk to you, deacon. Mr. Laevsky's career lies open before you, like a long Chinese puzzle, and you can read it from beginning to end. What has he been doing these two years that he has been living here? We will reckon his doings on our fingers. First, he has taught the inhabitants of the town to play vint : two years ago that game was unknown here; now they all play it from morning till late at night, even the women and the boys. Secondly, he has taught the residents to drink beer, which was not known here either; the inhabitants are indebted to him for the knowledge of various sorts of spirits, so that now they can distinguish Kospelov's vodka from Smirnov's No. 21, blindfold. Thirdly, in former days, people here made love to other men's wives in secret, from the same motives as thieves steal in secret and not openly; adultery was considered something they were ashamed to make a public display of. Laevsky has come as a pioneer in that line; he lives with another man's wife openly... Fourthly..."

Von Koren hurriedly ate up his soup and gave his plate to the orderly.

"I understood Laevsky from the first month of our acquaintance," he went on, addressing the deacon. "We arrived here at the same time. Men like him are very fond of friendship, intimacy, solidarity, and all the rest of it, because they always want company for vint , drinking, and eating; besides, they are talkative and must have listeners. We made friends--that is, he turned up every day, hindered me working, and indulged in confidences in regard to his mistress. From the first he struck me by his exceptional falsity, which simply made me sick. As a friend I pitched into him, asking him why he drank too much, why he lived beyond his means and got into debt, why he did nothing and read nothing, why he had so little culture and so little knowledge; and in answer to all my questions he used to smile bitterly, sigh, and say: 'I am a failure, a superfluous man'; or: 'What do you expect, my dear fellow, from us, the debris of the serf-owning class?' or: 'We are degenerate...' Or he would begin a long rigmarole about Onyegin, Petchorin, Byron's Cain, and Bazarov, of whom he would say: 'They are our fathers in flesh and in spirit.' So we are to understand that it was not his fault that Government envelopes lay unopened in his office for weeks together, and that he drank and taught others to drink, but Onyegin, Petchorin, and Turgenev, who had invented the failure and the superfluous man, were responsible for it. The cause of his extreme dissoluteness and unseemliness lies, do you see, not in himself, but somewhere outside in space. And so--an ingenious idea!--it is not only he who is dissolute, false, and disgusting, but we... 'we men of the eighties,' 'we the spiritless, nervous offspring of the serf-owning class'; 'civilisation has crippled us'... in fact, we are to understand that such a great man as Laevsky is great even in his fall: that his dissoluteness, his lack of culture and of moral purity, is a phenomenon of natural history, sanctified by inevitability; that the causes of it are world-wide, elemental; and that we ought to hang up a lamp before Laevsky, since he is the fated victim of the age, of influences, of heredity, and so on.

All the officials and their ladies were in ecstasies when they listened to him, and I could not make out for a long time what sort of man I had to deal with, a cynic or a clever rogue. Such types as he, on the surface intellectual with a smattering of education and a great deal of talk about their own nobility, are very clever in posing as exceptionally complex natures."

"Hold your tongue!" Samoylenko flared up. "I will not allow a splendid fellow to be spoken ill of in my presence!"

"Don't interrupt, Alexandr Daviditch," said Von Koren coldly; "I am just finishing. Laevsky is by no means a complex organism. Here is his moral skeleton: in the morning, slippers, a bathe, and coffee; then till dinner-time, slippers, a constitutional, and conversation; at two o'clock slippers, dinner, and wine; at five o'clock a bathe, tea and wine, then vint and lying; at ten o'clock supper and wine; and after midnight sleep and la femme . His existence is confined within this narrow programme like an egg within its shell. Whether he walks or sits, is angry, writes, rejoices, it may all be reduced to wine, cards, slippers, and women. Woman plays a fatal, overwhelming part in his life. He tells us himself that at thirteen he was in love; that when he was a student in his first year he was living with a lady who had a good influence over him, and to whom he was indebted for his musical education. In his second year he bought a prostitute from a brothel and raised her to his level--that is, took her as his kept mistress, and she lived with him for six months and then ran away back to the brothel-keeper, and her flight caused him much spiritual suffering. Alas! his sufferings were so great that he had to leave the university and spend two years at home doing nothing. But this was all for the best. At home he made friends with a widow who advised him to leave the Faculty of Jurisprudence and go into the Faculty of Arts. And so he did. When he had taken his degree, he fell passionately in love with his present... what's her name?... married lady, and was obliged to flee with her here to the Caucasus for the sake of his ideals, he would have us believe, seeing that... to-morrow, if not to-day, he will be tired of her and flee back again to Petersburg, and that, too, will be for the sake of his ideals."

"How do you know?" growled Samoylenko, looking angrily at the zoologist. "You had better eat your dinner."

The next course consisted of boiled mullet with Polish sauce. Samoylenko helped each of his companions to a whole mullet and poured out the sauce with his own hand. Two minutes passed in silence.

"Woman plays an essential part in the life of every man," said the deacon. "You can't help that."

"Yes, but to what degree? For each of us woman means mother, sister, wife, friend. To Laevsky she is everything, and at the same time nothing but a mistress. She--that is, cohabitation with her-- is the happiness and object of his life; he is gay, sad, bored, disenchanted--on account of woman; his life grows disagreeable --woman is to blame; the dawn of a new life begins to glow, ideals turn up--and again look for the woman... He only derives enjoyment from books and pictures in which there is woman. Our age is, to his thinking, poor and inferior to the forties and the sixties only because we do not know how to abandon ourselves obviously to the passion and ecstasy of love. These voluptuaries must have in their brains a special growth of the nature of sarcoma, which stifles the brain and directs their whole psychology. Watch Laevsky when he is sitting anywhere in company. You notice: when one raises any general question in his presence, for instance, about the cell or instinct, he sits apart, and neither speaks nor listens; he looks languid and disillusioned; nothing has any interest for him, everything is vulgar and trivial. But as soon as you speak of male and female--for instance, of the fact that the female spider, after fertilisation, devours the male--his eyes glow with curiosity, his face brightens, and the man revives, in fact. All his thoughts, however noble, lofty, or neutral they may be, they all have one point of resemblance. You walk along the street with him and meet a donkey, for instance... 'Tell me, please,' he asks, 'what would happen if you mated a donkey with a camel?' And his dreams! Has he told you of his dreams? It is magnificent! First, he dreams that he is married to the moon, then that he is summoned before the police and ordered to live with a guitar..."

The deacon burst into resounding laughter; Samoylenko frowned and wrinkled up his face angrily so as not to laugh, but could not restrain himself, and laughed.

"And it's all nonsense!" he said, wiping his tears. "Yes, by Jove, it's nonsense!"

IV

The deacon was very easily amused, and laughed at every trifle till he got a stitch in his side, till he was helpless. It seemed as though he only liked to be in people's company because there was a ridiculous side to them, and because they might be given ridiculous nicknames. He had nicknamed Samoylenko "the tarantula," his orderly "the drake," and was in ecstasies when on one occasion Von Koren spoke of Laevsky and Nadyezhda Fyodorovna as "Japanese monkeys." He watched people's faces greedily, listened without blinking, and it could be seen that his eyes filled with laughter and his face was tense with expectation of the moment when he could let himself go and burst into laughter.

"He is a corrupt and depraved type," the zoologist continued, while the deacon kept his eyes riveted on his face, expecting he would say something funny. "It is not often one can meet with such a nonentity. In body he is inert, feeble, prematurely old, while in intellect he differs in no respect from a fat shopkeeper's wife who does nothing but eat, drink, and sleep on a feather-bed, and who keeps her coachman as a lover."

The deacon began guffawing again.

"Don't laugh, deacon," said Von Koren. "It grows stupid, at last. I should not have paid attention to his insignificance," he went on, after waiting till the deacon had left off laughing; "I should have passed him by if he were not so noxious and dangerous. His noxiousness lies first of all in the fact that he has great success with women, and so threatens to leave descendants--that is, to present the world with a dozen Laevskys as feeble and as depraved as himself. Secondly, he is in the highest degree contaminating. I have spoken to you already of vint and beer. In another year or two he will dominate the whole Caucasian coast. You know how the mass, especially its middle stratum, believe in intellectuality, in a university education, in gentlemanly manners, and in literary language. Whatever filthy thing he did, they would all believe that it was as it should be, since he is an intellectual man, of liberal ideas and university education. What is more, he is a failure, a superfluous man, a neurasthenic, a victim of the age, and that means he can do anything. He is a charming fellow, a regular good sort, he is so genuinely indulgent to human weaknesses; he is compliant, accommodating, easy and not proud; one can drink with him and gossip and talk evil of people... The masses, always inclined to anthropomorphism in religion and morals, like best of all the little gods who have the same weaknesses as themselves. Only think what a wide field he has for contamination! Besides, he is not a bad actor and is a clever hypocrite, and knows very well how to twist things round. Only take his little shifts and dodges, his attitude to civilisation, for instance. He has scarcely sniffed at civilisation, yet: 'Ah, how we have been crippled by civilisation! Ah, how I envy those savages, those children of nature, who know nothing of civilisation!' We are to understand, you see, that at one time, in ancient days, he has been devoted to civilisation with his whole soul, has served it, has sounded it to its depths, but it has exhausted him, disillusioned him, deceived him; he is a Faust, do you see?--a second Tolstoy... As for Schopenhauer and Spencer, he treats them like small boys and slaps them on the shoulder in a fatherly way: 'Well, what do you say, old Spencer?' He has not read Spencer, of course, but how charming he is when with light, careless irony he says of his lady friend: 'She has read Spencer!' And they all listen to him, and no one cares to understand that this charlatan has not the right to kiss the sole of Spencer's foot, let alone speaking about him in that tone! Sapping the foundations of civilisation, of authority, of other people's altars, spattering them with filth, winking jocosely at them only to justify and conceal one's own rottenness and moral poverty is only possible for a very vain, base, and nasty creature."

"I don't know what it is you expect of him, Kolya," said Samoylenko, looking at the zoologist, not with anger now, but with a guilty air. "He is a man the same as every one else. Of course, he has his weaknesses, but he is abreast of modern ideas, is in the service, is of use to his country. Ten years ago there was an old fellow serving as agent here, a man of the greatest intelligence... and he used to say..."

"Nonsense, nonsense!" the zoologist interrupted. "You say he is in the service; but how does he serve? Do you mean to tell me that things have been done better because he is here, and the officials are more punctual, honest, and civil? On the contrary, he has only sanctioned their slackness by his prestige as an intellectual university man. He is only punctual on the 20th of the month, when he gets his salary; on the other days he lounges about at home in slippers and tries to look as if he were doing the Government a great service by living in the Caucasus. No, Alexandr Daviditch, don't stick up for him. You are insincere from beginning to end. If you really loved him and considered him your neighbour, you would above all not be indifferent to his weaknesses, you would not be indulgent to them, but for his own sake would try to make him innocuous."

"That is?"

"Innocuous. Since he is incorrigible, he can only be made innocuous in one way..." Von Koren passed his finger round his throat. "Or he might be drowned...", he added. "In the interests of humanity and in their own interests, such people ought to be destroyed. They certainly ought."

"What are you saying?" muttered Samoylenko, getting up and looking with amazement at the zoologist's calm, cold face. "Deacon, what is he saying? Why--are you in your senses?"

"I don't insist on the death penalty," said Von Koren. "If it is proved that it is pernicious, devise something else. If we can't destroy Laevsky, why then, isolate him, make him harmless, send him to hard labour."

"What are you saying!" said Samoylenko in horror. "With pepper, with pepper," he cried in a voice of despair, seeing that the deacon was eating stuffed aubergines without pepper. "You with your great intellect, what are you saying! Send our friend, a proud intellectual man, to penal servitude!"

"Well, if he is proud and tries to resist, put him in fetters!"

Samoylenko could not utter a word, and only twiddled his fingers; the deacon looked at his flabbergasted and really absurd face, and laughed.

"Let us leave off talking of that," said the zoologist. "Only remember one thing, Alexandr Daviditch: primitive man was preserved from such as Laevsky by the struggle for existence and by natural selection; now our civilisation has considerably weakened the struggle and the selection, and we ought to look after the destruction of the rotten and worthless for ourselves; otherwise, when the Laevskys multiply, civilisation will perish and mankind will degenerate utterly. It will be our fault."

"If it depends on drowning and hanging," said Samoylenko, "damnation take your civilisation, damnation take your humanity! Damnation take it! I tell you what: you are a very learned and intelligent man and the pride of your country, but the Germans have ruined you. Yes, the Germans! The Germans!"

Since Samoylenko had left Dorpat, where he had studied medicine, he had rarely seen a German and had not read a single German book, but, in his opinion, every harmful idea in politics or science was due to the Germans. Where he had got this notion he could not have said himself, but he held it firmly.

"Yes, the Germans!" he repeated once more. "Come and have some tea."

All three stood up, and putting on their hats, went out into the little garden, and sat there under the shade of the light green maples, the pear-trees, and a chestnut-tree. The zoologist and the deacon sat on a bench by the table, while Samoylenko sank into a deep wicker chair with a sloping back. The orderly handed them tea, jam, and a bottle of syrup.

It was very hot, thirty degrees Reaumur in the shade. The sultry air was stagnant and motionless, and a long spider-web, stretching from the chestnut-tree to the ground, hung limply and did not stir.

The deacon took up the guitar, which was constantly lying on the ground near the table, tuned it, and began singing softly in a thin voice:

"'Gathered round the tavern were the seminary lads,'"

but instantly subsided, overcome by the heat, mopped his brow and glanced upwards at the blazing blue sky. Samoylenko grew drowsy; the sultry heat, the stillness and the delicious after-dinner languor, which quickly pervaded all his limbs, made him feel heavy and sleepy; his arms dropped at his sides, his eyes grew small, his head sank on his breast. He looked with almost tearful tenderness at Von Koren and the deacon, and muttered:

"The younger generation... A scientific star and a luminary of the Church... I shouldn't wonder if the long-skirted alleluia will be shooting up into a bishop; I dare say I may come to kissing his hand... Well... please God..."

Soon a snore was heard. Von Koren and the deacon finished their tea and went out into the street.

"Are you going to the harbour again to catch sea-gudgeon?" asked the zoologist.

"No, it's too hot."

"Come and see me. You can pack up a parcel and copy something for me. By the way, we must have a talk about what you are to do. You must work, deacon. You can't go on like this."

"Your words are just and logical," said the deacon. "But my laziness finds an excuse in the circumstances of my present life. You know yourself that an uncertain position has a great tendency to make people apathetic. God only knows whether I have been sent here for a time or permanently. I am living here in uncertainty, while my wife is vegetating at her father's and is missing me. And I must confess my brain is melting with the heat."

"That's all nonsense," said the zoologist. "You can get used to the heat, and you can get used to being without the deaconess. You mustn't be slack; you must pull yourself together."

V

Nadyezhda Fyodorovna went to bathe in the morning, and her cook, Olga, followed her with a jug, a copper basin, towels, and a sponge. In the bay stood two unknown steamers with dirty white funnels, obviously foreign cargo vessels. Some men dressed in white and wearing white shoes were walking along the harbour, shouting loudly in French, and were answered from the steamers. The bells were ringing briskly in the little church of the town.

"To-day is Sunday!" Nadyezhda Fyodorovna remembered with pleasure.

She felt perfectly well, and was in a gay holiday humour. In a new loose-fitting dress of coarse thick tussore silk, and a big wide-brimmed straw hat which was bent down over her ears, so that her face looked out as though from a basket, she fancied she looked very charming. She thought that in the whole town there was only one young, pretty, intellectual woman, and that was herself, and that she was the only one who knew how to dress herself cheaply, elegantly, and with taste. That dress, for example, cost only twenty-two roubles, and yet how charming it was! In the whole town she was the only one who could be attractive, while there were numbers of men, so they must all, whether they would or not, be envious of Laevsky.

She was glad that of late Laevsky had been cold to her, reserved and polite, and at times even harsh and rude; in the past she had met all his outbursts, all his contemptuous, cold or strange incomprehensible glances, with tears, reproaches, and threats to leave him or to starve herself to death; now she only blushed, looked guiltily at him, and was glad he was not affectionate to her. If he had abused her, threatened her, it would have been better and pleasanter, since she felt hopelessly guilty towards him. She felt she was to blame, in the first place, for not sympathising with the dreams of a life of hard work, for the sake of which he had given up Petersburg and had come here to the Caucasus, and she was convinced that he had been angry with her of late for precisely that. When she was travelling to the Caucasus, it seemed that she would find here on the first day a cosy nook by the sea, a snug little garden with shade, with birds, with little brooks, where she could grow flowers and vegetables, rear ducks and hens, entertain her neighbours, doctor poor peasants and distribute little books amongst them. It had turned out that the Caucasus was nothing but bare mountains, forests, and huge valleys, where it took a long time and a great deal of effort to find anything and settle down; that there were no neighbours of any sort; that it was very hot and one might be robbed. Laevsky had been in no hurry to obtain a piece of land; she was glad of it, and they seemed to be in a tacit compact never to allude to a life of hard work. He was silent about it, she thought, because he was angry with her for being silent about it.

In the second place, she had without his knowledge during those two years bought various trifles to the value of three hundred roubles at Atchmianov's shop. She had bought the things by degrees, at one time materials, at another time silk or a parasol, and the debt had grown imperceptibly.

"I will tell him about it to-day...", she used to decide, but at once reflected that in Laevsky's present mood it would hardly be convenient to talk to him of debts.

Thirdly, she had on two occasions in Laevsky's absence received a visit from Kirilin, the police captain: once in the morning when Laevsky had gone to bathe, and another time at midnight when he was playing cards. Remembering this, Nadyezhda Fyodorovna flushed crimson, and looked round at the cook as though she might overhear her thoughts. The long, insufferably hot, wearisome days, beautiful languorous evenings and stifling nights, and the whole manner of living, when from morning to night one is at a loss to fill up the useless hours, and the persistent thought that she was the prettiest young woman in the town, and that her youth was passing and being wasted, and Laevsky himself, though honest and idealistic, always the same, always lounging about in his slippers, biting his nails, and wearying her with his caprices, led by degrees to her becoming possessed by desire, and as though she were mad, she thought of nothing else day and night. Breathing, looking, walking, she felt nothing but desire. The sound of the sea told her she must love; the darkness of evening-- the same; the mountains--the same... And when Kirilin began paying her attentions, she had neither the power nor the wish to resist, and surrendered to him...

Now the foreign steamers and the men in white reminded her for some reason of a huge hall; together with the shouts of French she heard the strains of a waltz, and her bosom heaved with unaccountable delight. She longed to dance and talk French.

She reflected joyfully that there was nothing terrible about her infidelity. Her soul had no part in her infidelity; she still loved Laevsky, and that was proved by the fact that she was jealous of him, was sorry for him, and missed him when he was away. Kirilin had turned out to be very mediocre, rather coarse though handsome; everything was broken off with him already and there would never be anything more. What had happened was over; it had nothing to do with any one, and if Laevsky found it out he would not believe in it.

There was only one bathing-house for ladies on the sea-front; men bathed under the open sky. Going into the bathing-house, Nadyezhda Fyodorovna found there an elderly lady, Marya Konstantinovna

Bityugov, and her daughter Katya, a schoolgirl of fifteen; both of them were sitting on a bench undressing. Marya Konstantinovna was a good-natured, enthusiastic, and genteel person, who talked in a drawling and pathetic voice. She had been a governess until she was thirty-two, and then had married Bityugov, a Government official--a bald little man with his hair combed on to his temples and with a very meek disposition. She was still in love with him, was jealous, blushed at the word "love," and told every one she was very happy.

"My dear," she cried enthusiastically, on seeing Nadyezhda Fyodorovna, assuming an expression which all her acquaintances called "almond-oily." "My dear, how delightful that you have come! We'll bathe together --that's enchanting!"

Olga quickly flung off her dress and chemise, and began undressing her mistress.

"It's not quite so hot to-day as yesterday?" said Nadyezhda Fyodorovna, shrinking at the coarse touch of the naked cook. "Yesterday I almost died of the heat."

"Oh, yes, my dear; I could hardly breathe myself. Would you believe it? I bathed yesterday three times! Just imagine, my dear, three times! Nikodim Alexandritch was quite uneasy."

"Is it possible to be so ugly?" thought Nadyezhda Fyodorovna, looking at Olga and the official's wife; she glanced at Katya and thought: "The little girl's not badly made."

"Your Nikodim Alexandritch is very charming!" she said. "I'm simply in love with him."

"Ha, ha, ha!" cried Marya Konstantinovna, with a forced laugh; "that's quite enchanting."

Free from her clothes, Nadyezhda Fyodorovna felt a desire to fly. And it seemed to her that if she were to wave her hands she would fly upwards. When she was undressed, she noticed that Olga looked scornfully at her white body. Olga, a young soldier's wife, was living with her lawful husband, and so considered herself superior to her mistress. Marya Konstantinovna and Katya were afraid of her, and did not respect her. This was disagreeable, and to raise herself in their opinion, Nadyezhda Fyodorovna said:

"At home, in Petersburg, summer villa life is at its height now. My husband and I have so many friends! We ought to go and see them."

"I believe your husband is an engineer?" said Marya Konstantinovna timidly.

"I am speaking of Laevsky. He has a great many acquaintances. But unfortunately his mother is a proud aristocrat, not very intelligent..."

Nadyezhda Fyodorovna threw herself into the water without finishing; Marya Konstantinovna and Katya made their way in after her.

"There are so many conventional ideas in the world," Nadyezhda Fyodorovna went on, "and life is not so easy as it seems."

Marya Konstantinovna, who had been a governess in aristocratic families and who was an authority on social matters, said:

"Oh yes! Would you believe me, my dear, at the Garatynskys' I was expected to dress for lunch as well as for dinner, so that, like an actress, I received a special allowance for my wardrobe in addition to my salary."

She stood between Nadyezhda Fyodorovna and Katya as though to screen her daughter from the water that washed the former.

Through the open doors looking out to the sea they could see some one swimming a hundred paces from their bathing-place.

"Mother, it's our Kostya," said Katya.

"Ach, ach!" Marya Konstantinovna cackled in her dismay. "Ach, Kostya!" she shouted, "Come back! Kostya, come back!"

Kostya, a boy of fourteen, to show off his prowess before his mother and sister, dived and swam farther, but began to be exhausted and hurried back, and from his strained and serious face it could be seen that he could not trust his own strength.

"The trouble one has with these boys, my dear!" said Marya Konstantinovna, growing calmer. "Before you can turn round, he will break his neck. Ah, my dear, how sweet it is, and yet at the same time how difficult, to be a mother! One's afraid of everything."

Nadyezhda Fyodorovna put on her straw hat and dashed out into the open sea. She swam some thirty feet and then turned on her back. She could see the sea to the horizon, the steamers, the people on the sea-front, the town; and all this, together with the sultry heat and the soft, transparent waves, excited her and whispered that she must live, live... A sailing-boat darted by her rapidly and vigorously, cleaving the waves and the air; the man sitting at the helm looked at her, and she liked being looked at...

After bathing, the ladies dressed and went away together.

"I have fever every alternate day, and yet I don't get thin," said Nadyezhda Fyodorovna, licking her lips, which were salt from the bathe, and responding with a smile to the bows of her acquaintances. "I've always been plump, and now I believe I'm plumper than ever."

"That, my dear, is constitutional. If, like me, one has no constitutional tendency to stoutness, no diet is of any use... But you've wetted your hat, my dear."

"It doesn't matter; it will dry."

Nadyezhda Fyodorovna saw again the men in white who were walking on the sea-front and talking French; and again she felt a sudden thrill of joy, and had a vague memory of some big hall in which she had once danced, or of which, perhaps, she had once dreamed. And something at the bottom of her soul dimly and obscurely whispered to her that she was a pretty, common, miserable, worthless woman...

Marya Konstantinovna stopped at her gate and asked her to come in and sit down for a little while.

"Come in, my dear," she said in an imploring voice, and at the same time she looked at Nadyezhda Fyodorovna with anxiety and hope; perhaps she would refuse and not come in!

"With pleasure," said Nadyezhda Fyodorovna, accepting. "You know how I love being with you!"

And she went into the house. Marya Konstantinovna sat her down and gave her coffee, regaled her with milk rolls, then showed her photographs of her former pupils, the Garatynskys, who were by now married. She showed her, too, the examination reports of Kostya and Katya. The reports were very good, but to make them seem even better, she complained, with a sigh, how difficult the lessons at school were now... She made much of her visitor, and was sorry for her, though at the same time she was harassed by the thought that Nadyezhda Fyodorovna might have a corrupting influence on the morals of Kostya and Katya, and was glad that her Nikodim Alexandritch was not at home. Seeing that in her opinion all men are fond of "women like that," Nadyezhda Fyodorovna might have a bad effect on Nikodim Alexandritch too.

As she talked to her visitor, Marya Konstantinovna kept remembering that they were to have a picnic that evening, and that Von Koren had particularly begged her to say nothing about it to the "Japanese monkeys"--that is, Laevsky and Nadyezhda Fyodorovna; but she dropped a word about it unawares, crimsoned, and said in confusion:

"I hope you will come too!"

VI

It was agreed to drive about five miles out of town on the road to the south, to stop near a duhan at the junction of two streams --the Black River and the Yellow River--and to cook fish soup. They started out soon after five. Foremost of the party in a char-a-banc drove Samoylenko and Laevsky; they were followed by Marya Konstantinovna, Nadyezhda Fyodorovna, Katya and Kostya, in a coach with three horses, carrying with them the crockery and a basket with provisions. In the next carriage came the police captain, Kirilin, and the young Atchmianov, the son of the shopkeeper to whom Nadyezhda Fyodorovna owed three hundred roubles; opposite them, huddled up on the little seat with his feet tucked under him, sat Nikodim Alexandritch, a neat little man with hair combed on to his temples. Last of all came Von Koren and the deacon; at the deacon's feet stood a basket of fish.

"R-r-right!" Samoylenko shouted at the top of his voice when he met a cart or a mountaineer riding on a donkey.

"In two years' time, when I shall have the means and the people ready, I shall set off on an expedition," Von Koren was telling the deacon. "I shall go by the sea-coast from Vladivostok to the Behring Straits, and then from the Straits to the mouth of the Yenisei. We shall make the map, study the fauna and the flora, and make detailed geological, anthropological, and ethnographical researches. It depends upon you to go with me or not."

"It's impossible," said the deacon.

"Why?"

"I'm a man with ties and a family."

"Your wife will let you go; we will provide for her. Better still if you were to persuade her for the public benefit to go into a nunnery; that would make it possible for you to become a monk, too, and join the expedition as a priest. I can arrange it for you."

The deacon was silent.

"Do you know your theology well?" asked the zoologist.

"No, rather badly."

"H'm!... I can't give you any advice on that score, because I don't know much about theology myself. You give me a list of books you need, and I will send them to you from Petersburg in the winter. It will be necessary for you to read the notes of religious travellers, too; among them are some good ethnologists and Oriental scholars. When you are familiar with their methods, it will be easier for you to set to work. And you needn't waste your time till you get the books; come to me, and we will study the compass and go through a course of meteorology. All that's indispensable."

"To be sure..." muttered the deacon, and he laughed. "I was trying to get a place in Central Russia, and my uncle, the head priest, promised to help me. If I go with you I shall have troubled them for nothing."

"I don't understand your hesitation. If you go on being an ordinary deacon, who is only obliged to hold a service on holidays, and on the other days can rest from work, you will be exactly the same as you are now in ten years' time, and will have gained nothing but a beard and moustache; while on returning from this expedition in ten years' time you will be a different man, you will be enriched by the consciousness that something has been done by you."

From the ladies' carriage came shrieks of terror and delight. The carriages were driving along a road hollowed in a literally overhanging precipitous cliff, and it seemed to every one that they were galloping along a shelf on a steep wall, and that in a moment the carriages would drop into the abyss. On the right stretched the sea; on the left was a rough brown wall with black blotches and red veins and with climbing roots; while on the summit stood shaggy fir-trees bent over, as though looking down in terror and curiosity. A minute later there were shrieks and laughter again: they had to drive under a huge overhanging rock.

"I don't know why the devil I'm coming with you," said Laevsky. "How stupid and vulgar it is! I want to go to the North, to run away, to escape; but here I am, for some reason, going to this stupid picnic."

"But look, what a view!" said Samoylenko as the horses turned to the left, and the valley of the Yellow River came into sight and the stream itself gleamed in the sunlight, yellow, turbid, frantic.

"I see nothing fine in that, Sasha," answered Laevsky. "To be in continual ecstasies over nature shows poverty of imagination. In comparison with what my imagination can give me, all these streams and rocks are trash, and nothing else."

The carriages now were by the banks of the stream. The high mountain banks gradually grew closer, the valley shrank together and ended in a gorge; the rocky mountain round which they were driving had been piled together by nature out of huge rocks, pressing upon each other with such terrible weight, that Samoylenko could not help gasping every time he looked at them. The dark and beautiful mountain was cleft in places by narrow fissures and gorges from which came a breath of dewy moisture and mystery; through the gorges could be seen other mountains, brown, pink, lilac, smoky, or bathed in vivid sunlight. From time to time as they passed a gorge they caught the sound of water falling from the heights and splashing on the stones.

"Ach, the damned mountains!" sighed Laevsky. "How sick I am of them!"

At the place where the Black River falls into the Yellow, and the water black as ink stains the yellow and struggles with it, stood the Tatar Kerbalay's duhan , with the Russian flag on the roof and with an inscription written in chalk: "The Pleasant duhan ." Near it was a little garden, enclosed in a hurdle fence, with tables and chairs set out in it, and in the midst of a thicket of wretched thornbushes stood a single solitary cypress, dark and beautiful.

Kerbalay, a nimble little Tatar in a blue shirt and a white apron, was standing in the road, and, holding his stomach, he bowed low to welcome the carriages, and smiled, showing his glistening white teeth.

"Good-evening, Kerbalay," shouted Samoylenko. "We are driving on a little further, and you take along the samovar and chairs! Look sharp!"

Kerbalay nodded his shaven head and muttered something, and only those sitting in the last carriage could hear: "We've got trout, your Excellency."

"Bring them, bring them!" said Von Koren.

Five hundred paces from the duhan the carriages stopped. Samoylenko selected a small meadow round which there were scattered stones convenient for sitting on, and a fallen tree blown down by the storm with roots overgrown by moss and dry yellow needles. Here there was a fragile wooden bridge over the stream, and just opposite on the other bank there was a little barn for drying maize, standing on four low piles, and looking like the hut on hen's legs in the fairy tale; a little ladder sloped from its door.

The first impression in all was a feeling that they would never get out of that place again. On all sides wherever they looked, the mountains rose up and towered above them, and the shadows of evening were stealing rapidly, rapidly from the duhan and dark cypress, making the narrow winding valley of the Black River narrower and the mountains higher. They could hear the river murmuring and the unceasing chirrup of the grasshoppers.

"Enchanting!" said Marya Konstantinovna, heaving deep sighs of ecstasy. "Children, look how fine! What peace!"

"Yes, it really is fine," assented Laevsky, who liked the view, and for some reason felt sad as he looked at the sky and then at the blue smoke rising from the chimney of the duhan . "Yes, it is fine," he repeated.

"Ivan Andreitch, describe this view," Marya Konstantinovna said tearfully.

"Why?" asked Laevsky. "The impression is better than any description. The wealth of sights and sounds which every one receives from nature by direct impression is ranted about by authors in a hideous and unrecognisable way."

"Really?" Von Koren asked coldly, choosing the biggest stone by the side of the water, and trying to clamber up and sit upon it. "Really?" he repeated, looking directly at Laevsky. "What of 'Romeo and Juliet'? Or, for instance, Pushkin's 'Night in the Ukraine'? Nature ought to come and bow down at their feet."

"Perhaps," said Laevsky, who was too lazy to think and oppose him. "Though what is 'Romeo and Juliet' after all?" he added after a short pause. "The beauty of poetry and holiness of love are simply the roses under which they try to hide its rottenness. Romeo is just the same sort of animal as all the rest of us."

"Whatever one talks to you about, you always bring it round to…" Von Koren glanced round at Katya and broke off.

"What do I bring it round to?" asked Laevsky.

"One tells you, for instance, how beautiful a bunch of grapes is, and you answer: 'Yes, but how ugly it is when it is chewed and digested in one's stomach!' Why say that? It's not new, and... altogether it is a queer habit."

Laevsky knew that Von Koren did not like him, and so was afraid of him, and felt in his presence as though every one were constrained and some one were standing behind his back. He made no answer and walked away, feeling sorry he had come.

"Gentlemen, quick march for brushwood for the fire!" commanded Samoylenko.

They all wandered off in different directions, and no one was left but Kirilin, Atchmianov, and Nikodim Alexandritch. Kerbalay brought chairs, spread a rug on the ground, and set a few bottles of wine.

The police captain, Kirilin, a tall, good-looking man, who in all weathers wore his great-coat over his tunic, with his haughty deportment, stately carriage, and thick, rather hoarse voice, looked like a young provincial chief of police; his expression was mournful and sleepy, as though he had just been waked against his will.

"What have you brought this for, you brute?" he asked Kerbalay, deliberately articulating each word. "I ordered you to give us kvarel , and what have you brought, you ugly Tatar? Eh? What?"

"We have plenty of wine of our own, Yegor Alekseitch," Nikodim Alexandritch observed, timidly and politely.

"What? But I want us to have my wine, too; I'm taking part in the picnic and I imagine I have full right to contribute my share. I im-ma-gine so! Bring ten bottles of kvarel ."

"Why so many?" asked Nikodim Alexandritch, in wonder, knowing Kirilin had no money.

"Twenty bottles! Thirty!" shouted Kirilin.

"Never mind, let him," Atchmianov whispered to Nikodim Alexandritch; "I'll pay."

Nadyezhda Fyodorovna was in a light-hearted, mischievous mood; she wanted to skip and jump, to laugh, to shout, to tease, to flirt. In her cheap cotton dress with blue pansies on it, in her red shoes and the same straw hat, she seemed to herself, little, simple, light, ethereal as a butterfly. She ran over the rickety bridge and looked for a minute into the water, in order to feel giddy; then, shrieking and laughing, ran to the other side to the drying-shed, and she fancied that all the men were admiring her, even Kerbalay. When in the rapidly falling darkness the trees began to melt into the mountains and the horses into the carriages, and a light gleamed in the windows of the duhan , she climbed up the mountain by the little path which zigzagged between stones and thorn-bushes and sat on a stone. Down below, the camp-fire was burning. Near the fire, with his sleeves tucked up, the deacon was moving to and fro, and his long black shadow kept describing a circle round it; he put on wood, and with a spoon tied to a long stick he stirred the cauldron. Samoylenko, with a copper-red face, was fussing round the fire just as though he were in his own kitchen, shouting furiously:

"Where's the salt, gentlemen? I bet you've forgotten it. Why are you all sitting about like lords while I do the work?"

Laevsky and Nikodim Alexandritch were sitting side by side on the fallen tree looking pensively at the fire. Marya Konstantinovna, Katya, and Kostya were taking the cups, saucers, and plates out of the baskets. Von Koren, with his arms folded and one foot on a stone, was standing on a bank at the very edge of the water, thinking about something. Patches of red light from the fire moved together with the shadows over the ground near the dark human figures, and quivered on the mountain, on the trees, on the bridge, on the drying-shed; on the other side the steep, scooped-out bank was all lighted up and glimmering in the stream, and the rushing turbid water broke its reflection into little bits.

The deacon went for the fish which Kerbalay was cleaning and washing on the bank, but he stood still half-way and looked about him.

"My God, how nice it is!" he thought. "People, rocks, the fire, the twilight, a monstrous tree--nothing more, and yet how fine it is!"

On the further bank some unknown persons made their appearance near the drying-shed. The flickering light and the smoke from the camp-fire puffing in that direction made it impossible to get a full view of them all at once, but glimpses were caught now of a shaggy hat and a grey beard, now of a blue shirt, now of a figure, ragged from shoulder to knee, with a dagger across the body; then a swarthy young face with black eyebrows, as thick and bold as though they had been drawn in charcoal. Five of them sat in a circle on the ground, and the other five went into the drying-shed. One was standing at the door with his back to the fire, and with his hands behind his back was telling something, which must have been very interesting, for when Samoylenko threw on twigs and the fire flared up, and scattered sparks and threw a glaring light on the shed, two calm countenances with an expression on them of deep attention could be seen, looking out of the door, while those who were sitting in a circle turned round and began listening to the speaker. Soon after, those sitting in a circle began softly singing something slow and melodious, that sounded like Lenten Church music... Listening to them, the deacon imagined how it would be with him in ten years' time, when he would come back from the expedition: he would be a young priest and monk, an author with a name and a splendid past; he would be consecrated an archimandrite, then a bishop; and he would serve mass in the cathedral; in a golden mitre he would come out into the body of the church with the ikon on his breast, and blessing the mass of the people with the triple and the double candelabra, would proclaim: "Look down from Heaven, O God, behold and visit this vineyard which Thy Hand has planted," and the children with their angel voices would sing in response: "Holy God..."

"Deacon, where is that fish?" he heard Samoylenko's voice.

As he went back to the fire, the deacon imagined the Church procession going along a dusty road on a hot July day; in front the peasants carrying the banners and the women and children the ikons, then the boy choristers and the sacristan with his face tied up and a straw in his hair, then in due order himself, the deacon, and behind him the priest wearing his calotte and carrying a cross, and behind them, tramping in the dust, a crowd of peasants--men, women, and children; in the crowd his wife and the priest's wife with kerchiefs on their heads. The choristers sing, the babies cry, the corncrakes call, the lark carols... Then they make a stand and sprinkle the herd with holy water... They go on again, and then kneeling pray for rain. Then lunch and talk...

"And that's nice too..." thought the deacon.

VII

Kirilin and Atchmianov climbed up the mountain by the path. Atchmianov dropped behind and stopped, while Kirilin went up to Nadyezhda Fyodorovna.

"Good-evening," he said, touching his cap.

"Good-evening."

"Yes!" said Kirilin, looking at the sky and pondering.

"Why 'yes'?" asked Nadyezhda Fyodorovna after a brief pause, noticing that Atchmianov was watching them both.

"And so it seems," said the officer, slowly, "that our love has withered before it has blossomed, so to speak. How do you wish me to understand it? Is it a sort of coquetry on your part, or do you look upon me as a nincompoop who can be treated as you choose."

"It was a mistake! Leave me alone!" Nadyezhda Fyodorovna said sharply, on that beautiful, marvellous evening, looking at him with terror and asking herself with bewilderment, could there really have been a moment when that man attracted her and had been near to her?

"So that's it!" said Kirilin; he thought in silence for a few minutes and said: "Well, I'll wait till you are in a better humour, and meanwhile I venture to assure you I am a gentleman, and I don't allow any one to doubt it. Adieu!"

He touched his cap again and walked off, making his way between the bushes. After a short interval Atchmianov approached hesitatingly.

"What a fine evening!" he said with a slight Armenian accent.

He was nice-looking, fashionably dressed, and behaved unaffectedly like a well-bred youth, but Nadyezhda Fyodorovna did not like him because she owed his father three hundred roubles; it was displeasing to her, too, that a shopkeeper had been asked to the picnic, and she was vexed at his coming up to her that evening when her heart felt so pure.

"The picnic is a success altogether," he said, after a pause.

"Yes," she agreed, and as though suddenly remembering her debt, she said carelessly: "Oh, tell them in your shop that Ivan Andreitch will come round in a day or two and will pay three hundred roubles... I don't remember exactly what it is."

"I would give another three hundred if you would not mention that debt every day. Why be prosaic?"

Nadyezhda Fyodorovna laughed; the amusing idea occurred to her that if she had been willing and sufficiently immoral she might in one minute be free from her debt. If she, for instance, were to turn the head of this handsome young fool! How amusing, absurd, wild it would be really! And she suddenly felt a longing to make him love her, to plunder him, throw him over, and then to see what would come of it.

"Allow me to give you one piece of advice," Atchmianov said timidly. "I beg you to beware of Kirilin. He says horrible things about you everywhere."

"It doesn't interest me to know what every fool says of me," Nadyezhda Fyodorovna said coldly, and the amusing thought of playing with handsome young Atchmianov suddenly lost its charm.

"We must go down," she said; "they're calling us."

The fish soup was ready by now. They were ladling it out by platefuls, and eating it with the religious solemnity with which this is only done at a picnic; and every one thought the fish soup very good, and thought that at home they had never eaten anything so nice. As is always the case at picnics, in the mass of dinner napkins, parcels, useless greasy papers fluttering in the wind, no one knew where was his glass or where his bread. They poured the wine on the carpet and on their own knees, spilt the salt, while it was dark all round them and the fire burnt more dimly, and every one was too lazy to get up and put wood on. They all drank wine, and even gave Kostya and Katya half a glass each. Nadyezhda Fyodorovna drank one glass and then another, got a little drunk and forgot about Kirilin.

"A splendid picnic, an enchanting evening," said Laevsky, growing lively with the wine. "But I should prefer a fine winter to all this. 'His beaver collar is silver with hoar-frost.'"

"Every one to his taste," observed Von Koren.

Laevsky felt uncomfortable; the heat of the campfire was beating upon his back, and the hatred of Von Koren upon his breast and face: this hatred on the part of a decent, clever man, a feeling in which there probably lay hid a well-grounded reason, humiliated him and enervated him, and unable to stand up against it, he said in a propitiatory tone:

"I am passionately fond of nature, and I regret that I'm not a naturalist. I envy you."

"Well, I don't envy you, and don't regret it," said Nadyezhda Fyodorovna. "I don't understand how any one can seriously interest himself in beetles and ladybirds while the people are suffering."

Laevsky shared her opinion. He was absolutely ignorant of natural science, and so could never reconcile himself to the authoritative tone and the learned and profound air of the people who devoted themselves to the whiskers of ants and the claws of beetles, and he always felt vexed that these people, relying on these whiskers, claws, and something they called protoplasm (he always imagined it in the form of an oyster), should undertake to decide questions involving the origin and life of man. But in Nadyezhda Fyodorovna's words he heard a note of falsity, and simply to contradict her he said: "The point is not the ladybirds, but the deductions made from them."

VIII

It was late, eleven o'clock, when they began to get into the carriages to go home. They took their seats, and the only ones missing were Nadyezhda Fyodorovna and Atchmianov, who were running after one another, laughing, the other side of the stream.

"Make haste, my friends," shouted Samoylenko.

"You oughtn't to give ladies wine," said Von Koren in a low voice.

Laevsky, exhausted by the picnic, by the hatred of Von Koren, and by his own thoughts, went to meet Nadyezhda Fyodorovna, and when, gay and happy, feeling light as a feather, breathless and laughing, she took him by both hands and laid her head on his breast, he stepped back and said dryly:

"You are behaving like a... cocotte."

It sounded horribly coarse, so that he felt sorry for her at once. On his angry, exhausted face she read hatred, pity and vexation with himself, and her heart sank at once. She realised instantly that she had gone too far, had been too free and easy in her behaviour, and overcome with misery, feeling herself heavy, stout, coarse, and drunk, she got into the first empty carriage together with Atchmianov. Laevsky got in with Kirilin, the zoologist with Samoylenko, the deacon with the ladies, and the party set off.

"You see what the Japanese monkeys are like," Von Koren began, rolling himself up in his cloak and shutting his eyes. "You heard she doesn't care to take an interest in beetles and ladybirds because the people are suffering. That's how all the Japanese monkeys look upon people like us. They're a slavish, cunning race, terrified by the whip and the fist for ten generations; they tremble and burn incense only before violence; but let the monkey into a free state where there's no one to take it by the collar, and it relaxes at once and shows itself in its true colours. Look how bold they are in picture galleries, in museums, in theatres, or when they talk of science: they puff themselves out and get excited, they are abusive and critical... they are bound to criticise--it's the sign of the slave. You listen: men of the liberal professions are more often sworn at than pickpockets--that's because three-quarters of society are made up of slaves, of just such monkeys. It never happens that a slave holds out his hand to you and sincerely says 'Thank you' to you for your work."

"I don't know what you want," said Samoylenko, yawning; "the poor thing, in the simplicity of her heart, wanted to talk to you of scientific subjects, and you draw a conclusion from that. You're cross with him for something or other, and with her, too, to keep him company. She's a splendid woman."

"Ah, nonsense! An ordinary kept woman, depraved and vulgar. Listen, Alexandr Daviditch; when you meet a simple peasant woman, who isn't living with her husband, who does nothing but giggle, you tell her to go and work. Why are you timid in this case and afraid to tell the truth? Simply because Nadyezhda Fyodorovna is kept, not by a sailor, but by an official."

"What am I to do with her?" said Samoylenko, getting angry. "Beat her or what?

"Not flatter vice. We curse vice only behind its back, and that's like making a long nose at it round a corner. I am a zoologist or a sociologist, which is the same thing; you are a doctor; society believes in us; we ought to point out the terrible harm which threatens it and the next generation from the existence of ladies like Nadyezhda Ivanovna."

"Fyodorovna," Samoylenko corrected. "But what ought society to do?"

"Society? That's its affair. To my thinking the surest and most direct method is--compulsion. Manu militari she ought to be returned to her husband; and if her husband won't take her in, then she ought to be sent to penal servitude or some house of correction."

"Ouf!" sighed Samoylenko. He paused and asked quietly: "You said the other day that people like Laevsky ought to be destroyed... Tell me, if you... if the State or society commissioned you to destroy him, could you... bring yourself to it?"

"My hand would not tremble."

IX

When they got home, Laevsky and Nadyezhda Fyodorovna went into their dark, stuffy, dull rooms. Both were silent. Laevsky lighted a candle, while Nadyezhda Fyodorovna sat down, and without taking off her cloak and hat, lifted her melancholy, guilty eyes to him.

He knew that she expected an explanation from him, but an explanation would be wearisome, useless and exhausting, and his heart was heavy because he had lost control over himself and been rude to her. He chanced to feel in his pocket the letter which he had been intending every day to read to her, and thought if he were to show her that letter now, it would turn her thoughts in another direction.

"It is time to define our relations," he thought. "I will give it her; what is to be will be."

He took out the letter and gave it her.

"Read it. It concerns you."

Saying this, he went into his own room and lay down on the sofa in the dark without a pillow. Nadyezhda Fyodorovna read the letter, and it seemed to her as though the ceiling were falling and the walls were closing in on her. It seemed suddenly dark and shut in and terrible. She crossed herself quickly three times and said:

"Give him peace, O Lord... give him peace..."

And she began crying.

"Vanya," she called. "Ivan Andreitch!"

There was no answer. Thinking that Laevsky had come in and was standing behind her chair, she sobbed like a child, and said:

"Why did you not tell me before that he was dead? I wouldn't have gone to the picnic; I shouldn't have laughed so horribly... The men said horrid things to me. What a sin, what a sin! Save me, Vanya, save me... I have been mad... I am lost..."

Laevsky heard her sobs. He felt stifled and his heart was beating violently. In his misery he got up, stood in the middle of the room, groped his way in the dark to an easy-chair by the table, and sat down.

"This is a prison..." he thought. "I must get away... I can't bear it."

It was too late to go and play cards; there were no restaurants in the town. He lay down again and covered his ears that he might not hear her sobbing, and he suddenly remembered that he could go to Samoylenko. To avoid going near Nadyezhda Fyodorovna, he got out of the window into the garden, climbed over the garden fence and went along the street. It was dark. A steamer, judging by its lights, a big passenger one, had just come in. He heard the clank of the anchor chain. A red light was moving rapidly from the shore in the direction of the steamer: it was the Customs boat going out to it.

"The passengers are asleep in their cabins..." thought Laevsky, and he envied the peace of mind of other people.

The windows in Samoylenko's house were open. Laevsky looked in at one of them, then in at another; it was dark and still in the rooms.

"Alexandr Daviditch, are you asleep?" he called. "Alexandr Daviditch!"

He heard a cough and an uneasy shout:

"Who's there? What the devil?"

"It is I, Alexandr Daviditch; excuse me."

A little later the door opened; there was a glow of soft light from the lamp, and Samoylenko's huge figure appeared all in white, with a white nightcap on his head.

"What now?" he asked, scratching himself and breathing hard from sleepiness. "Wait a minute; I'll open the door directly."

"Don't trouble; I'll get in at the window..."

Laevsky climbed in at the window, and when he reached Samoylenko, seized him by the hand.

"Alexandr Daviditch," he said in a shaking voice, "save me! I beseech you, I implore you. Understand me! My position is agonising. If it goes on for another two days I shall strangle myself like... like a dog."

"Wait a bit... What are you talking about exactly?"

"Light a candle."

"Oh... oh!..." sighed Samoylenko, lighting a candle. "My God! My God!... Why, it's past one, brother."

"Excuse me, but I can't stay at home," said Laevsky, feeling great comfort from the light and the presence of Samoylenko. "You are my best, my only friend, Alexandr Daviditch... You are my only hope. For God's sake, come to my rescue, whether you want to or not. I must get away from here, come what may!... Lend me the money!"

"Oh, my God, my God!..." sighed Samoylenko, scratching himself. "I was dropping asleep and I hear the whistle of the steamer, and now you... Do you want much?"

"Three hundred roubles at least. I must leave her a hundred, and I need two hundred for the journey... I owe you about four hundred already, but I will send it you all... all..."

Samoylenko took hold of both his whiskers in one hand, and standing with his legs wide apart, pondered.

"Yes..." he muttered, musing. "Three hundred... Yes... But I haven't got so much. I shall have to borrow it from some one."

"Borrow it, for God's sake!" said Laevsky, seeing from Samoylenko's face that he wanted to lend him the money and certainly would lend it. "Borrow it, and I'll be sure to pay you back. I will send it from Petersburg as soon as I get there. You can set your mind at rest about that. I'll tell you what, Sasha," he said, growing more animated; "let us have some wine."

"Yes... we can have some wine, too."

They both went into the dining-room.

"And how about Nadyezhda Fyodorovna?" asked Samoylenko, setting three bottles and a plate of peaches on the table. "Surely she's not remaining?"

"I will arrange it all, I will arrange it all," said Laevsky, feeling an unexpected rush of joy. "I will send her the money afterwards and she will join me... Then we will define our relations. To your health, friend."

"Wait a bit," said Samoylenko. "Drink this first... This is from my vineyard. This bottle is from Navaridze's vineyard and this one is from Ahatulov's... Try all three kinds and tell me candidly... There seems a little acidity about mine. Eh? Don't you taste it?"

"Yes. You have comforted me, Alexandr Daviditch. Thank you... I feel better."

"Is there any acidity?"

"Goodness only knows, I don't know. But you are a splendid, wonderful man!"

Looking at his pale, excited, good-natured face, Samoylenko remembered Von Koren's view that men like that ought to be destroyed, and Laevsky seemed to him a weak, defenceless child, whom any one could injure and destroy.

"And when you go, make it up with your mother," he said. "It's not right."

"Yes, yes; I certainly shall."

They were silent for a while. When they had emptied the first bottle, Samoylenko said:

"You ought to make it up with Von Koren too. You are both such splendid, clever fellows, and you glare at each other like wolves."

"Yes, he's a fine, very intelligent fellow," Laevsky assented, ready now to praise and forgive every one. "He's a remarkable man, but it's impossible for me to get on with him. No! Our natures are too different. I'm an indolent, weak, submissive nature. Perhaps in a good minute I might hold out my hand to him, but he would turn away from me... with contempt."

Laevsky took a sip of wine, walked from corner to corner and went on, standing in the middle of the room:

"I understand Von Koren very well. His is a resolute, strong, despotic nature. You have heard him continually talking of 'the expedition,' and it's not mere talk. He wants the wilderness, the moonlit night: all around in little tents, under the open sky, lie sleeping his sick and hungry Cossacks, guides, porters, doctor, priest, all exhausted with their weary marches, while only he is awake, sitting like Stanley on a camp-stool, feeling himself the monarch of the desert and the master of these men. He goes on and on and on, his men groan and die, one after another, and he goes on and on, and in the end perishes himself, but still is monarch and ruler of the desert, since the cross upon his tomb can be seen by the caravans for thirty or forty miles over the desert. I am sorry the man is not in the army. He would have made a splendid military genius. He would not have hesitated to drown his cavalry in the river and make a bridge out of dead bodies. And such hardihood is more needed in war than any kind of fortification or strategy. Oh, I understand him perfectly! Tell me: why is he wasting his substance here? What does he want here?"

"He is studying the marine fauna."

"No, no, brother, no!" Laevsky sighed. "A scientific man who was on the steamer told me the Black Sea was poor in animal life, and that in its depths, thanks to the abundance of sulphuric hydrogen, organic life was impossible. All the serious zoologists work at the biological station at Naples or Villefranche. But Von Koren is independent and obstinate: he works on the Black Sea because nobody else is working there; he is at loggerheads with the university, does not care to know his comrades and other scientific men because he is first of all a despot and only secondly a zoologist. And you'll see he'll do something. He is already dreaming that when he comes back from his expedition he will purify our universities from intrigue and mediocrity, and will make the scientific men mind their p's and q's. Despotism is just as strong in science as in the army. And he is spending his second summer in this stinking little town because he would rather be first in a village than second in a town. Here he is a king and an eagle; he keeps all the inhabitants under his thumb and oppresses them with his authority. He has appropriated every one, he meddles in other people's affairs; everything is of use to him, and every one is afraid of him. I am slipping out of his clutches, he feels that and hates me. Hasn't he told you that I ought to be destroyed or sent to hard labour?"

"Yes," laughed Samoylenko.

Laevsky laughed too, and drank some wine.

"His ideals are despotic too," he said, laughing, and biting a peach. "Ordinary mortals think of their neighbour--me, you, man in fact--if they work for the common weal. To Von Koren men are puppets and nonentities, too trivial to be the object of his life. He works, will go for his expedition and break his neck there, not for the sake of love for his neighbour, but for the sake of such abstractions as humanity, future generations, an ideal race of men. He exerts himself for the improvement of the human race, and we are in his eyes only slaves, food for the cannon, beasts of burden; some he would destroy or stow away in Siberia, others he would break by discipline, would, like Araktcheev, force them to get up and go to bed to the sound of the drum; would appoint eunuchs to preserve our chastity and morality, would order them to fire at any one who steps out of the circle of our narrow conservative morality; and all this in the name of the improvement of the human race... And what is the human race? Illusion, mirage... despots have always been illusionists. I understand him very well, brother. I appreciate him and don't deny his importance; this world rests on men like him, and if the world were left only to such men as us, for all our good-nature and good intentions, we should make as great a mess of it as the flies have of that picture. Yes."

Laevsky sat down beside Samoylenko, and said with genuine feeling: "I'm a foolish, worthless, depraved man. The air I breathe, this wine, love, life in fact--for all that, I have given nothing in exchange so far but lying, idleness, and cowardice. Till now I have deceived myself and other people; I have been miserable about it, and my misery was cheap and common. I bow my back humbly before Von Koren's hatred because at times I hate and despise myself."

Laevsky began again pacing from one end of the room to the other in excitement, and said:

"I'm glad I see my faults clearly and am conscious of them. That will help me to reform and become a different man. My dear fellow, if only you knew how passionately, with what anguish, I long for such a change. And I swear to you I'll be a man! I will! I don't know whether it is the wine that is speaking in me, or whether it really is so, but it seems to me that it is long since I have spent such pure and lucid moments as I have just now with you."

"It's time to sleep, brother," said Samoylenko.

"Yes, yes... Excuse me; I'll go directly."

Laevsky moved hurriedly about the furniture and windows, looking for his cap.

"Thank you," he muttered, sighing. "Thank you... Kind and friendly words are better than charity. You have given me new life."

He found his cap, stopped, and looked guiltily at Samoylenko.

"Alexandr Daviditch," he said in an imploring voice.

"What is it?"

"Let me stay the night with you, my dear fellow!"

"Certainly... Why not?"

Laevsky lay down on the sofa, and went on talking to the doctor for a long time.

X

Three days after the picnic, Marya Konstantinovna unexpectedly called on Nadyezhda Fyodorovna, and without greeting her or taking off her hat, seized her by both hands, pressed them to her breast and said in great excitement:

"My dear, I am deeply touched and moved: our dear kind-hearted doctor told my Nikodim Alexandritch yesterday that your husband was dead. Tell me, my dear... tell me, is it true?

"Yes, it's true; he is dead," answered Nadyezhda Fyodorovna.

"That is awful, awful, my dear! But there's no evil without some compensation; your husband was no doubt a noble, wonderful, holy man, and such are more needed in Heaven than on earth."

Every line and feature in Marya Konstantinovna's face began quivering as though little needles were jumping up and down under her skin; she gave an almond-oily smile and said, breathlessly, enthusiastically:

"And so you are free, my dear. You can hold your head high now, and look people boldly in the face. Henceforth God and man will bless your union with Ivan Andreitch. It's enchanting. I am trembling with joy, I can find no words. My dear, I will give you away... Nikodim Alexandritch and I have been so fond of you, you will allow us to give our blessing to your pure, lawful union. When, when do you think of being married?"

"I haven't thought of it," said Nadyezhda Fyodorovna, freeing her hands.

"That's impossible, my dear. You have thought of it, you have."

"Upon my word, I haven't," said Nadyezhda Fyodorovna, laughing. "What should we be married for? I see no necessity for it. We'll go on living as we have lived."

"What are you saying!" cried Marya Konstantinovna in horror. "For God's sake, what are you saying!"

"Our getting married won't make things any better. On the contrary, it will make them even worse. We shall lose our freedom."

"My dear, my dear, what are you saying!" exclaimed Marya Konstantinovna, stepping back and flinging up her hands. "You are talking wildly! Think what you are saying. You must settle down!"

"'Settle down.' How do you mean? I have not lived yet, and you tell me to settle down."

Nadyezhda Fyodorovna reflected that she really had not lived. She had finished her studies in a boarding-school and had been married to a man she did not love; then she had thrown in her lot with Laevsky, and had spent all her time with him on this empty, desolate coast, always expecting something better. Was that life?

"I ought to be married though," she thought, but remembering Kirilin and Atchmianov she flushed and said:

"No, it's impossible. Even if Ivan Andreitch begged me to on his knees--even then I would refuse."

Marya Konstantinovna sat on the sofa for a minute in silence, grave and mournful, gazing fixedly into space; then she got up and said coldly:

"Good-bye, my dear! Forgive me for having troubled you. Though it's not easy for me, it's my duty to tell you that from this day all is over between us, and, in spite of my profound respect for Ivan Andreitch, the door of my house is closed to you henceforth."

She uttered these words with great solemnity and was herself overwhelmed by her solemn tone. Her face began quivering again; it assumed a soft almond-oily expression. She held out both hands to Nadyezhda Fyodorovna, who was overcome with alarm and confusion, and said in an imploring voice:

"My dear, allow me if only for a moment to be a mother or an elder sister to you! I will be as frank with you as a mother."

Nadyezhda Fyodorovna felt in her bosom warmth, gladness, and pity for herself, as though her own mother had really risen up and were standing before her. She impulsively embraced Marya Konstantinovna and pressed her face to her shoulder. Both of them shed tears. They sat down on the sofa and for a few minutes sobbed without looking at one another or being able to utter a word.

"My dear child," began Marya Konstantinovna, "I will tell you some harsh truths, without sparing you."

"For God's sake, for God's sake, do!

"Trust me, my dear. You remember of all the ladies here, I was the only one to receive you. You horrified me from the very first day, but I had not the heart to treat you with disdain like all the rest. I grieved over dear, good Ivan Andreitch as though he were my son --a young man in a strange place, inexperienced, weak, with no mother; and I was worried, dreadfully worried... My husband was opposed to our making his acquaintance, but I talked him over... persuaded him... We began receiving Ivan Andreitch, and with him, of course, you. If we had not, he would have been insulted. I have a daughter, a son... You understand the tender mind, the pure heart of childhood... 'who so offendeth one of these little ones.'... I received you into my house and trembled for my children. Oh, when you become a mother, you will understand my fears. And every one was surprised at my receiving you, excuse my saying so, as a respectable woman, and hinted to me... well, of course, slanders, suppositions... At the bottom of my heart I blamed you, but you were unhappy, flighty, to be pitied, and my heart was wrung with pity for you."

"But why, why?" asked Nadyezhda Fyodorovna, trembling all over. "What harm have I done any one?"

"You are a terrible sinner. You broke the vow you made your husband at the altar. You seduced a fine young man, who perhaps had he not met you might have taken a lawful partner for life from a good family in his own circle, and would have been like every one else now. You have ruined his youth. Don't speak, don't speak, my dear! I never believe that man is to blame for our sins. It is always the woman's fault. Men are frivolous in domestic life; they are guided by their minds, and not by their hearts. There's a great deal they don't understand; woman understands it all. Everything depends on her. To her much is given and from her much will be required. Oh, my dear, if she had been more foolish or weaker than man on that side, God would not have entrusted her with the education of boys and girls. And then, my dear, you entered on the path of vice, forgetting all modesty; any other woman in your place would have hidden herself from people, would have sat shut up at home, and would only have been seen in the temple of God, pale, dressed all in black and weeping, and every one would have said in genuine compassion: 'O Lord, this erring angel is coming back again to Thee...' But you, my dear, have forgotten all discretion; have lived openly, extravagantly; have seemed to be proud of your sin; you have been gay and laughing, and I, looking at you, shuddered with horror, and have been afraid that thunder from Heaven would strike our house while you were sitting with us. My dear, don't speak, don't speak," cried Marya Konstantinovna, observing that Nadyezhda Fyodorovna wanted to speak. "Trust me, I will not deceive you, I will not hide one truth from the eyes of your soul. Listen to me, my dear... God marks great sinners, and you have been marked-out: only think- -your costumes have always been appalling."

Nadyezhda Fyodorovna, who had always had the highest opinion of her costumes, left off crying and looked at her with surprise.

"Yes, appalling," Marya Konstantinovna went on. "Any one could judge of your behaviour from the elaboration and gaudiness of your attire. People laughed and shrugged their shoulders as they looked at you, and I grieved, I grieved... And forgive me, my dear; you are not nice in your person! When we met in the bathing-place, you made me tremble. Your outer clothing was decent enough, but your petticoat, your chemise... My dear, I blushed! Poor Ivan Andreitch! No one ever ties his cravat properly, and from his linen and his boots, poor fellow! one can see he has no one at home to look after him. And he is always hungry, my darling, and of course, if there is no one at home to think of the samovar and the coffee, one is forced to spend half one's salary at the pavilion. And it's simply awful, awful in your home! No one else in the town has flies, but there's no getting rid of them in your rooms: all the plates and dishes are black with them. If you look at the windows and the chairs, there's nothing but dust, dead flies, and glasses... What do you want glasses standing about for? And, my dear, the table's not cleared till this time in the day. And one's ashamed to go into your bedroom: underclothes flung about everywhere, india-rubber tubes hanging on the walls, pails and basins standing about... My dear! A husband ought to know nothing, and his wife ought to be as neat as a little angel in his presence. I wake up every morning before it is light, and wash my face with cold water that my Nikodim Alexandritch may not see me looking drowsy."

"That's all nonsense," Nadyezhda Fyodorovna sobbed. "If only I were happy, but I am so unhappy!"

"Yes, yes; you are very unhappy!" Marya Konstantinovna sighed, hardly able to restrain herself from weeping. "And there's terrible grief in store for you in the future! A solitary old age, ill-health; and then you will have to answer at the dread judgment seat... It's awful, awful. Now fate itself holds out to you a helping hand, and you madly thrust it from you. Be married, make haste and be married!"

"Yes, we must, we must," said Nadyezhda Fyodorovna; "but it's impossible!"

"Why?"

"It's impossible. Oh, if only you knew!"

Nadyezhda Fyodorovna had an impulse to tell her about Kirilin, and how the evening before she had met handsome young Atchmianov at the harbour, and how the mad, ridiculous idea had occurred to her of cancelling her debt for three hundred; it had amused her very much, and she returned home late in the evening feeling that she had sold herself and was irrevocably lost. She did not know herself how it had happened. And she longed to swear to Marya Konstantinovna that she would certainly pay that debt, but sobs and shame prevented her from speaking.

"I am going away," she said. "Ivan Andreitch may stay, but I am going."

"Where?"

"To Russia."

"But how will you live there? Why, you have nothing."

"I will do translation, or... or I will open a library..."

"Don't let your fancy run away with you, my dear. You must have money for a library. Well, I will leave you now, and you calm yourself and think things over, and to-morrow come and see me, bright and happy. That will be enchanting! Well, good-bye, my angel. Let me kiss you."

Marya Konstantinovna kissed Nadyezhda Fyodorovna on the forehead, made the sign of the cross over her, and softly withdrew. It was getting dark, and Olga lighted up in the kitchen. Still crying, Nadyezhda Fyodorovna went into the bedroom and lay down on the bed. She began to be very feverish. She undressed without getting up, crumpled up her clothes at her feet, and curled herself up under the bedclothes. She was thirsty, and there was no one to give her something to drink.

"I'll pay it back!" she said to herself, and it seemed to her in delirium that she was sitting beside some sick woman, and recognised her as herself. "I'll pay it back. It would be stupid to imagine that it was for money I... I will go away and send him the money from Petersburg. At first a hundred... then another hundred... and then the third hundred..."

It was late at night when Laevsky came in.

"At first a hundred..." Nadyezhda Fyodorovna said to him, "then another hundred..."

"You ought to take some quinine," he said, and thought, "To-morrow is Wednesday; the steamer goes and I am not going in it. So I shall have to go on living here till Saturday."

Nadyezhda Fyodorovna knelt up in bed.

"I didn't say anything just now, did I?" she asked, smiling and screwing up her eyes at the light.

"No, nothing. We shall have to send for the doctor to-morrow morning. Go to sleep."

He took his pillow and went to the door. Ever since he had finally made up his mind to go away and leave Nadyezhda Fyodorovna, she had begun to raise in him pity and a sense of guilt; he felt a little ashamed in her presence, as though in the presence of a sick or old horse whom one has decided to kill. He stopped in the doorway and looked round at her.

"I was out of humour at the picnic and said something rude to you. Forgive me, for God's sake!"

Saying this, he went off to his study, lay down, and for a long while could not get to sleep.

Next morning when Samoylenko, attired, as it was a holiday, in full-dress uniform with epaulettes on his shoulders and decorations on his breast, came out of the bedroom after feeling Nadyezhda Fyodorovna's pulse and looking at her tongue, Laevsky, who was standing in the doorway, asked him anxiously: "Well? Well?"

There was an expression of terror, of extreme uneasiness, and of hope on his face.

"Don't worry yourself; there's nothing dangerous," said Samoylenko; "it's the usual fever."

"I don't mean that." Laevsky frowned impatiently. "Have you got the money?"

"My dear soul, forgive me," he whispered, looking round at the door and overcome with confusion.

"For God's sake, forgive me! No one has anything to spare, and I've only been able to collect by five- and by ten-rouble notes... Only a hundred and ten in all. To-day I'll speak to some one else. Have patience."

"But Saturday is the latest date," whispered Laevsky, trembling with impatience. "By all that's sacred, get it by Saturday! If I don't get away by Saturday, nothing's any use, nothing! I can't understand how a doctor can be without money!"

"Lord have mercy on us!" Samoylenko whispered rapidly and intensely, and there was positively a breaking note in his throat. "I've been stripped of everything; I am owed seven thousand, and I'm in debt all round. Is it my fault?"

"Then you'll get it by Saturday? Yes?"

"I'll try."

"I implore you, my dear fellow! So that the money may be in my hands by Friday morning!"

Samoylenko sat down and prescribed solution of quinine and kalii bromati and tincture of rhubarb, tincturae gentianae, aquae foeniculi --all in one mixture, added some pink syrup to sweeten it, and went away.

XI

"You look as though you were coming to arrest me," said Von Koren, seeing Samoylenko coming in, in his full-dress uniform.

"I was passing by and thought: 'Suppose I go in and pay my respects to zoology,'" said Samoylenko, sitting down at the big table, knocked together by the zoologist himself out of plain boards. "Good-morning, holy father," he said to the deacon, who was sitting in the window, copying something. "I'll stay a minute and then run home to see about dinner. It's time... I'm not hindering you?"

"Not in the least," answered the zoologist, laying out over the table slips of paper covered with small writing. "We are busy copying."

"Ah!... Oh, my goodness, my goodness!..." sighed Samoylenko. He cautiously took up from the table a dusty book on which there was lying a dead dried spider, and said: "Only fancy, though; some little green beetle is going about its business, when suddenly a monster like this swoops down upon it. I can fancy its terror."

"Yes, I suppose so."

"Is poison given it to protect it from its enemies?"

"Yes, to protect it and enable it to attack."

"To be sure, to be sure... And everything in nature, my dear fellows, is consistent and can be explained," sighed Samoylenko; "only I tell you what I don't understand. You're a man of very great intellect, so explain it to me, please. There are, you know, little beasts no bigger than rats, rather handsome to look at, but nasty and immoral in the extreme, let me tell you. Suppose such a little beast is running in the woods. He sees a bird; he catches it and devours it. He goes on and sees in the grass a nest of eggs; he does not want to eat them--he is not hungry, but yet he tastes one egg and scatters the others out of the nest with his paw. Then he meets a frog and begins to play with it; when he has tormented the frog he goes on licking himself and meets a beetle; he crushes the beetle with his paw... and so he spoils and destroys everything on his way... He creeps into other beasts' holes, tears up the anthills, cracks the snail's shell. If he meets a rat, he fights with it; if he meets a snake or a mouse, he must strangle it; and so the whole day long. Come, tell me: what is the use of a beast like that? Why was he created?"

"I don't know what animal you are talking of," said Von Koren; "most likely one of the insectivora. Well, he got hold of the bird because it was incautious; he broke the nest of eggs because the bird was not skilful, had made the nest badly and did not know how to conceal it. The frog probably had some defect in its colouring or he would not have seen it, and so on. Your little beast only destroys the weak, the unskilful, the careless--in fact, those who have defects which nature does not think fit to hand on to posterity. Only the cleverer, the stronger, the more careful and developed survive; and so your little beast, without suspecting it, is serving the great ends of perfecting creation."

"Yes, yes, yes... By the way, brother," said Samoylenko carelessly, "lend me a hundred roubles."

"Very good. There are some very interesting types among the insectivorous mammals. For instance, the mole is said to be useful because he devours noxious insects. There is a story that some German sent William I. a fur coat made of moleskins, and the Emperor ordered him to be reproved for having destroyed so great a number of useful animals. And yet the mole is not a bit less cruel than your little beast, and is very mischievous besides, as he spoils meadows terribly."

Von Koren opened a box and took out a hundred-rouble note.

"The mole has a powerful thorax, just like the bat," he went on, shutting the box; "the bones and muscles are tremendously developed, the mouth is extraordinarily powerfully furnished. If it had the proportions of an elephant, it would be an all-destructive, invincible animal. It is interesting when two moles meet underground; they begin at once as though by agreement digging a little platform; they need the platform in order to have a battle more conveniently. When they have made it they enter upon a ferocious struggle and fight till the weaker one falls. Take the hundred roubles," said Von Koren, dropping his voice, "but only on condition that you're not borrowing it for Laevsky."

"And if it were for Laevsky," cried Samoylenko, flaring up, "what is that to you?"

"I can't give it to you for Laevsky. I know you like lending people money. You would give it to Kerim, the brigand, if he were to ask you; but, excuse me, I can't assist you in that direction."

"Yes, it is for Laevsky I am asking it," said Samoylenko, standing up and waving his right arm. "Yes! For Laevsky! And no one, fiend or devil, has a right to dictate to me how to dispose of my own money. It doesn't suit you to lend it me? No?"

The deacon began laughing.

"Don't get excited, but be reasonable," said the zoologist. "To shower benefits on Mr. Laevsky is, to my thinking, as senseless as to water weeds or to feed locusts."

"To my thinking, it is our duty to help our neighbours!" cried Samoylenko.

"In that case, help that hungry Turk who is lying under the fence! He is a workman and more useful and indispensable than your Laevsky. Give him that hundred-rouble note! Or subscribe a hundred roubles to my expedition!"

"Will you give me the money or not? I ask you!"

"Tell me openly: what does he want money for?"

"It's not a secret; he wants to go to Petersburg on Saturday."

"So that is it!" Von Koren drawled out. "Aha!... We understand. And is she going with him, or how is it to be?"

"She's staying here for the time. He'll arrange his affairs in Petersburg and send her the money, and then she'll go."

"That's smart!" said the zoologist, and he gave a short tenor laugh. "Smart, well planned."

He went rapidly up to Samoylenko, and standing face to face with him, and looking him in the eyes, asked: "Tell me now honestly: is he tired of her? Yes? tell me: is he tired of her? Yes?"

"Yes," Samoylenko articulated, beginning to perspire.

"How repulsive it is!" said Von Koren, and from his face it could be seen that he felt repulsion. "One of two things, Alexandr Daviditch: either you are in the plot with him, or, excuse my saying so, you are a simpleton. Surely you must see that he is taking you in like a child in the most shameless way? Why, it's as clear as day that he wants to get rid of her and abandon her here. She'll be left a burden on you. It is as clear as day that you will have to send her to Petersburg at your expense. Surely your fine friend can't have so blinded you by his dazzling qualities that you can't see the simplest thing?"

"That's all supposition," said Samoylenko, sitting down.

"Supposition? But why is he going alone instead of taking her with him? And ask him why he doesn't send her off first. The sly beast!"

Overcome with sudden doubts and suspicions about his friend, Samoylenko weakened and took a humbler tone.

"But it's impossible," he said, recalling the night Laevsky had spent at his house. "He is so unhappy!"

"What of that? Thieves and incendiaries are unhappy too!"

"Even supposing you are right..." said Samoylenko, hesitating. "Let us admit it... Still, he's a young man in a strange place... a student. We have been students, too, and there is no one but us to come to his assistance."

"To help him to do abominable things, because he and you at different times have been at universities, and neither of you did anything there! What nonsense!"

"Stop; let us talk it over coolly. I imagine it will be possible to make some arrangement..." Samoylenko reflected, twiddling his fingers. "I'll give him the money, you see, but make him promise on his honour that within a week he'll send Nadyezhda Fyodorovna the money for the journey."

"And he'll give you his word of honour--in fact, he'll shed tears and believe in it himself; but what's his word of honour worth? He won't keep it, and when in a year or two you meet him on the Nevsky Prospect with a new mistress on his arm, he'll excuse himself on the ground that he has been crippled by civilisation, and that he is made after the pattern of Rudin. Drop him, for God's sake! Keep away from the filth; don't stir it up with both hands!"

Samoylenko thought for a minute and said resolutely:

"But I shall give him the money all the same. As you please. I can't bring myself to refuse a man simply on an assumption."

"Very fine, too. You can kiss him if you like."

"Give me the hundred roubles, then," Samoylenko asked timidly.

"I won't."

A silence followed. Samoylenko was quite crushed; his face wore a guilty, abashed, and ingratiating expression, and it was strange to see this pitiful, childish, shamefaced countenance on a huge man wearing epaulettes and orders of merit.

"The bishop here goes the round of his diocese on horseback instead of in a carriage," said the deacon, laying down his pen. "It's extremely touching to see him sit on his horse. His simplicity and humility are full of Biblical grandeur."

"Is he a good man?" asked Von Koren, who was glad to change the conversation.

"Of course! If he hadn't been a good man, do you suppose he would have been consecrated a bishop?"

"Among the bishops are to be found good and gifted men," said Von Koren. "The only drawback is that some of them have the weakness to imagine themselves statesmen. One busies himself with Russification, another criticises the sciences. That's not their business. They had much better look into their consistory a little."

"A layman cannot judge of bishops."

"Why so, deacon? A bishop is a man just the same as you or I."

"The same, but not the same." The deacon was offended and took up his pen. "If you had been the same, the Divine Grace would have rested upon you, and you would have been bishop yourself; and since you are not bishop, it follows you are not the same."

"Don't talk nonsense, deacon," said Samoylenko dejectedly. "Listen to what I suggest," he said, turning to Von Koren. "Don't give me that hundred roubles. You'll be having your dinners with me for three months before the winter, so let me have the money beforehand for three months."

"I won't."

Samoylenko blinked and turned crimson; he mechanically drew towards him the book with the spider on it and looked at it, then he got up and took his hat.

Von Koren felt sorry for him.

"What it is to have to live and do with people like this," said the zoologist, and he kicked a paper into the corner with indignation. "You must understand that this is not kindness, it is not love, but cowardice, slackness, poison! What's gained by reason is lost by your flabby good-for-nothing hearts! When I was ill with typhoid as a schoolboy, my aunt in her sympathy gave me pickled mushrooms to eat, and I very nearly died. You, and my aunt too, must understand that love for man is not to be found in the heart or the stomach or the bowels, but here!"

Von Koren slapped himself on the forehead.

"Take it," he said, and thrust a hundred-rouble note into his hand.

"You've no need to be angry, Kolya," said Samoylenko mildly, folding up the note. "I quite understand you, but... you must put yourself in my place."

"You are an old woman, that's what you are."

The deacon burst out laughing.

"Hear my last request, Alexandr Daviditch," said Von Koren hotly. "When you give that scoundrel the money, make it a condition that he takes his lady with him, or sends her on ahead, and don't give it him without. There's no need to stand on ceremony with him. Tell him so, or, if you don't, I give you my word I'll go to his office and kick him downstairs, and I'll break off all acquaintance with you. So you'd better know it."

"Well! To go with her or send her on beforehand will be more convenient for him," said Samoylenko. "He'll be delighted indeed. Well, goodbye."

He said good-bye affectionately and went out, but before shutting the door after him, he looked round at Von Koren and, with a ferocious face, said:

"It's the Germans who have ruined you, brother! Yes! The Germans!"

XII

Next day, Thursday, Marya Konstantinovna was celebrating the birthday of her Kostya. All were invited to come at midday and eat pies, and in the evening to drink chocolate. When Laevsky and Nadyezhda Fyodorovna arrived in the evening, the zoologist, who was already sitting in the drawing-room, drinking chocolate, asked Samoylenko:

"Have you talked to him?"

"Not yet."

"Mind now, don't stand on ceremony. I can't understand the insolence of these people! Why, they know perfectly well the view taken by this family of their cohabitation, and yet they force themselves in here."

"If one is to pay attention to every prejudice," said Samoylenko, "one could go nowhere."

"Do you mean to say that the repugnance felt by the masses for illicit love and moral laxity is a prejudice?"

"Of course it is. It's prejudice and hate. When the soldiers see a girl of light behaviour, they laugh and whistle; but just ask them what they are themselves."

"It's not for nothing they whistle. The fact that girls strangle their illegitimate children and go to prison for it, and that Anna Karenin flung herself under the train, and that in the villages they smear the gates with tar, and that you and I, without knowing why, are pleased by Katya's purity, and that every one of us feels a vague craving for pure love, though he knows there is no such love--is all that prejudice? That is the one thing, brother, which has survived intact from natural selection, and, if it were not for that obscure force regulating the relations of the sexes, the Laevskys would have it all their own way, and mankind would degenerate in two years."

Laevsky came into the drawing-room, greeted every one, and shaking hands with Von Koren, smiled ingratiatingly. He waited for a favourable moment and said to Samoylenko:

"Excuse me, Alexandr Daviditch, I must say two words to you."

Samoylenko got up, put his arm round Laevsky's waist, and both of them went into Nikodim Alexandritch's study.

"To-morrow's Friday," said Laevsky, biting his nails. "Have you got what you promised?"

"I've only got two hundred. I'll get the rest to-day or to-morrow. Don't worry yourself."

"Thank God..." sighed Laevsky, and his hands began trembling with joy. "You are saving me, Alexandr Daviditch, and I swear to you by God, by my happiness and anything you like, I'll send you the money as soon as I arrive. And I'll send you my old debt too."

"Look here, Vanya..." said Samoylenko, turning crimson and taking him by the button. "You must forgive my meddling in your private affairs, but... why shouldn't you take Nadyezhda Fyodorovna with you?"

"You queer fellow. How is that possible? One of us must stay, or our creditors will raise an outcry. You see, I owe seven hundred or more to the shops. Only wait, and I will send them the money. I'll stop their mouths, and then she can come away."

"I see... But why shouldn't you send her on first?"

"My goodness, as though that were possible!" Laevsky was horrified. "Why, she's a woman; what would she do there alone? What does she know about it? That would only be a loss of time and a useless waste of money."

"That's reasonable..." thought Samoylenko, but remembering his conversation with Von Koren, he looked down and said sullenly: "I can't agree with you. Either go with her or send her first; otherwise... otherwise I won't give you the money. Those are my last words..."

He staggered back, lurched backwards against the door, and went into the drawing-room, crimson, and overcome with confusion.

"Friday... Friday," thought Laevsky, going back into the drawing-room. "Friday..."

He was handed a cup of chocolate; he burnt his lips and tongue with the scalding chocolate and thought: "Friday... Friday..."

For some reason he could not get the word "Friday" out of his head;

he could think of nothing but Friday, and the only thing that was clear to him, not in his brain but somewhere in his heart, was that he would not get off on Saturday. Before him stood Nikodim Alexandritch, very neat, with his hair combed over his temples, saying:

"Please take something to eat..."

Marya Konstantinovna showed the visitors Katya's school report and said, drawling:

"It's very, very difficult to do well at school nowadays! So much is expected..."

"Mamma!" groaned Katya, not knowing where to hide her confusion at the praises of the company.

Laevsky, too, looked at the report and praised it. Scripture, Russian language, conduct, fives and fours, danced before his eyes, and all this, mixed with the haunting refrain of "Friday," with the carefully combed locks of Nikodim Alexandritch and the red cheeks of Katya, produced on him a sensation of such immense overwhelming boredom that he almost shrieked with despair and asked himself: "Is it possible, is it possible I shall not get away?"

They put two card tables side by side and sat down to play post. Laevsky sat down too.

"Friday... Friday..." he kept thinking, as he smiled and took a pencil out of his pocket. "Friday..."

He wanted to think over his position, and was afraid to think. It was terrible to him to realise that the doctor had detected him in the deception which he had so long and carefully concealed from himself. Every time he thought of his future he would not let his thoughts have full rein. He would get into the train and set off, and thereby the problem of his life would be solved, and he did not let his thoughts go farther. Like a far-away dim light in the fields, the thought sometimes flickered in his mind that in one of the side-streets of Petersburg, in the remote future, he would have to have recourse to a tiny lie in order to get rid of Nadyezhda Fyodorovna and pay his debts; he would tell a lie only once, and then a completely new life would begin. And that was right: at the price of a small lie he would win so much truth.

Now when by his blunt refusal the doctor had crudely hinted at his deception, he began to understand that he would need deception not only in the remote future, but to-day, and to-morrow, and in a month's time, and perhaps up to the very end of his life. In fact, in order to get away he would have to lie to Nadyezhda Fyodorovna, to his creditors, and to his superiors in the Service; then, in order to get money in Petersburg, he would have to lie to his mother, to tell her that he had already broken with Nadyezhda Fyodorovna; and his mother would not give him more than five hundred roubles, so he had already deceived the doctor, as he would not be in a position to pay him back the money within a short time. Afterwards, when Nadyezhda Fyodorovna came to Petersburg, he would have to resort to a regular series of deceptions, little and big, in order to get free of her; and again there would be tears, boredom, a disgusting existence, remorse, and so there would be no new life. Deception and nothing more. A whole mountain of lies rose before Laevsky's imagination. To leap over it at one bound and not to do his lying piecemeal, he would have to bring himself to stern, uncompromising action; for instance, to getting up without saying a word, putting on his hat, and at once setting off without money and without explanation. But Laevsky felt that was impossible for him.

"Friday, Friday..." he thought. "Friday..."

They wrote little notes, folded them in two, and put them in Nikodim Alexandritch's old top-hat. When there were a sufficient heap of notes, Kostya, who acted the part of postman, walked round the table and delivered them. The deacon, Katya, and Kostya, who received amusing notes and tried to write as funnily as they could, were highly delighted.

"We must have a little talk," Nadyezhda Fyodorovna read in a little note; she glanced at Marya Konstantinovna, who gave her an almond-oily smile and nodded.

"Talk of what?" thought Nadyezhda Fyodorovna. "If one can't tell the whole, it's no use talking."

Before going out for the evening she had tied Laevsky's cravat for him, and that simple action filled her soul with tenderness and sorrow. The anxiety in his face, his absent-minded looks, his pallor, and the incomprehensible change that had taken place in him of late, and the fact that she had a terrible revolting secret from him, and the fact that her hands trembled when she tied his cravat--all this seemed to tell her that they had not long left to be together. She looked at him as though he were an ikon, with terror and penitence, and thought: "Forgive, forgive."

Opposite her was sitting Atchmianov, and he never took his black, love-sick eyes off her. She was stirred by passion; she was ashamed of herself, and afraid that even her misery and sorrow would not prevent her from yielding to impure desire to-morrow, if not to-day --and that, like a drunkard, she would not have the strength to stop herself.

She made up her mind to go away that she might not continue this life, shameful for herself, and humiliating for Laevsky. She would beseech him with tears to let her go; and if he opposed her, she would go away secretly. She would not tell him what had happened; let him keep a pure memory of her.

"I love you, I love you, I love you," she read. It was from Atchmianov.

She would live in some far remote place, would work and send Laevsky, "anonymously," money, embroidered shirts, and tobacco, and would return to him only in old age or if he were dangerously ill and needed a nurse. When in his old age he learned what were her reasons for leaving him and refusing to be his wife, he would appreciate her sacrifice and forgive.

"You've got a long nose." That must be from the deacon or Kostya.

Nadyezhda Fyodorovna imagined how, parting from Laevsky, she would embrace him warmly, would kiss his hand, and would swear to love him all her life, all her life, and then, living in obscurity among strangers, she would every day think that somewhere she had a friend, some one she loved--a pure, noble, lofty man who kept a pure memory of her.

"If you don't give me an interview to-day, I shall take measures, I assure you on my word of honour. You can't treat decent people like this; you must understand that." That was from Kirilin.

XIII

Laevsky received two notes; he opened one and read: "Don't go away, my darling."

"Who could have written that?" he thought. "Not Samoylenko, of course. And not the deacon, for he doesn't know I want to go away. Von Koren, perhaps?"

The zoologist bent over the table and drew a pyramid. Laevsky fancied that his eyes were smiling.

"Most likely Samoylenko... has been gossiping," thought Laevsky.

In the other note, in the same disguised angular handwriting with long tails to the letters, was written: "Somebody won't go away on Saturday."

"A stupid gibe," thought Laevsky. "Friday, Friday..."

Something rose in his throat. He touched his collar and coughed, but instead of a cough a laugh broke from his throat.

"Ha-ha-ha!" he laughed. "Ha-ha-ha! What am I laughing at? Ha-ha-ha!"

He tried to restrain himself, covered his mouth with his hand, but the laugh choked his chest and throat, and his hand could not cover his mouth.

"How stupid it is!" he thought, rolling with laughter. "Have I gone out of my mind?"

The laugh grew shriller and shriller, and became something like the bark of a lap-dog. Laevsky tried to get up from the table, but his legs would not obey him and his right hand was strangely, without his volition, dancing on the table, convulsively clutching and crumpling up the bits of paper. He saw looks of wonder, Samoylenko's grave, frightened face, and the eyes of the zoologist full of cold irony and disgust, and realised that he was in hysterics.

"How hideous, how shameful!" he thought, feeling the warmth of tears on his face. "... Oh, oh, what a disgrace! It has never happened to me..."

They took him under his arms, and supporting his head from behind, led him away; a glass gleamed before his eyes and knocked against his teeth, and the water was spilt on his breast; he was in a little room, with two beds in the middle, side by side, covered by two snow-white quilts. He dropped on one of the beds and sobbed.

"It's nothing, it's nothing," Samoylenko kept saying; "it does happen... it does happen..."

Chill with horror, trembling all over and dreading something awful, Nadyezhda Fyodorovna stood by the bedside and kept asking:

"What is it? What is it? For God's sake, tell me."

"Can Kirilin have written him something?" she thought.

"It's nothing," said Laevsky, laughing and crying; "go away, darling."

His face expressed neither hatred nor repulsion: so he knew nothing; Nadyezhda Fyodorovna was somewhat reassured, and she went into the drawing-room.

"Don't agitate yourself, my dear!" said Marya Konstantinovna, sitting down beside her and taking her hand. "It will pass. Men are just as weak as we poor sinners. You are both going through a crisis... One can so well understand it! Well, my dear, I am waiting for an answer. Let us have a little talk."

"No, we are not going to talk," said Nadyezhda Fyodorovna, listening to Laevsky's sobs. "I feel depressed... You must allow me to go home."

"What do you mean, what do you mean, my dear?" cried Marya Konstantinovna in alarm. "Do you think I could let you go without supper? We will have something to eat, and then you may go with my blessing."

"I feel miserable..." whispered Nadyezhda Fyodorovna, and she caught at the arm of the chair with both hands to avoid falling.

"He's got a touch of hysterics," said Von Koren gaily, coming into the drawing-room, but seeing Nadyezhda Fyodorovna, he was taken aback and retreated.

When the attack was over, Laevsky sat on the strange bed and thought.

"Disgraceful! I've been howling like some wretched girl! I must have been absurd and disgusting. I will go away by the back stairs... But that would seem as though I took my hysterics too seriously. I ought to take it as a joke..."

He looked in the looking-glass, sat there for some time, and went back into the drawing-room.

"Here I am," he said, smiling; he felt agonisingly ashamed, and he felt others were ashamed in his presence. "Fancy such a thing happening," he said, sitting down. "I was sitting here, and all of a sudden, do you know, I felt a terrible piercing pain in my side... unendurable, my nerves could not stand it, and... and it led to this silly performance. This is the age of nerves; there is no help for it."

At supper he drank some wine, and, from time to time, with an abrupt sigh rubbed his side as though to suggest that he still felt the pain. And no one, except Nadyezhda Fyodorovna, believed him, and he saw that.

After nine o'clock they went for a walk on the boulevard. Nadyezhda Fyodorovna, afraid that Kirilin would speak to her, did her best to keep all the time beside Marya Konstantinovna and the children. She felt weak with fear and misery, and felt she was going to be feverish; she was exhausted and her legs would hardly move, but she did not go home, because she felt sure that she would be followed by Kirilin or Atchmianov or both at once. Kirilin walked behind her with Nikodim Alexandritch, and kept humming in an undertone:

"I don't al-low people to play with me! I don't al-low it."

From the boulevard they went back to the pavilion and walked along the beach, and looked for a long time at the phosphorescence on the water. Von Koren began telling them why it looked phosphorescent.

XIV

"It's time I went to my vint... They will be waiting for me," said Laevsky. "Good-bye, my friends."

"I'll come with you; wait a minute," said Nadyezhda Fyodorovna, and she took his arm.

They said good-bye to the company and went away. Kirilin took leave too, and saying that he was going the same way, went along beside them.

"What will be, will be," thought Nadyezhda Fyodorovna. "So be it..."

And it seemed to her that all the evil memories in her head had taken shape and were walking beside her in the darkness, breathing heavily, while she, like a fly that had fallen into the inkpot, was crawling painfully along the pavement and smirching Laevsky's side and arm with blackness.

If Kirilin should do anything horrid, she thought, not he but she would be to blame for it. There was a time when no man would have talked to her as Kirilin had done, and she had torn up her security like a thread and destroyed it irrevocably--who was to blame for it? Intoxicated by her passions she had smiled at a complete stranger, probably just because he was tall and a fine figure. After two meetings she was weary of him, had thrown him over, and did not that, she thought now, give him the right to treat her as he chose?

"Here I'll say good-bye to you, darling," said Laevsky. "Ilya Mihalitch will see you home."

He nodded to Kirilin, and, quickly crossing the boulevard, walked along the street to Sheshkovsky's, where there were lights in the windows, and then they heard the gate bang as he went in.

"Allow me to have an explanation with you," said Kirilin. "I'm not a boy, not some Atchkasov or Latchkasov, Zatchkasov... I demand serious attention."

Nadyezhda Fyodorovna's heart began beating violently. She made no reply.

"The abrupt change in your behaviour to me I put down at first to coquetry," Kirilin went on; "now I see that you don't know how to behave with gentlemanly people. You simply wanted to play with me, as you are playing with that wretched Armenian boy; but I'm a gentleman and I insist on being treated like a gentleman. And so I am at your service..."

"I'm miserable," said Nadyezhda Fyodorovna beginning to cry, and to hide her tears she turned away.

"I'm miserable too," said Kirilin, "but what of that?"

Kirilin was silent for a space, then he said distinctly and emphatically:

"I repeat, madam, that if you do not give me an interview this evening, I'll make a scandal this very evening."

"Let me off this evening," said Nadyezhda Fyodorovna, and she did not recognise her own voice, it was so weak and pitiful.

"I must give you a lesson... Excuse me for the roughness of my tone, but it's necessary to give you a lesson. Yes, I regret to say I must give you a lesson. I insist on two interviews--to-day and to-morrow. After to-morrow you are perfectly free and can go wherever you like with any one you choose. To-day and to-morrow."

Nadyezhda Fyodorovna went up to her gate and stopped.

"Let me go," she murmured, trembling all over and seeing nothing before her in the darkness but his white tunic. "You're right: I'm a horrible woman... I'm to blame, but let me go... I beg you." She touched his cold hand and shuddered. "I beseech you..."

"Alas!" sighed Kirilin, "alas! it's not part of my plan to let you go; I only mean to give you a lesson and make you realise. And what's more, madam, I've too little faith in women."

"I'm miserable..."

Nadyezhda Fyodorovna listened to the even splash of the sea, looked at the sky studded with stars, and longed to make haste and end it all, and get away from the cursed sensation of life, with its sea, stars, men, fever.

"Only not in my home," she said coldly. "Take me somewhere else."

"Come to Muridov's. That's better."

"Where's that?"

"Near the old wall."

She walked quickly along the street and then turned into the side-street that led towards the mountains. It was dark. There were pale streaks of light here and there on the pavement, from the lighted windows, and it seemed to her that, like a fly, she kept falling into the ink and crawling out into the light again. At one point he stumbled, almost fell down and burst out laughing.

"He's drunk," thought Nadyezhda Fyodorovna. "Never mind... Never mind... So be it."

Atchmianov, too, soon took leave of the party and followed Nadyezhda Fyodorovna to ask her to go for a row. He went to her house and looked over the fence: the windows were wide open, there were no lights.

"Nadyezhda Fyodorovna!" he called.

A moment passed, he called again.

"Who's there?" he heard Olga's voice.

"Is Nadyezhda Fyodorovna at home?"

"No, she has not come in yet."

"Strange... very strange," thought Atchmianov, feeling very uneasy. "She went home..."

He walked along the boulevard, then along the street, and glanced in at the windows of Sheshkovsky's. Laevsky was sitting at the table without his coat on, looking attentively at his cards.

"Strange, strange," muttered Atchmianov, and remembering Laevsky's hysterics, he felt ashamed. "If she is not at home, where is she?"

He went to Nadyezhda Fyodorovna's lodgings again, and looked at the dark windows.

"It's a cheat, a cheat..." he thought, remembering that, meeting him at midday at Marya Konstantinovna's, she had promised to go in a boat with him that evening.

The windows of the house where Kirilin lived were dark, and there was a policeman sitting asleep on a little bench at the gate. Everything was clear to Atchmianov when he looked at the windows and the policeman. He made up his mind to go home, and set off in that direction, but somehow found himself near Nadyezhda Fyodorovna's lodgings again. He sat down on the bench near the gate and took off his hat, feeling that his head was burning with jealousy and resentment.

The clock in the town church only struck twice in the twenty-four hours--at midday and midnight. Soon after it struck midnight he heard hurried footsteps.

"To-morrow evening, then, again at Muridov's," Atchmianov heard, and he recognised Kirilin's voice. "At eight o'clock; good-bye!"

Nadyezhda Fyodorovna made her appearance near the garden. Without noticing that Atchmianov was sitting on the bench, she passed beside him like a shadow, opened the gate, and leaving it open, went into the house. In her own room she lighted the candle and quickly undressed, but instead of getting into bed, she sank on her knees before a chair, flung her arms round it, and rested her head on it.

It was past two when Laevsky came home.

XV

Having made up his mind to lie, not all at once but piecemeal, Laevsky went soon after one o'clock next day to Samoylenko to ask for the money that he might be sure to get off on Saturday. After his hysterical attack, which had added an acute feeling of shame to his depressed state of mind, it was unthinkable to remain in the town. If Samoylenko should insist on his conditions, he thought it would be possible to agree to them and take the money, and next day, just as he was starting, to say that Nadyezhda Fyodorovna refused to go. He would be able to persuade her that evening that the whole arrangement would be for her benefit. If Samoylenko, who was obviously under the influence of Von Koren, should refuse the money altogether or make fresh conditions, then he, Laevsky, would go off that very evening in a cargo vessel, or even in a sailing-boat, to Novy Athon or Novorossiisk, would send from there an humiliating telegram, and would stay there till his mother sent him the money for the journey.

When he went into Samoylenko's, he found Von Koren in the drawing-room. The zoologist had just arrived for dinner, and, as usual, was turning over the album and scrutinising the gentlemen in top-hats and the ladies in caps.

"How very unlucky!" thought Laevsky, seeing him. "He may be in the way. Good-morning."

"Good-morning," answered Von Koren, without looking at him.

"Is Alexandr Daviditch at home?"

"Yes, in the kitchen."

Laevsky went into the kitchen, but seeing from the door that Samoylenko was busy over the salad, he went back into the drawing-room and sat down. He always had a feeling of awkwardness in the zoologist's presence, and now he was afraid there would be talk about his attack of hysterics. There was more than a minute of silence. Von Koren suddenly raised his eyes to Laevsky and asked:

"How do you feel after yesterday?"

"Very well indeed," said Laevsky, flushing. "It really was nothing much..."

"Until yesterday I thought it was only ladies who had hysterics, and so at first I thought you had St. Vitus's dance."

Laevsky smiled ingratiatingly, and thought:

"How indelicate on his part! He knows quite well how unpleasant it is for me..."

"Yes, it was a ridiculous performance," he said, still smiling. "I've been laughing over it the whole morning. What's so curious in an attack of hysterics is that you know it is absurd, and are laughing at it in your heart, and at the same time you sob. In our neurotic age we are the slaves of our nerves; they are our masters and do as they like with us. Civilisation has done us a bad turn in that way..."

As Laevsky talked, he felt it disagreeable that Von Koren listened to him gravely, and looked at him steadily and attentively as though studying him; and he was vexed with himself that in spite of his dislike of Von Koren, he could not banish the ingratiating smile from his face.

"I must admit, though," he added, "that there were immediate causes for the attack, and quite sufficient ones too. My health has been terribly shaky of late. To which one must add boredom, constantly being hard up... the absence of people and general interests... My position is worse than a governor's."

"Yes, your position is a hopeless one," answered Von Koren.

These calm, cold words, implying something between a jeer and an uninvited prediction, offended Laevsky. He recalled the zoologist's eyes the evening before, full of mockery and disgust. He was silent for a space and then asked, no longer smiling:

"How do you know anything of my position?"

"You were only just speaking of it yourself. Besides, your friends take such a warm interest in you, that I am hearing about you all day long."

"What friends? Samoylenko, I suppose?"

"Yes, he too."

"I would ask Alexandr Daviditch and my friends in general not to trouble so much about me."

"Here is Samoylenko; you had better ask him not to trouble so much about you."

"I don't understand your tone," Laevsky muttered, suddenly feeling as though he had only just realised that the zoologist hated and despised him, and was jeering at him, and was his bitterest and most inveterate enemy.

"Keep that tone for some one else," he said softly, unable to speak aloud for the hatred with which his chest and throat were choking, as they had been the night before with laughter.

Samoylenko came in in his shirt-sleeves, crimson and perspiring from the stifling kitchen.

"Ah, you here?" he said. "Good-morning, my dear boy. Have you had dinner? Don't stand on ceremony. Have you had dinner?"

"Alexandr Daviditch," said Laevsky, standing up, "though I did appeal to you to help me in a private matter, it did not follow that I released you from the obligation of discretion and respect for other people's private affairs."

"What's this?" asked Samoylenko, in astonishment.

"If you have no money," Laevsky went on, raising his voice and shifting from one foot to the other in his excitement, "don't give it; refuse it. But why spread abroad in every back street that my position is hopeless, and all the rest of it? I can't endure such benevolence and friend's assistance where there's a shilling-worth of talk for a ha'porth of help! You can boast of your benevolence as much as you please, but no one has given you the right to gossip about my private affairs!"

"What private affairs?" asked Samoylenko, puzzled and beginning to be angry. "If you've come here to be abusive, you had better clear out. You can come again afterwards!"

He remembered the rule that when one is angry with one's neighbour, one must begin to count a hundred, and one will grow calm again; and he began rapidly counting.

"I beg you not to trouble yourself about me," Laevsky went on. "Don't pay any attention to me, and whose business is it what I do and how I live? Yes, I want to go away. Yes, I get into debt, I drink, I am living with another man's wife, I'm hysterical, I'm ordinary. I am not so profound as some people, but whose business is that? Respect other people's privacy."

"Excuse me, brother," said Samoylenko, who had counted up to thirty-five, "but..."

"Respect other people's individuality!" interrupted Laevsky. "This continual gossip about other people's affairs, this sighing and groaning and everlasting prying, this eavesdropping, this friendly sympathy... damn it all! They lend me money and make conditions as though I were a schoolboy! I am treated as the devil knows what! I don't want anything," shouted Laevsky, staggering with excitement and afraid that it might end in another attack of hysterics. "I shan't get away on Saturday, then," flashed through his mind. "I want nothing. All I ask of you is to spare me your protecting care. I'm not a boy, and I'm not mad, and I beg you to leave off looking after me."

The deacon came in, and seeing Laevsky pale and gesticulating, addressing his strange speech to the portrait of Prince Vorontsov, stood still by the door as though petrified.

"This continual prying into my soul," Laevsky went on, "is insulting to my human dignity, and I beg these volunteer detectives to give up their spying! Enough!"

"What's that... what did you say?" said Samoylenko, who had counted up to a hundred. He turned crimson and went up to Laevsky.

"It's enough," said Laevsky, breathing hard and snatching up his cap.

"I'm a Russian doctor, a nobleman by birth, and a civil councillor," said Samoylenko emphatically. "I've never been a spy, and I allow no one to insult me!" he shouted in a breaking voice, emphasising the last word. "Hold your tongue!"

The deacon, who had never seen the doctor so majestic, so swelling with dignity, so crimson and so ferocious, shut his mouth, ran out into the entry and there exploded with laughter.

As though through a fog, Laevsky saw Von Koren get up and, putting his hands in his trouser-pockets, stand still in an attitude of expectancy, as though waiting to see what would happen. This calm attitude struck Laevsky as insolent and insulting to the last degree.

"Kindly take back your words," shouted Samoylenko.

Laevsky, who did not by now remember what his words were, answered:

"Leave me alone! I ask for nothing. All I ask is that you and German upstarts of Jewish origin should let me alone! Or I shall take steps to make you! I will fight you!"

"Now we understand," said Von Koren, coming from behind the table. "Mr. Laevsky wants to amuse himself with a duel before he goes away. I can give him that pleasure. Mr. Laevsky, I accept your challenge."

"A challenge," said Laevsky, in a low voice, going up to the zoologist and looking with hatred at his swarthy brow and curly hair. "A challenge? By all means! I hate you! I hate you!"

"Delighted. To-morrow morning early near Kerbalay's. I leave all details to your taste. And now, clear out!"

"I hate you," Laevsky said softly, breathing hard. "I have hated you a long while! A duel! Yes!"

"Get rid of him, Alexandr Daviditch, or else I'm going," said Von Koren. "He'll bite me."

Von Koren's cool tone calmed the doctor; he seemed suddenly to come to himself, to recover his reason; he put both arms round Laevsky's waist, and, leading him away from the zoologist, muttered in a friendly voice that shook with emotion:

"My friends... dear, good... you've lost your tempers and that's enough... and that's enough, my friends."

Hearing his soft, friendly voice, Laevsky felt that something unheard of, monstrous, had just happened to him, as though he had been nearly run over by a train; he almost burst into tears, waved his hand, and ran out of the room.

"To feel that one is hated, to expose oneself before the man who hates one, in the most pitiful, contemptible, helpless state. My God, how hard it is!" he thought a little while afterwards as he sat in the pavilion, feeling as though his body were scarred by the hatred of which he had just been the object.

"How coarse it is, my God!"

Cold water with brandy in it revived him. He vividly pictured Von Koren's calm, haughty face; his eyes the day before, his shirt like a rug, his voice, his white hand; and heavy, passionate, hungry hatred rankled in his breast and clamoured for satisfaction. In his thoughts he felled Von Koren to the ground, and trampled him underfoot. He remembered to the minutest detail all that had happened, and wondered how he could have smiled ingratiatingly to that insignificant man, and how he could care for the opinion of wretched petty people whom nobody knew, living in a miserable little town which was not, it seemed, even on the map, and of which not one decent person in Petersburg had heard. If this wretched little town suddenly fell into ruins or caught fire, the telegram with the news would be read in Russia with no more interest than an advertisement of the sale of second-hand furniture. Whether he killed Von Koren next day or left him alive, it would be just the same, equally useless and uninteresting. Better to shoot him in the leg or hand, wound him, then laugh at him, and let him, like an insect with a broken leg lost in the grass--let him be lost with his obscure sufferings in the crowd of insignificant people like himself.

Laevsky went to Sheshkovsky, told him all about it, and asked him to be his second; then they both went to the superintendent of the postal telegraph department, and asked him, too, to be a second, and stayed to dinner with him. At dinner there was a great deal of joking and laughing. Laevsky made jests at his own expense, saying he hardly knew how to fire off a pistol, calling himself a royal archer and William Tell.

"We must give this gentleman a lesson..." he said.

After dinner they sat down to cards. Laevsky played, drank wine, and thought that duelling was stupid and senseless, as it did not decide the question but only complicated it, but that it was sometimes impossible to get on without it. In the given case, for instance, one could not, of course, bring an action against Von Koren. And this duel was so far good in that it made it impossible for Laevsky to remain in the town afterwards. He got a little drunk and interested in the game, and felt at ease.

But when the sun had set and it grew dark, he was possessed by a feeling of uneasiness. It was not fear at the thought of death, because while he was dining and playing cards, he had for some reason a confident belief that the duel would end in nothing; it was dread at the thought of something unknown which was to happen next morning for the first time in his life, and dread of the coming night... He knew that the night would be long and sleepless, and that he would have to think not only of Von Koren and his hatred, but also of the mountain of lies which he had to get through, and which he had not strength or ability to dispense with. It was as though he had been taken suddenly ill; all at once he lost all interest in the cards and in people, grew restless, and began asking them to let him go home. He was eager to get into bed, to lie without moving, and to prepare his thoughts for the night. Sheshkovsky and the postal superintendent saw him home and went on to Von Koren's to arrange about the duel.

Near his lodgings Laevsky met Atchmianov. The young man was breathless and excited.

"I am looking for you, Ivan Andreitch," he said. "I beg you to come quickly..."

"Where?"

"Some one wants to see you, some one you don't know, about very important business; he earnestly begs you to come for a minute. He wants to speak to you of something... For him it's a question of life and death..." In his excitement Atchmianov spoke in a strong Armenian accent.

"Who is it?" asked Laevsky.

"He asked me not to tell you his name."

"Tell him I'm busy; to-morrow, if he likes..."

"How can you!" Atchmianov was aghast. "He wants to tell you something very important for you... very important! If you don't come, something dreadful will happen."

"Strange..." muttered Laevsky, unable to understand why Atchmianov was so excited and what mysteries there could be in this dull, useless little town.

"Strange," he repeated in hesitation. "Come along, though; I don't care."

Atchmianov walked rapidly on ahead and Laevsky followed him. They walked down a street, then turned into an alley.

"What a bore this is!" said Laevsky.

"One minute, one minute... it's near."

Near the old rampart they went down a narrow alley between two empty enclosures, then they came into a sort of large yard and went towards a small house.

"That's Muridov's, isn't it?" asked Laevsky.

"Yes."

"But why we've come by the back yards I don't understand. We might have come by the street; it's nearer..."

"Never mind, never mind..."

It struck Laevsky as strange, too, that Atchmianov led him to a back entrance, and motioned to him as though bidding him go quietly and hold his tongue.

"This way, this way..." said Atchmianov, cautiously opening the door and going into the passage on tiptoe. "Quietly, quietly, I beg you... they may hear."

He listened, drew a deep breath and said in a whisper:

"Open that door, and go in... don't be afraid."

Laevsky, puzzled, opened the door and went into a room with a low ceiling and curtained windows.

There was a candle on the table.

"What do you want?" asked some one in the next room. "Is it you, Muridov?"

Laevsky turned into that room and saw Kirilin, and beside him Nadyezhda Fyodorovna.

He didn't hear what was said to him; he staggered back, and did not know how he found himself in the street. His hatred for Von Koren and his uneasiness--all had vanished from his soul. As he went home he waved his right arm awkwardly and looked carefully at the ground under his feet, trying to step where it was smooth. At home in his study he walked backwards and forwards, rubbing his hands, and awkwardly shrugging his shoulders and neck, as though his jacket and shirt were too tight; then he lighted a candle and sat down to the table...

XVI

"The 'humane studies' of which you speak will only satisfy human thought when, as they advance, they meet the exact sciences and progress side by side with them. Whether they will meet under a new microscope, or in the monologues of a new Hamlet, or in a new religion, I do not know, but I expect the earth will be covered with a crust of ice before it comes to pass. Of all humane learning the most durable and living is, of course, the teaching of Christ; but look how differently even that is interpreted! Some teach that we must love all our neighbours but make an exception of soldiers, criminals, and lunatics. They allow the first to be killed in war, the second to be isolated or executed, and the third they forbid to marry. Other interpreters teach that we must love all our neighbours without exception, with no distinction of plus or minus . According to their teaching, if a consumptive or a murderer or an epileptic asks your daughter in marriage, you must let him have her. If cretins go to war against the physically and mentally healthy, don't defend yourselves. This advocacy of love for love's sake, like art for art's sake, if it could have power, would bring mankind in the long run to complete extinction, and so would become the vastest crime that has ever been committed upon earth. There are very many interpretations, and since there are many of them, serious thought is not satisfied by any one of them, and hastens to add its own individual interpretation to the mass. For that reason you should never put a question on a philosophical or so-called Christian basis; by so doing you only remove the question further from solution."

The deacon listened to the zoologist attentively, thought a little, and asked:

"Have the philosophers invented the moral law which is innate in every man, or did God create it together with the body?"

"I don't know. But that law is so universal among all peoples and all ages that I fancy we ought to recognise it as organically connected with man. It is not invented, but exists and will exist. I don't tell you that one day it will be seen under the microscope, but its organic connection is shown, indeed, by evidence: serious affections of the brain and all so-called mental diseases, to the best of my belief, show themselves first of all in the perversion of the moral law."

"Good. So then, just as our stomach bids us eat, our moral sense bids us love our neighbours. Is that it? But our natural man through self-love opposes the voice of conscience and reason, and this gives rise to many brain-racking questions. To whom ought we to turn for the solution of those questions if you forbid us to put them on the philosophic basis?"

"Turn to what little exact science we have. Trust to evidence and the logic of facts. It is true it is but little, but, on the other hand, it is less fluid and shifting than philosophy. The moral law, let us suppose, demands that you love your neighbour. Well? Love ought to show itself in the removal of everything which in one way or another is injurious to men and threatens them with danger in the present or in the future. Our knowledge and the evidence tells us that the morally and physically abnormal are a menace to humanity. If so you must struggle against the abnormal; if you are not able to raise them to the normal standard you must have strength and ability to render them harmless--that is, to destroy them."

"So love consists in the strong overcoming the weak."

"Undoubtedly."

"But you know the strong crucified our Lord Jesus Christ," said the deacon hotly.

"The fact is that those who crucified Him were not the strong but the weak. Human culture weakens and strives to nullify the struggle for existence and natural selection; hence the rapid advancement of the weak and their predominance over the strong. Imagine that you succeeded in instilling into bees humanitarian ideas in their crude and elementary form. What would come of it? The drones who ought to be killed would remain alive, would devour the honey, would corrupt and stifle the bees, resulting in the predominance of the weak over the strong and the degeneration of the latter. The same process is taking place now with humanity; the weak are oppressing the strong. Among savages untouched by civilisation the strongest, cleverest, and most moral takes the lead; he is the chief and the master. But we civilised men have crucified Christ, and we go on crucifying Him, so there is something lacking in us... And that something one ought to raise up in ourselves, or there will be no end to these errors."

"But what criterion have you to distinguish the strong from the weak?"

"Knowledge and evidence. The tuberculous and the scrofulous are recognised by their diseases, and the insane and the immoral by their actions."

"But mistakes may be made!"

"Yes, but it's no use to be afraid of getting your feet wet when you are threatened with the deluge!"

"That's philosophy," laughed the deacon.

"Not a bit of it. You are so corrupted by your seminary philosophy that you want to see nothing but fog in everything. The abstract studies with which your youthful head is stuffed are called abstract just because they abstract your minds from what is obvious. Look the devil straight in the eye, and if he's the devil, tell him he's the devil, and don't go calling to Kant or Hegel for explanations."

The zoologist paused and went on:

"Twice two's four, and a stone's a stone. Here to-morrow we have a duel. You and I will say it's stupid and absurd, that the duel is out of date, that there is no real difference between the aristocratic duel and the drunken brawl in the pot-house, and yet we shall not stop, we shall go there and fight. So there is some force stronger than our reasoning. We shout that war is plunder, robbery, atrocity, fratricide; we cannot look upon blood without fainting; but the French or the Germans have only to insult us for us to feel at once an exaltation of spirit; in the most genuine way we shout 'Hurrah!' and rush to attack the foe. You will invoke the blessing of God on our weapons, and our valour will arouse universal and general enthusiasm. Again it follows that there is a force, if not higher, at any rate stronger, than us and our philosophy. We can no more stop it than that cloud which is moving upwards over the sea. Don't be hypocritical, don't make a long nose at it on the sly; and don't say, 'Ah, old-fashioned, stupid! Ah, it's inconsistent with Scripture!' but look it straight in the face, recognise its rational lawfulness, and when, for instance, it wants to destroy a rotten, scrofulous, corrupt race, don't hinder it with your pilules and misunderstood quotations from the Gospel. Leskov has a story of a conscientious Danila who found a leper outside the town, and fed and warmed him in the name of love and of Christ. If that Danila had really loved humanity, he would have dragged the leper as far as possible from the town, and would have flung him in a pit, and would have gone to save the healthy. Christ, I hope, taught us a rational, intelligent, practical love."

"What a fellow you are!" laughed the deacon. "You don't believe in Christ. Why do you mention His name so often?"

"Yes, I do believe in Him. Only, of course, in my own way, not in yours. Oh, deacon, deacon!" laughed the zoologist; he put his arm round the deacon's waist, and said gaily: "Well? Are you coming with us to the duel to-morrow?"

"My orders don't allow it, or else I should come."

"What do you mean by 'orders'?"

"I have been consecrated. I am in a state of grace."

"Oh, deacon, deacon," repeated Von Koren, laughing, "I love talking to you."

"You say you have faith," said the deacon. "What sort of faith is it? Why, I have an uncle, a priest, and he believes so that when in time of drought he goes out into the fields to pray for rain, he takes his umbrella and leather overcoat for fear of getting wet through on his way home. That's faith! When he speaks of Christ, his face is full of radiance, and all the peasants, men and women, weep floods of tears. He would stop that cloud and put all those forces you talk about to flight. Yes... faith moves mountains."

The deacon laughed and slapped the zoologist on the shoulder.

"Yes..." he went on; "here you are teaching all the time, fathoming the depths of the ocean, dividing the weak and the strong, writing books and challenging to duels--and everything remains as it is; but, behold! some feeble old man will mutter just one word with a holy spirit, or a new Mahomet, with a sword, will gallop from Arabia, and everything will be topsy-turvy, and in Europe not one stone will be left standing upon another."

"Well, deacon, that's on the knees of the gods."

"Faith without works is dead, but works without faith are worse still--mere waste of time and nothing more."

The doctor came into sight on the sea-front. He saw the deacon and the zoologist, and went up to them.

"I believe everything is ready," he said, breathing hard. "Govorovsky and Boyko will be the seconds. They will start at five o'clock in the morning. How it has clouded over," he said, looking at the sky. "One can see nothing; there will be rain directly."

"I hope you are coming with us?" said the zoologist.

"No, God preserve me; I'm worried enough as it is. Ustimovitch is going instead of me. I've spoken to him already."

Far over the sea was a flash of lightning, followed by a hollow roll of thunder.

"How stifling it is before a storm!" said Von Koren. "I bet you've been to Laevsky already and have been weeping on his bosom."

"Why should I go to him?" answered the doctor in confusion. "What next?"

Before sunset he had walked several times along the boulevard and the street in the hope of meeting Laevsky. He was ashamed of his hastiness and the sudden outburst of friendliness which had followed it. He wanted to apologise to Laevsky in a joking tone, to give him a good talking to, to soothe him and to tell him that the duel was a survival of mediaeval barbarism, but that Providence itself had brought them to the duel as a means of reconciliation; that the next day, both being splendid and highly intelligent people, they would, after exchanging shots, appreciate each other's noble qualities and would become friends. But he could not come across Laevsky.

"What should I go and see him for?" repeated Samoylenko. "I did not insult him; he insulted me. Tell me, please, why he attacked me. What harm had I done him? I go into the drawing-room, and, all of a sudden, without the least provocation: 'Spy!' There's a nice thing! Tell me, how did it begin? What did you say to him?"

"I told him his position was hopeless. And I was right. It is only honest men or scoundrels who can find an escape from any position, but one who wants to be at the same time an honest man and a scoundrel --it is a hopeless position. But it's eleven o'clock, gentlemen, and we have to be up early to-morrow."

There was a sudden gust of wind; it blew up the dust on the seafront, whirled it round in eddies, with a howl that drowned the roar of the sea.

"A squall," said the deacon. "We must go in, our eyes are getting full of dust."

As they went, Samoylenko sighed and, holding his hat, said:

"I suppose I shan't sleep to-night."

"Don't you agitate yourself," laughed the zoologist. "You can set your mind at rest; the duel will end in nothing. Laevsky will magnanimously fire into the air--he can do nothing else; and I daresay I shall not fire at all. To be arrested and lose my time on Laevsky's account--the game's not worth the candle. By the way, what is the punishment for duelling?"

"Arrest, and in the case of the death of your opponent a maximum of three years' imprisonment in the fortress."

"The fortress of St. Peter and St. Paul?"

"No, in a military fortress, I believe."

"Though this fine gentleman ought to have a lesson!"

Behind them on the sea, there was a flash of lightning, which for an instant lighted up the roofs of the houses and the mountains. The friends parted near the boulevard. When the doctor disappeared in the darkness and his steps had died away, Von Koren shouted to him:

"I only hope the weather won't interfere with us to-morrow!"

"Very likely it will! Please God it may!"

"Good-night!"

"What about the night? What do you say?"

In the roar of the wind and the sea and the crashes of thunder, it was difficult to hear.

"It's nothing," shouted the zoologist, and hurried home.

XVII

"Upon my mind, weighed down with woe,
Crowd thoughts, a heavy multitude:
In silence memory unfolds
Her long, long scroll before my eyes.
Loathing and shuddering I curse
And bitterly lament in vain,
And bitter though the tears I weep
I do not wash those lines away."

PUSHKIN.

Whether they killed him next morning, or mocked at him--that is, left him his life--he was ruined, anyway. Whether this disgraced woman killed herself in her shame and despair, or dragged on her pitiful existence, she was ruined anyway.

So thought Laevsky as he sat at the table late in the evening, still rubbing his hands. The windows suddenly blew open with a bang; a violent gust of wind burst into the room, and the papers fluttered from the table. Laevsky closed the windows and bent down to pick up the papers. He was aware of something new in his body, a sort of awkwardness he had not felt before, and his movements were strange to him. He moved timidly, jerking with his elbows and shrugging his shoulders; and when he sat down to the table again, he again began rubbing his hands. His body had lost its suppleness.

On the eve of death one ought to write to one's nearest relation. Laevsky thought of this. He took a pen and wrote with a tremulous hand:

"Mother!"

He wanted to write to beg his mother, for the sake of the merciful God in whom she believed, that she would give shelter and bring a little warmth and kindness into the life of the unhappy woman who, by his doing, had been disgraced and was in solitude, poverty, and weakness, that she would forgive and forget everything, everything, everything, and by her sacrifice atone to some extent for her son's terrible sin. But he remembered how his mother, a stout, heavily-built old woman in a lace cap, used to go out into the garden in the morning, followed by her companion with the lap-dog; how she used to shout in a peremptory way to the gardener and the servants, and how proud and haughty her face was--he remembered all this and scratched out the word he had written.

There was a vivid flash of lightning at all three windows, and it was followed by a prolonged, deafening roll of thunder, beginning with a hollow rumble and ending with a crash so violent that all the window-panes rattled. Laevsky got up, went to the window, and pressed his forehead against the pane. There was a fierce, magnificent storm. On the horizon lightning-flashes were flung in white streams from the storm-clouds into the sea, lighting up the high, dark waves over the far-away expanse. And to right and to left, and, no doubt, over the house too, the lightning flashed.

"The storm!" whispered Laevsky; he had a longing to pray to some one or to something, if only to the lightning or the storm-clouds. "Dear storm!"

He remembered how as a boy he used to run out into the garden without a hat on when there was a storm, and how two fair-haired girls with blue eyes used to run after him, and how they got wet through with the rain; they laughed with delight, but when there was a loud peal of thunder, the girls used to nestle up to the boy confidingly, while he crossed himself and made haste to repeat: "Holy, holy, holy..." Oh, where had they vanished to! In what sea were they drowned, those dawning days of pure, fair life? He had no fear of the storm, no

love of nature now; he had no God. All the confiding girls he had ever
known had by now been ruined by him and those like him. All his life
he had not planted one tree in his own garden, nor grown one blade
of grass; and living among the living, he had not saved one fly; he had
done nothing but destroy and ruin, and lie, lie...

"What in my past was not vice?" he asked himself, trying to clutch
at some bright memory as a man falling down a precipice clutches at
the bushes.

School? The university? But that was a sham. He had neglected
his work and forgotten what he had learnt. The service of his country?
That, too, was a sham, for he did nothing in the Service, took a salary
for doing nothing, and it was an abominable swindling of the State for
which one was not punished.

He had no craving for truth, and had not sought it; spellbound by
vice and lying, his conscience had slept or been silent. Like a stranger,
like an alien from another planet, he had taken no part in the common
life of men, had been indifferent to their sufferings, their ideas, their
religion, their sciences, their strivings, and their struggles. He had not
said one good word, not written one line that was not useless and
vulgar; he had not done his fellows one ha'p'orth of service, but had
eaten their bread, drunk their wine, seduced their wives, lived on their
thoughts, and to justify his contemptible, parasitic life in their eyes
and in his own, he had always tried to assume an air of being higher
and better than they. Lies, lies, lies...

He vividly remembered what he had seen that evening at
Muridov's, and he was in an insufferable anguish of loathing and
misery. Kirilin and Atchmianov were loathsome, but they were only
continuing what he had begun; they were his accomplices and his
disciples. This young weak woman had trusted him more than a
brother, and he had deprived her of her husband, of her friends and
of her country, and had brought her here--to the heat, to fever, and to
boredom; and from day to day she was bound to reflect, like a mirror,
his idleness, his viciousness and falsity--and that was all she had had

to fill her weak, listless, pitiable life. Then he had grown sick of her, had begun to hate her, but had not had the pluck to abandon her, and he had tried to entangle her more and more closely in a web of lies... These men had done the rest.

Laevsky sat at the table, then got up and went to the window; at one minute he put out the candle and then he lighted it again. He cursed himself aloud, wept and wailed, and asked forgiveness; several times he ran to the table in despair, and wrote:

"Mother!"

Except his mother, he had no relations or near friends; but how could his mother help him? And where was she? He had an impulse to run to Nadyezhda Fyodorovna, to fall at her feet, to kiss her hands and feet, to beg her forgiveness; but she was his victim, and he was afraid of her as though she were dead.

"My life is ruined," he repeated, rubbing his hands. "Why am I still alive, my God!..."

He had cast out of heaven his dim star; it had fallen, and its track was lost in the darkness of night. It would never return to the sky again, because life was given only once and never came a second time. If he could have turned back the days and years of the past, he would have replaced the falsity with truth, the idleness with work, the boredom with happiness; he would have given back purity to those whom he had robbed of it. He would have found God and goodness, but that was as impossible as to put back the fallen star into the sky, and because it was impossible he was in despair.

When the storm was over, he sat by the open window and thought calmly of what was before him. Von Koren would most likely kill him. The man's clear, cold theory of life justified the destruction of the rotten and the useless; if it changed at the crucial moment, it would be the hatred and the repugnance that Laevsky inspired in him that would save him. If he missed his aim or, in mockery of his hated opponent, only wounded him, or fired in the air, what could he do then? Where could he go?

"Go to Petersburg?" Laevsky asked himself. But that would mean beginning over again the old life which he cursed. And the man who seeks salvation in change of place like a migrating bird would find nothing anywhere, for all the world is alike to him. Seek salvation in men? In whom and how? Samoylenko's kindness and generosity could no more save him than the deacon's laughter or Von Koren's hatred. He must look for salvation in himself alone, and if there were no finding it, why waste time? He must kill himself, that was all...

He heard the sound of a carriage. It was getting light. The carriage passed by, turned, and crunching on the wet sand, stopped near the house. There were two men in the carriage.

"Wait a minute; I'm coming directly," Laevsky said to them out of the window. "I'm not asleep. Surely it's not time yet?"

"Yes, it's four o'clock. By the time we get there..."

Laevsky put on his overcoat and cap, put some cigarettes in his pocket, and stood still hesitating. He felt as though there was something else he must do. In the street the seconds talked in low voices and the horses snorted, and this sound in the damp, early morning, when everybody was asleep and light was hardly dawning in the sky, filled Laevsky's soul with a disconsolate feeling which was like a presentiment of evil. He stood for a little, hesitating, and went into the bedroom.

Nadyezhda Fyodorovna was lying stretched out on the bed, wrapped from head to foot in a rug. She did not stir, and her whole appearance, especially her head, suggested an Egyptian mummy. Looking at her in silence, Laevsky mentally asked her forgiveness, and thought that if the heavens were not empty and there really were a God, then He would save her; if there were no God, then she had better perish--there was nothing for her to live for.

All at once she jumped up, and sat up in bed. Lifting her pale face and looking with horror at Laevsky, she asked:

"Is it you? Is the storm over?"

"Yes."

She remembered; put both hands to her head and shuddered all over.

"How miserable I am!" she said. "If only you knew how miserable I am! I expected," she went on, half closing her eyes, "that you would kill me or turn me out of the house into the rain and storm, but you delay... delay..."

Warmly and impulsively he put his arms round her and covered her knees and hands with kisses. Then when she muttered something and shuddered with the thought of the past, he stroked her hair, and looking into her face, realised that this unhappy, sinful woman was the one creature near and dear to him, whom no one could replace.

When he went out of the house and got into the carriage he wanted to return home alive.

XVIII

The deacon got up, dressed, took his thick, gnarled stick and slipped quietly out of the house. It was dark, and for the first minute when he went into the street, he could not even see his white stick. There was not a single star in the sky, and it looked as though there would be rain again. There was a smell of wet sand and sea.

"It's to be hoped that the mountaineers won't attack us," thought the deacon, hearing the tap of the stick on the pavement, and noticing how loud and lonely the taps sounded in the stillness of the night.

When he got out of town, he began to see both the road and his stick. Here and there in the black sky there were dark cloudy patches, and soon a star peeped out and timidly blinked its one eye. The deacon walked along the high rocky coast and did not see the sea; it was slumbering below, and its unseen waves broke languidly and heavily on the shore, as though sighing "Ouf!" and how slowly! One wave broke--the deacon had time to count eight steps; then another broke, and six steps; later a third. As before, nothing could be seen, and in the darkness one could hear the languid, drowsy drone of the sea. One could hear the infinitely faraway, inconceivable time when God moved above chaos.

The deacon felt uncanny. He hoped God would not punish him for keeping company with infidels, and even going to look at their duels. The duel would be nonsensical, bloodless, absurd, but however that might be, it was a heathen spectacle, and it was altogether unseemly for an ecclesiastical person to be present at it. He stopped and wondered--should he go back? But an intense, restless curiosity triumphed over his doubts, and he went on.

"Though they are infidels they are good people, and will be saved," he assured himself. "They are sure to be saved," he said aloud, lighting a cigarette.

By what standard must one measure men's qualities, to judge rightly of them? The deacon remembered his enemy, the inspector of the clerical school, who believed in God, lived in chastity, and did not fight duels; but he used to feed the deacon on bread with sand in it, and on one occasion almost pulled off the deacon's ear. If human life was so artlessly constructed that every one respected this cruel and dishonest inspector who stole the Government flour, and his health and salvation were prayed for in the schools, was it just to shun such men as Von Koren and Laevsky, simply because they were unbelievers? The deacon was weighing this question, but he recalled how absurd Samoylenko had looked yesterday, and that broke the thread of his ideas. What fun they would have next day! The deacon imagined how he would sit under a bush and look on, and when Von Koren began boasting next day at dinner, he, the deacon, would begin laughing and telling him all the details of the duel.

"How do you know all about it?" the zoologist would ask.

"Well, there you are! I stayed at home, but I know all about it."

It would be nice to write a comic description of the duel. His father-in-law would read it and laugh. A good story, told or written, was more than meat and drink to his father-in-law.

The valley of the Yellow River opened before him. The stream was broader and fiercer for the rain, and instead of murmuring as before, it was raging. It began to get light. The grey, dingy morning, and the clouds racing towards the west to overtake the storm-clouds, the mountains girt with mist, and the wet trees, all struck the deacon as ugly and sinister. He washed at the brook, repeated his morning prayer, and felt a longing for tea and hot rolls, with sour cream, which were served every morning at his father-in-law's. He remembered his wife and the "Days past Recall," which she played on the piano. What sort of woman was she? His wife had been introduced, betrothed, and married to him all in one week: he had lived with her less than a month when he was ordered here, so that he had not had time to find out what she was like. All the same, he rather missed her.

"I must write her a nice letter..." he thought. The flag on the duhan hung limp, soaked by the rain, and the duhan itself with its wet roof seemed darker and lower than it had been before. Near the door was standing a cart; Kerbalay, with two mountaineers and a young Tatar woman in trousers--no doubt Kerbalay's wife or daughter--were bringing sacks of something out of the duhan , and putting them on maize straw in the cart.

Near the cart stood a pair of asses hanging their heads. When they had put in all the sacks, the mountaineers and the Tatar woman began covering them over with straw, while Kerbalay began hurriedly harnessing the asses.

"Smuggling, perhaps," thought the deacon.

Here was the fallen tree with the dried pine-needles, here was the blackened patch from the fire. He remembered the picnic and all its incidents, the fire, the singing of the mountaineers, his sweet dreams of becoming a bishop, and of the Church procession... The Black River had grown blacker and broader with the rain. The deacon walked cautiously over the narrow bridge, which by now was reached by the topmost crests of the dirty water, and went up through the little copse to the drying-shed.

"A splendid head," he thought, stretching himself on the straw, and thinking of Von Koren. "A fine head--God grant him health; only there is cruelty in him..."

Why did he hate Laevsky and Laevsky hate him? Why were they going to fight a duel? If from their childhood they had known poverty as the deacon had; if they had been brought up among ignorant, hard-hearted, grasping, coarse and ill-mannered people who grudged you a crust of bread, who spat on the floor and hiccoughed at dinner and at prayers; if they had not been spoilt from childhood by the pleasant surroundings and the select circle of friends they lived in--how they would have rushed at each other, how readily they would have overlooked each other's shortcomings and would have prized each other's strong points! Why, how few even outwardly decent people there were in the world! It was true that Laevsky was flighty, dissipated, queer, but he did not steal, did not spit loudly on the floor; he did not abuse his wife and say, "You'll eat till you burst, but you don't want to work;" he would not beat a child with reins, or give his servants stinking meat to eat-- surely this was reason enough to be indulgent to him? Besides, he was the chief sufferer from his failings, like a sick man from his sores. Instead of being led by boredom and some sort of misunderstanding to look for degeneracy, extinction, heredity, and other such incomprehensible things in each other, would they not do better to stoop a little lower and turn their hatred and anger where whole streets resounded with moanings from coarse ignorance, greed, scolding, impurity, swearing, the shrieks of women...

The sound of a carriage interrupted the deacon's thoughts. He glanced out of the door and saw a carriage and in it three persons: Laevsky, Sheshkovsky, and the superintendent of the post-office.

"Stop!" said Sheshkovsky.

All three got out of the carriage and looked at one another.

"They are not here yet," said Sheshkovsky, shaking the mud off. "Well? Till the show begins, let us go and find a suitable spot; there's not room to turn round here."

They went further up the river and soon vanished from sight. The Tatar driver sat in the carriage with his head resting on his shoulder and fell asleep. After waiting ten minutes the deacon came out of the drying-shed, and taking off his black hat that he might not be noticed, he began threading his way among the bushes and strips of maize along the bank, crouching and looking about him. The grass and maize were wet, and big drops fell on his head from the trees and bushes. "Disgraceful!" he muttered, picking up his wet and muddy skirt. "Had I realised it, I would not have come."

Soon he heard voices and caught sight of them. Laevsky was walking rapidly to and fro in the small glade with bowed back and hands thrust in his sleeves; his seconds were standing at the water's edge, rolling cigarettes.

"Strange," thought the deacon, not recognising Laevsky's walk; "he looks like an old man..."

"How rude it is of them!" said the superintendent of the post-office, looking at his watch. "It may be learned manners to be late, but to my thinking it's hoggish."

Sheshkovsky, a stout man with a black beard, listened and said:

"They're coming!"

XIX

"It's the first time in my life I've seen it! How glorious!" said Von Koren, pointing to the glade and stretching out his hands to the east. "Look: green rays!"

In the east behind the mountains rose two green streaks of light, and it really was beautiful. The sun was rising.

"Good-morning!" the zoologist went on, nodding to Laevsky's seconds. "I'm not late, am I?"

He was followed by his seconds, Boyko and Govorovsky, two very young officers of the same height, wearing white tunics, and

Ustimovitch, the thin, unsociable doctor; in one hand he had a bag of some sort, and in the other hand, as usual, a cane which he held behind him. Laying the bag on the ground and greeting no one, he put the other hand, too, behind his back and began pacing up and down the glade.

Laevsky felt the exhaustion and awkwardness of a man who is soon perhaps to die, and is for that reason an object of general attention. He wanted to be killed as soon as possible or taken home. He saw the sunrise now for the first time in his life; the early morning, the green rays of light, the dampness, and the men in wet boots, seemed to him to have nothing to do with his life, to be superfluous and embarrassing. All this had no connection with the night he had been through, with his thoughts and his feeling of guilt, and so he would have gladly gone away without waiting for the duel.

Von Koren was noticeably excited and tried to conceal it, pretending that he was more interested in the green light than anything. The seconds were confused, and looked at one another as though wondering why they were here and what they were to do.

"I imagine, gentlemen, there is no need for us to go further," said Sheshkovsky. "This place will do."

"Yes, of course," Von Koren agreed.

A silence followed. Ustimovitch, pacing to and fro, suddenly turned sharply to Laevsky and said in a low voice, breathing into his face:

"They have very likely not told you my terms yet. Each side is to pay me fifteen roubles, and in the case of the death of one party, the survivor is to pay thirty."

Laevsky was already acquainted with the man, but now for the first time he had a distinct view of his lustreless eyes, his stiff moustaches, and wasted, consumptive neck; he was a money-grubber, not a doctor; his breath had an unpleasant smell of beef.

"What people there are in the world!" thought Laevsky, and answered: "Very good."

The doctor nodded and began pacing to and fro again, and it was evident he did not need the money at all, but simply asked for it from hatred. Every one felt it was time to begin, or to end what had been begun, but instead of beginning or ending, they stood about, moved to and fro and smoked. The young officers, who were present at a duel for the first time in their lives, and even now hardly believed in this civilian and, to their thinking, unnecessary duel, looked critically at their tunics and stroked their sleeves. Sheshkovsky went up to them and said softly: "Gentlemen, we must use every effort to prevent this duel; they ought to be reconciled."

He flushed crimson and added:

"Kirilin was at my rooms last night complaining that Laevsky had found him with Nadyezhda Fyodorovna, and all that sort of thing."

"Yes, we know that too," said Boyko.

"Well, you see, then... Laevsky's hands are trembling and all that sort of thing... he can scarcely hold a pistol now. To fight with him is as inhuman as to fight a man who is drunk or who has typhoid. If a reconciliation cannot be arranged, we ought to put off the duel, gentlemen, or something... It's such a sickening business, I can't bear to see it."

"Talk to Von Koren."

"I don't know the rules of duelling, damnation take them, and I don't want to either; perhaps he'll imagine Laevsky funks it and has sent me to him, but he can think what he likes--I'll speak to him."

Sheshkovsky hesitatingly walked up to Von Koren with a slight limp, as though his leg had gone to sleep; and as he went towards him, clearing his throat, his whole figure was a picture of indolence.

"There's something I must say to you, sir," he began, carefully scrutinising the flowers on the zoologist's shirt. "It's confidential. I don't know the rules of duelling, damnation take them, and I don't want to, and I look on the matter not as a second and that sort of thing, but as a man, and that's all about it."

"Yes. Well?"

"When seconds suggest reconciliation they are usually not listened to; it is looked upon as a formality. Amour propre and all that. But I humbly beg you to look carefully at Ivan Andreitch. He's not in a normal state, so to speak, to-day--not in his right mind, and a pitiable object. He has had a misfortune. I can't endure gossip..."

Sheshkovsky flushed crimson and looked round.

"But in view of the duel, I think it necessary to inform you, Laevsky found his madam last night at Muridov's with... another gentleman."

"How disgusting!" muttered the zoologist; he turned pale, frowned, and spat loudly. "Tfoo!"

His lower lip quivered, he walked away from Sheshkovsky, unwilling to hear more, and as though he had accidentally tasted something bitter, spat loudly again, and for the first time that morning looked with hatred at Laevsky. His excitement and awkwardness passed off; he tossed his head and said aloud:

"Gentlemen, what are we waiting for, I should like to know? Why don't we begin?"

Sheshkovsky glanced at the officers and shrugged his shoulders.

"Gentlemen," he said aloud, addressing no one in particular. "Gentlemen, we propose that you should be reconciled."

"Let us make haste and get the formalities over," said Von Koren. "Reconciliation has been discussed already. What is the next formality? Make haste, gentlemen, time won't wait for us."

"But we insist on reconciliation all the same," said Sheshkovsky in a guilty voice, as a man compelled to interfere in another man's business; he flushed, laid his hand on his heart, and went on: "Gentlemen, we see no grounds for associating the offence with the duel. There's nothing in common between duelling and offences against one another of which we are sometimes guilty through human weakness. You are university men and men of culture, and no doubt you see in the duel nothing but a foolish and out-of-date formality, and all that sort of thing. That's how we look at it ourselves, or we shouldn't have come, for we cannot allow that in our presence men should fire at one another, and all that."

Sheshkovsky wiped the perspiration off his face and went on: "Make an end to your misunderstanding, gentlemen; shake hands, and let us go home and drink to peace. Upon my honour, gentlemen!"

Von Koren did not speak. Laevsky, seeing that they were looking at him, said:

"I have nothing against Nikolay Vassilitch; if he considers I'm to blame, I'm ready to apologise to him."

Von Koren was offended.

"It is evident, gentlemen," he said, "you want Mr. Laevsky to return home a magnanimous and chivalrous figure, but I cannot give you and him that satisfaction. And there was no need to get up early and drive eight miles out of town simply to drink to peace, to have breakfast, and to explain to me that the duel is an out-of-date formality. A duel is a duel, and there is no need to make it more false and stupid than it is in reality. I want to fight!"

A silence followed. Boyko took a pair of pistols out of a box; one was given to Von Koren and one to Laevsky, and then there followed a difficulty which afforded a brief amusement to the zoologist and the seconds. It appeared that of all the people present not one had ever in his life been at a duel, and no one knew precisely how they ought to stand, and what the seconds ought to say and do. But then Boyko remembered and began, with a smile, to explain.

"Gentlemen, who remembers the description in Lermontov?" asked Von Koren, laughing. "In Turgenev, too, Bazarov had a duel with some one..."

"There's no need to remember," said Ustimovitch impatiently. "Measure the distance, that's all."

And he took three steps as though to show how to measure it. Boyko counted out the steps while his companion drew his sabre and scratched the earth at the extreme points to mark the barrier. In complete silence the opponents took their places.

"Moles," the deacon thought, sitting in the bushes.

Sheshkovsky said something, Boyko explained something again, but Laevsky did not hear--or rather heard, but did not understand. He cocked his pistol when the time came to do so, and raised the cold, heavy weapon with the barrel upwards. He forgot to unbutton his overcoat, and it felt very tight over his shoulder and under his arm, and his arm rose as awkwardly as though the sleeve had been cut out of tin. He remembered the hatred he had felt the night before for the swarthy brow and curly hair, and felt that even yesterday at the moment of intense hatred and anger he could not have shot a man. Fearing that the bullet might somehow hit Von Koren by accident, he raised the pistol higher and higher, and felt that this too obvious magnanimity was indelicate and anything but magnanimous, but he did not know how else to do and could do nothing else. Looking at the pale, ironically smiling face of Von Koren, who evidently had been convinced from the beginning that his opponent would fire in the air, Laevsky thought that, thank God, everything would be over directly, and all that he had to do was to press the trigger rather hard...

He felt a violent shock on the shoulder; there was the sound of a shot and an answering echo in the mountains: ping-ting!

Von Koren cocked his pistol and looked at Ustimovitch, who was pacing as before with his hands behind his back, taking no notice of any one.

"Doctor," said the zoologist, "be so good as not to move to and fro like a pendulum. You make me dizzy."

The doctor stood still. Von Koren began to take aim at Laevsky.

"It's all over!" thought Laevsky.

The barrel of the pistol aimed straight at his face, the expression of hatred and contempt in Von Koren's attitude and whole figure, and the murder just about to be committed by a decent man in broad daylight, in the presence of decent men, and the stillness and the unknown force that compelled Laevsky to stand still and not to run --how mysterious it all was, how incomprehensible and terrible!

The moment while Von Koren was taking aim seemed to Laevsky longer than a night: he glanced imploringly at the seconds; they were pale and did not stir.

"Make haste and fire," thought Laevsky, and felt that his pale, quivering, and pitiful face must arouse even greater hatred in Von Koren.

"I'll kill him directly," thought Von Koren, aiming at his forehead, with his finger already on the catch. "Yes, of course I'll kill him."

"He'll kill him!" A despairing shout was suddenly heard somewhere very close at hand.

A shot rang out at once. Seeing that Laevsky remained standing where he was and did not fall, they all looked in the direction from which the shout had come, and saw the deacon. With pale face and wet hair sticking to his forehead and his cheeks, wet through and muddy, he was standing in the maize on the further bank, smiling rather queerly and waving his wet hat. Sheshkovsky laughed with joy, burst into tears, and moved away...

XX

A little while afterwards, Von Koren and the deacon met near the little bridge. The deacon was excited; he breathed hard, and avoided looking in people's faces. He felt ashamed both of his terror and his muddy, wet garments.

"I thought you meant to kill him..." he muttered. "How contrary to human nature it is! How utterly unnatural it is!"

"But how did you come here?" asked the zoologist.

"Don't ask," said the deacon, waving his hand. "The evil one tempted me, saying: 'Go, go...' So I went and almost died of fright in the maize. But now, thank God, thank God... I am awfully pleased with you," muttered the deacon. "Old Grandad Tarantula will be glad... It's funny, it's too funny! Only I beg of you most earnestly don't tell anybody I was there, or I may get into hot water with the authorities. They will say: 'The deacon was a second.'"

"Gentlemen," said Von Koren, "the deacon asks you not to tell any one you've seen him here. He might get into trouble."

"How contrary to human nature it is!" sighed the deacon. "Excuse my saying so, but your face was so dreadful that I thought you were going to kill him."

"I was very much tempted to put an end to that scoundrel," said Von Koren, "but you shouted close by, and I missed my aim. The whole procedure is revolting to any one who is not used to it, and it has exhausted me, deacon. I feel awfully tired. Come along..."

"No, you must let me walk back. I must get dry, for I am wet and cold."

"Well, as you like," said the zoologist, in a weary tone, feeling dispirited, and, getting into the carriage, he closed his eyes. "As you like..."

While they were moving about the carriages and taking their seats, Kerbalay stood in the road, and, laying his hands on his stomach, he bowed low, showing his teeth; he imagined that the gentry had come to enjoy the beauties of nature and drink tea, and could not understand why they were getting into the carriages. The party set off in complete silence and only the deacon was left by the duhan .

"Come to the duhan , drink tea," he said to Kerbalay. "Me wants to eat."

Kerbalay spoke good Russian, but the deacon imagined that the Tatar would understand him better if he talked to him in broken Russian. "Cook omelette, give cheese..."

"Come, come, father," said Kerbalay, bowing. "I'll give you everything... I've cheese and wine... Eat what you like."

"What is 'God' in Tatar?" asked the deacon, going into the duhan .

"Your God and my God are the same," said Kerbalay, not understanding him. "God is the same for all men, only men are different. Some are Russian, some are Turks, some are English--there are many sorts of men, but God is one."

"Very good. If all men worship the same God, why do you Mohammedans look upon Christians as your everlasting enemies?"

"Why are you angry?" said Kerbalay, laying both hands on his stomach. "You are a priest; I am a Mussulman: you say, 'I want to eat'--I give it you... Only the rich man distinguishes your God from my God; for the poor man it is all the same. If you please, it is ready."

While this theological conversation was taking place at the duhan , Laevsky was driving home thinking how dreadful it had been driving there at daybreak, when the roads, the rocks, and the mountains were wet and dark, and the uncertain future seemed like a terrible abyss, of which one could not see the bottom; while now the raindrops hanging on the grass and on the stones were sparkling in the sun like diamonds, nature was smiling joyfully, and the terrible future was left behind. He looked at Sheshkovsky's sullen, tear-stained face, and at the two carriages ahead of them in which Von Koren, his seconds, and the doctor were sitting, and it seemed to him as though they were all coming back from a graveyard in which a wearisome, insufferable man who was a burden to others had just been buried.

"Everything is over," he thought of his past, cautiously touching his neck with his fingers.

On the right side of his neck was a small swelling, of the length and breadth of his little finger, and he felt a pain, as though some one had passed a hot iron over his neck. The bullet had bruised it.

Afterwards, when he got home, a strange, long, sweet day began for him, misty as forgetfulness. Like a man released from prison or from hospital, he stared at the long-familiar objects and wondered that the tables, the windows, the chairs, the light, and the sea stirred in him a keen, childish delight such as he had not known for long, long years. Nadyezhda Fyodorovna, pale and haggard, could not understand his gentle voice and strange movements; she made haste to tell him everything that had happened to her... It seemed to her that very likely he scarcely heard and did not understand her, and that if he did know everything he would curse her and kill her, but he listened to her, stroked her face and hair, looked into her eyes and said:

"I have nobody but you..."

Then they sat a long while in the garden, huddled close together, saying nothing, or dreaming aloud of their happy life in the future, in brief, broken sentences, while it seemed to him that he had never spoken at such length or so eloquently.

XXI

More than three months had passed.

The day came that Von Koren had fixed on for his departure. A cold, heavy rain had been falling from early morning, a north-east wind was blowing, and the waves were high on the sea. It was said that the steamer would hardly be able to come into the harbour in such weather. By the time-table it should have arrived at ten o'clock in the morning, but Von Koren, who had gone on to the sea-front at midday and again after dinner, could see nothing through the field-glass but grey waves and rain covering the horizon.

Towards the end of the day the rain ceased and the wind began to drop perceptibly. Von Koren had already made up his mind that he would not be able to get off that day, and had settled down to play chess with Samoylenko; but after dark the orderly announced that there were lights on the sea and that a rocket had been seen.

Von Koren made haste. He put his satchel over his shoulder, and kissed Samoylenko and the deacon. Though there was not the slightest necessity, he went through the rooms again, said good-bye to the orderly and the cook, and went out into the street, feeling that he had left something behind, either at the doctor's or his lodging. In the street he walked beside Samoylenko, behind them came the deacon with a box, and last of all the orderly with two portmanteaus. Only

Samoylenko and the orderly could distinguish the dim lights on the sea. The others gazed into the darkness and saw nothing. The steamer had stopped a long way from the coast.

"Make haste, make haste," Von Koren hurried them. "I am afraid it will set off."

As they passed the little house with three windows, into which Laevsky had moved soon after the duel, Von Koren could not resist peeping in at the window. Laevsky was sitting, writing, bent over the table, with his back to the window.

"I wonder at him!" said the zoologist softly. "What a screw he has put on himself!"

"Yes, one may well wonder," said Samoylenko. "He sits from morning till night, he's always at work. He works to pay off his debts. And he lives, brother, worse than a beggar!"

Half a minute of silence followed. The zoologist, the doctor, and the deacon stood at the window and went on looking at Laevsky.

"So he didn't get away from here, poor fellow," said Samoylenko. "Do you remember how hard he tried?"

"Yes, he has put a screw on himself," Von Koren repeated. "His marriage, the way he works all day long for his daily bread, a new expression in his face, and even in his walk--it's all so extraordinary that I don't know what to call it."

The zoologist took Samoylenko's sleeve and went on with emotion in his voice:

"You tell him and his wife that when I went away I was full of admiration for them and wished them all happiness... and I beg him, if he can, not to remember evil against me. He knows me. He knows that if I could have foreseen this change, then I might have become his best friend."

"Go in and say good-bye to him."

"No, that wouldn't do."

"Why? God knows, perhaps you'll never see him again."

The zoologist reflected, and said:

"That's true."

Samoylenko tapped softly at the window. Laevsky started and looked round.

"Vanya, Nikolay Vassilitch wants to say goodbye to you," said Samoylenko. "He is just going away."

Laevsky got up from the table, and went into the passage to open the door. Samoylenko, the zoologist, and the deacon went into the house.

"I can only come for one minute," began the zoologist, taking off his galoshes in the passage, and already wishing he had not given way to his feelings and come in, uninvited. "It is as though I were forcing myself on him," he thought, "and that's stupid."

"Forgive me for disturbing you," he said as he went into the room with Laevsky, "but I'm just going away, and I had an impulse to see you. God knows whether we shall ever meet again."

"I am very glad to see you... Please come in," said Laevsky, and he awkwardly set chairs for his visitors as though he wanted to bar their way, and stood in the middle of the room, rubbing his hands.

"I should have done better to have left my audience in the street," thought Von Koren, and he said firmly: "Don't remember evil against me, Ivan Andreitch. To forget the past is, of course, impossible --it is too painful, and I've not come here to apologise or to declare that I was not to blame. I acted sincerely, and I have not changed my convictions since then... It is true that I see, to my great delight, that I was mistaken in regard to you, but it's easy to make a false step even on a smooth road, and, in fact, it's the natural human lot: if one is not mistaken in the main, one is mistaken in the details. Nobody knows the real truth."

"No, no one knows the truth," said Laevsky.

"Well, good-bye... God give you all happiness."

Von Koren gave Laevsky his hand; the latter took it and bowed.

"Don't remember evil against me," said Von Koren. "Give my greetings to your wife, and say I am very sorry not to say good-bye to her."

"She is at home."

Laevsky went to the door of the next room, and said:

"Nadya, Nikolay Vassilitch wants to say goodbye to you."

Nadyezhda Fyodorovna came in; she stopped near the doorway and looked shyly at the visitors. There was a look of guilt and dismay on her face, and she held her hands like a schoolgirl receiving a scolding.

"I'm just going away, Nadyezhda Fyodorovna," said Von Koren, "and have come to say good-bye."

She held out her hand uncertainly, while Laevsky bowed.

"What pitiful figures they are, though!" thought Von Koren. "The life they are living does not come easy to them. I shall be in Moscow and Petersburg; can I send you anything?" he asked.

"Oh!" said Nadyezhda Fyodorovna, and she looked anxiously at her husband. "I don't think there's anything..."

"No, nothing..." said Laevsky, rubbing his hands. "Our greetings."

Von Koren did not know what he could or ought to say, though as he went in he thought he would say a very great deal that would be warm and good and important. He shook hands with Laevsky and his wife in silence, and left them with a depressed feeling.

"What people!" said the deacon in a low voice, as he walked behind them. "My God, what people! Of a truth, the right hand of God has planted this vine! Lord! Lord! One man vanquishes thousands and another tens of thousands. Nikolay Vassilitch," he said ecstatically, "let me tell you that to-day you have conquered the greatest of man's enemies--pride."

"Hush, deacon! Fine conquerors we are! Conquerors ought to look like eagles, while he's a pitiful figure, timid, crushed; he bows like a Chinese idol, and I, I am sad..."

They heard steps behind them. It was Laevsky, hurrying after them to see him off. The orderly was standing on the quay with the two portmanteaus, and at a little distance stood four boatmen.

"There is a wind, though... Brrr!" said Samoylenko. "There must be a pretty stiff storm on the sea now! You are not going off at a nice time, Koyla."

"I'm not afraid of sea-sickness."

"That's not the point... I only hope these rascals won't upset you. You ought to have crossed in the agent's sloop. Where's the agent's sloop?" he shouted to the boatmen.

"It has gone, Your Excellency."

"And the Customs-house boat?"

"That's gone, too."

"Why didn't you let us know," said Samoylenko angrily. "You dolts!"

"It's all the same, don't worry yourself..." said Von Koren. "Well, good-bye. God keep you."

Samoylenko embraced Von Koren and made the sign of the cross over him three times.

"Don't forget us, Kolya... Write... We shall look out for you next spring."

"Good-bye, deacon," said Von Koren, shaking hands with the deacon. "Thank you for your company and for your pleasant conversation. Think about the expedition."

"Oh Lord, yes! to the ends of the earth," laughed the deacon. "I've nothing against it."

Von Koren recognised Laevsky in the darkness, and held out his hand without speaking. The boatmen were by now below, holding the boat, which was beating against the piles, though the breakwater screened it from the breakers. Von Koren went down the ladder, jumped into the boat, and sat at the helm.

"Write!" Samoylenko shouted to him. "Take care of yourself."

"No one knows the real truth," thought Laevsky, turning up the collar of his coat and thrusting his hands into his sleeves.

The boat turned briskly out of the harbour into the open sea. It vanished in the waves, but at once from a deep hollow glided up onto a high breaker, so that they could distinguish the men and even the oars. The boat moved three yards forward and was sucked two yards back.

"Write!" shouted Samoylenko; "it's devilish weather for you to go in."

"Yes, no one knows the real truth..." thought Laevsky, looking wearily at the dark, restless sea.

"It flings the boat back," he thought; "she makes two steps forward and one step back; but the boatmen are stubborn, they work the oars unceasingly, and are not afraid of the high waves. The boat goes on and on. Now she is out of sight, but in half an hour the boatmen will see the steamer lights distinctly, and within an hour they will be by the steamer ladder. So it is in life... In the search for truth man makes two steps forward and one step back. Suffering, mistakes, and weariness of life thrust them back, but the thirst for truth and stubborn will drive them on and on. And who knows? Perhaps they will reach the real truth at last."

"Go--o--od-by--e," shouted Samoylenko.

"There's no sight or sound of them," said the deacon. "Good luck on the journey!"

It began to spot with rain.

At Home

I

The don railway. A quiet, cheerless station, white and solitary in the steppe, with its walls baking in the sun, without a speck of shade, and, it seems, without a human being. The train goes on after leaving one here; the sound of it is scarcely audible and dies away at last. Outside the station it is a desert, and there are no horses but one's own. One gets into the carriage--which is so pleasant after the train--and is borne along the road through the steppe, and by degrees there are unfolded before one views such as one does not see near Moscow--immense, endless, fascinating in their monotony. The steppe, the steppe, and nothing more; in the distance an ancient barrow or a windmill; ox-waggons laden with coal trail by... Solitary birds fly low over the plain, and a drowsy feeling comes with the monotonous beat of their wings. It is hot. Another hour or so passes, and still the steppe, the steppe, and still in the distance the barrow. The driver tells you something, some long unnecessary tale, pointing into the distance with his whip. And tranquillity takes possession of the soul; one is loth to think of the past...

A carriage with three horses had been sent to fetch Vera Ivanovna Kardin. The driver put in her luggage and set the harness to rights.

"Everything just as it always has been," said Vera, looking about her. "I was a little girl when I was here last, ten years ago. I remember old Boris came to fetch me then. Is he still living, I wonder?"

The driver made no reply, but, like a Little Russian, looked at her angrily and clambered on to the box.

It was a twenty-mile drive from the station, and Vera, too, abandoned herself to the charm of the steppe, forgot the past, and thought only of the wide expanse, of the freedom. Healthy, clever, beautiful, and young--she was only three-and-twenty--she had hitherto lacked nothing in her life but just this space and freedom.

The steppe, the steppe... The horses trotted, the sun rose higher and higher; and it seemed to Vera that never in her childhood had the steppe been so rich, so luxuriant in June; the wild flowers were green, yellow, lilac, white, and a fragrance rose from them and from the warmed earth; and there were strange blue birds along the roadside... Vera had long got out of the habit of praying, but now, struggling with drowsiness, she murmured:

"Lord, grant that I may be happy here."

And there was peace and sweetness in her soul, and she felt as though she would have been glad to drive like that all her life, looking at the steppe.

Suddenly there was a deep ravine overgrown with oak saplings and alder-trees; there was a moist feeling in the air--there must have been a spring at the bottom. On the near side, on the very edge of the ravine, a covey of partridges rose noisily. Vera remembered that in old days they used to go for evening walks to this ravine; so it must be near home! And now she could actually see the poplars, the barn, black smoke rising on one side--they were burning old straw. And there was Auntie Dasha coming to meet her and waving her handkerchief; grandfather was on the terrace. Oh dear, how happy she was!

"My darling, my darling!" cried her aunt, shrieking as though she were in hysterics. "Our real mistress has come! You must understand you are our mistress, you are our queen! Here everything is yours! My darling, my beauty, I am not your aunt, but your willing slave!"

Vera had no relations but her aunt and her grandfather; her mother had long been dead; her father, an engineer, had died three months before at Kazan, on his way from Siberia. Her grandfather had a big grey beard. He was stout, red-faced, and asthmatic, and walked leaning on a cane and sticking his stomach out. Her aunt, a lady of forty-two, drawn in tightly at the waist and fashionably dressed with sleeves high on the shoulder, evidently tried to look young and was still anxious to be charming; she walked with tiny steps with a wriggle of her spine.

"Will you love us?" she said, embracing Vera, "You are not proud?"

At her grandfather's wish there was a thanksgiving service, then they spent a long while over dinner--and Vera's new life began. She was given the best room. All the rugs in the house had been put in it, and a great many flowers; and when at night she lay down in her snug, wide, very soft bed and covered herself with a silk quilt that smelt of old clothes long stored away, she laughed with pleasure. Auntie Dasha came in for a minute to wish her good-night.

"Here you are home again, thank God," she said, sitting down on the bed. "As you see, we get along very well and have everything we want. There's only one thing: your grandfather is in a poor way! A terribly poor way! He is short of breath and he has begun to lose his memory. And you remember how strong, how vigorous, he used to be! There was no doing anything with him... In old days, if the servants didn't please him or anything else went wrong, he would jump up at once and shout: 'Twenty-five strokes! The birch!' But now he has grown milder and you never hear him. And besides, times are changed, my precious; one mayn't beat them nowadays. Of course, they oughtn't to be beaten, but they need looking after."

"And are they beaten now, auntie?" asked Vera.

"The steward beats them sometimes, but I never do, bless their hearts! And your grandfather sometimes lifts his stick from old habit, but he never beats them."

Auntie Dasha yawned and crossed herself over her mouth and her right ear.

"It's not dull here?" Vera inquired.

"What shall I say? There are no landowners living here now, but there have been works built near, darling, and there are lots of engineers, doctors, and mine managers. Of course, we have theatricals and concerts, but we play cards more than anything. They come to us, too. Dr. Neshtchapov from the works comes to see us--such a handsome, interesting man! He fell in love with your photograph. I made up my mind: he is Verotchka's destiny, I thought. He's young, handsome, he has means--a good match, in fact. And of course you're a match for any one. You're of good family. The place is mortgaged, it's true, but it's in good order and not neglected; there is my share in it, but it will all come to you; I am your willing slave. And my brother, your father, left you fifteen thousand roubles... But I see you can't keep your eyes open. Sleep, my child."

Next day Vera spent a long time walking round the house. The garden, which was old and unattractive, lying inconveniently upon the slope, had no paths, and was utterly neglected; probably the care of it was regarded as an unnecessary item in the management. There were numbers of grass-snakes. Hoopoes flew about under the trees calling "Oo-too-toot!" as though they were trying to remind her of something. At the bottom of the hill there was a river overgrown with tall reeds, and half a mile beyond the river was the village. From the garden Vera went out into the fields; looking into the distance, thinking of her new life in her own home, she kept trying to grasp what was in store for her. The space, the lovely peace of the steppe, told her that happiness was near at hand, and perhaps was here already; thousands of people, in fact, would have said: "What happiness to be young, healthy, well-educated, to be living on one's own estate!" And at the same time the endless plain, all alike, without one living soul, frightened her, and at moments it was clear to her that its peaceful green vastness would swallow up her life and reduce it to nothingness. She was very young, elegant, fond of life; she had finished her studies at an aristocratic boarding-school, had learnt three languages, had read a great deal, had travelled with her father--and could all this have been meant to lead to nothing but settling down in a remote country-house in the steppe, and wandering day after day from the garden into the fields and from the fields into the garden to while away the time, and then sitting at home listening to her grandfather's breathing? But what could she do? Where could she go? She could find no answer, and as she was returning home she doubted whether she would be happy here, and thought that driving from the station was far more interesting than living here.

Dr. Neshtchapov drove over from the works. He was a doctor, but three years previously he had taken a share in the works, and had become one of the partners; and now he no longer looked upon medicine as his chief vocation, though he still practised. In appearance he was a pale, dark man in a white waistcoat, with a good figure; but to guess what there was in his heart and his brain was difficult. He kissed Auntie Dasha's hand on greeting her, and was continually leaping up to set a chair or give his seat to some one. He was very silent and grave all the while, and, when he did speak, it was for some reason impossible to hear and understand his first sentence, though he spoke correctly and not in a low voice.

"You play the piano?" he asked Vera, and immediately leapt up, as she had dropped her handkerchief.

He stayed from midday to midnight without speaking, and Vera found him very unattractive. She thought that a white waistcoat in the country was bad form, and his elaborate politeness, his manners, and his pale, serious face with dark eyebrows, were mawkish; and it seemed to her that he was perpetually silent, probably because he was stupid. When he had gone her aunt said enthusiastically:

"Well? Isn't he charming?"

II

Auntie Dasha looked after the estate. Tightly laced, with jingling bracelets on her wrists, she went into the kitchen, the granary, the cattle-yard, tripping along with tiny steps, wriggling her spine; and whenever she talked to the steward or to the peasants, she used, for some reason, to put on a pince-nez. Vera's grandfather always sat in the same place, playing patience or dozing. He ate a very great deal at dinner and supper; they gave him the dinner cooked to-day and what was left from yesterday, and cold pie left from Sunday, and salt meat from the servants' dinner, and he ate it all greedily. And every dinner left on Vera such an impression, that when she saw afterwards a flock of sheep driven by, or flour being brought from the mill, she thought, "Grandfather will eat that." For the most part he was silent, absorbed in eating or in patience; but it sometimes happened at dinner that at the sight of Vera he would be touched and say tenderly:

"My only grandchild! Verotchka!"

And tears would glisten in his eyes. Or his face would turn suddenly crimson, his neck would swell, he would look with fury at the servants, and ask, tapping with his stick:

"Why haven't you brought the horse-radish?"

In winter he led a perfectly inactive existence; in summer he sometimes drove out into the fields to look at the oats and the hay; and when he came back he would flourish his stick and declare that everything was neglected now that he was not there to look after it.

"Your grandfather is out of humour," Auntie Dasha would whisper. "But it's nothing now to what it used to be in the old days: 'Twenty-five strokes! The birch!'"

Her aunt complained that every one had grown lazy, that no one did anything, and that the estate yielded no profit. Indeed, there was no systematic farming; they ploughed and sowed a little simply from habit, and in reality did nothing and lived in idleness. Meanwhile there was a running to and fro, reckoning and worrying all day long; the bustle in the house began at five o'clock in the morning; there were continual sounds of "Bring it," "Fetch it," "Make haste," and by the evening the servants were utterly exhausted. Auntie Dasha changed her cooks and her housemaids every week; sometimes she discharged them for immorality; sometimes they went of their own accord, complaining that they were worked to death. None of the village people would come to the house as servants; Auntie Dasha had to hire them from a distance. There was only one girl from the village living in the house, Alyona, and she stayed because her whole family--old people and children--were living upon her wages. This Alyona, a pale, rather stupid little thing, spent the whole day turning out the rooms, waiting at table, heating the stoves, sewing, washing; but it always seemed as though she were only pottering about, treading heavily with her boots, and were nothing but a hindrance in the house. In her terror that she might be dismissed and sent home, she often dropped and broke the crockery, and they stopped the value of it out of her wages, and then her mother and grandmother would come and bow down at Auntie Dasha's feet.

Once a week or sometimes oftener visitors would arrive. Her aunt would come to Vera and say:

"You should sit a little with the visitors, or else they'll think that you are stuck up."

Vera would go in to the visitors and play vint with them for hours together, or play the piano for the visitors to dance; her aunt, in high spirits and breathless from dancing, would come up and whisper to her:

"Be nice to Marya Nikiforovna."

On the sixth of December, St. Nikolay's Day, a large party of about thirty arrived all at once; they played vint until late at night, and many of them stayed the night. In the morning they sat down to cards again, then they had dinner, and when Vera went to her room after dinner to rest from conversation and tobacco smoke, there were visitors there too, and she almost wept in despair. And when they began to get ready to go in the evening, she was so pleased they were going at last, that she said:

"Do stay a little longer."

She felt exhausted by the visitors and constrained by their presence; yet every day, as soon as it began to grow dark, something drew her out of the house, and she went out to pay visits either at the works or at some neighbours', and then there were cards, dancing, forfeits, suppers...The young people in the works or in the mines sometimes sang Little Russian songs, and sang them very well. It made one sad to hear them sing. Or they all gathered together in one room and talked in the dusk of the mines, of the treasures that had once been buried in the steppes, of Saur's Grave... Later on, as they talked, a shout of "Help!" sometimes reached them. It was a drunken man going home, or some one was being robbed by the pit near by. Or the wind howled in the chimneys, the shutters banged; then, soon afterwards, they would hear the uneasy church bell, as the snow-storm began.

At all the evening parties, picnics, and dinners, Auntie Dasha was invariably the most interesting woman and the doctor the most interesting man. There was very little reading either at the works or at the country-houses; they played only marches and polkas; and the young people always argued hotly about things they did not understand, and the effect was crude. The discussions were loud and heated, but, strange to say, Vera had nowhere else met people so indifferent and careless as these. They seemed to have no fatherland, no religion, no public interests. When they talked of literature or debated some abstract question, it could be seen from Dr. Neshtchapov's face that the question had no interest for him whatever, and that for long, long years he had read nothing and cared to read nothing. Serious and expressionless, like a badly painted portrait, for ever in his white waistcoat, he was silent and incomprehensible as before; but the ladies, young and old, thought him interesting and were enthusiastic over his manners. They envied Vera, who appeared to attract him very much. And Vera always came away from the visits with a feeling of vexation, vowing inwardly to remain at home; but the day passed, the evening came, and she hurried off to the works again, and it was like that almost all the winter.

She ordered books and magazines, and used to read them in her room. And she read at night, lying in bed. When the clock in the corridor struck two or three, and her temples were beginning to ache from reading, she sat up in bed and thought, "What am I to do? Where am I to go?" Accursed, importunate question, to which there were a number of ready-made answers, and in reality no answer at all.

Oh, how noble, how holy, how picturesque it must be to serve the people, to alleviate their sufferings, to enlighten them! But she, Vera, did not know the people. And how could she go to them? They were strange and uninteresting to her; she could not endure the stuffy smell of the huts, the pot-house oaths, the unwashed children, the women's talk of illnesses. To walk over the snow-drifts, to feel cold, then to sit in a stifling hut, to teach children she disliked--no, she would rather die! And to teach the peasants' children while Auntie Dasha made money out of the pot-houses and fined the peasants--it was too great a farce! What a lot of talk there was of schools, of village libraries, of universal education; but if all these engineers, these mine-owners and ladies of her acquaintance, had not been hypocrites, and really had believed that enlightenment was necessary, they would not have paid the schoolmasters fifteen roubles a month as they did now, and would not have let them go hungry. And the schools and the talk about ignorance--it was all only to stifle the voice of conscience because they were ashamed to own fifteen or thirty thousand acres and to be indifferent to the peasants' lot. Here the ladies said about Dr. Neshtchapov that he was a kind man and had built a school at the works. Yes, he had built a school out of the old bricks at the works for some eight hundred roubles, and they sang the prayer for "long life" to him when the building was opened, but there was no chance of his giving up his shares, and it certainly never entered his head that the peasants were human beings like himself, and that they, too, needed university teaching, and not merely lessons in these wretched schools.

And Vera felt full of anger against herself and every one else. She took up a book again and tried to read it, but soon afterwards sat down and thought again. To become a doctor? But to do that one must pass an examination in Latin; besides, she had an invincible repugnance to corpses and disease. It would be nice to become a mechanic, a judge, a commander of a steamer, a scientist; to do something into which she could put all her powers, physical and spiritual, and to be tired out and sleep soundly at night; to give up her life to something that would make her an interesting person, able to attract interesting people, to love, to have a real family of her own... But what was she to do? How was she to begin?

One Sunday in Lent her aunt came into her room early in the morning to fetch her umbrella. Vera was sitting up in bed clasping her head in her hands, thinking.

"You ought to go to church, darling," said her aunt, "or people will think you are not a believer."

Vera made no answer.

"I see you are dull, poor child," said Auntie Dasha, sinking on her knees by the bedside; she adored Vera. "Tell me the truth, are you bored?"

"Dreadfully."

"My beauty, my queen, I am your willing slave, I wish you nothing but good and happiness... Tell me, why don't you want to marry Nestchapov? What more do you want, my child? You must forgive me, darling; you can't pick and choose like this, we are not princes... Time is passing, you are not seventeen... And I don't understand it! He loves you, idolises you!"

"Oh, mercy!" said Vera with vexation. "How can I tell? He sits dumb and never says a word."

"He's shy, darling... He's afraid you'll refuse him!"

And when her aunt had gone away, Vera remained standing in the middle of her room uncertain whether to dress or to go back to bed. The bed was hateful; if one looked out of the window there were the bare trees, the grey snow, the hateful jackdaws, the pigs that her grandfather would eat...

"Yes, after all, perhaps I'd better get married!" she thought.

III

For two days Auntie Dasha went about with a tear-stained and heavily powdered face, and at dinner she kept sighing and looking towards the ikon. And it was impossible to make out what was the matter with her. But at last she made up her mind, went in to Vera, and said in a casual way:

"The fact is, child, we have to pay interest on the bank loan, and the tenant hasn't paid his rent. Will you let me pay it out of the fifteen thousand your papa left you?"

All day afterwards Auntie Dasha spent in making cherry jam in the garden. Alyona, with her cheeks flushed with the heat, ran to and from the garden to the house and back again to the cellar.

When Auntie Dasha was making jam with a very serious face as though she were performing a religious rite, and her short sleeves displayed her strong, little, despotic hands and arms, and when the servants ran about incessantly, bustling about the jam which they would never taste, there was always a feeling of martyrdom in the air...

The garden smelt of hot cherries. The sun had set, the charcoal stove had been carried away, but the pleasant, sweetish smell still lingered in the air. Vera sat on a bench in the garden and watched a new labourer, a young soldier, not of the neighbourhood, who was, by her express orders, making new paths. He was cutting the turf with a spade and heaping it up on a barrow.

"Where were you serving?" Vera asked him.

"At Berdyansk."

"And where are you going now? Home?"

"No," answered the labourer. "I have no home."

"But where were you born and brought up?"

"In the province of Oryol. Till I went into the army I lived with my mother, in my step-father's house; my mother was the head of the house, and people looked up to her, and while she lived I was cared for. But while I was in the army I got a letter telling me my mother was dead... And now I don't seem to care to go home. It's not my own father, so it's not like my own home."

"Then your father is dead?"

"I don't know. I am illegitimate."

At that moment Auntie Dasha appeared at the window and said:

" Il ne faut pas parler aux gens... Go into the kitchen, my good man. You can tell your story there," she said to the soldier.

And then came as yesterday and every day supper, reading, a sleepless night, and endless thinking about the same thing. At three o'clock the sun rose; Alyona was already busy in the corridor, and Vera was not asleep yet and was trying to read. She heard the creak of the barrow: it was the new labourer at work in the garden... Vera sat at the open window with a book, dozed, and watched the soldier making the paths for her, and that interested her. The paths were as even and level as a leather strap, and it was pleasant to imagine what they would be like when they were strewn with yellow sand.

She could see her aunt come out of the house soon after five o'clock, in a pink wrapper and curl-papers. She stood on the steps for three minutes without speaking, and then said to the soldier:

"Take your passport and go in peace. I can't have any one illegitimate in my house."

An oppressive, angry feeling sank like a stone on Vera's heart. She was indignant with her aunt, she hated her; she was so sick of her aunt that her heart was full of misery and loathing. But what was she to do? To stop her mouth? To be rude to her? But what would be the use? Suppose she struggled with her, got rid of her, made her harmless, prevented her grandfather from flourishing his stick-- what would be the use of it? It would be like killing one mouse or one snake in the boundless steppe. The vast expanse, the long winters, the monotony and dreariness of life, instil a sense of helplessness; the position seems hopeless, and one wants to do nothing--everything is useless.

Alyona came in, and bowing low to Vera, began carrying out the arm-chairs to beat the dust out of them.

"You have chosen a time to clean up," said Vera with annoyance. "Go away."

Alyona was overwhelmed, and in her terror could not understand what was wanted of her. She began hurriedly tidying up the dressing-table.

"Go out of the room, I tell you," Vera shouted, turning cold; she had never had such an oppressive feeling before. "Go away!"

Alyona uttered a sort of moan, like a bird, and dropped Vera's gold watch on the carpet.

"Go away!" Vera shrieked in a voice not her own, leaping up and trembling all over. "Send her away; she worries me to death!" she went on, walking rapidly after Alyona down the passage, stamping her feet. "Go away! Birch her! Beat her!" Then suddenly she came to herself, and just as she was, unwashed, uncombed, in her dressing-gown and slippers, she rushed out of the house. She ran to the familiar ravine and hid herself there among the sloe-trees, so that she might see no one and be seen by no one. Lying there motionless on the grass, she did not weep, she was not horror-stricken, but gazing at the sky open-eyed, she reflected coldly and clearly that something had happened which she could never forget and for which she could never forgive herself all her life.

"No, I can't go on like this," she thought. "It's time to take myself in hand, or there'll be no end to it... I can't go on like this..."

At midday Dr. Neshtchapov drove by the ravine on his way to the house. She saw him and made up her mind that she would begin a new life, and that she would make herself begin it, and this decision calmed her. And following with her eyes the doctor's well-built figure, she said, as though trying to soften the crudity of her decision:

"He's a nice man... We shall get through life somehow."

She returned home. While she was dressing, Auntie Dasha came into the room, and said:

"Alyona upset you, darling; I've sent her home to the village. Her mother's given her a good beating and has come here, crying."

"Auntie," said Vera quickly, "I'm going to marry Dr. Neshtchapov. Only talk to him yourself... I can't."

And again she went out into the fields. And wandering aimlessly about, she made up her mind that when she was married she would look after the house, doctor the peasants, teach in the school, that she would do all the things that other women of her circle did. And this perpetual dissatisfaction with herself and every one else, this series of crude mistakes which stand up like a mountain before one whenever one looks back upon one's past, she would accept as her real life to which she was fated, and she would expect nothing better... Of course there was nothing better! Beautiful nature, dreams, music, told one story, but reality another. Evidently truth and happiness existed somewhere outside real life... One must give up one's own life and merge oneself into this luxuriant steppe, boundless and indifferent as eternity, with its flowers, its ancient barrows, and its distant horizon, and then it would be well with one...

A month later Vera was living at the works.

Expensive Lessons

For a cultivated man to be ignorant of foreign languages is a great inconvenience. Vorotov became acutely conscious of it when, after taking his degree, he began upon a piece of research work.

"It's awful," he said, breathing hard (although he was only twenty-six he was fat, heavy, and suffered from shortness of breath).

"It's awful! Without languages I'm like a bird without wings. I might just as well give up the work."

And he made up his mind at all costs to overcome his innate laziness, and to learn French and German; and began to look out for a teacher.

One winter noon, as Vorotov was sitting in his study at work, the servant told him that a young lady was inquiring for him.

"Ask her in," said Vorotov.

And a young lady elaborately dressed in the last fashion walked in. She introduced herself as a teacher of French, Alice Osipovna Enquete, and told Vorotov that she had been sent to him by one of his friends.

"Delighted! Please sit down," said Vorotov, breathing hard and putting his hand over the collar of his nightshirt (to breathe more freely he always wore a nightshirt at work instead of a stiff linen one with collar). "It was Pyotr Sergeitch sent you? Yes, yes... I asked him about it. Delighted!"

As he talked to Mdlle. Enquete he looked at her shyly and with curiosity. She was a genuine Frenchwoman, very elegant and still quite young. Judging from her pale, languid face, her short curly hair, and her unnaturally slim waist, she might have been eighteen; but looking at her broad, well-developed shoulders, the elegant lines of her back and her severe eyes, Vorotov thought that she was not less than three-and-twenty and might be twenty-five; but then again he began to think she was not more than eighteen. Her face looked as cold and business-like as the face of a person who has come to speak about money. She did not once smile or frown, and only once a look of perplexity flitted over her face when she learnt that she was not required to teach children, but a stout grown-up man.

"So, Alice Osipovna," said Vorotov, "we'll have a lesson every evening from seven to eight. As regards your terms--a rouble a lesson--I've nothing to say against that. By all means let it be a rouble..."

And he asked her if she would not have some tea or coffee, whether it was a fine day, and with a good-natured smile, stroking the baize of the table, he inquired in a friendly voice who she was, where she had studied, and what she lived on.

With a cold, business-like expression, Alice Osipovna answered that she had completed her studies at a private school and had the diploma of a private teacher, that her father had died lately of scarlet fever, that her mother was alive and made artificial flowers; that she, Mdlle. Enquete, taught in a private school till dinnertime, and after dinner was busy till evening giving lessons in different good families.

She went away leaving behind her the faint fragrance of a woman's clothes. For a long time afterwards Vorotov could not settle to work, but, sitting at the table stroking its green baize surface, he meditated.

"It's very pleasant to see a girl working to earn her own living," he thought. "On the other hand, it's very unpleasant to think that poverty should not spare such elegant and pretty girls as Alice Osipovna, and that she, too, should have to struggle for existence. It's a sad thing!"

Having never seen virtuous Frenchwomen before, he reflected also that this elegantly dressed young lady with her well-developed shoulders and exaggeratedly small waist in all probability followed another calling as well as giving French lessons.

The next evening when the clock pointed to five minutes to seven, Mdlle. Enquete appeared, rosy from the frost. She opened Margot, which she had brought with her, and without introduction began:

"French grammar has twenty-six letters. The first letter is called A , the second B..."

"Excuse me," Vorotov interrupted, smiling. "I must warn you, mademoiselle, that you must change your method a little in my case. You see, I know Russian, Greek, and Latin well... I've studied comparative philology, and I think we might omit Margot and pass straight to reading some author."

And he explained to the French girl how grown-up people learn languages.

"A friend of mine," he said, "wanting to learn modern languages, laid before him the French, German, and Latin gospels, and read them side by side, carefully analysing each word, and would you believe it, he attained his object in less than a year. Let us do the same. We'll take some author and read him."

The French girl looked at him in perplexity. Evidently the suggestion seemed to her very naive and ridiculous. If this strange proposal had been made to her by a child, she would certainly have been angry and have scolded it, but as he was a grown-up man and very stout and she could not scold him, she only shrugged her shoulders hardly perceptibly and said:

"As you please."

Vorotov rummaged in his bookcase and picked out a dog's-eared French book.

"Will this do?"

"It's all the same," she said.

"In that case let us begin, and good luck to it! Let's begin with the title... 'Memoires.'"

"Reminiscences," Mdlle. Enquete translated.

With a good-natured smile, breathing hard, he spent a quarter of an hour over the word "Memoires," and as much over the word de , and this wearied the young lady. She answered his questions languidly, grew confused, and evidently did not understand her pupil well, and did not attempt to understand him. Vorotov asked her questions, and at the same time kept looking at her fair hair and thinking:

"Her hair isn't naturally curly; she curls it. It's a strange thing! She works from morning to night, and yet she has time to curl her hair."

At eight o'clock precisely she got up, and saying coldly and dryly, "Au revoir, monsieur," walked out of the study, leaving behind her the same tender, delicate, disturbing fragrance. For a long time again her pupil did nothing; he sat at the table meditating.

During the days that followed he became convinced that his teacher was a charming, conscientious, and precise young lady, but that she was very badly educated, and incapable of teaching grown-up people, and he made up his mind not to waste his time, to get rid of her, and to engage another teacher. When she came the seventh time he took out of his pocket an envelope with seven roubles in it, and holding it in his hand, became very confused and began:

"Excuse me, Alice Osipovna, but I ought to tell you... I'm under painful necessity..."

Seeing the envelope, the French girl guessed what was meant, and for the first time during their lessons her face quivered and her cold, business-like expression vanished. She coloured a little, and dropping her eyes, began nervously fingering her slender gold chain. And Vorotov, seeing her perturbation, realised how much a rouble meant to her, and how bitter it would be to her to lose what she was earning.

"I ought to tell you," he muttered, growing more and more confused, and quavering inwardly; he hurriedly stuffed the envelope into his pocket and went on: "Excuse me, I... I must leave you for ten minutes."

And trying to appear as though he had not in the least meant to get rid of her, but only to ask her permission to leave her for a short time, he went into the next room and sat there for ten minutes. And then "he returned more embarrassed than ever: it struck him that she might have interpreted his brief absence in some way of her own, and he felt awkward.

The lessons began again. Yorotov felt no interest in them. Realising that he would gain nothing from the lessons, he gave the French girl liberty to do as she liked, asking her nothing and not interrupting her. She translated away as she pleased ten pages during a lesson, and he did not listen, breathed hard, and having nothing better to do, gazed at her curly head, or her soft white hands or her neck and sniffed the fragrance of her clothes. He caught himself thinking very unsuitable thoughts, and felt ashamed, or he was moved to tenderness, and then he felt vexed and wounded that she was so cold and business-like with him, and treated him as a pupil, never smiling and seeming afraid that he might accidentally touch her. He kept wondering how to inspire her with confidence and get to know her better, and to help her, to make her understand how badly she taught, poor thing.

One day Mdlle. Enquete came to the lesson in a smart pink dress, slightly decollete , and surrounded by such a fragrance that she seemed to be wrapped in a cloud, and, if one blew upon her, ready to fly away into the air or melt away like smoke. She apologised and said she could stay only half an hour for the lesson, as she was going straight from the lesson to a dance.

He looked at her throat and the back of her bare neck, and thought he understood why Frenchwomen had the reputation of frivolous creatures easily seduced; he was carried away by this cloud of fragrance, beauty, and bare flesh, while she, unconscious of his thoughts and probably not in the least interested in them, rapidly turned over the pages and translated at full steam:

"'He was walking the street and meeting a gentleman his friend and saying, "Where are you striving to seeing your face so pale it makes me sad."'"

The "Memoires" had long been finished, and now Alice was translating some other book. One day she came an hour too early for the lesson, apologizing and saying that she wanted to leave at seven and go to the Little Theatre. Seeing her out after the lesson, Vorotov dressed and went to the theatre himself. He went, and fancied that he was going simply for change and amusement, and that he was not thinking about Alice at all. He could not admit that a serious man, preparing for a learned career, lethargic in his habits, could fling up his work and go to the theatre simply to meet there a girl he knew very little, who was unintelligent and utterly unintellectual.

Yet for some reason his heart was beating during the intervals, and without realizing what he was doing, he raced about the corridors and foyer like a boy impatiently looking for some one, and he was disappointed when the interval was over. And when he saw the familiar pink dress and the handsome shoulders under the tulle, his heart quivered as though with a foretaste of happiness; he smiled joyfully, and for the first time in his life experienced the sensation of jealousy.

Alice was walking with two unattractive-looking students and an officer. She was laughing, talking loudly, and obviously flirting. Vorotov had never seen her like that. She was evidently happy, contented, warm, sincere. What for? Why? Perhaps because these men were her friends and belonged to her own circle. And Vorotov felt there was a terrible gulf between himself and that circle. He bowed to his teacher, but she gave him a chilly nod and walked quickly by; she evidently did not care for her friends to know that she had pupils, and that she had to give lessons to earn money.

After the meeting at the theatre Vorotov realised that he was in love... During the subsequent lessons he feasted his eyes on his elegant teacher, and without struggling with himself, gave full rein to his imaginations, pure and impure. Mdlle. Enquete's face did not cease to be cold; precisely at eight o'clock every evening she said coldly, "Au revoir, monsieur," and he felt she cared nothing about him, and never would care anything about him, and that his position was hopeless.

Sometimes in the middle of a lesson he would begin dreaming, hoping, making plans. He inwardly composed declarations of love, remembered that Frenchwomen were frivolous and easily won, but it was enough for him to glance at the face of his teacher for his ideas to be extinguished as a candle is blown out when you bring it into the wind on the verandah. Once, overcome, forgetting himself as though in delirium, he could not restrain himself, and barred her way as she was going from the study into the entry after the lesson, and, gasping for breath and stammering, began to declare his love:

"You are dear to me! I... I love you! Allow me to speak."

And Alice turned pale--probably from dismay, reflecting that after this declaration she could not come here again and get a rouble a lesson. With a frightened look in her eyes she said in a loud whisper:

"Ach, you mustn't! Don't speak, I entreat you! You mustn't!"

And Vorotov did not sleep all night afterwards; he was tortured by shame; he blamed himself and thought intensely. It seemed to him that he had insulted the girl by his declaration, that she would not come to him again.

He resolved to find out her address from the address bureau in the morning, and to write her a letter of apology. But Alice came without a letter. For the first minute she felt uncomfortable, then she opened a book and began briskly and rapidly translating as usual:

"'Oh, young gentleman, don't tear those flowers in my garden which I want to be giving to my ill daughter...'"

She still comes to this day. Four books have already been translated, but Vorotov knows no French but the word "Memoires," and when he is asked about his literary researches, he waves his hand, and without answering, turns the conversation to the weather.

The Chemist's Wife

The little town of B----, consisting of two or three crooked streets, was sound asleep. There was a complete stillness in the motionless air. Nothing could be heard but far away, outside the town no doubt, the barking of a dog in a thin, hoarse tenor. It was close upon daybreak.

Everything had long been asleep. The only person not asleep was the young wife of Tchernomordik, a qualified dispenser who kept a chemist's shop at B----. She had gone to bed and got up again three times, but could not sleep, she did not know why. She sat at the open window in her nightdress and looked into the street. She felt bored, depressed, vexed... so vexed that she felt quite inclined to cry--again she did not know why. There seemed to be a lump in her chest that kept rising into her throat... A few paces behind her Tchernomordik lay curled up close to the wall, snoring sweetly. A greedy flea was stabbing the bridge of his nose, but he did not feel it, and was positively smiling, for he was dreaming that every one in the town had a cough, and was buying from him the King of Denmark's cough-drops. He could not have been wakened now by pinpricks or by cannon or by caresses.

The chemist's shop was almost at the extreme end of the town, so that the chemist's wife could see far into the fields. She could see the eastern horizon growing pale by degrees, then turning crimson as though from a great fire. A big broad-faced moon peeped out unexpectedly from behind bushes in the distance. It was red (as a rule when the moon emerges from behind bushes it appears to be blushing).

Suddenly in the stillness of the night there came the sounds of footsteps and a jingle of spurs. She could hear voices.

"That must be the officers going home to the camp from the Police Captain's," thought the chemist's wife.

Soon afterwards two figures wearing officers' white tunics came into sight: one big and tall, the other thinner and shorter... They slouched along by the fence, dragging one leg after the other and talking loudly together. As they passed the chemist's shop, they walked more slowly than ever, and glanced up at the windows.

"It smells like a chemist's," said the thin one. "And so it is! Ah, I remember... I came here last week to buy some castor-oil. There's a chemist here with a sour face and the jawbone of an ass! Such a jawbone, my dear fellow! It must have been a jawbone like that Samson killed the Philistines with."

"M'yes," said the big one in a bass voice. "The pharmacist is asleep. And his wife is asleep too. She is a pretty woman, Obtyosov."

"I saw her. I liked her very much... Tell me, doctor, can she possibly love that jawbone of an ass? Can she?"

"No, most likely she does not love him," sighed the doctor, speaking as though he were sorry for the chemist. "The little woman is asleep behind the window, Obtyosov, what? Tossing with the heat, her little mouth half open... and one little foot hanging out of bed. I bet that fool the chemist doesn't realise what a lucky fellow he is... No doubt he sees no difference between a woman and a bottle of carbolic!"

"I say, doctor," said the officer, stopping. "Let us go into the shop and buy something. Perhaps we shall see her."

"What an idea--in the night!"

"What of it? They are obliged to serve one even at night. My dear fellow, let us go in!"

"If you like..."

The chemist's wife, hiding behind the curtain, heard a muffled ring. Looking round at her husband, who was smiling and snoring sweetly as before, she threw on her dress, slid her bare feet into her slippers, and ran to the shop.

On the other side of the glass door she could see two shadows. The chemist's wife turned up the lamp and hurried to the door to open it, and now she felt neither vexed nor bored nor inclined to cry, though her heart was thumping. The big doctor and the slender Obtyosov walked in. Now she could get a view of them. The doctor was corpulent and swarthy; he wore a beard and was slow in his movements. At the slightest motion his tunic seemed as though it would crack, and perspiration came on to his face. The officer was rosy, clean-shaven, feminine-looking, and as supple as an English whip.

"What may I give you? asked the chemist's wife, holding her dress across her bosom.

"Give us... er-er... four pennyworth of peppermint lozenges!"

Without haste the chemist's wife took down a jar from a shelf and began weighing out lozenges. The customers stared fixedly at her back; the doctor screwed up his eyes like a well-fed cat, while the lieutenant was very grave.

"It's the first time I've seen a lady serving in a chemist's shop," observed the doctor.

"There's nothing out of the way in it," replied the chemist's wife, looking out of the corner of her eye at the rosy-cheeked officer. "My husband has no assistant, and I always help him."

"To be sure... You have a charming little shop! What a number of different... jars! And you are not afraid of moving about among the poisons? Brrr!"

The chemist's wife sealed up the parcel and handed it to the doctor. Obtyosov gave her the money. Half a minute of silence followed... The men exchanged glances, took a step towards the door, then looked at one another again.

"Will you give me two pennyworth of soda?" said the doctor.

Again the chemist's wife slowly and languidly raised her hand to the shelf.

"Haven't you in the shop anything... such as..." muttered Obtyosov, moving his fingers, "something, so to say, allegorical... revivifying...

seltzer-water, for instance. Have you any seltzer-water?"

"Yes," answered the chemist's wife.

"Bravo! You're a fairy, not a woman! Give us three bottles!"

The chemist's wife hurriedly sealed up the soda and vanished through the door into the darkness.

"A peach!" said the doctor, with a wink. "You wouldn't find a pineapple like that in the island of Madeira! Eh? What do you say? Do you hear the snoring, though? That's his worship the chemist enjoying sweet repose."

A minute later the chemist's wife came back and set five bottles on the counter. She had just been in the cellar, and so was flushed and rather excited.

"Sh-sh!... quietly!" said Obtyosov when, after uncorking the bottles, she dropped the corkscrew. "Don't make such a noise; you'll wake your husband."

"Well, what if I do wake him?"

"He is sleeping so sweetly... he must be dreaming of you... To your health!"

"Besides," boomed the doctor, hiccupping after the seltzer-water, "husbands are such a dull business that it would be very nice of them to be always asleep. How good a drop of red wine would be in this water!"

"What an idea!" laughed the chemist's wife.

"That would be splendid. What a pity they don't sell spirits in chemist's shops! Though you ought to sell wine as a medicine. Have you any vinum gallicum rubrum ?"

"Yes."

"Well, then, give us some! Bring it here, damn it!"

"How much do you want?"

" Quantum satis... Give us an ounce each in the water, and afterwards we'll see... Obtyosov, what do you say? First with water and afterwards per se..."

The doctor and Obtyosov sat down to the counter, took off their caps, and began drinking the wine.

"The wine, one must admit, is wretched stuff! Vinum nastissimum! Though in the presence of... er... it tastes like nectar. You are enchanting, madam! In imagination I kiss your hand."

"I would give a great deal to do so not in imagination," said Obtyosov. "On my honour, I'd give my life."

"That's enough," said Madame Tchernomordik, flushing and assuming a serious expression.

"What a flirt you are, though!" the doctor laughed softly, looking slyly at her from under his brows. "Your eyes seem to be firing shot: piff-paff! I congratulate you: you've conquered! We are vanquished!"

The chemist's wife looked at their ruddy faces, listened to their chatter, and soon she, too, grew quite lively. Oh, she felt so gay! She entered into the conversation, she laughed, flirted, and even, after repeated requests from the customers, drank two ounces of wine.

"You officers ought to come in oftener from the camp," she said; "it's awful how dreary it is here. I'm simply dying of it."

"I should think so!" said the doctor indignantly. "Such a peach, a miracle of nature, thrown away in the wilds! How well Griboyedov said, 'Into the wilds, to Saratov'! It's time for us to be off, though. Delighted to have made your acquaintance... very. How much do we owe you?"

The chemist's wife raised her eyes to the ceiling and her lips moved for some time.

"Twelve roubles forty-eight kopecks," she said.

Obtyosov took out of his pocket a fat pocket-book, and after fumbling for some time among the notes, paid.

"Your husband's sleeping sweetly... he must be dreaming," he muttered, pressing her hand at parting.

"I don't like to hear silly remarks..."

"What silly remarks? On the contrary, it's not silly at all... even Shakespeare said: 'Happy is he who in his youth is young.'"

"Let go of my hand."

At last after much talk and after kissing the lady's hand at parting, the customers went out of the shop irresolutely, as though they were wondering whether they had not forgotten something.

She ran quickly into the bedroom and sat down in the same place. She saw the doctor and the officer, on coming out of the shop, walk lazily away a distance of twenty paces; then they stopped and began whispering together. What about? Her heart throbbed, there was a pulsing in her temples, and why she did not know... Her heart beat violently as though those two whispering outside were deciding her fate.

Five minutes later the doctor parted from Obtyosov and walked on, while Obtyosov came back. He walked past the shop once and a second time... He would stop near the door and then take a few steps again. At last the bell tinkled discreetly.

"What? Who is there?" the chemist's wife heard her husband's voice suddenly. "There's a ring at the bell, and you don't hear it," he said severely. "Is that the way to do things?"

He got up, put on his dressing-gown, and staggering, half asleep, flopped in his slippers to the shop.

"What... is it?" he asked Obtyosov.

"Give me... give me four pennyworth of peppermint lozenges."

Sniffing continually, yawning, dropping asleep as he moved, and knocking his knees against the counter, the chemist went to the shelf and reached down the jar.

Two minutes later the chemist's wife saw Obtyosov go out of the shop, and, after he had gone some steps, she saw him throw the packet of peppermints on the dusty road. The doctor came from behind a corner to meet him... They met and, gesticulating, vanished in the morning mist.

"How unhappy I am!" said the chemist's wife, looking angrily at her husband, who was undressing quickly to get into bed again. "Oh, how unhappy I am!" she repeated, suddenly melting into bitter tears. "And nobody knows, nobody knows..."

"I forgot fourpence on the counter," muttered the chemist, pulling the quilt over him. "Put it away in the till, please..."

And at once he fell asleep again.